More praise for
The Painter from Shanghai

"In this age of memoir and thinly veiled autobiographical fiction, writers who take high dives into deeply imagined waters have become increasingly rare—and valuable. What a pleasure, then, to discover that Jennifer Cody Epstein, whose luminous first novel, *The Painter from Shanghai*, is based on the actual life of Pan Yuliang, a former child prostitute turned celebrated painter, also happens to be one such writer . . . an irresistible story."　　　　—*New York Times*

"A page turner. . . . non-Chinese-speaking Epstein writes about historical China and the Chinese in a surprisingly authentic way. Her descriptions of brothel life and the landscape of Shanghai, and her rendering of traditional weddings, funerals and foot bindings, makes the book feel like a cross between Zhang Yimou's movies and Chen Yifei's oil paintings."　　　　—*South China Morning Post*

"Epstein's debut novel thwarts the barriers of language, time and space. With its vivid narration, the book takes readers to the colorful arts and unusual life of the 'Chinese Vincent Van Gogh' in the early 20th Century."　　　　—*Sing Tao Daily*

"[A] sensitive and persuasive telling . . . one of the most remarkable things about this book is Epstein's imaginative ability to make it all come alive through the precision of detail and evocative image. She manages to convey a sense of the ambience of the period that is at once poetic and steeped in realism."

　　　　—*Buddha Diaries / Huffington Post*

"Moving, evocative and well-researched. Pan makes a good protagonist: prostitute to painter is quite a transition. The story is also apropos, as Chinese art comes to the forefront of the world's art market: knowing something about of the pioneers of Chinese oils and the tensions between Chinese and Western influences is useful and illuminating." —*Asian Review of Books*

"Jennifer Epstein has written a historical novel on a grand scale that reads like a fable, a dark love story, a triumphant tale of survival. Pan Yuliang, a girl sold to the mythical, though all too real, degradations of a brothel makes her way to distinction as an artist. From the promise of her first charcoal sketches to the triumphant exhibition in Paris, she is fully realized. Yuliang's doubt of her talent, her every determination to cross borders—East to West, constraints of gender, art as it attempts to render life—is fully imagined in Epstein's work. She is as learned in the enchantments of storytelling as she is in the real politics of Chinese and expatriate life."

—Maureen Howard, author of *The Silver Screen*

"*The Painter from Shanghai* by Jennifer Cody Epstein is an exquisitely rendered tale about the artist's struggle for self-realization. The novel is set primarily in China during the first part of the twentieth century with rumbles of the coming Chinese Revolution. And although character-driven, *The Painter from Shanghai* abounds in plot as our young heroine, Yuliang, moves from one perilous position to another until she achieves in heart's dream. One could not have a more humble background—orphan, prostitute—than our young heroine, yet it seems that adversity fuels her art. The author relishes her character's struggle and does not stint on descriptive detail or psychological insight, as the reader comes to understand the heroine's insecurities as a new painter, and to sympathize with her effort to achieve autonomy despite her love for her powerful and wealthy Chinese husband. This is a magnificent book, a fascinating read." —Frances Sherwood, author of *Night of Sorrows*

"What astonishes most about *The Painter from Shanghai* is not just its epic scale, its exhaustive research or its wildly ambitious subject matter, but the fact that Jennifer Cody Epstein has woven these elements together with such lush and inventive writing. This is a phenomenal debut."

—Joanna Hershon, author of *Swimming* and *The German Bride*

"Like Tracy Chevalier did with *Girl with a Pearl Earring*, Jennifer Epstein has written a truly fascinating and sympathetic portrait of an artist in *The Painter from Shanghai*. Yuliang's story is by turns harrowing, passionate, and inspiring. A moving story, and a real page-turner too."

—Binnie Kirshenbaum, author of *An Almost Perfect Moment*

"In *The Painter from Shanghai*, Jennifer Epstein has given us a luminous, compelling debut novel. Yuliang's story is as captivating as it is chilling, vividly told, hard to put down."

—Helen Schulman, author of *A Day at the Beach*

"Plush and vibrant, Jennifer Cody Epstein's *The Painter from Shanghai* combines the sweep of an epic with the persuasive, textured detail of daily life. It is a portrait of the artist who succeeds because she insists upon it, a captivating glimpse into history, and—when you least expect it—a gently layered, bittersweet love story."

—Michelle Wildgen, author of *You're Not You*

"Masterfully told, *The Painter from Shanghai* offers a brilliant and gripping portrait of one of art history's most fascinating figures. With prose as vivid and luminous as one of her subject's paintings, Epstein brings to life Pan Yuliang's incredible saga. At once deeply intimate and sweepingly epic, heart-wrenching and inspiring. I honestly could not put this wonderful novel down. A tremendous achievement. One of the best books I've read in years."

—Scott Snyder, author of *Voodoo Heart*

"Jennifer Epstein has created a world of extraordinary imagination out of a world of extraordinary historical fact, and in the process has demonstrated, with verve, that art can redeem misery."

—David Plante, author of *ABC*

"Among the new names worth keeping an eye on."

—*The Observer* (London)

"Real-life painter Pan Yuliang's journey from concubine to famous artist, reimagined, [is one of] a hot new crop of reads . . . featuring kick-ass women."

—*Glamour*

"Epstein's sweeping debut novel, set in early 20th-century China, fictionalizes the life of Chinese painter Pan Yuliang. . . . [Her] take on Yuliang's life is captivating to the last line."

—*Publishers Weekly*

"[An] engrossing story of a woman forced to choose between following her heart and pursuing her art."

—*Library Journal*

"A compelling, sensuous imagining of the life of 20th-century Chinese artist Pan Yuliang. Orphaned by her mother and betrayed by her uncle who sold her to a brothel at age 14, Yuliang survives degradation, tragedy and loss to build a remarkable life for herself in Shanghai and France. With clear, striking prose, rich historical details and enchanting characters, Jennifer Cody Epstein paints a masterpiece of her own."

—*Roanoke Times*

"The history of China from the last Manchus into the 20th Century, the roles of women and family, the hard-earned self-reliance that moves Pan Yuliang inside her art to an inner existence initially impossible to imagine, make this novel unique."

—*Poisoned Pen Reviews*

"Epstein has written a beautifully-crafted, intelligent and thoroughly entertaining novel about Pan Yuliang. I savored every moment of this book and it was particularly fun, once I realized she actually existed, to go onto the internet and look at her many paintings."

"If Yuliang's brush strokes are delicate, so are Epstein's descriptions; but the debut novelist does not let details crowd out the characters, much like the artist who gave her bathing women neat, bold contours."

"Yuliang is one of the most interesting characters I've ever read about, be it fiction or non-. . . . Don't let this author get away!"

"*The Painter from Shanghai* is a real page-turner, a compelling read and a witness to bigotry and prejudice in China. Jennifer Cody Epstein has imbued this saga with authentic scenes, sights, smells, language and paintings. She has brought forth the harrowing life of this much maligned painter from Shanghai."

"The moment I started reading this book, I became totally engrossed in the story. . . . It is difficult to believe that this is a debut book from Jennifer Cody Epstein. She tells this story in such a way that the reader will think the words have come from a seasoned writer who has been mastering novels for many years."

The *PAINTER* from

SHANGHAI

Jennifer Cody Epstein

W. W. NORTON & COMPANY · NEW YORK · LONDON

For information about permission to reproduce
selections from this book, write to Permissions,
W. W. Norton & Company, Inc.,
500 Fifth Avenue, New York, NY 10110

For information about special discounts for bulk
purchases, please contact W. W. Norton Special Sales at
specialsales@wwnorton.com or 800-233-4830

Manufacturing by RR Donnelley, Bloomsburg
Book design by Judith Stagnitto Abbate, Abbate Design
Production manager: Anna Oler

Library of Congress Cataloging-in-Publication Data

Epstein, Jennifer Cody.
The painter from Shanghai / Jennifer Cody Epstein. — 1st ed.
p. cm.
ISBN 978-0-393-06528-2 (hardcover)
1. Pan, Yuliang, 1895–1977—Fiction. 2. Women artists—
China—Fiction. 3. China—History—20th century—Fiction.
4. Biographical fiction. I. Title.
PS3605.P646P35 2008
813'.6—dc22

                                        2007041805

ISBN 978-0-393-33531-6 pbk.

W. W. Norton & Company, Inc.
500 Fifth Avenue, New York, N.Y. 10110
www.wwnorton.com

W. W. Norton & Company Ltd.
Castle House, 75/76 Wells Street, London W1T 3QT

2 3 4 5 6 7 8 9 0

For Michael.

For everything.

Author's Note

While this novel is based on the life and works of Pan Yuliang, it is a work of the imagination. It attempts to stay true to the broad strokes of Madame Pan's life as depicted in the few sources available. For the most part, however, the characters, events, and places depicted here are—like the paintings that inspired them—impressionistic portraits.

Here is a sketch by Leonardo da Vinci. I enter this sketch and I see him at work and in trouble and I meet him there.

————

ROBERT HENRI
The Art Spirit

Part ONE

The *ATELIER*

Though a living cannot be made at art, art makes life worth living. It makes starving, living. It makes worry, it makes trouble, it makes a life that would be barren of everything—living. It brings life to life.

———

JOHN SLOAN

Montparnasse, 1957

W HEN THE SESSION IS OVER, Yuliang retreats to the chipped sink in the atelier's corner. Of her two models, one leaves immediately. The other, Leanne, lingers a little, straightening her slip and shimmying her garters back into place high on her thighs. As she hooks the straps to her stockings, she leans over Yuliang's painting and the still-damp fruits of the past five hours: a tree, a lake. Herself kneeling by another nude.

Wiping her spattered palms on her painting smock, Yuliang observes Leanne observing the girl she has just been made into. She did well today, Yuliang decides. New models often need extra time to undress, to settle into their nudity before strangers. But Leanne surprised her, stepping out of her Orlon shift and underwear as blithely as though she'd undressed publicly all her life. She didn't fuss over her flesh; didn't apologize for or try to hide the pimple on her left thigh. But at each break in the five-hour session she crossed the room and, still unabashedly naked, silently inspected Yuliang's progress.

Yuliang, who usually works through her model's rest times, found these attentions disconcerting. She didn't stop working. But she worked differently than she'd planned, reluctant to retouch the girl's painted flesh under her real-life gaze. She worked on other things—her willow tree, the rumpled blanket—all the while inhaling her observer's scent: her cheap perfume, her old smokes, a sour-sweet hint of sweat. Something clean and cloverlike too, like sun-dried sheets. Leanne has said that her father runs a laundry shop near the Gare de Lyon.

Water rushes from the faucet, rust-flecked. Yuliang waits, fingertips pressing the soap-filmed chill of the tap. When the stream runs pure, she pushes her brushes beneath it. Colors wash into their neutralizing counterparts: ultramarine into cadmium into blue into yellow ocher, the brilliant shades blending into a mud-toned flow that disappears down the drain.

She is starting on her hands when Leanne sneezes, a breathy explosion so high-pitched it's almost sweet.

"*Pardon,*" Leanne says.

"*Non, non,*" says Yuliang. "I'm sorry it's so cold in here." She says it in French; Leanne's Chinese is, she's found, limited.

"The cat, perhaps. Sometimes they make my nose itch." The girl presses a handkerchief against her upper lip.

"Ah." Yuliang turns back to her brushes, the cloth momentarily etched in her mind's eye: the starry whiteness, the sheen endowed by hot iron and starch. Leanne's family, from Guangxi originally, ran one of Hanoi's Chinese banks until '54. Leanne hasn't offered more than this; Yuliang assumes the Communists took the bank when they took the rest of the north. *Does she miss it?* she wonders.

For she herself certainly misses China—despite everything. "Do you consider going home?" a reporter asked her at her last exhibition. "*Naturellement, parfois,*" she replied, although in truth she "considers" it all the time. The truth is, "home" feels less like a place now than an inner part of her, an organ cancerously riddled with longing. The hurt recedes when she's painting. But the ache of it, of all she's lost—that never leaves. Places and people still appear in an eyeblink, so tremblingly real she could touch them. The Parisian grace of Fouzhou Road, its elm-lined streets and Tudor mansions. A Shanghai marketplace, its air saturated with dialects and the fierce smell of seared meat. Women washing food and dishes on a riverbank, nursing their howling red babies. The damp clatter of Yangtze commerce, its endlessly inventive curses.

She shuts her eyes. In an instant she is back on the steamship landing, Zanhua's arms stiff and desperate around her, that ridiculous cane poking right into her shoulder blade. It seemed so clear to her then—back in 1937—that Chiang Kai-shek's so-called New Life was already half dead. Chaipei lay in charred ruins. Hirohito's soldiers roamed Shanghai like wolves circling before another attack. But the true danger came from Yuliang's own countrymen, Chiang's Blue Shirts and Green Gang thugs—the Generalissimo's own oppressive little palette. Everyone knew at that point that Yuliang was a marked target—if not her body, then certainly her work. And yet Zanhua still begged her to reconsider. *You can stay,* he'd insisted. *It's not too late. Things here are on the verge of change. I feel it.* Even now—is it really twenty full years later?—Yuliang all but hears his voice. And for just an instant, doubt wells. *Should* she have stayed?

Don't be ridiculous. Opening her eyes, Yuliang shuts off the emotion as ruthlessly as she twists shut the tap. Her work is her life. She is lonely here, yes. But she has her painting, her cats. Her clients and admirers. Her small circle of intimates. Each one would confirm that her decision was the right one. Her friend Junbi said as much the other day, studying Yuliang's latest self-portrait: "There's something new in this one."

"You mean the fact that I've shown myself smoking, gambling, *and* drinking?" Yuliang didn't mention the nudity. Of course, that's not new.

"That's not it." Junbi thought for a moment, her soft brow furrowed. "Ah! I see it now. You are smiling. You actually look happy."

"Oh, really." But staring at herself—the flushed face, the round contours, the unusually relaxed stance, Yuliang had to admit she saw it too: she looked, at last, like a woman enjoying her life.

Her reverie is interrupted by the bells of Chapelle des Auxiliatrices. She looks at her watch, then up at Leanne, still standing in stocking feet by the table. Has the girl really been here for an entire half-hour?

As though hearing Yuliang's unspoken groan, Leanne steps back from the painting. She is chewing her lower lip.

"Is something wrong?" Yuliang asks her.

"My legs. You've made them—how do I put it? Rather . . . fat."

Ah-ha. So that's what she's been mooning around for. "I apologize," Yuliang says curtly. And yet even as she says it, she sees in the girl's face that it isn't that, isn't vanity after all. It is simply a question. *Why? Why did you do it this way?*

It is not Yuliang's habit to explain her art. Not to critics. Certainly not to models. Nevertheless, she finds herself stepping to the girl's side. *"Alors,"* she says, and with her brush handle traces over the painting's surface. Three lines: from Leanne's thigh to the tip of her head; from her head to Xiahe's buttocks; finally, along Xiahe's outstretched leg to the toe that nestles against Leanne's bare knee. "They are not your legs alone. They're legs for the compositional structure. A triangle. See? If I make them too thin, it throws off the balance. Even the lines are thick. You know some calligraphy?" And when the girl shakes her head: "Well, if you did, you'd recognize the stroke. It's very similar to those used in scrolls."

Leanne drops her gaze to the floor. She twists a foot into a patent-leather pump. Yuliang follows the movement musingly. Then she does the one thing she absolutely should not do at this instant: she looks back at her picture.

What she sees sinks her spirits: a hundred flaws bloom. Brushstrokes that seemed precise a half-hour ago shapeshift into gaping mistakes. The willow tree is flaccid. Leanne's hair—painted, she had thought, so as to create a sense of translucence—now simply appears to be stringy. And, yes, no doubt about it—the girl's legs are too thick.

Defeated, she leans against the table. *I'm a farce,* she thinks. *Even after all these years . . .*

"Madame. Are you all right?"

With her shoes on, Leanne stands a good seven centimeters above her. For a moment there's an urge to throw her arms around the white neck, to confess. To weep. But then Leanne touches her arm, and Yuliang stiffens as she always does when touched without permission. "We said five francs, correct?" She picks up her purse, snaps it open, and offers the bills stiffly. Leanne blinks.

"Thank you," she says, and takes the fee. There's an uncomfortable pause. "I like your purse," she adds.

Yuliang smiles coolly. The girl turns to pick up her salmon swing coat. "Tomorrow at eleven again?"

"Tomorrow we rest." Yuliang says, although in fact she's only just made this decision. She will take a day alone. To repair the damage. "Come Friday at four." And when Leanne hesitates, "Friday is no good?"

"No, it's fine. I finish with my father at three."

"Good." Yuliang reseats herself. It is late. What she wants is to smoke, to lose herself in the soothing, circular work of ink-grinding. But she has a student coming at six, one of the boys from the Beaux Arts. A baby, but very handsome: a liquid-eyed Italian. He indulges her by letting her attempt to instruct him in his native language—although these days Yuliang's Italian surely isn't much better than his Chinese.

She fumbles for her Gitanes, awaiting the woolly rustle of Leanne's coat, the calm *click* of the door closing. When neither comes she glances at the small mirror she's hung opposite the door (less to deflect spirits than to detect their more annoying mortal counterparts). The mirror reveals Leanne, still at the threshold, one gloved hand on the knob.

"My dear," Yuliang says, "I have *work.*"

"I'm sorry. I just . . ." The girl's voice is deferential but assured. She seems to know Yuliang will hear her out. Sighing, Yuliang sits back and waits, her eyes on the building across the street.

"Since we met last week," Leanne begins quietly, "I've been feeling like it was more than . . . coincidence. The way you found me."

"You mean destiny."

Yuliang says it wryly enough that the girl looks at her quickly. "Perhaps. Yes."

You have much to learn, Yuliang thinks to herself. But what she says is, "I didn't find *you*, my dear. I simply saw a pretty face." Though what had stopped her, as Leanne emerged from a Quai de Bercy cake shop, her egg tart in hand and warm sweet smells uncoiling in her path, wasn't so much the girl's classic features—the wide red mouth, the sweeping brow. It was a sense that something elusive and yet brittle underscored them—an emotional veneer, left by sorrow or hardship.

"At the girls' school back home," Leanne is continuing (so Hanoi is still home), "we studied art. I loved it." She takes a breath. "I suppose that part of me had always hoped that someday—"

"You want to paint," Yuliang interjects.

Leanne colors. "I've wanted to. I just haven't known where to start." She plays with her jade bracelet, the one accessory she hasn't removed today. "I can't pay much. But I'll model for free. I can help with washing, too."

Her hope is raw enough to make Yuliang blanch. Tightening her lips, she turns back to the window. The tenement is a brick glow in evening lamplight. She watches a window brighten as a light within is switched on. A small silhouette—child? dog?—darkens the pane. Then vanishes.

It must seem so easy, just to shift positions. Cross the studio, pick up a brush. And *voilà*, another Valadon. Unsurprisingly, Leanne is not the first model to ask this of her. They have no idea, these girls, of the pain—real pain—involved. The truth is that Yuliang's purse may be in vogue but her work certainly isn't. People don't want girls and flowers right now. They want splashes and gashes. Inkblot tests. Fingerpaints . . . What was it that dealer from the avenue Montaigne said? "Our clients want work that goes beyond the figurative. They want"—and this with a straight face—"metaphorical multivalence. Humor. Puns on form. You understand?"

In fact, Yuliang did not. In fact, she still doesn't. The very thought of that term (she couldn't find it in any of her six dictionaries) makes her want to laugh. But she understands one thing: If *multivalence de metaphor* is what is selling, she certainly can't afford to offer lessons at a discount. Especially not to a beginner.

What she hears herself say as Leanne shrugs on her coat is, "You have drawings? Bring them next time."

The girl's eyes widen. "Thank you, madame."

"I haven't said yes yet," Yuliang lies crisply, and turns away a second time. "Please don't let the cat out," she adds to the mirror. "He's something of a Houdini."

A muffled *thunk* as the cat is tossed to a chair. Then—at last!—the door shuts. The high heels tap away down the stairs.

Still unsettled for some reason, Yuliang pours herself a glass of Bordeaux. She pulls out a cigarette, lights it. *I'm still too soft*, she thinks, exhaling haze over her lake. *It's why I'm where I am: barely covering the cat food.* Lifting her enameled cup, she studies the painted phoenix that glowers (faded now, but still proud) from its side. Then she studies her own hand. The gold band on her heart finger is scratched and tarnished. A mesh of blue veins and wrinkles stretches from cuticles to wrist: age is tightening its net. When the cat lands in her lap and begins kneading her leg, small needles of discomfort prickle through her thin skirt. The pain, like a winter draft, brings her back to herself. She drinks some more, strokes the cat's white back. "You're spoiled," she reprimands it, in Chinese. "You have had a very easy life. Do you know that? Do you, Master Cat?"

He slits his eyes sleepily. She follows his slow gaze to the picture. "I really should just start over," she tells him.

But strangely—and perhaps it is only the wine's impact—her painting seems more redeemable. The sky at least works. Leanne's apple-plump breasts are nice, too. And that sad, small smile that says nothing. Little Mona Lisa in Heibei. Yuliang thinks of the burnlike wound she saw on the girl's back. A rash? A tryst? A battle with a masked attacker? She's curious about this French Chinese girl from Indochina. Perhaps that's why she agreed. If Leanne does end up joining her students (and she will, why deny it?), they'll have a session. They'll drink cheap *vin de table*, discuss what brought them here. Yuliang does it with all her new recruits. It seems only fair, since most come as much for the story as for the skill. What they want is a lusty fable: bordellos, brutish men, and, at the end, the magic brush that painted her escape, the way Liang's did in the old story. Yuliang doesn't give them that, of course. She paints around the dangerous parts of her past, ending up with a dozen versions that tell only what is most important. She's wise enough by now to know that history—especially her history—sells. And she needs the publicity. Having sworn off the dealers.

Outside, bells chime again. Just once: six-fifteen. A door slams; she hears the tread of Italian shoes on the stairwell. Yuliang looks longingly at her inkstone. Then she sighs. *I need the money*, she reminds herself.

Heaving herself to her feet, she checks her hair in the mirror, wipes an ultramarine paint fleck from her otherwise unpainted cheek. She thinks ahead to tomorrow, a day alone with her ladies and her lake. A light rain on the shutters further lifts her spirits. Yuliang loves painting in rain, loves how the rain makes the world feel close and safe. She'll grind new ink to thicken Leanne's hair, make grasstrokes glisten with the dawn. When it is done, she'll triumphantly place her name. In Chinese:

潘玉良
Pan-Yu-Liang

That the buyer, if she finds one, probably won't be able to read it means little. Yuliang doesn't sign for him. She signs for herself, to bind her work to her. To tattoo it with a message: she has won.

Part TWO

The JOURNEY

My body is white; my fate, softly rounded
Rising and sinking like mountains in streams.

Whatever way hands may shape me,
At center my heart is red and true.

———

Ho Xuan Huong
(an eighteenth-century
Vietnamese concubine)

One

Zhenjiang, 1913

AT NOON SHE HEARS her uncle's voice, buoyant, backed by velvet rain-patter:

> *Flute and drum keep time with the rover's song*
> *Amidst revel and feasting, sad thoughts come . . .*

The singing stops as he addresses the cat: "Hello, Turtle! Have you eaten yet?" Xiuqing pictures him stooping, stroking. His thin fingers limp on the arched black back; his wan face filled with wonder, even though he's had the cat for seven years now—a year longer than he's had Xiuqing. Still, he greets them both the same way. As though they are treats unexpectedly encountered in the pantry.

Cat patted, her *jiujiu* resumes his song. He's back later today than usual, Xiuqing realizes. Usually he leaves the little house at dusk and returns with the pale seep of sunrise. Xiuqing senses rather than hears these returns: the heavy vibration of his step; the cloying whiff of smoke-soaked clothes as he passes her door. The wall between them quavering slightly as he drops to his rickety bed.

Sometime after that, she'll sit, then rise. Creep out to see what's missing.

What's missing: it used to be things of scant consequence, things only Lina, their one young serving girl, would miss. The kitchen's extra ladle, a rice pot. In the past year, though, as Wu Ding's visits to the smoke houses near the All Heaven Temple have increased, it's become items of more value. The hanging scroll of Heaven and Earth, which Xiuqing would stand and stare at for hours in those first bleak days after she was brought here (wondering, *How do black brushstrokes become the Earth? How is an ink wash Heaven?*). The little pig they'd been fattening in the courtyard disappeared too, right ahead of the New Year's feast. And yesterday, Xiuqing found, even rice was missing: on her last trip to the storeroom there were three empty jars, mouths gaping. Xiuqing asked Lina about it. Lina said she didn't know. But her eyes shifted a little, oblique and anxious. Xiuqing knew what the serving girl must be thinking: when rice is carried off in the night, it's a sure sign that a house is headed for trouble.

"Little Xiu," she hears now, in his sleepy, singsong tenor.

"Yes." She puts down the doll that she'd been holding on her bent knees and giving a little ride to. The doll falls onto its back and stares blandly at the rooftop tiles. Its face is a dried-out pomelo rind her uncle carved two years ago, for Xiuqing's twelfth birthday. Its dress is Xiuqing's mother's apron, wrapped twice and tightly tied. The apron smells like her mother did, of rice water, ash, and cedar. At least, Xiuqing thinks she can smell these things as she hugs the little toy each night in bed. She also thinks sometimes she hears her mother's voice, although in truth she barely recalls now what it sounded like. Still, she wills herself to hear it in the presleep daze before dreams: mama. Singing her name softly: *"Xiuqing."*

The courtyard stones are slick and silvered with the rain. Xiuqing picks her way over them carefully. Her uncle sits beneath an awning, the cat a plush mound in his lap. Gray half-moons border his eyes. He straightens the spectacles he sometimes lets her try on (worn for show; their lenses are clear glass). "How are you?" he cries, beaming. "What's for dinner?"

"I thought river butterfish in creamy sauce. And some cabbage rolls." *And small portions of rice*, Xiuqing adds silently. She doesn't ask where he's been. She knows he'd only lie anyway. He lies to her often, just as he leaves her often. As long as he comes back, she doesn't mind.

"Wonderful," he says. "I'm famished." Which is actually another lie: except for those few times he has tried to shake his smoking habit, Wu Ding eats with a sparrow's stomach. But he likes it when Xiuqing and Lina cook as though for company. He likes the look and smell of a full table.

"I brought you something," he adds, and reaches below his chair.

Xiuqing takes the gift and sits on the ground to open it. She unwinds the dingy string. Inside the brown paper is a stack of Western catalogues. Their covers feature curvaceous, flush-cheeked *yangguizi*—white-ghost women—in Western clothes.

"New republic," her uncle says, beaming, "new look. This is what modern girls will start to wear now." A self-declared intellectual despite his artisan background, he considers himself an authority on both the old and the new China. "I found them at the mission. I know how you like pretty pictures. You can look at them on our journey."

"Journey?" Xiuqing looks up. She doesn't go out much. Aside from the physical discomfort of walking on her folded feet, her mother believed that proper women remain indoors. And since bringing her here, Wu Ding, for all his talk of modern girls, has more or less abided by his sister's wishes. He hired Lina to teach Xiuqing cooking and household skills and to take her to a neighbor's house to embroider. Other than these brief trips, though, Xiuqing has left her uncle's little house exactly twelve times: five festivals, three operas, and four New Year's trips to the Zhenfeng Pagoda. Plus one surreptitious, teetering trip up the street, just to prove she could do it; though as a boar by birth, Xiuqing knows she's destined to stay close to home.

Darting down the street after dark is one thing, however. Taking a journey is quite another. The only trip she's really taken was the three-day sail here from Yangzhou after her mama's funeral. All she recalls are her own white mourning clothes, slowly growing gray with soot. "What . . . what about Lina?" she asks now with a quaver. "What about the housekeeping?"

"Don't worry about these things, little Xiu. Your life is about to change." He lets the words linger, pleased by their prescience. Then he breaks into song again: " 'All is quiet. The moon lingers, and the emerald screen hangs low . . .' " He pauses, quirks a brow.

"Li Qingzhao?" It's a little game they have: he recites, she identifies. Modern girls, her *jiujiu* says, should have a grasp of the classics.

"Right!" He beams. "And she was . . ."

"A *ci* poetess, of the Song, Dynasty."

"Not just *a* poetess, little Xiu. One of the best our nation has ever seen, though many dismiss her poems as women's work. She lost everything at one point—her husband, home, wealth. But her misfortune didn't break her. She bent, like bamboo. She turned her grief into verse so pure and true that nearly a thousand years later she is still revered . . ." He drifts off for a moment, staring at his knobby knuckles. Then he pulls out a cracked pocket watch. "We need to leave," he adds, "in just about . . . oh, seventeen hours." He snaps the watch shut, an emphatic *snick*. "Why don't you go pack?"

"Pack?" He is serious.

"Yes. Pack a lot. Warm things too." He looks skyward. "And one nice outfit. Perhaps the red cheongsam I bought you to wear for New Year's." He makes a kiss-kiss sound at the cat and lifts his feet to the table to form a spindly bridge. Turtle eyes it, leaps, lands. He circles on his master's thighs and lies down. Xiuqing kicks a heel against her chair, faintly panicked. When she looks up, Wu Ding's eyes are shut: he is going to sleep.

BACK IN HER ROOM she lays the catalogues out so they overlap, a slick secondhand fan. She flips through them distractedly as two or three raindrops tap on the papered window, testing for a downpour. From the kitchen comes the sound of Lina's butcher's knife, sparking thoughts of the green frost of cabbage. *I hope she cuts it finely enough*, Xiuqing thinks.

And, almost as afterthought, *I hope we can pay her this month*.

In his more capable modes her uncle letter-writes for the illiterate and peddles the shoes and handkerchiefs Xiuqing embroiders. But since she took over the household accounts (last year, after one of his longer clinic visits coincided with bill collectors carting off most of the little house's furniture), Xiuqing is well aware of the sword's-edge dance of their finances. It's only thanks to Lina's connections—and her fishing skills—that the household is eating at all.

Sighing, Xiuqing opens her pine chest, one of the few items she convinced the bill collectors to leave, and begins making a pile:

Two thick-weave cotton tunics.

Two pairs of cotton trousers.

A woven sash for holidays and special occasions.

The cheap, knee-length cheongsam her uncle bought her to wear on their few New Year's visits this year.

A padded winter jacket (*warm things too*).

After a moment's hesitation she adds a pair of plain cotton slippers, passing over another pair that is newer but too big for her now. When she last wore them her feet were freshly bound, the pain a raw shock, a silent scream. The soles are clean because she'd crawled on hands and knees for four months. Still, the training shoes prompt her to remember something else. Turning, she pulls out a pair of shoes wrapped in yellowing tissue. These haven't touched the ground either. In fact, they've never been worn at all. The red silk is intricately embroidered, with rows of Beijing knots plumping out magpies' breasts. Delicate stem and split stitches outline hills full of peonies. In places the technique is so delicate and skilled that the bare silk is itself a motif. But there is one small patch by the back of the left heel that is blank in a different way. Unintentional; unfinished. A small mouth, crying.

Xiuqing holds the shoes in her palms. Lifts them a little: one, two. They were made for her wedding day, to flutter over floor and ground. Her mama spoke of this someday wedding nearly every day toward the end, half reclining on her bed. Sewing, knotting, biting. It took Xiuqing a long time to realize that her mother was stitching more than just shoes. She was stitching her daughter a promise: after the binding, the finding. The making of a good match. *Your uncle improved his lot with his mind: he learned to read. But a girl's feet are her best chance to better herself. If we make them small enough, we'll get our fortunes back. When you've grown, when your feet are perfect lilies.*

But Xiuqing's feet never were perfect lilies. Her mother died before the bones had fully broken to the midwife's specifications, and she'd lacked the strength, at the end, to make Xiuqing walk upon them properly. By the time Xiuqing reached Zhenjiang, her feet had grown by three full fingers, and she'd lacked the determination to break them back again. The result is that now, when she is fourteen, her feet are even bigger than those the neighborhood grandmothers scornfully call "Yangzhou style"—six inches long, twice the size of the tiny lilies favored by Souzhou's famed beauties. Bigger feet make for easier walking, of course. But her mother would have been aghast. "Sea bass," she would have called them. Xiuqing tries not to think about it.

She can't help wondering now, however, whether this journey might be about the long-awaited making of a match. Is it possible? Has her odd old uncle actually found someone for her to marry? Xiuqing can't imagine him living on his own, without her. But she also can't imagine living here forever. As her mama always said, girls are raised for others . . .

In the end she sets the shoes on the "pack" pile, just in case. If she can't wear them, then at least they'll bring her luck.

Sitting back, Xiuqing scans the room for anything else she might need, her gaze coming to rest on her broken looking glass. Her most steadfast companion here, the Mirror Girl, gazes back at her blankly.

Her face is pale and slightly square, with a broad forehead and a strong chin. Her eyes are large, heavily lashed, her lips full and fresh, if slow to smile. Xiuqing knows she's considered pretty. Still all she sees now is a tight-faced, tired-looking girl. "We're going to be fine," Xiuqing tells her. "This will be an adventure."

The girl just stares back, her lips tense with unease.

AT THE ROYAL BRITANNICA Steamship Company's ticket office the signs are in Roman characters, with smaller Chinese characters beneath and even smaller characters and letters beneath that. All, for Xiuqing, are equally unreadable, although her uncle claims to differentiate between the five foreign languages (in order: English, Japanese, German, French, and "possibly American").

The *yangguizi* themselves queue at a window manned by another white devil, and Xiuqing studies them with some interest. The two women in line look nothing like her buxom magazine ladies; they are older, fatter, distinctly less fashionable. One of them returns Xiuqing's gaze with annoyance. Xiuqing stares right back, with all the impunity of a visitor to a zoo.

Her uncle edges toward the crowd's shoreline, describing how they'll travel. "Like the foreigners—like gentry. Two beds, one great window. A lovely view of the water." Xiuqing looks at the water, where the stripped hull of an old steamship serves as the landing for the newer one they'll be taking—the *Crying Loon*. To Xiuqing, the ship, with its myriad windows and mysterious lack of sails, looks like an enormous honeycomb. Passengers line the railings like indolent bees. Stark-naked coolies tow the huge hulk through the shallows to the makeshift landing, hemp ropes sawing at the sun-darkened skin of their backs. When they'd first arrived, Xiuqing had tried to make out what they looked like from the waist down. She got one glimpse of a purplish, wormlike stretch of dripping flesh before her *jiujiu*, following her gaze, primly hustled her off toward the office.

Now, facing her fellow travelers, Xiuqing shifts from foot to foot, trying to ease the cutting itch of her bindings, which she wound extra-tight this morning. "Will we really have a window, Uncle?"

"A window!" he reiterates grandly. "The silvery river. The blue of the sky." He lights a cigarette, adding, "The fresh green face of the new nation."

Both the Yangtze and the sky are gray, almost the same color as the pigeons that make feathery lumps both inside and outside the office. To Xiuqing, all three grays are beautiful, in different ways. The cloudbank is blue, white, and black furled together. The Yangtze is a thick flow of gray-gold. Even the pigeons hint at gleaming rainbows: aqua, violet, jade green, as though their drab feathers hide jewels.

Uncle Wu stands and stares at the three lines, fingering his spectacles. Finally he throws back his shoulders and leads them into the crowd, which sucks them in. Everyone seems to be shouting, a dozen dialects melding into a single singsong wail: *Walawala, wa-la.* Xiuqing feels elbows, backs, ribs pressing against her. The man behind her has just eaten salted fish, perhaps with old beer. She breathes through her mouth and looks at him from the corner of her eyes. It's a soldier, just a few years older than she. Perhaps the age of her soon-to-be fiancé. He is wearing a khaki vest cut in a Western style but the pigtail and ballooning pants of the old imperial army. Xiuqing wonders whether he is being called to Nanjing. Her uncle has told her about the fighting there. One side fights for China's provisional premier, Yuan Shikai, whom Uncle Wu hates. The other is fighting for something called either *parliamentary procedure* or *electoral outcome,* terms her *jiujiu* won't clarify because as an opium addict he was barred from voting.

When the soldier catches Xiuqing's eye and grins, Xiuqing feels herself flush. She pushes ahead to escape his stare, but the surging crowd pushes him forward right along with her. Soon she feels his hand brushing her back. Then dropping a little bit lower. Then lower still. Then—he does it so quickly and assuredly that at first she's not even sure she's reading her own body correctly—it's deftly nestled between her thighs.

There.

He doesn't leer; doesn't even acknowledge her shock. He acts as though this were simply ticket-crowd custom. *Is it?* Xiuqing wonders. What do people do in situations like this? If she were Washing Silk Woman from the *Tales of Honorable and Virtuous Women*, she would throw herself in the river. But then again, the river looks very dirty. And while the ancients may have lauded Washing Silk Woman's chasteness (for the soldier merely spoke to her; he never even touched her!), Xiuqing senses somehow that her uncle wouldn't feel the same way.

She twitches her hips tentatively, but the hand just wedges further into the split of her buttocks. Finally she puts her own small hand behind her and presses back. A gruff chuckle; another blast of salty fish-breath. Eventually the hand moves away. But her backside quivers with shame.

"Almost there," her *jiujiu* calls back encouragingly. "First class awaits!"

IN THE END, however, both first and second class prove too expensive. "They've raised it," huffs her uncle. "Must be all these rich foreigners." They travel third class, deep within the steamer's windowless hull, boxed in like steaming dumplings. Their only access to the water is a small rear deck barely the size of a small courtyard, its floor coated with hardened phlegm and ossified seagull excretions. "Perfect," Wu Ding mutters, staking out their small space on the floor. "Room to breathe here. Near the water. More than fine." He rolls out a blanket and anchors it with shoes. One of the pairs is his. The other is Xiuqing's. Not the wedding slippers, of course. Xiuqing knows little of opium, but she knows enough about her uncle to know that he wouldn't see what she does: a mother's failing fingers, the lush thread-gardens they'd tended. He'd see pellets of opium balls, stacked up like a stagnant black mountain.

Even now, in fact, Wu Ding's eyes rove the crowd restlessly: he must not have much opium left. It occurs to Xiuqing that she may lose him for the night. The thought terrifies her even more than that of sleeping beside him directly, without their customary wall between them. In this room full of mostly men, she feels like a peach without its skin. *Get him to talk*, she thinks. "*Jiujiu*. I've a question."

Her uncle is rolling up a jacket, plumping it with small blows. "Look," he says. "Isn't this nice? It will make a comfy pillow. Give me your jacket, little Xiu. I'll make one for you too."

Xiuqing hands him the padded silk coat she's brought. Her *jiujiu* rolls it up as well. "You see, this isn't so bad!" He looks up, pleased. "What is it, little Xiu?"

She asks the first thing that comes to her mind: "I was just wondering whether you've thought at all. About my—about my future. What I want to know is, are you finding me a—" *This was a bad choice*, she realizes. How does one bring up what one isn't supposed to bring up? "My mother always said," she goes on, carefully, "that marriage is the most important thing. She said every woman must have children. She said . . ."

Drifting off, she looks up from her feet. Her uncle's face has abruptly emptied of mirth. For a moment he just licks his lips. Then he shakes his head. "Marriage!" he thunders, so loudly that the family next to them turns to stare. "Are you some simpering little fool who has no value without a husband?"

Xiuqing pulls her hands into her sleeves. It makes her feel less conspicuous.

"No, my girl, noooooo," he says, still loudly enough to elicit disapproving glares two rows over. Oblivious to them, he settles back on his mat, cross-legged. He is winding up for a lecture. Xiuqing heaves a silent sigh of relief. "I'm giving you an opportunity that goes beyond marriage," he goes on. "I'm sending you into the workforce, niece. You're headed to Wuhu. To work."

It takes a moment for the meaning of the words to settle. *Work?* Xiuqing pictures the straining coolies, their corded muscles, their backs covered with rope-wide welts. She pictures Lina scrubbing the floor by the stove, killing a chicken by calmly snapping its neck. "Work," she says, trying to associate herself with the concept.

"*You're going to work*," he replies, beaming. "You're going to be your own woman." He closes his eyes, sings softly, but with feeling:

The moon setting, heaven's mirror in flight
Clouds build, spreading to seascape towers.

"Li Bai," guesses Xiuqing.

"Correct again," says her uncle. "You see? You're very smart. You could be just about anything. A lady poet. A teacher."

"I'm going to work as a teacher?" Xiuqing asks, incredulous. She's always thought teachers were men. Old men. With long beards, and canes they use to beat misbehaving schoolboys.

Her uncle scratches his head. "Well, no. The place I've gotten for you is—well, you'll be doing something else first. But the money's good. The money's very good." He sucks a tooth contemplatively. Almost to himself, he adds, "And after a while, after you've saved, you can move on to something else."

"Am I going to be doing embroidery?"

His hesitation is beat-quick; Xiuqing barely registers it before he slaps his thigh energetically in approval. "Yes!" he cries. "Embroidery! It's just as Masters Hume and Emerson tell us. It's about realizing your own potential." Shutting his eyes, he recites with bravado: " 'Man is his own star. And the soul that can render an honest and a perfect man commands all light, all influence, all fate.' "

Xiuqing nods—purely from reflex, since her uncle still has his eyes closed, and she has no idea at all who the masters "YuMee" and "AyMah Soon" are. He enjoys bringing up such foreign names, especially after visits to his mission clinic and its reading room. Xiuqing is never certain he has them straight in his mist-filled head. But for now it's enough: her *jiujiu* is pleased with her. He isn't leaving. And the soldier is nowhere in sight.

Embroidery, Xiuqing thinks, settling back a little on her new pillow. Of course there'd be money in that. Her parents had made a good living at it. Until, that is, the bad men came. Mama never said exactly what they did—the subject sewed her red lips together almost as tightly as her expert seams. But Xiuqing gathered it involved things like characters and written contracts, and the fact that her *baba* couldn't read. It is one of the reasons that Xiuqing has promised herself that one day, like her uncle, she will learn.

The boy from the ticket window sticks his head through the doors. "Anyone who doesn't have a ticket, off," he calls. "Next stop, Wuxi."

There's some stirring, some pocket-patting. No one leaves. Wu Ding grunts and lowers himself back onto the mat. "We're off." He pulls his hat over his eyes. Xiuqing lies down on her own mat and thinks of her mother. Long, fragrant hair. A face as round and pale and essential as the moon. Soft, strong hands pulling thread through the metal embroidery frame. Full lips chanting the last line of Li Qingzhao's poem:

> I caress the withered flower, fondle the fragrant petals
> Trying to bring back the lost time.

Two

"WHY DID HE FALL?" Xiuqing asks three days later, and gives a little push with her toes. She's leaning over the ship's railing, tipping forward, almost to the limit of her balance.

Her uncle doesn't answer: He seems to have lost the slim thread of his lecture about Li Bai. Not on the poems of the itinerate bard, but on his death: He fell from a boat more than a thousand years ago. Perhaps near here, or even on this very stretch of gold-gray water somewhere between Tongling and Wuhu.

Xiuqing pulls her jacket tight around her waist. After three days on the water she feels wind-whipped and shrunken, smaller inside her clothes. For a moment she imagines that that's all she is: clothes. Creased and dust-streaked pants, a top. Rumpled cotton soaked in boat smells, hung on a railing to air. As her eyes reach the level of her thighs, she sees oily shadows of sloshed butterfly noodles. If they were home she could tell Lina to do laundry today, to soak their things in river water and pine ash. To spread it all on a boulder to dry. *Little on earth,* her mother used to say, *is as sweet as sun-dried laundry.* In the days before her foot-binding, Xiuqing would go along, chasing tadpoles and minnows while her mother beat clothes against a rock. *That's far enough, Xiuqing!* her mama would shrill when Xiuqing strayed too far. *Stay where I can see you!*

"That's far enough, little Xiu," Uncle Wu says now. "Any farther and you'll fall right off." He crushes his fifth cigarette of the morning under one of his heels. "He fell the same way you very well might, if you don't start acting your age."

Just for a moment she defies him, testing gravity's tug and tumble. She looks past her legs to where they've just been. The boat leaves bile-colored pleats in the river's wake.

"Little Xiu." Her uncle's voice is beginning to tighten. With a small grunt, Xiuqing pulls herself upright. "He fell," Wu Ding resumes, "in the middle of an evening cruise. He was reaching for the moon."

"The moon?"

"It was under the boat. Underwater. The old bastard had had too much to drink." He lights a sixth cigarette, fingers dancing a little. He's beginning to reach his limit. Xiuqing does a quick mental calculation: It's been two days since she spied him squatting in the ship's soiled stern patio, sharing a pipe with a second-class merchant. They ran into the merchant this morning, strolling on deck. Her uncle gave him an ingratiating greeting and then hustled Xiuqing off. "Not a very refined man," he murmured vaguely. "Best to avoid him, in such small quarters." And Xiuqing knew without asking that he now owed this man too, just as he owed all the lenders and pawnshops back home.

"He drowned," he says now, firmly, as though settling a debate. "The man couldn't swim."

"That doesn't seem very sensible. Reaching for the moon in the water."

"Artists aren't interested in sense. They're interested in the *senses*." He coughs, the sound harsh and wet in the wind. He pats himself for his handkerchief, comes up empty. "They're after life's reflections, not life itself."

Xiuqing hops back on one foot, tries to balance again. She contemplates this gap: things and reflections. Objects and images. She stares at the sinking sun, its rays chipping gemlike off the river. The moon—Li Bai's mirror—is a silver disk to the east. She'd like to string it on a silken cord around her neck.

Her uncle breaks into another round of coughing. Xiuqing hands over her handkerchief, watches him shudder into it. He glances at the blood flecks before hastily tucking the cloth into his pocket.

"I could get you some water," she offers worriedly. "I could go looking for the tea man."

"Ahhh, Xiuqing," he says softly, as he always does. "Little Xiu. What would I do without you?"

A gull slopes toward them, its wings stiff and still. Its cry is a raspy echo of Wu's cough. Below them, a swarm of coolies strip down and prepare to wade out to meet the boat. Her uncle watches them, the wind whipping a tear from his left eye. Then, abruptly, he looks up. "Wuhu awaits," he exclaims, as though this were a long-awaited surprise. "Let's get ready."

AS THEIR LAUNCH BOBS TOWARD SHORE, Xiuqing squints ahead into the gathering darkness. She makes out the tiled tops of the riverbank shops, the flickering winks of new streetlamps. A single, soaring spire rises before the mountains, its point brushed into softness by dusk. The cathedral, her uncle tells her, was built by Europeans who were part of Wuhu's small community of foreign traders and missionaries. When antiforeigner feeling ran highest during the Boxer Rebellion, they had to hide in their building. They boarded up the candy-colored windows, nailed the elaborate doors shut. The townsfolk, goaded on by the Boxers, stood outside shouting *Hairy devils!* and *Mother-sexers!* They called the Europeans *washed-out ghosts* and *eaters of our babies.* Eventually they destroyed most of the structure. The foreigners and orphans fled down the river.

"The foreigners eat babies?" Xiuqing says now, horrified.

"No," her uncle says. "But people thought they did. They thought when they took the children in, they were planning a holiday feast. It didn't help that they were feeding them pig food. Cow's milk. Boiled potatoes and corn."

Xiuqing shudders. Chewing wax, she thinks, would have more flavor.

The launch is being hailed by bobbing lights. A swarm of sampans approach like vengeful bugs, all eyes and wriggling arms. As they draw nearer, Xiuqing sees that the eyes are just paint: white-and-black dots with the sharp points of bows as noses. The arms belong to people, whole families shouting urgently as though they're coming to put out a fire:

Three yang for baggage and transport, good deal! Good deal!
No, no; that dog-fart is lying. He'll steal you blind. Don't listen to him!
Come with me—my boat is brand-new! You'll ride in the lap of luxury!

When the boats reach them, a riverman with an egglike nose grabs their bundle and smiles a foul-smelling smile. Another takes Xiuqing's arm, his hand squeezing around it in a greasy clamp. The launch rocks, water spilling over both sides. The navigator shouts, "Who are you pushing, snout-face! Were you born in the year of the boar? You'll drown us!"

"I was born in the year of the boar," Xiuqing murmurs. But no one pays any attention.

Somehow her uncle manages to negotiate through the chaos, and soon Xiuqing finds herself sitting beneath the arched bamboo of a boat. The riverwoman who steers has big shoes with strange, sharp points and smells of sweat, salt, and drying fish. When she sees Xiuqing, she smiles and says something in a tongue as incomprehensible as that of the gulls, still crying overhead.

Three

IN THE MORNING she awakens from thick, disturbing dreams to the sound of her uncle's knuckles on the door: *crack, crack, crack.* "Up, up, little Xiu! An inch of time is an inch of gold."

Xiuqing opens her eyes. The door opens a sliver. Her uncle peers in, pupils swollen from smoking.

"Why don't you put on your dress?" he says. "Brush your hair. Look pretty for breakfast." He shuts the door with a bang.

Xiuqing stands and stretches. She pushes back the window's shutters. Outside, two sparrows bathe, twitching and fluttering in a puddle by a pump. Xiuqing thinks, *Come on, walk.* Lina says that when sparrows walk, it's good luck.

One of the birds bobs its head, takes a drink. Droplets fly from its beak like flung diamonds.

DOWNSTAIRS, HER *JIUJIU* SITS at a cluttered table across from a man in an emerald-green silk coat. The man looks up as Xiuqing stands in the doorway. He takes in the red cheongsam, her carefully combed hair. The directness of his gaze shames her slightly.

"There you are. Join us. Have some tea." Her uncle pats the seat next to him.

"This is the niece," the green-coated man says blandly.

"It is."

Xiuqing spends the short silence that follows rubbing her tea-cup's rim against her lips. The man studies her some more, his jaw wagging from side to side like a goat's as he chews. Crumbs of prawn paste stick pinkly to his mustache.

"This is Master Gao," her uncle eventually says. "He's helping us to secure your position."

"There are still some details to settle," Master Gao says, and spits something onto the floor.

This is a practice Uncle Wu condemns as outmoded, unsanitary, and uncultured. But he doesn't say so now. What he says, very mildly, is, "We understand that."

Xiuqing fixes her eyes on the little teapot, on its picture of the Yellow Mountains in indigo. Pinnacles soar toward the handles; narrow rivers wend their way up the spout. When she pours, it's as though the yellow river water comes to life and splashes into her cup.

Master Gao wipes his hands, then climbs to his feet. "If all is as you say, I believe we can use her. The Hall used to take only younger ones. But recently we've changed our policy. Too much money invested. Girls of this age—how old is she?"

"Fourteen."

The man nods. "A bit old, but still young enough to learn. If she's obedient."

Xiuqing waits for her uncle to tell the man that she's already learned what she needs to embroider. But he just says, "Oh, she's very obedient, my niece."

He begins folding and unfolding his newspaper, and Xiuqing watches ink spread like soot over his fingers. The man indicates the serving woman with a jut of his chin. "Zheng *niangyi* can handle the details and contract. If everything's in order, she'll take her over this afternoon."

The woman looks up at the sound of her name. An eye skims

Xiuqing, narrow and assessing. The other is cloaked in a moist white veil that fits the cornea like a shield.

Master Gao scratches himself between his legs, strolls around the table. "More loans," he reads over Uncle Wu's sloping shoulder. "They're yanking at their own balls, this fancy Western-style government. Why do we need wider streets?"

"I suppose for the automobiles."

The man snorts. "No one's going to be able to afford even a jackass if this keeps up. We're going to owe everything to the damned long-noses." He frowns. "I hear, by the way, that we share a friend."

"Yes. Master Fang," her uncle says in a tight voice. "I did mention that he sends his greetings." Xiuqing looks up. Master Fang, she knows, owns Uncle Wu's favorite opium den and the house that adjoins it, where men buy girls ("Buy them for what?" she asked Lina once. But the maid just pressed her lips together).

"I'm thinking of someone else," Master Gao says. "Merchant Deng? From Chibi."

Her uncle blanches. "Ah yes. We met aboard the *Crying Loon*." He stands reluctantly, wringing his hands in a smudging self-caress. "We had a very interesting discussion."

"He'd very much like to finish it," Master Gao says meaningfully.

Xiuqing sees her uncle swallow hard. Then—stunningly—the other man reaches out and puts his hand on her shoulder. Easily. As if she's his daughter. Or a wife.

Xiuqing looks to her uncle. She waits for him to speak. But he just shifts from foot to foot like a nervous schoolboy.

"Perhaps," Master Gao says, rubbing Xiuqing's neck gently, "you can stop by and see him. On your way back home." His fingers smell like smoked fish. Xiuqing stares at her uncle, so wide-eyed that her lids ache. *Help. Help me.*

But Wu Ding is looking at his hands; he seems finally to have noticed the inkstains. "Certainly," he says, accepting a hot, damp towel from the old woman. "I was planning to do that. In fact, I was going to go buy my ticket tonight."

Tonight? Xiuqing's pounding heart skips again. Her uncle said he'd stay here for a few days. They would see the town together. Make her introductions. Then he'd take her to a fine, final meal before he went home. Just for a few weeks . . .

"Good," says Master Gao. He lets his fingers trace her ear. Then, abruptly, he steps away, throwing two coins on the table. "I'll send a runner so he'll know to expect your visit."

After he leaves, her uncle sits back down heavily. *"Jiujiu?"* Xiuqing asks quaveringly.

He stares into his cup. "Perhaps," he murmurs, "we should get started."

He's not speaking to her. But when Zheng *niangyi* puts a gnarled hand on Xiuqing's shoulder, he says sternly, "Cooperate, niece."

"Obey your uncle," the woman caws as Xiuqing twitches herself free.

Wu Ding turns his back. He studies the sole piece of wall art, a strange painting done entirely in iron. Its blunt lines portray a man fishing in a stream. The woman drops to her knees with a grunt, as though preparing to perform the kowtow. Xiuqing fights back an unplanned giggle, though she doesn't find it especially funny. The old fingers probe through Xiuqing's flimsy shoes, measuring length and width. They insert themselves into the peach-like clefts, testing for depth and tightness. When she is finished, she clambers to her own big feet and unties Xiuqing's shirtwaist. Xiuqing feels her hands again, cold this time, and hard, on her belly, her neck, her arms. She yanks her shirt back down. "Stop. Stop that!"

Zheng *niangyi* pauses. She looks at Wu Ding's fixed back. Then she cuffs Xiuqing on the side of her head. Hard. "Stay put." She takes the soft flesh of the girl's forearm and twists it like a key in a lock. "There's nothing else for it—you'll just have to endure. Try to think of something else."

Xiuqing's helplessness wells up from somewhere deep inside her. Her breath slows with the sheer rush of it. Her arms and lips are numb; the place where the blow landed tingles. She feels leathery fingerpads brush her neck and nipples. *Something else.* Feels the nipples harden like two copper coins. *Think. Something else. Think.* She searches for something to cling to, some idea or image that will help, make it stop. She settles on flesh, its various tones and hues. The way it changes with touch. A slap mark glows red at first but fades slowly to peach-pink. Then to nothing at all. Pinches and punches, which she's seen on Lina (her father beats her sometimes), darken the skin. They leave purple marks but gradually lighten into streaking blues, reds, yellows. They can be covered, Lina has shown her, by a mixture made up carefully at the apothecary's. The ingredients are talcum powder and grease and rouge.

Oh, Lina.

Her uncle stretches a lazy finger out and touches the little iron man's iron fishing rod.

"Come," the woman says. "We'll finish upstairs."

THEY STAND IN XIUQING'S RENTED ROOM before the bamboo bed, the half-sorted clothes on top of it. The things that need washing lie heaped to the left. The still-clean things are folded flat on the right. The red shoes sit on top of the latter pile, where Xiuqing put them before breakfast. The catalogues are stacked neatly on the small, low table.

The woman picks up the shoes, turns them over. She leafs briefly through one of the catalogues. She looks at Xiuqing, puzzled. Then she shrugs and sweeps everything off the bed, onto the floor in a heap. Her good eye finds Xiuqing in the mirror. "Tell me, child," she says, pushing back her sleeves, "your uncle says you have yet to light the big candles. Is that true? I've seen enough opium-eaters in my time to know. I'll bet this one lies every hour."

Mirror Girl just stares back, as expressionless as a girl in a poster. Xiuqing, in fact, studies the framed reflection as though she were merely considering a poster. Perhaps an advertisement for youth cream: an old woman and a young one. The way time molds our faces.

"Your melon," the woman prompts. "He says it hasn't been broken yet."

Xiuqing's mind presents melon: wet yellow-green flesh. Shiny, eye-shaped black seeds. Her uncle, in another of his peculiarities, hates the fruit. He says it takes too much work to eat.

"*Aiyaa*," groans the woman. "Are you as empty-headed as a melon as well?"

She turns toward Xiuqing, positions her. Ungently, she pushes her down to the bed. She checks Xiuqing's feet again, clucking in disapproval. Then she unties Xiuqing's trousers and yanks them down, down around her little ankles.

Xiuqing feels the woman's hands fumbling at her thighs. She registers air from the window washing her skin. *I will need to remember this,* she thinks numbly. *I'll need to tell them everything. When they come for me.* And yet, who will come for her? Lina? Her mother's hungry ghost? The fiancé she'd imagined a lifetime earlier? Besides, what's happening isn't something she'll ever have words for. It will simply be shame—the head-splitting shame of it.

It's the shame that makes her throw back her head back and call: "Uncle! Please! *Jiujiu!*" And then: "Mama!"

The scream rings through the stillness; a child's voice, cracked and broken. A chair shifts abruptly against a floor somewhere. There is no further response.

AGES LATER, IT SEEMS, the fingers pull stickily out. Xiuqing hears steps, then splashing from the washbasin. The woman's voice seems to travel from some faraway point: "All's in order. I'll go have him draw up the papers." Her footsteps pad heavily off down the hallway.

Two images float past: of sparrows not walking, of Mirror Girl lying here on the bed. In her head the girl lies still, barely breathing. Her pulse has slowed to almost the same still pace as that of the catalogue ladies, staring blithely at the ceiling.

When Xiuqing finally returns downstairs Wu Ding sits at the breakfast table, just as he did when she first came down. Now, however, it's Zheng *niangyi* who sits across from him, face-to-face. Like a man. The papers they both hold are slightly wet; her uncle has just copied them out with his pen. The woman squints at her version with the tense overfocus Xiuqing quickly recognizes as illiteracy.

Wu Ding reads:

The sale being effected, she can be taken away, her name changed, and when she is grown up she shall abide by the will of the purchaser who may make use of her for any purpose he pleases, whether the same be respectable or otherwise. In the case of disobedience, she may be disposed of without hindrance. By this consignment her relations have yielded up all interest in her, and intercourse between her and her relations will cease forever and she shall not be redeemed. In the case of death, which is mutually to be regarded as the order of heaven, no complaints are to be preferred.

A shuffling pause.

"What was that part about relatives?" Zheng *niangyi* asks.

"I have a grandmother," Xiuqing announces abruptly. She is speaking loudly, in the same little-girl voice that emerged from her, unsummoned, upstairs. "I have a mother, too. Back home, in Yuang-zhou. They'll both be very angry—"

"*Hush!*" roars her uncle, and pounds the table.

Xiuqing hushes.

Slowly, as though it takes tremendous effort, her uncle relaxes each finger.

"I," he says, "am her last living relative." When the woman looks dubious, he adds, "My mother died seven years ago. My sister a year later." He puts down the papers, neatens them with his fingers. Aligns the corners and edges.

"How did they die?" the broker asks suspiciously.

"My mother was simply old. My sister died of disease with the blossoms. There was another sister, but she died as a child. When this one was still a baby."

"How?"

"Of the water sickness."

"Water," repeats the innkeeper reflectively. "And the father?"

"Threw himself into the river when this one was two." He says it flatly, as though the words mean nothing to him. "They say he'd lost all his money."

"And she is how old, you said?"

"Fourteen." He smiles, a little sadly. "Year of the boar. Which, as you know, means she'll never stray too far from home."

"But is she stubborn?"

Xiuqing stares at him beseechingly. "Not at all," he says, meeting her eyes directly for the first time this morning. "She is strong, but like bamboo. She'll bend if the wind forces her to. But she will not break."

He holds her gaze a moment longer. Then he clears his throat and looks away.

THE NEXT TIME the old woman gives Xiuqing a blow, Xiuqing isn't thinking about the colors of her skin. She is thinking about her feet, how they must be red with blood now. She has never, ever walked this far before.

The broker hits her again. "Hurry up. Are you a girl or a log with legs?" The hitting hurts, yet there's something oddly affectionate, almost half-pat, to it. As though they share some sort of camaraderie. *We'll make it*, the light blows seem to say. *We've been through a hard time together.* Xiuqing forces herself to walk faster, if only to avoid the woman's touch.

"You know," her captor says, scurrying now to keep up, "you are actually very lucky. My mother died too. I was around your age." Her withered lips purse around her little silver pipe, making small kissing sounds as she sucks out smoke. "I got a good-for-nothing husband. An opium-eater, like your uncle. He didn't talk or dress as fancily. But they are all the same, such men."

Xiuqing thinks of her *jiujiu* waving gaily from the door at the inn. Reciting—as Xiuqing's innards turned to stone—the final stanza of his steamboat verse:

> *Poor waters of home. I know how it feels:*
> *Ten thousand miles of farewell on this boat . . .*

"As for me," the woman is continuing, "I couldn't keep anything in the house. He sold my pots, my sewing things. He even sold my daughters—all but the baby. When that money ran out he leased me to Old Man Cao. For six years I cleaned his dog-fart kitchen by day, slept with the old prick by night. My husband, he spent three years on his back in a better state." She spits spitefully.

Xiuqing looks up, curious despite herself. "What happened then?"

"My husband died. Old Man Cao sent me back but kept my son. I came home to a daughter who didn't know me." Her face creases, at first in pain, then into something that almost looks like a pride. *See,* it seems to say, *I've endured.*

The streets have thickened with activity as they walk. Merchants hustle by, wheeling barrows of wheat flour, kerosene. A blacksmith with a portable forge almost runs Xiuqing over, his face a black smudge of soot and sweat. The forge's breath is like dragon's fire on her neck, doubly hot in the midsummer swelter. Xiuqing welcomes it as though it could burn the morning's filth right off her. She thinks of leaping on the man's cart, and pressing herself hard against his anvil.

"What you're doing will be better," the woman is saying. "And at least you'll get a variety of men. Not just one old prick over and over."

"They have *men*? Doing the embroidery?"

The *niangyi* looks at Xiuqing as though she's just offered up a bad joke. "He didn't tell you anything, did he?"

"He did," Xiuqing says, defensive again. "He told me about manifest destiny. And about how a perfect man commands all light, and influence, and—and all fate."

The verse rolls from her tongue, as elegant and opaque as anything Wu Ding ever recited. And for a moment, as the older woman squints in incomprehension, Xiuqing feels she has won something. But triumph dissipates with Zheng *niangyi*'s next words: "My little seamstress. Let me tell you something. This house is all about men and their needles. And they won't be poking them into your fine wedding shoes, either." She chuckles. "Or at least, not just into the shoes . . . But you'll find out for yourself soon enough." She shades her eyes. "You see that green roof? That's it. That's the Hall of Eternal Splendor."

Xiuqing looks. What she sees is somewhat short of splendid: a two-story house, its shutters painted a garish jade. Its doorway is crowded with elaborate signs, sculptures, and hangings, sprawling latticework, gold and red paint. Slips of paper hang on cords over the door, the print on them thick and stylized, the words winking in and out of view in the breeze.

As Xiuqing gazes, a moment comes to her unbidden: not just the sight, but the sounds and smell of summer. It was a morning two years back, maybe three. Hot and white like this one, the crickets sawing out a rasping chorus. She'd been scouring the courtyard jasmine trees for beetles with iridescent shells. She captured close to a dozen and then tried something she'd once heard of: tying linen threads around the insects' hairy hind legs, flagging the threads with slips of paper, and adding porcelain shards from a broken teacup for ballast. Then she released them on their leashes.

Weighed down by the shards, marked by fluttering confetti, the beetles flew in circles around her. She'd been thrilled with herself, thrilled with her power. She could make blizzards, she thought. Put nature on a leash . . . But by the third day all the beetles were dead.

They lay like luminous beads on the dirt, their little legs crabbed and still. Xiuqing buried them in a mass grave in the back courtyard.

They reach the fancy door. Woman Zheng raps on it sharply. It opens. "It's me," the woman says. "I've brought a harbor lily. A nice one this time. Well-shaped nose and chin. Fine hands." She doesn't, Xiuqing notes, mention the feet.

The manservant looks her up and down without apparent interest. His hair looks like it's been cut with a knife.

"Welcome," he says.

Part THREE

The HALL

Don woman's skirt and hairpin
Bright purple flowers open
Heart takes fire
Peony flowers open
Study stringed instruments, singing ah!

———

Chinese folk song

Four

Xiuqing sits in the courtyard as Zheng *niangyi* discusses her contract with a fat woman in makeup heavy for so early. They smoke and haggle, cackle, argue. Then the broker departs, without so much as a backward glance at her former charge.

The fat lady turns to Xiuqing. "Well, that's settled. That white ant certainly drives a hard bargain. I only hope you are worth it." She waddles in a small circle around Xiuqing as she speaks, looking at her. "Up," she adds, pleasantly enough. "I'll adopt you officially next week. For now, though, you may call me Ganma." *Godmother?* Xiuqing thinks.

When she neither rises nor responds, the woman steps closer. "Really, there's no shame in what we do here. Lots of girls like you do it." She steps back, taps her tiny foot. Xiuqing hugs her knees harder.

"It's the virtuous thing," Godmother says, wheedling. "You're just doing what any honorable daughter would do for her family." Xiuqing studies some ants at her feet: little creatures with shiny, tiny bodies. Not white, but tar black. They tug and pull at a flesh-colored worm as Godmother's voice rises in agitation. "I've no time for this, you little cunt. I'm a businesswoman. Stand *up*."

But Xiuqing keeps her eyes on the worm. It is, she observes, half flattened, presumably from where someone stepped on it. The ants' efforts make it shudder as though it were still alive.

It's only after the woman leaves that Xiuqing dares to lift her eyes. One of the shutters from the second floor has swung open a little. Inside, she makes out a woman standing by a looking glass. She is brushing and brushing her long hair. Her red lips move; she appears to be counting the strokes. Absently, Xiuqing counts with her: *One. Two. Three.*

By ten, Godmother is back with a leather whip. She beats Xiuqing —mostly on her back, although she takes one well-aimed swing at her feet. The blows are less painful than faintly sickening, and Xiuqing stays where she is.

Eventually Godmother shrills something and the manservant appears. "The little cunt is supposed to be a boar," she grumbles. "In truth she's as obstinate as a horse. That's probably why he got rid of her—no one marries a horse."

"Some men like them stubborn," the servant replies. "As they say, the harder the battle, the sweeter the victory." He picks Xiuqing up—casually, as though it's something he does often—and slings her over his shoulder like a sack of corn. He smacks her bottom, makes another salty comment she doesn't understand. Then he carries her to a dark room, where he throws her down amid oil urns and baskets of onions. When he leaves, he shuts and locks the door.

XIUQING LIES IN THE HALL'S PANTRY for several hours, motionless. She watches light from the one window make a single shifting square across the room. Sensation returns with its orbit: her feet hurt. Her eyes sting. Her skin smarts where the woman's leather whip landed. She becomes aware of smells; garlic, peanut oil, spicy beef. After dark, laughter bubbles through the walls. There are sounds of glasses clinking, of passing plates and girls complaining. A slap rings out like a firecracker. "I don't care if he's got every illness known under heaven," Godmother cries. "You borrowed the money, now you earn it back. You *always* finish the job."

Later come the men's voices. First the manservant's, just inside the main gate. It drones a steady stream of names: Master Kai. Master Peng. Master Yao. Sometimes simply Honored Guest. Xiuqing identifies Master Gao, who for some unfathomable reason the girls here all seem to call Papa. Other men's tones blend in slowly, adding banter and shouts. Shrieks merge with heavy footsteps, doors slammed and reopened. A zither sounds like the sobbing of a child. It is one of her favorite of Li Qingzhao's *ci,* "The Double Ninth Festival." Xiuqing mouths the words against the darkness:

> *Light mists and heavy clouds*
> *Melancholy the long dreary day*
> *In the golden censer*
> *the burning incense is dying away.*

Somehow, though, the very familiarity of the lyrics makes her feel even more displaced. It's as though the meanings of even known things are shifting.

IT'S WELL INTO THE NEXT DAY when Godmother unlocks the door. She asks if Xiuqing has come to her senses. Xiuqing replies quietly that she has.

Wordlessly, the young girl follows the older woman down the Hall's tunnel-like corridors, past the room where she'd heard the men and music. Then there were the odors of incense, spicy beef. Now the smell is of stale plum wine and vomit.

Xiuqing follows Godmother to the bathing room and strips down as directed. She steps, shivering, into the cold tin tub. The water is filthy, full of strands of hair floating in dreamy squiggles, clumps of sloughed-off skin like dirty snow. But Xiuqing savors it anyway; it's the first bath she's had in nearly a week. She tries to disregard the way Godmother studies her naked body, though when she's made to strut back and forth, dripping, she can't help flushing.

"A name," the madam says briskly.

"What?"

"You'll need a new name." And as Xiuqing blinks at her blankly: "*Aiyaaa.* As stupid as a wooden chicken." Covering her eyes, she heaves an injured sigh. "I pay too much. I *trust* people . . ."

When Godmother removes the hand, her eye makeup, dislodged by her palm's pressure and the room's steam, drips a single black tear. Xiuqing waits, hiding her privates with her palms.

"I think," Godmother says finally, "we'll start with Yuliang. Good Jade." She cocks her head thoughtfully. "Zhang Yuliang. Yes. It suits you well." She looks balefully downward. "Your feet are too big, of course. But we can work on the rest. Yes, certainly. Zhang Yuliang." She hands Xiuqing her clothes.

"What about my own family's name?"

"Don't you know that troubles come to those who are talkative? Especially here. Men don't like it when women natter the nights away." Godmother wipes her dripping brow and glowers. Then, as though explaining the sky's color to a small child, very slowly and simply, she says, "We're your family now. We're all our own family. We're all that any of us need."

Xiuqing's head reels as she is led, damp but dressed, to the kitchen. *Zhang,* she is thinking. *Yu-liang. Yu. Yu. Liang. Liang.* The sounds feel alien and false; she wouldn't even know what they look like on paper. She knows the characters for her own name. (Old name? *No.* It's like renouncing her own arm.) Her uncle wrote them for her the day he brought her home. "See?" Wu Ding said, carefully etching the sloping strokes. "That's you. Xiu: *clever.* Qing: *innocent.*" It was the first thing, in the month since her mother's sudden death, that had broken through the eight-year-old's fog of loss. Beguiled, Xiuqing had taken the tallow-toned rice paper to her room. She practiced writing her name nearly until dawn.

She has no idea, however, how to write *Good Jade.* She catches herself wishing suddenly for her *jiujiu*. To punish herself, she pinches her arm hard. "He's dead," she mutters fiercely. It was one of the resolutions she made last night, in the dark: she will neither think nor speak of him. Even to herself.

"What *now?*" asks Godmother over her shoulder. "Still nattering?"

"No," Xiuxing says. "I just coughed."

It comes out unconvincingly; unlike her uncle, Xiuqing isn't a particularly good liar. But this is another thing she resolved to change last night. She will lie to them, and fight them, and in the end she will leave them. Boar or no boar, she will escape.

IN THE KITCHEN Xiuqing is presented, as Yuliang, to two sullen-faced maids and the cook. The latter gives her hot tea, a bowl of fried rice with pork, and a small helping of the day's lunch, shrimp with green tea leaves. Godmother waits impatiently while Xiuqing, suddenly ravenous, crams it all into her mouth. Then she gives her a fresh teapot and steers her through the screened doorway.

Girls straggle into the dining room, rubbing eyes, limping, grumbling. Speaking of being tired, and sore. Godmother chastises some, pats others. She introduces Xiuqing as *the new leaf*. She calls the other girls *my flowers*, though at first Xiuqing can't believe she uses the term seriously. With their tangled hair and peeling patches of slept-in makeup, the women seem singularly unfloral to her, and smell even less so.

The one exception is Jinling, the girl Xiuqing had seen in the window. She sails in last, trailing scent like an elegant scarf, an exotic blend of gardenia and musk. Even half asleep she is as breathtaking as a girl in an old scroll painting: fashionably delicate and pallid, with a sweeping brow and eyes like calm black pools. Her mouth is little and red and full of small teeth that are charmingly and childishly uneven. Her hair is trimmed into long bangs that frame her face like the glossy feathers of an exotic bird. While the other girls jab at their food and jabber with full mouths, Jinling sits as straight as a sapling and pushes *fan* into her mouth with small, ladylike gestures. She looks for all the world as if she is hosting the meal.

Godmother tells Xiuqing that Jinling is the Hall's top girl. She came to the Hall from Shanghai's French Concession. "From a real Flower and Willow Lane," she adds proudly. "You are very lucky. I'm making her your teacher here."

Xiuqing's pulse leaps a little, despite herself. But Jinling just frowns. "Why should I teach anyone? It will take money and time from me. Two things I'm short of." She gazes at Xiuqing, cocks her head. "Such a sour face!" she adds.

The other girls titter. Godmother brushes off the protest with a *tskkk.* "Please," she wheedles. "Her hair-combing ceremony will be just after the New Year. And just *look* at her. She has more refinement than Suyin, I suppose. But there's really not very much time."

At these words the other young girl who is serving pauses. She looks Xiuqing up and down, chewing her lip.

"After New Year?" interrupts one of the seated girls, Dai, who is rather fat—who looks, in fact, like she could be Godmother's real daughter. "Where are you going to put her? There aren't any rooms free."

"There will be."

Sleep-crusted gazes flick toward the table's foot, where the woman named Xiaochen sits. Apart from the top girl, she's the only one to appear in full makeup. But the pastelike layers of powder can't hide the harsh lines by her eyes and lips. Her pupils are abnormally large and empty. Xiuqing sees them and thinks of Uncle Wu.

Jinling sniffs. Her chopsticks hover over the main dish. Xiuqing watches the red-tipped hands as though they speak a silent code. "He never puts enough yams in," Jinling says, pouting.

"He puts in as many as we can afford," Godmother retorts crossly.

"Tea!" someone else squeals. "What's her name again? Hey, Yuliang!" And then, because Xiuqing keeps forgetting that her name is now Yuliang, "*New girl!* Little idiot! More hot water!"

Obediently, Xiuqing takes the pot into the kitchen. It's empty at the moment, and she edges over to the stove. She eyes the contents of a pan for a moment. Then, quickly, she slides an extra bowl from a shelf.

Back in the dining hall, she puts the bowl by Jinling's elbow, just close enough to be within reach. The other young girl, Suyin, looks at Xiuqing curiously. She catches Xiuqing's eye and slowly parts her lips. A little orange tongue emerges, flickering. It takes Xiuqing a moment to see that it's actually a prawn tail. Xiuqing gazes, entranced, until a small breathy yelp pulls her attention back to the table. She realizes she's just missed Jinling's cup entirely with the tea. The spill cuts a watery brown path across the table.

Jinling picks her arm up quickly, strokes it like a hurt cat. Xiuqing waits for a rebuke, or another blow.

But when she looks up, Jinling's not looking at her. She is frowning at the bowl of yams Xiuqing has just set before her. And when she lifts her hand, it is just to produce a handkerchief and mournfully dab at her silk sleeve.

Then she looks up. "You certainly *need* training," she says.

Five

I**N THE END** Y**ULIANG** **ACCLIMATES** to this harsh and glittering new name, much as she acclimates to her harsh and glittering new life. It is Jinling who helps her with both tasks. In fact, just tumbling from the courtesan's red lips ("Ai, Yu *Liang*!"), the words seem less punishment than a playful new song.

The top girl guides her new charge through the nightly schedule of primping, preparing, and cleaning up. She shows Yuliang how to pare the end of her kohl eye pencil so it makes a clean line. She shows her how to refill her rouge locket for the nights when she is summoned out on call. She shows her how to brush her hair with just the right number of strokes—one hundred and sixty-eight, for prosperity.

It's Jinling who explains the rituals that must be performed, the incense that must be lit, the prayers that must be chanted. The gold paper ingots that must be tucked monthly under her mattress, to ensure guest satisfaction and healthy tips. She shows Yuliang the store of seed pearls that she keeps locked in her drawer, and she teaches her to steam them in a white cloth, and to grind up the moistened gems with a pestle and some sugar. Jinling eats the gritty paste in three or four small bites, grimacing. No one else in the Hall can afford to eat pearls. But Jinling says the custom pays for itself in her luminous skin. Plus, it helps with her digestion; regularity, she explains delicately, is key to maintaining one's balance and womanly composure. "It's like when chickens eat sand," she says. And then giggles, because *chicken*, as she has also taught Yuliang, is another term for *whore*.

The Hall's top girl shows Yuliang the other fruits of her years of labor: nearly two dozen dresses, stiff with gold trim and brocade that, while not quite as skillfully created as Yuliang's mama might have done, is nevertheless impressive. She has so many scarves that when she opens up their drawer they burst out in a gauzy, jewel-toned gust. She has boxes of hair ornaments, strings of gems to wind through the glossy wrap of her hair. Lacquered wine cups, as black as jet, emblazoned with gold-painted phoenixes. A lucky-ball locket she wears around her neck, and a key bigger than Yuliang's thumb-nail. The key fits Jinling's three-tiered chest with the dancing crane on its cover. Yuliang adores this chest—its cunning inlay, its gleaming wood. But inside lies Jinling's real treasure. She lays it out for Yuliang one evening: the diamond rings and emerald necklaces, the gold-dipped bracelet with intricate designs of flowers and fish, the jade pendant as pale as mutton fat, carved into a rooster—her sign, she tells Yuliang. Little stories accompany each piece: "This one's from a wealthy magistrate back in Shanghai. He wanted to marry me, but his wife wouldn't let him . . . This one's from the son of a Mongolian prince. He wanted to take me to the plains, to make love on horse-back . . . This one's from one of the top lieutenants of General Sun Yat-sen—he's fled to Japan. I'd like to see Japan. Wouldn't you?" And Yuliang says she would, even though traditionally (she knows) boars are supposed to dislike travel.

All of this is Jinling's dowry. It is her Shanghai legacy. She puts it all back reverently, save for two or three items she will wear. She disdains girls who dangle knickknacks from every hair, finger, and hole. No one in Shanghai was that unrefined: "It was more than just beds and money. We danced, and played *pipa*, and wrote poems. We learned the classic of taoism, the *Tao Te Ching*, by heart. There were nights when I didn't have to sleep with anyone at all. I would just sit and chat and pour wine."

"Why did you leave?" Yuliang asks. She is trying to ignore the noises filtering through the wall: a man snorting and thumping like a pig, Dai squealing *oooh* and *eeeeee-eeeee* and—sometimes—*ow!*

Jinling studies her protégé. "You need to relax," she chides. "You'll never survive here otherwise. I think I'll ask Godmother about having a demonstration session for you. One of my customers likes to be watched." She lifts a filigree necklace to her breast, cocks her head. "What do you think?"

"That one would be better." Yuliang points to the jade.

Jinling shoots her a dubious glance: "Really?" She tries it; frowns. Then smiles. "Well! Maybe you're right."

She lifts her hair and bends her head so Yuliang can do the clasp. "Money," she continues. "I left Shanghai for the money. The old centipede paid a lot for my contract. And she gave me a bonus." By *old centipede* she means Godmother, whose puffy ringed hands seem to be everywhere at once: counting and recounting the girls' earnings at dawn, feeling hems and robe linings for secret tips, squeezing fingers and elbows for lumps and swelling and other telltale sexsickness signs, running down the red "moon" book in which she records monthly cycles. Or the black book where she records her flowers' debt—and where the numbers only seem to grow and grow and grow. All but Jinling's—as the top girl, she brings in the most money. Xiaochen, a twenty-year veteran, brings in the least.

"She has Guangzhou sores," Suyin confides a few days later.

"Guangzhou . . . ?" Yuliang asks, baffled.

"Big red welts. The *fan kuei* brought them with them when they first came to Guangzhou. They spread them among the singsong girls there." Suyin's voice whistles around the clothespins in her mouth. The girls are hanging the weekly fine laundry of silk underthings and sheer linen robes.

"Anyway, Xiaochen rarely has customers anymore. She says she's sixteen. Everyone says they're sixteen. But I think she's actually closer to forty. Can you imagine?"

She shakes her head, pulls a clip. She secures a pair of shoes to the line, and they dangle between the two girls like gaudy butterflies. "Godmother makes her take mercury sometimes. And I have to help give her boiled milk injections in her buttocks." She rolls her eyes, exasperated by Yuliang's confusion. "*Sickness*," she shouts. "You get it from the night rooms. From men. You don't even have to touch them to get it. You can just sit down after someone gets up." She pulls a pink petticoat flat with her hands. "You get it," she says, "from the cushion."

"If that's true, then almost everyone must have it. The sickness. Do they? Do *we*?"

Suyin just shrugs. "You'll know if you do. But most keep it a secret."

Suyin seems to know a lot of secrets. She knows that Lirong, for example, paints herself every night with red lipstick.

"So what?" Yuliang asks. "Doesn't everyone paint their lips?"

"Not *those* lips, idiot," Suyin says. She spits the last pin from her mouth as she doubles over, laughing. It's only eleven o'clock; her titters stream through the quiet of the back courtyard. "She thinks her overhanging cliff is too dark," she finally explains. "She thinks painting it makes it look younger."

And though it isn't particularly funny, Yuliang finds herself laughing too. Soon she's laughing so hard that her stomach knots in pain. And when voices rise crankily from the sleeping quarters ("*Haiii!* Keep it down, you little cunts! We need sleep!"), the two girls use bright *qipao* sleeves and satin drawers as gags. Trying, with very little success, to sop up the spilling giggles.

A WEEK LATER, Godmother schedules Yuliang's first official appearance, after the yearly Burning Road ceremony. The maids pile oranges and paper money around a golden bodhisattva. Candles form a flickering path to his feet. After the ritual comes a banquet to which the most honored clients are invited, though what they're really invited to do is come and spend their money. Jinling takes it upon herself to groom her protégé for display. She lends Yuliang an eye-catching blue jacket, and long earrings, and an orchid clip for her hair. She gives her her very first makeup application. Her tongue pokes out like a plum tip as she lines Yuliang's blinking eyes in black and powders her nose and forehead smooth and white. Yuliang wrinkles her face, sneezes at the tickle. She fights the urge to wince as Jinling coaxes her lashes around a little metal rod.

"Stay still," Jinling says. "You need to look your best. Some wealthy man may see you today and make a big bid for your hair-combing. It's how it happened for me."

"In Shanghai?"

The top girl gives her a hard look as she rubs in rouge. "Of course, in Shanghai."

Yuliang's scalp still tingles from where Jinling combed, twisted, and pinned her hair. She knows what *hair-combing* is supposed to mean here. It's not the rite Mama described to her so often, in the days when marriage still beckoned in the future: *The night before, I'll comb your hair for you. For prosperity.*

How many times, Mama? Xiuqing would ask, although she already knew the answer.

Three times, her mother would answer, although she knew Xiuqing knew. *The first comb is for longevity. The second comb brings love and respect until your old age. The third comb will make sure that you—*

Have lots of children! Xiuqing would interrupt. *And I will!*

And her mother would laugh and say, *And with luck they'll be sons, who will make your life easy in your old age.*

At the Hall no one cares if a flower has longevity or not. Certainly no one expects love or respect. As for children—well, Yuliang already knows what bitter lengths Godmother's girls go to to quell their fertility. There are teas and potions, oversized foreign coins. When those fail, there are adoptions and abortions. There is depression, infection. Sometimes—often, even—there is death. One girl, Linyao, has died already since Yuliang arrived. Four months pregnant, she hurled herself from the top of Zheta Pagoda when her lover failed to make her his concubine. "How ridiculous," Jinling scoffed later. "Killing herself. Over a *man*." It was her same verdict on Washing Silk Woman: "What a waste. She was quite pretty, from the way I've heard the story. She could probably have made a good match."

Now, frowning in concentration, she finishes coloring Yuliang's lips. "Rub," she commands.

The lipstick tastes like greasy soap. But when Yuliang looks into Jinling's jade-handled looking glass, Mirror Girl looks lovely. Her eyes are larger and clearer than Yuliang has ever seen them. Her nose looks less like a button. Her lips seem to smile without her even moving them. Jinling, gazing at her over her shoulder, reaches out and strokes Yuliang's cheek. "Won't Godmother be pleased," she says softly. "You hardly look like your old self at all."

And in fact Yuliang does feel different—almost separated from herself. As though Mirror Girl has finally taken over. It's a new sensation, a little dizzying. Yet unlike so many other new things here, she doesn't fight it. The disconnection feels strangely like freedom.

TWO WEEKS LATER, when all's back to normal, Yuliang sits stiffly in a fraying bamboo chair. She is staring at a portrait, a portrait of a woman. The woman's face is a smooth moon of calm, her arms a pale nimbus around the boy in her lap. The smile on her lips is a mirage: when Yuliang looks at it with her left eye, it vanishes. When Yuliang closes the left and peers with the right, however, it reappears, clandestine, tempting. It's the implication of emotion rather than its actual expression. It is the perfect womanly smile. *When you smile,* her mother used to say, *don't move your lips. When you walk, don't move your skirts.*

A woman's keening call breaks into her thoughts: "Ahhhh, ahhhhhhhh, ah-ah-ah."

"Is she watching? Is she?" Wood creaks and wheezes. A long, drawn-out groan. Then the man speaks again. "I don't think that she *was* watching."

"Yuliang," Jinling chides. Yuliang pretends to hear. *Smile-smile.* It's occurred to her that there's something fundamentally wrong with the picture. She finally realizes what it is: the blank little spot above the goddess's lip. A real woman would have something there, a subtle double line. A soft flesh-furrow to the nose.

"Yu-*liang*! Look at me! Are you deaf as well as blind?"

Sighing, Yuliang finally lets her eyes slide: down the wall, past the small, shuttered window, directly to the bed below. Jinling is lying on her side. Merchant Yi is behind her, his big arm heavily clamping Jinling's neck. "She was watching," Jinling says. "You were watching, Yuliang, weren't you?" She pants a little as she speaks.

"I saw everything," Yuliang says. "It was . . ." But she doesn't know what it was. She twines her hands in her lap.

The merchant's eyes stroke her face as he reaches down, adjusts something. "I'm glad you found it so edifying." He sits up, stretching his long arms toward the ceiling. His big hands flop about as though sloppily sewn to his wrists.

Jinling sits up too, with an exasperated grimace at Yuliang. She caresses her client's neck, croons. "Don't pay any attention to her. You are formidable. You almost pierced me!" She darts another look at Yuliang, who obediently stores the term with the other expressions Jinling has taught her: *You're as hard as iron! I almost died in your arms!* It's the first time she's actually seen a man's cock up close, and she understands now why it's sometimes called a turtle. Merchant Yi's shrinks and shrivels shyly under her open gaze. His testicles look like plucked chicken skin.

"Washing," Jinling prompts softly, arching one perfect brow. Yuliang stands quickly, a line of sweat trickling down her knee. As she goes to the basin, carrying the little Buddha bowl, her thoughts return to the picture of Lady Guanyin. It was done by a local artist, with Jinling as its model. In merchant circles she is something of a celebrity. She's almost always included in the Merchant Guild's yearly flower calendar, which features a different local beauty for each month.

The merchant stands up. Yuliang kneels before him. The perfumed water meets the fish-sweat smell of sex. Yi Gan's hand absently plays with her hair as she washes his flaccid member. His thick fingers pull small strands from the bun that signifies her virginity.

AFTER HE HAS LEFT THE ROOM, Yuliang refills the little Buddha bowl. She adds a half-teacup of salt and carries it over to Jinling. The brothel cat, Money, who is always either deeply in heat or asleep, winds urgently around her ankles. "Out," Jinling intones. Yuliang dutifully picks up the animal and drops it in the hall, where it tucks a leg behind its ear like a festival contortionist and begins animatedly to lick itself.

When Yuliang returns Jinling is examining her breast, which has been bitten. "That old bastard deserves a thousand cuts," she says, pouting. "It's the second time he's done this. I should tell Godmother. I never want to see him again."

"You should," Yuliang agrees. But she knows that Jinling won't. Yi Gan is head of the Merchant Guild. He's the kind of client the girls here call a "bean curd": ever-present, easy to squeeze money from. Offending him would hurt everyone: girls, servants, Godmother. Especially Jinling herself.

But it's the thought of offending Jinling that sends a shiver down Yuliang's neck. "You're not really angry with me, are you?"

Jinling hoists her leg onto a chair. "Angry?" She holds out her hand for the cloth.

"For not watching."

Jinling fingers herself a moment, then gets to work. "Oh, that. No. Not really." She winces. "It may even tempt him into the bidding. You know: 'This one's so innocent, she can't even bear to watch!' Men like that in a virgin." Her white fingers deftly delve the pink folds the merchant has just purchased. Yuliang watches beneath her lashes, both ashamed and entranced. "Later, though," the top girl adds, "you'd better learn to be more jolly. No one wants to bed a corpse."

She grits her teeth as the salt goes to work. "Well, almost no one," she adds. And giggles.

Six

I N THE FOLLOWING MONTHS, Yuliang seeks safety in small tasks, little rituals. She forges armor out of routine. At the Hall, the "leaves" sleep at two or three and are roused promptly at seven. They take turns perching on the chamber pot's chipped rim, behind the screen that screens nothing but their bodies. They wash up with water from a pitcher on the bureau, rub and rebind their sore feet. They put on their "chore" clothes. Yuliang saves the cheongsam Wu Ding gave her for the dirtiest work—floor-scrubbing, collecting chamber pots for the night-soil man. She thrills at each rip and slop, revels in the spreading stains. As the fabric unravels, she pictures it as her uncle's frayed spirit. Disintegrating.

After eating the girls sweep the courtyard, attacking bottle shards and crumpled call-cards. As winter approaches, lines of snow fill in the spaces between stones, creating an illusion of checkered smooth-ness. Yuliang sweeps the snow out, along with used matches that look like twisted and burned little bones. Though she's not supposed to she sweeps the trash into the gutter. She defiantly hopes it will cause a flood when spring comes.

The afternoons are devoted to more formal training, which

Yuliang and Suyin receive in the spare pantry. They're taught music, deportment, "love." The music teacher has a face that droops as though made out of warming wax. She picks out songs on her three-stringed *pipa,* teaches the girls popular tunes about the moon's reflection on water, on icy lakes. Yuliang sings these back without missing a note, and is oddly strong with the male verses. The teacher tells Godmother that she has an "unusual talent" and that she holds "great promise" in entertainment. The truth, of course, is that Yuliang already knows most of the pieces. It's one of her uncle's few and sad little legacies.

In "love" classes, the girls pull the pleasure beads strung on a stained silk cord through their fists. They study pictures in the seventeenth-century classic *Gold Plum Vase, or the Adventurous History of His Men and His Six Wives,* and puzzle over little statues of people portrayed at various intersects. The books are Godmother's, the statues brought by the Taoist nun who teaches them about bedding matters. The girls drone the names of the positions like insects in summer: Dragon Turning. Tiger Slinking. The Rabbit Nibbling the Hare. "In Cicada Clinging," the nun instructs, "the woman lies on her stomach. The man stands behind her. He pulls her hips right into his. His jade stem is plunged so deeply within that it isn't visible at all."

"If it's Feng Yitmien's jade stem," Suyin whispers to Yuliang, "then it's barely visible to begin with." Feng Yitmien is a tea vendor who visits Mingmei. His hands and feet are as dainty as a woman's.

"Ideally," the nun continues frowning, "the man thrusts fifty-four times. Fifty-four brings mutual pleasure."

Godmother, who has poked her head in to supervise, objects. "If he wants to push two thousand times, so be it," she says. "So long as you finish the job."

It is one of her most frequent injunctions: no matter how a job goes, you must finish. And it isn't just advice. Those who don't finish, who don't have an excuse—and for Godmother, only bloodshed is an excuse—are beaten. Often (ironically) until they bleed.

In the evenings Suyin and Yuliang sometimes go on call with older girls. Their first job is to take the card and the required deposit from the runner bearing them. The deposit is generally fifteen percent of a night's total, which can vary, depending on how elaborate the client's demands are. The card comes originally from the girl herself, who will have left stacks of them at restaurants or with favored clients. On the front is the girl's name and the Hall's address. On the back the client will have filled in the location the girl is being summoned to: the opera, a banquet, a party for a birthday or a business achievement. Godmother will read them: *Zao Tong requests Lirong's honorable presence at the Jade Garden Restaurant, the back courtyard. Hu Zinyang aks Dai to Yuan Shikai Hall.* The madam will carefully count out the deposit, mark it down, and give it and the card back to Yuliang or Suyin. The girls will then help the girl on call dress and powder, and then climb into one of the Hall's two sedan chairs. Whichever of the virgins has been chosen to go along will follow her on the manservant's shoulders.

On these nights, her feet interlocking like little charms under the manservant's chin, her hands clutching his rough-cut, greasy hair, Yuliang snatches glimpses of life beyond the Hall walls. She sees mostly men, jostling their way through the streets, coming home from work, going to dinners or meetings. Occasionally she'll see foreigners from one of the churches: pasty, large-limbed people in dark clothing. One woman outside the foreign settlement has hair the color and texture of stiff wet straw, bunched awkwardly on the back of her head. A little girl with the woman has locks of almost the same color. They flow like a tangled mane down her back. The girl says something to her mother as Yuliang and the man pass. Her voice hisses like a little snake's. Yuliang, intrigued by words that sound and seem so very different from her own, leans over enough to throw off the manservant's balance.

Once at the event, Yuliang waters the older girl's wine cup so she doesn't get too tipsy as she talks and flirts. She keeps track of call-cards and is careful to keep them in order. She's under strict instructions not to leave the manservant's sight; Godmother doesn't want her virgins "mingling" or running off. So the man follows Yuliang everywhere, even on outhouse trips. He stands guard while she sits, hotly shamed, trying vainly to pass water without splashing.

Despite such humiliations, however, such nights feel like tiny escapes. Sometimes Yuliang even imagines slipping away unnoticed, off the man's shoulders, away from the room. Cloakless, breathless, racing down the street despite her bound feet. Perhaps someone would help her. Or perhaps she'd just slip onto a houseboat docked by the shore. On the long journey down the gloomy, cowshit-brown river, she could show herself to the boat's owners. They would be a real, proper family. A real mother, not a Godmother. A real father, not an uncle. Maybe even a little baby; Yuliang would love to play with a baby! She would appear like a genie to embroider tiny clothes and caps. She'd cook southern specialties she would magically have mastered: fish-head casserole, clay-pot rice. She'd win the surprised family right over. *You've made our lives so much better,* the mother would say. *Please come home with us. Become our eldest daughter.*

And Yuliang would. She'd sleep with the baby and the mother like a kitten in a snug litter. Safe from men. Blissful in the knowledge that the next day would start at six in the morning, and not six at night.

SIX AT NIGHT is when Hall life starts in earnest. In Jinling's room Yuliang lines up her mentor's accessories and appliances. She helps Jinling with her toilette, bringing water, mixing makeup. She now knows how to clean a downy upper lip with a taut piece of thread. She can redraw Jinling's eyebrows with a charcoal pencil; can give her elegant spider legs or flying arches like bird wings. It makes her feel oddly powerful to be able to make such choices.

After makeup, she also helps choose Jinling's first outfit of the night. Jinling is the only girl in the Hall who changes for each of her guests. The maids complain that it makes extra work, and Xiaochen mutters that it's "uppity." But Jinling always makes sure to tip the maids a little extra. And no one pays attention to anything Xiaochen says these days. "Listen, Yuliang," Jinling instructs. "A fresh dress makes a guest feel special, welcomed. It makes him feel like he's your first customer of the evening."

Yuliang tucks this advice away along with Godmother's promise of her own new wardrobe: six new dresses once her calyx has been opened. For now, she focuses on the colors and textures of Jinling's trousseau. She learns the characters embossed on jackets and scarves, and matches them up in what she imagines must be auspicious combinations: Luck and happiness. Happiness and good fortune. Good fortune with wealth with wisdom. She thinks of new ways to pair tones: the sea greens, sky blues, the starry silvers. At first Jinling eyes some of these choices dubiously. "I've never worn that dress with that shawl," she'll say, and send out for a second opinion. But as the months pass and the opinions concur, the top girl stops her questioning. She even tells Godmother that Yuliang's eye is becoming refined. "She'll be good, this one," she says. And gives Yuliang's knee a soft squeeze beneath the table.

By seven the manservant is announcing arrivals, using the Hall's own special code. *A guest has arrived* means someone unknown, since return guests are always announced by name. If the guest has a preferred girl, her name is announced too. *Jinling, Yi Gan has honored you with a visit. He requests that you prepare him some tea.*

By ten, the Hall is filled with smoke and liquored chatter. Voices rise in counting for the finger-game. Yuliang and Suyin ferry plates back and forth from the kitchen: the plump bodies of crabs doused with black beans and chili, shiny red pork and potatoes, bowls and more bowls of steaming rice. The girls weave around the gambling tables to the slick click of tiles. They pass the musician with her lined face and tired arias, fending off groping hands and twisting themselves away from ubiquitous, lumpy laps. ("No laps!" orders Godmother. She will beat them if she finds them there, even involuntarily.) They watch older girls rising, leaving, returning, smudged and flushed or bored, or simply tired. *Did the old buzzard get it up all right?* the men shout. *Did the old cannon manage to blast?*

Godmother serves and observes, banters and barters. She writes sums owed and paid in her books. She samples food, waves it on, although sometimes she sends it back. She creeps up to the night wing, listening at closed doors for unsanctioned trysts, unreported tips and gifts, and sounds more alarming than the flesh-slap of a rough tumble. And occasionally cries of real pain do drift in: *Aiiiiii. Stop it—stop it! Help!*

The shrieks float like ghosts into the mirth and smoke, make little dents of silence amid the clamor. Usually it's Godmother who heaves onto her little feet when this happens, and bustles heavily up the stairs into the night wing. A little commonplace beating is expected, she says. But killing or disfiguring her girls is not. It will result in surcharges and doctor's fees. The very worst cases will go to court.

"What are the very worst cases?" Yuliang asks Jinling, early one morning after Mingmei is attacked. The soft-spoken girl from Suzhou erupted from the night rooms with red cords trailing from her wrists and ankles. Blood ran in a thick stream down her left leg. The cut was high on her thigh, nearly half a finger deep in some places. A soldier wearing the slapdash uniform of some warlord's private army followed her out, smoking, smiling. Still tying his trousers. The knife had slipped, he said, shrugging. They were playing a game. He called the wound *a scratch,* Mingmei *an actress.* He threatened not to pay; he hadn't had a chance to finish. But Godmother demanded and received payment—and well more than a single night's price. She tacked on an inflated estimate for the doctor's fee, and a penalty for the scar Mingmei would have later. She demanded a fee for not taking the soldier to court, and a fee for cleaning the bloody footprints off the floor. In the end, with the help of the manservant and several guests (including a judge), she succeeded in emptying the man's wallet. "Good iron is not used for nails," she'd said later, almost fondly. "Good men do not become soldiers."

"I don't know," says Jinling grimly now, as young sunlight seeps through the window. "I don't know what the worst cases are."

She grimaces as Yuliang yanks at a pearl-sized frog button on her *qipao,* one of the dozens that run from knee to nape. The top girl can never undo them all herself. When she's drunk or tired she sometimes rips them right off.

Her dark eyes meet Yuliang's in the faint light of the mirror. She is lavender, gilded by the nascent light. Yuliang thinks: *She looks older.* It's not a criticism, for she's not a man, or Godmother. She just forgets sometimes how tired even Jinling, flawless Jinling, can get here.

She lets her fingers descend to her mentor's neck, then from there to her shoulders. She shapes softly descending circles with her thumbs, then her forefingers. She presses tentatively at first, then—as Jinling shuts her eyes and leans her head back into Yuliang's belly—with more force. She leans forward to massage the spare flesh shielding the top girl's lungs, her heart. Her own pulse quickens. "Is this all right?" she murmurs.

Jinling opens her eyes. She looks confused, as though she's torn between two answers. But all she says is "Yes." And, sighing, shuts her eyes again.

Seven

THE HOLIDAYS END in a whirlwind of prayers and bright light. Over Yuan Shikai Hall, fireworks etch flaming fish and dragons into the sky. At the other Hall—of Eternal Splendor—those who are able clear their debts and begin racking up new ones.

The girls, for their part, are well rested for the first time in the year. They've passed the past week—spent by most clients with family and friends—gambling, gossiping, and eating. All, that is, but Xiaochen, who has finally been sent away. It's said she's been sold (for little more than a single smoke) to the "nail shed," the meanest of Wuhu's brothels. It sits behind the railroad depot, a dirty shack with no entrance fee and no amenities. Customers—rickshaw runners, dockhands, even the occasional beggar—pay a pittance for its offerings. In some rooms there's not even a bed.

The disappearance of the Hall's oldest whore is a relief in some ways. In the weeks past, Xiaochen's appearance was disheveled, her face and neck layered with makeup which, however thickly mixed, couldn't hide her deep wrinkles and scarred skin. Her dresses were out of fashion, their colors and cuts dating back to the long-gone days when she still had credit. Everyone knew she hadn't had a "wet" guest, one who stayed and stripped and spent the night, since the dragon-boat races. Sometimes men let her sit with them, and warble a token song or two. Most buzzed off like swatted flies at the sight of her.

"They were afraid," Suyin speculates one day, as she and Yuliang are shelling peanuts. "They thought she was like that girl who told her husband never to look at her at night. But he did once, soon after she had his son."

"What did he see?" Yuliang asks. But warily: Suyin enjoys shocking people. She embellishes stories with far-off relatives and friends to lend them a patina of credibility.

"He discovered that she was only flesh-and-blood up above," her roommate says, sure enough. "From the waist down she was a rotting skeleton."

"How could they have done it to begin with, if she didn't have any skin?" Yuliang objects. "And how could she carry the baby without its falling out? He would have known. He would have had to."

"Some men are so self-centered they wouldn't know if they were thrusting into a teapot," offers Dai helpfully. The plump flower has been put on a vinegar diet to lose weight, but she often noses in for a snack during Godmother's naptime.

"It happened," Suyin retorts firmly, handing her a handful of nuts to crunch. "My uncle's wife's sister knew the man."

"Well, then," says Dai, chewing. "Show us. Go to the nail shed and get Xiaochen to lower her trousers. I dare you."

Yuliang eyes her fellow "leaf" in amusement, half expecting her to take the challenge, just for show. Before she can, though, Godmother materializes in the doorway. Dai squeals and swallows simultaneously. But it's not her the madam is seeking.

"Yuliang," she says. "Suyin will finish your kitchen duties this afternoon. You are to go pull together your things." As the girls stare at her in surprise, she adds, "You're a lucky girl. You're getting your own room."

Yuliang looks at Suyin, whose face registers the same shock

she feels. But Godmother isn't finished yet. "Also," she continues, "your hair-combing takes place in a week. Have Jinling mark it in her book."

She turns to go. Then, remembering something, she turns back. Stepping lightly across the room, she slaps Dai on the face, hard enough to leave a red mark. "No dinner for you tonight, my piglet," she says. "Now go upstairs and change."

"It's going to be Yi Gan."

Yuliang stares at her friend and mentor. "No."

"Oh, Yuliang. Don't act so surprised." Jinling shakes her head. But she steps back from the doorway and waves Yuliang in. Then, carefully, she shuts the door behind her. "Yes," she says, turning to face her. "He bid the highest."

"How long have you known?"

"Godmother told me last week." The top girl walks slowly to the window, her white hands twisting and clasping at her waist. "I was going to tell you. But then . . ." Yuliang hears rather than sees the gesture, the soft, rustling sound of a shrug. "It's just skin."

She staggers to the bed, pressing her palms to her eyes. She sees Yi Gan, his twining arms, his apelike hands.

"You knew this was coming," Jinling says softly, touching her shoulder. "It comes for each one of us."

I'm not one of you, Yuliang thinks. But what she says, in a tiny whisper of a voice, is, "I don't want him to touch me."

Jinling makes a small sound: "*Tsk.*" She strokes Yuliang's hand, her arm. Then she puts her hands on Yuliang's shoulders. "Lie down," she whispers.

Numbly, Yuliang lets herself be pulled, lets Jinling curl around her like a little cat. The top girl murmurs soft and comfortless phrases into Yuliang's hair. "Think about the big party beforehand. All the nice things you'll get to eat and wear. A red silk dress that's so stiff with embroidery that it will stand up by itself. I've seen it! And there will be a big banquet—almost as big as tonight's. Merchant Yi will pay for everything. The best food. Anything you ask for."

"I ask for nothing."

"Hush. Ask for *everything*. It's the only way. You'll be able to start saving."

"I can't." She feels Jinling's heartbeat through the thin cotton of her nightshirt. Beating, a small finger tapping her back. "Let's leave," she says. "We can beg for a living. Or stow away on a boat. People would take pity on us and help us. I'm sure they would!"

"They'd find us. We're registered with the police now. They have lists and descriptions. Soon they'll even have photographs."

"We'd just run away again," says Yuliang. "They'd give up eventually. They'd have to."

"They wouldn't!" Jinling says. "Listen to me, Yuliang. Listen." She turns Yuliang around. Her breath is sharp and faintly floral. She spritzes her mouth at night with her special French cologne. Not to please men, but to clean her tongue of their taste. "The other night you asked what the worst case was," she says. "I'll tell you." Her finger's pressure on Yuliang's arm deepens. "There was another girl here, before you. The apprentice leaf you replaced. She said the same things, and ran away. And when they brought her back, she ran away again."

"You see?"

Jinling holds up her hand. "The second time, they killed her. No one says so. But everyone knows."

Yuliang stiffens. In her brief time here she's seen plenty of violence. Papa Gao has beaten Mingmei within an inch of her life, then offered her bleeding body to his friends. Whores have attacked each other too—it is even whispered that Xiaochen once hired someone to disfigure a rival flower from the teahouse. The man threw burning acid on the girl's face. So far, though, Yuliang has never heard of anyone's being murdered. "Who—who did it?" she asks.

Jinling just looks at her meaningfully. "The police pulled her out of Wuhu Lake. They brought her here. Yuliang, I saw her. Her ankles were like puffed pig bladders. Her scalp—it was flaking off. Not just the skin, the whole thing. Bone and all." She shudders, shuts her eyes. "That was when I realized."

"Realized what?"

"That the only way to escape this place is by doing it their way. You bring the men in. You buy your way out."

Yuliang covers her eyes again. "How do you stand it?" she wails. "Their hands. Their mouths. Their——"

"Because you have to." Jinling tightens her pink lips. "You have to let them into your body." She strokes Yuliang's hair. "But here's a secret: you don't have to let them into your head. Your thoughts are yours alone. You must just think of something else."

Her words bring back, unexpectedly, the white ant who brought her here, the day her uncle so brutally betrayed her. *You'll just have to endure,* she hears the broker rasp. *Try to think of something else.* For a moment she almost feels them: the crabbed fingers pressing her legs apart . . . "I should kill myself. I should eat opium. Right now."

"Oh. Oh, no." Jinling pulls Yuliang to her, harder this time, and starts to rock. "You can't kill yourself," she croons. "What will I do then? What will I do without you?"

In the next room, maids debate over an old colonel, who has drunk himself completely unconscious. The manservant votes just to leave him: "Give him a dry bed in the night wing for the night. Just make sure he's out before the old centipede wakes."

The maids giggle. "Sir," they say. "Please, sir. Eminence. Wake up."

Yuliang can't breathe. The girl from the lake floats in the black space of her mind.

Jinling keeps rocking. Then she starts to sing. At first the tune is wordless. Then it isn't. Words shape themselves from the humming like small pearls, formed by the ocean: *"Shi shang zhi you ma ma hao . . . Mei ma de hai zi xiang ge cao . . ."*

Your mama is the best in the world
Without her, you're but a blade of grass

Away from your mama's heart
How will you ever find happiness?

Mama, Yuliang thinks numbly. *Mama, I'm so sorry.* The hurt doesn't stop, but breathing becomes easier. Overwhelmed, she buries her face in Jinling's white skin. For a moment she just lies there. Then, slowly, she begins to brush the soft expanse with her face. There's a little dimple, she discovers. A soft nook that marks where chest becomes neck. She rests her lips on the spot, and finds they fit.

Eight

IN THE EARLY MORNINGS that follow, Yuliang retreats to sleep (or not-sleep) in Jinling's room, in Jinling's bed. She burrows between her mentor's clean sheets and soft limbs like a small rabbit, seeking safety from a fox. There are names, she now knows, for the things that they do together: *laying slippery noodles. Polishing the mirror.* But these snide terms seem far removed from the warm, affirming acts the two girls share; and besides, they are terms the men give it. So Yuliang doesn't think about them—any more than she thinks of the men themselves. For a few hours each night, in fact, it's as though men don't even exist.

In her own new room, as in her old, Yuliang keeps the wedding shoes hidden. As always, she has avoided looking at them. But on the eve of her arranged "wedding" she parts the silken pile of her under-things and finds the little paper package.

She opens the tissue carefully and picks up the left shoe. Over the holidays she finally began to embroider in the little hole, although she practiced first, sometimes for hours at a time: couching stitches and chain stiches, split stitches and man-character stitches. Satin stitches, grass seed stitches, oblique stitches to make the stems of plants. She re-created each blossom perfectly on at least two or three handker-chiefs before even picking up the unfinished slipper. Her eyes ached, and her tired fingertips stung with pricks by the time she was done. But her effort paid off. Studying the shoe by candlelight now, she can hardly see where the past needle leaves off and her own picks up.

It should make her feel proud—that she's attained such skill. And yet, all Yuliang really feels is ill. The irony of it doesn't miss her—that she's completed her mother's gift, only to make a mockery of her dreams.

I should just burn them, Yuliang thinks. She pictures it: red silk, orange flame. A final funereal rite. The slippers, now black ghosts, would float back to her mama. They'd return to their rightful owner. In their rightful state.

When Yuliang opens her eyes, the silk's close enough to the candle that the flame senses fuel and shivers. Almost unthinkingly, she tilts the shoe a little closer, studying not the blossoms now but her own hands, these thin white servants that stroke cat fur and brush Jinling's hair and clothes and—these past, new nights—her soft thighs. "You have such beautiful fingers," Jinling has said more than once. "They are like the hands of a true artist."

Her mother's hands were slightly thinner, as Yuliang remembers them. And they were almost always in motion: cleaning dishes, smoothing her hair, and of course stitching, always stitching. As she stitched, her mama wove stories: about finding her husband (although never about losing him). About the troubles of the year of the boar. "It was so much worse than anyone had predicted," she'd murmur. "The rains poured into the Yangtze for days and days. The river boiled, as though cooked on some huge stove. The floods soaked the streets and the fields and washed the shoots of rice and corn until they were waterlogged, worthless. But we ate them anyway."

"Why, Mama?"

"There was nothing else. When the fields were empty, we plucked wet bark from the trees. We tried to cook it into stews. Eventually that went too. So we ate clay from the riverbanks, special clay that filled you and almost felt like food, if you were that hungry. Sometimes we pounded bricks and swallowed the dust as if it were rice flour."

"Did you really eat *dust?*"

"You were just out of my belly. And I was losing my milk." A gentle smile. "I did it for you. To save your life."

One of the small stitched peonies roughens, turns brown. Yuliang watches, mesmerized by the spreading, sootlike stain. Three rooms away Jinling cries out in something like pleasure, although Yuliang knows—she believes fervently—that it is not. "Listen, Yuliang," her friend has told her sternly. "You must never, never enjoy it with them. *That's* what makes you a whore. Not their money."

"Does *this* make us whores?" Yuliang asked her then, indicating their twined bodies, just half-teasing.

"No," Jinling said, still quite seriously. "This keeps us alive."

Yuliang doesn't see what happens next—she doesn't know quite how it happens. All she knows is that the candle clatters into the basin. The flame disappears in a wet and smoldering snuff. Molten wax sears her fingers and seeps through her shift, and the shoe tumbles right to the floor. Yuliang gasps. She snatches a hand towel, throws it over the flame. She stamps the sparks out, grinding them with her bare heel and gritting her teeth against the blister. "Fuck you," she mutters—to her uncle, to Papa Gao. To the "godmother," who is no mother at all. Perhaps even to Jinling, who two doors down is now giggling. "Fuck you all, you slave-girl bitches. You yellow she-dogs. You cursed-from-birth *women.*"

She stamps and sobs long after the smoke has vanished.

THE LIGHT SHE SEES the next morning is sweet and watery, a melony sort of yellow. It takes her a moment to register that the sounds outside are early morning's—a rooster's self-righteous outburst, a man singing as he shaves. Elsewhere, a wet nurse coos to a baby Yuliang has never seen, although she's seen the nurse.

Her face, though young, is wide, brown, and lined. Her breasts are as plump as two little pillows. Yuliang always wonders about the nursemaid's own child: Is it alive? Who gives *it* suck, once its mother's milk is sold?

Outside her room she hears the madam's short, cloth-soled footsteps. The plump fist lands on the door: *raprapraprapraprap.* "Up, up, my little bride. It's already late."

Yuliang rolls over, hides her head. Clinking copper coins greet the movement: the other flowers tossed money on the spread last night, for prosperity. If she were a real bride they'd have tossed oranges, pomegranates. Fruit, to encourage fruitfulness. But for this union, a child is not the goal. For a week now, Yuliang has swallowed tadpoles like the rest, squiggling mud-flavored morsels taken after dinner. Godmother says that the cold elements in the fetal frogs counter the warm elements that invite life to the body.

The rap comes again. "Yu-*liang.*" A tiny note of question now. Yuliang savors its implication: that she's not here at all. That after all the lessons and demonstration sessions, the new dresses commissioned and carefully columned in the black book, she isn't here. She has disappeared. Run away. For good.

"Don't make me beat you, today of all days," Godmother shouts crossly.

Across the street the wet nurse coos again, then laughs. An image comes: Yuliang's real mother, scooping up dust with her white fingers. *I did it for you. To save your life.*

"I'm coming," she calls, and throws off the quilt.

AFTER A BREAKFAST she can't eat, Yuliang sits for the first time in a year in a bath that hasn't already been sat in. Jinling has infused it with pomelo, sweet-sour juice, mottled rind—things to cleanse the new bride of evil elements. Jinling's eyes are still crumbed with sleep. She has never risen to a servant's schedule. But she'd insisted that she would do so today. "I want a chance to review," she'd told

Godmother. "If she does poorly, after all, I'll get the blame." To Yuliang, though, she simply murmured, "Don't worry. I will be there to help you."

Now she ladles fragrant water over Yuliang's shoulders and, in a surreal-seeming role reversal, neatens Yuliang's upper lip. The threading sends pin-like tears into Yuliang's eyes. But she doesn't complain: it's Jinling's touch. And this pain helps distract her from pain to come.

After the bath she is led back to her room, where Jinling lights candles shaped like dragons and phoenixes. She helps Yuliang into silky things picked out for her last week, when the seamstress came with a selection of undergarments and sheer robes in soft shades of crimson and pink. The top girl untangles Yuliang's hair, puts in oil to add gloss. She threads her hairline too, to make it "high" with the wisdom of a married woman. She combs it three times. But she intones nothing about longevity or children, the way a real bride's mother or "lucky" woman would do. Instead she whispers advice. "Eat something," she murmurs as she draws Yuliang's part. "You haven't been eating. Eat something light, but not spicy. Pork buns. Rice. To settle your stomach. Have two, maybe three cups of wine. To relax," she says, as she pins the knot to Yuliang's nape. "But no more. They get angry if you get too drunk. When you serve him, steer away from the garlic cloves," she says, as she helps Yuliang into the dress. "Otherwise, you'll be breathing them all night."

They still haven't spoken about Merchant Yi's switching his favors. But Jinling's features reflect nothing but an intent focus on making sure the dress's clasps are correctly aligned. The top girl takes out her phoenix wine cups. She pours rice wine into one, then into the other. She finishes hers in one gulp, hands the other to Yuliang. "Drink this. You need to relax."

Yuliang drinks, thinking of Yi Gan's breath. Of the yeasty blast on her face. The *shaoxing* in her stomach seems to sour, reawakening the nausea she has swallowed back since waking. She covers her mouth and lurches toward the basin. Jinling lifts the red veil just in time.

IN THE END, HE IS LATE. The banquet is called for six, but the Hall clock has chimed seven times and then once more by the time Yi Gan finally arrives. Yuliang, still draped in red and, for the first and last time, seated in one of the chairs of honor, feels her stomach tighten as his voice booms across the room: "So sorry to be late. Troubles down at the docks . . . Oh, my life."

The room cheers and claps. Yuliang takes advantage of the disruption to lift her veil a little. He is wearing not a groom's green robe and cap but dock-dusted work clothes. His windcap perches on his head, a flannel, flap-tailed bird. His nose and eyes are red already; it's clear that he's been drinking.

"Ah. Not at all. Girls! Let us begin!" Papa Gao cries cheerfully, even though the banquet's well under way. He waves his free hand over the table's shambles: the half-eaten pig, the soupy lobster. Godmother turns to Yuliang, spots her peeking. She frowns. "Cover yourself," she scolds, pinching Yuliang's upper arm. "Greet him. Offer him something to eat."

Yuliang starts to stand. But her dress's hem, which she's stepped on, stops her short. Her head spins as she tries to regain her balance. "Ask him," Godmother mutters.

Through the veil, she sees Yi Gan's dark shape. "Have you—have you eaten yet?" she squeaks.

"Eager, isn't she?" someone slurs.

Laughter booms. Tears burn Yuliang's eyelids, and she is suddenly grateful for her hot red curtain. She drops her head and waits for Merchang Yi's shadow. But it shifts in the other direction, flinging something away—cloak, hat? When it calls for a glass of *maotai* Jinling rises obediently from her seat.

For ten minutes or more Yuliang is ignored again. The hot rice wine heats and loosens the cramped space between her ribs. She feels warmly distant, sealed in red wax. She can smell her own wine-tart sighs. She is just reaching to scratch her nose when the red sea vanishes, replaced by a thousand red faces. She blinks in the flickering gaslight.

Merchant Yi is holding her veil in one hand, a bony chicken foot in the other. "A man pays a small fortune. He should at least be permitted to examine the goods." He steps closer. "Stand up, little Yu."

He plucks the glass from her hand. His fingers brush hers, just lightly, and without thinking Yuliang lifts her gaze. She stares into his face, his drink-sheened eyes. And somehow, the rage from last night reignites. She *hates* this man. She loathes him! "Yuliang," Jinling whispers sharply, sensing the shift in her mood, "stop it. Smile at him. He's your master."

But the merchant's eyes are intent, newly interested. "Well," he says, his voice thoughtful. "Well, well. Our little flower seems to have been hiding some thorns." He reaches out, chucks her under the chin. "I believe it's true, what they say about orphans and hot blood. I'll bet this one doesn't even need a quilt tonight."

"What quilt? She'll have you!" someone hoots.

"She looks like she can't wait," another calls out. "She'll be on the bridal bed before you are!"

"You'll have to be careful in the morning, though—with feet that size, you might put on her shoes by mistake!"

The table titters, enjoying the game—the Hall's version of the old tradition of jibing and taunting a new bride to test her composure. Merchant Yi ignores them, sitting heavily in the empty chair next to hers. "Here," he says, indicating the scattered plates, the jumbled food. "Aren't you hungry?"

The next hour passes like a magic lantern show Yuliang once saw at the market. Action feels interrupted. Faces are masklike, frozen in odd movements and garish expressions. Later she'll remember God-mother's head thrown back in a laugh, the fat pad of her double chin stretched and flattened. She'll remember Jinling's eyes, locked on hers for a moment before the top girl is called away to the night wing. She'll recall red-tipped fingers pushing more food—squab slices, fried rice, well-greased butterfly noodles—onto her plate. But Yuliang doesn't eat. She looks, listens. She sips wine. She watches the men drinking, the women flitting, serving. Watches their fluttering march to and from the night wing like butterflies from a farmer's field. She savors the sweet heat of the alcohol on her tongue, the slow glow of her lingering fury. Suyin takes her untouched dinner plate and replaces it with four more, each one filled with sweets. Yuliang ignores them, reaching for her cup.

"I thought all girls liked sweets," Yi Gan says, sinking his yellow teeth into a mooncake filled with black-purple bean paste. Then, more quietly, almost as if he actually cares, "Are you unwell?"

The question is so unexpected, and so utterly unanswerable, that Yuliang laughs—a high, sharp yelp that almost hurts. She sips some more wine, finally finding her voice: "I'm just a little tired. We all woke so early."

But by that point he is already gone. And when she looks up in confusion, the feasters are on their feet.

Perspiration traces a line down her spine. It is the same line Jinling's finger sometimes covers—*bump, bump, bump. Jinling,* she thinks. "Where is she?" she murmurs to Suyin.

"In the night wing," Suyin whispers, without asking whom she means. "With Actor Peng. She said to do what they say."

"What who say?" Yuliang turns. Then she sees Godmother and Papa Gao before her. Their lips smile, but their eyes are as hard as coins. Godmother leans and unhooks Yuliang's dangling earring, which has caught on the fabric of her shoulder. "You little fool," she hisses, jerking the trinket. "I hope you can walk."

Yuliang tries to shake her off. "Let me go." But they each take one red elbow and walk her past the kitchen and pantry and up the stairs. The feast fades into giggles and shrieks behind her. Mingmei's lute sobs, the last lines of her song fading with the rest:

At fourteen, I married you, my lord
I never laughed, being bashful . . .

They near Jinling's room. The door is shut tight, and as they pass there's an urge to fling herself on it: *Jinling. Jinling!* As if sensing the instinct, Godmother tightens her grip and hurries Yuliang down to her own door. She knocks, and a shout comes from within: "Who the hell is it?"

"She's ready," Godmother calls. She turns to Yuliang, her smile flattening to a frown. "Remember, whatever he wants. Anything. No scenes." Her eyes narrow. "And remember, *finish the job.*"

She pushes the door open. Two men explode from behind it, along with the smell of opium, alcohol, tobacco. "She is *come!*" one sings in an operatic falsetto. He pauses, looks Yuliang over. "Not bad." He turns to Godmother. "How much?"

Godmother gives a small smile. "I'll get my book after."

Then Yuliang is inside her room, and the door is shut and locked behind her.

For an instant she just stands there, disoriented and faintly sick. She makes out a red shape roughly her size, leaning weakly against the far wall. She squints. Mirror Girl squints back, rubs her eyes.

From the bed, Merchant Yi guffaws. "Such vanity. You don't need to worry about your looks. Why, you've always been as pretty as a picture."

He rolls onto his back. "Come here."

"TAKE DOWN YOUR HAIR. No, not like that. Do it slowly."

Endless pins. Jinling's pearls, woven so carefully through her new matron's knot, drop to the floor like popcorn. Yi Gan lights his cigarette, leans back reflectively. "Take that off too," he says, and points.

Her fingers pluck at one button, the next. She peels herself free of the dress. A draft from the window licks her bare arms. For a moment it almost feels good.

"Come."

In the corner of her eye, Mirror Girl walks with her as far as the edge of the glass.

"You know I'm not looking for another wife," he says. "But if I like you, I may clear some of your debts. I've done it for others." When he reaches for her, Yuliang winces. But he just fingers her earlobe, lifting the earring up and down. "Like catty weights," he comments. "Don't they hurt?"

SHE LIES ON TOP OF HIM, feeling precarious, unbalanced. Her face is pressed into the smoky damp of his tunic. His hips rise and fall, rise and fall, the movement even and yet somehow utterly without rhythm. His hands are warm, tracing the band of her drawers, her under-top. Pressing down, down. Up, down. Up, down. No pain yet, just a little discomfort. As though he were a rock she were napping on. She'd like to reach down, remove the lump. She'd like to sleep. That's what she'd really like.

"How is that?" he murmurs.

His eyes are shut: he can't see how lost she is for a response.

HE KICKS HIS TROUSERS and drawers free. She's supposed to be helping: Jinling said so. But she suddenly feels unable to move her arms. He rubs himself, eyes half shut, lips flaccid and half open. He looks dead. But his breath is quick and moist and hot. Sweat falls in streams from his hair. His legs push, opening hers and encountering no resistance. He hits her lightly anyway: "Don't fight." Jinling has told her he likes to be the aggressor.

He groans, reaches down, finds her in the place where she is as dry and as rough as wood. Jinling gave her an oil of some sort. *Put this on first.* But it's too late now. He is arching, pushing. She grits her teeth, anticipating the pain. Of course, she knew there'd be pain. Nothing good comes without pain, her mama often said. But surely she didn't mean this. Did she?

"Oh, yes," he says. "Yes."

SOMETHING STICKY AND SLIPPERY; the pain giving way to something deeper; a slow ache as though she is swelling inside. Yuliang grips the bed's edge. Yi Gan's eyes are like moon slivers, pure white as the pupils roll back. His dock-weathered face knots up with pleasure. Yuliang blinks, and suddenly he looks old, enormous, frenzied. Like Chung Qai, the black-faced keeper of Hell's gates . . .

It *hurts*!

But Yuliang won't cry. *No scenes,* they said. And besides, she has cried enough: when she woke this morning, her eyes were so swollen that Jinling had to layer cold tea dregs on them to soothe them.

He shifts slickly against her skin, and she suddenly panics: her torso is sticky with blood. But no, she's just wet; his sweat smears her face and breasts. *That's why it's called wetting the sheets* . . . A slow rip.

Oh. Oh. No.

You don't have to let them into your head, Jinling said. Think of something else. Mama's eyes. Godmother's garden. The moon on a still night. The feeling she got when she finally stitched a perfect flower . . . He pushes, two, three, four times. "Ahhh. You are sweet, girl. So sweet . . ." His throat is a black tunnel, a dangling glob of glistening pink. She shuts her eyes. She is a melon, and he's splitting her open. She will break.

She will *break* . . .

"*Aiiiiiiighhhhh,*" he says. "*Aiiighhhhhhhhhhhhhh.*" He gives two more calls, shudders as though shot. His eyes are wide; his lips are a rictus of ecstasy. Then he crumples over her, stops moving entirely. *Is he dead?* For this happens. It happens with old men, and very fat ones. Lirong says it happened to her once. But Suyin says she's lying . . .

His foot twitches against her calf. It feels oddly plush, oddly pointed. It takes a moment for her to understand: he never even took off his shoes.

Nine

F EW GIRLS WHO ENTER THIS WORLD survive it. Many end up like Xiaochen: skeletal, scarred by abuse, addiction, and sex-sickness. Some, like the girl from Wuhu Lake, are either killed or kill themselves. Others "demote" from flower to some other tangential position: musician, teacher, a top girl's maid. A select few, however, triumph over Fate's glum intentions, and Jinling plans to be among these.

Between Merchant Yi's assistance and her cache of jewelry, the top girl claims to be mere months from buying out her Hall contract. Yuliang tries, under her tutelage, to follow suit. The passing months and men are marked by a slow accumulation of glitter: a gold pendant in the shape of a boar. A butterfly hairpin of Cantonese filigree, with antennae that tremble at the slightest of movements. A Japanese doll in a gold-threaded kimono, her skin wax-white, like chrysanthemum petals. The most valuable gift Yuliang receives is a golden dragon, fashioned into a heavy bangle. Her patron pulls it from its tissue-paper lair on the eve of Yuliang's seventeenth birthday—the two-year anniversary of her hair-combing.

"I'm not worthy," Yuliang says, twisting the beast on her wrist. It stares balefully at its backside, biting its tail with its diamond-chip teeth. Its scales are waves of molten metal. Yuliang savors their scrape on her skin as Yi Gan takes her to bed.

Later he sleeps and she studies the beast again, wondering what artisan's fingers made it so lifelike, and how. The dragon itself gives nothing up. Its coral eyes glow derisively. But no matter which way she turns the trinket, they won't meet her own.

Later, after he's gone, Jinling tries on the piece before the glass. Naked, she steps back to see how it looks. Yuliang catches her breath at the sight of her like that—flushed and smooth, the golden monster twinkling at her wrist—and stores the image away to fall back on later.

"What do you think?" Jinling cocks her head thoughtfully.

"It suits you," Yuliang says. And laughs, because everything suits Jinling.

Her friend (and her only prized bedmate) smiles indulgently before returning to herself. She sucks in her cheeks and juts her hips, trying to look like a modern girl in a magazine. She shakes her arm, making the grumpy beast dance.

"It's my birth sign," she remarks.

Yuliang looks at her quickly. "Didn't you say you were a rat?"

"I'm too young to be a rat!" Jinling replies indignantly. "I'm a dragon, through and through." And in truth, Jinling, with her fiery spirit, her intense charm, her way of slipping past all the rules, does seem like a dragon. And yet Yuliang is almost certain her friend told her she was born in the year of the rat. *Rat and boar,* she recalls her saying one night, as they lay intertwined and panting. *The astrologers say they're destined for each other.* Then again, she also remembers something about her being a rooster . . .

"Can I borrow this for today?" Jinling is asking now. "It would go beautifully with my dragon jacket."

Yuliang agrees. She decides not to question further. Hall girls don't have many rights. But one of the few they do have is this: everyone is granted her own version of her story, which, like her name, she can change at will. Though Yuliang has sworn she won't change her name again. She needs one thing, at least, that she can hold on to for good.

LATER THAT NIGHT A TAP COMES on the door. Jinling pushes her head in. "Here's your dragon bracelet." She slides the piece from her wrist. "Can I borrow a wrap? None of mine match this new dress."

Yuliang studies her friend's slim curves and shadows, sheathed in a dress of plum-blossom lavender planted with silver flowers and butterflies. Yuliang helped to design it with the dressmaker. Seeing how well Jinling wears it still gives her a faint glow of ownership.

"Where's the call?" she asks, standing and rifling through her silks.

"At the teahouse. The deputy customs officer has been promoted to Beijing. Yi Gan didn't mention it to you?"

Yuliang shakes her head, studying her friend beneath her lashes. They still haven't discussed the fact that the merchant now visits Yuliang more often than he does Jinling—or that for all of his earlier protests, he recently offered to make Yuliang his third concubine. It's the sort of arrangement flowers are supposed to yearn for: a simplifying of life, sex, expenses. A promise of a future, perhaps children. Somehow, though, the thought of being slowly nibbled down like one of four sweets makes Yuliang shudder. She's relieved that he hasn't pressed her on the matter.

For her part, Jinling said she didn't care. "*Aiya*," she said, shrugging. "You need him more than I do." Still, the subject makes Yuliang uneasy. Jealousy is like a sex-sickness in the Hall. It can hover in the blood for months, or even years, before infecting even the closest friendships.

Scarf in hand, Jinling moves to the mirror. "Are you sure this matches?"

"It's very pretty. You look like a candle."

Jinling quirks an eyebrow. "You put things oddly sometimes, little sister."

Embarrassed, Yuliang tries to make the comment a joke. "It's the orange silk," she says, stepping over, running her hands down Jinling's arms. "That's the flame. See? And the purple is smoke. Take off the shawl, and *poof*." She blows lightly in Jinling's ear. "You've blown yourself out."

The top girl giggles and squirms. "I'll be late tonight," she says. "But wait for me—I want to see you." She turns once more to leave, then pauses. "I've an errand to do tomorrow after lunch. Come with me?"

Yuliang is actually looking forward to washing her hair tomorrow. But she hears herself saying, "All right." Just as she always does when Jinling asks her for a favor: *Can I borrow the dragon?* or *Can you embroider this bag with a lotus?* She watches her friend's figure flicker around the corner. What, she wonders, will it be this time? A new dress she needs advice on? An unplanned trip to the palm-reader? Or perhaps, for once, a surprise for *her*—for Yuliang?

From downstairs the call comes: *Master Feng for Miss Yuliang.* Yuliang winces and twists the ring on her finger. Feng Yitmieng comes once a month, when his business is good. A small man with thin white legs he saws over hers, he reminds her of a cricket in mating season.

"HE'S VERY DOWN-TO-EARTH, for gentry," Jinling says the next day, as they zip along on their appointed errand. "He comes out with all sorts of things that surprise me."

"Like what?" Yuliang asks. She grasps her seat as the rickshaw swerves to avoid what appears to be a pile of rags. But as they pass, bits of flesh and shriveled limbs take shape in it, and a head turns toward her weakly. The face is as dark and as crisscrossed with cracks as old leather. With a jolt, Yuliang also sees that it looks a bit like Xiaochen.

"I'm sorry," the boy calls. He doesn't look more than twelve, but his bare back is a mosaic of scars and dirt. His jacket is rolled under the girls' feet as an added amenity. Yuliang and Jinling splay their legs to avoid it: it is crawling with lice.

"Did you see that?" Yuliang asks.

"See what?"

But the woman is already behind them. And to mention her breaks an unsaid rule: when girls disappear, you act as though you never knew them. So Yuliang just shakes her head and turns her gaze back to the street.

At least she knows where they're going now: they are riding to Jinling's jeweler. The top girl has her jewelry box in her little blue bag. She wants to sell some things and to have others appraised. She hasn't told Yuliang why, although Yuliang has a sinking sense that she knows already. Moodily, she lets her friend babble on about the new client she's cultivating, the second son of a high-up family from town.

"The way he talks, for example. He comes up with the funniest curses."

"Really." Yuliang can't keep the skepticism from her voice. *She doesn't enjoy it,* she tells herself. *She never really enjoys it.* After all, isn't that what Jinling herself says? *You're only* really *a whore if you enjoy it* . . . At least, with the men.

"I think he's a populist," Jinling adds, and frowns. "Or was it anarchist?"

"There's a difference," Yuliang says. "Populists are for the people. Anarchists are for nothing at all."

It's something Yuliang's uncle explained to her once, although, as with many things Wu Ding explained, she's never been sure of its accuracy. Still, Jinling slaps her arm with feigned annoyance. "You always make me feel like such a simpleton. How on earth do you know these things?" She laughs. "Anyway, it's all only about fashion in the end, isn't it? About word fashion. It's strange, isn't it?" she adds thoughtfully. "Men can change what they're called. They can say, 'I'm a populist,' and people will call them that. And yet we can call ourselves anything—singers, entertainers, taxi dancers. In the end, they'll always call us whores."

They're unusually bitter words from the usually blithe top girl. Oddly enough, though, Jinling looks genuinely happy. Her pale cheeks are peach-toned with the chill. Yuliang feels her mood lift, just looking at her, even as she feels a tart envy at such effortless loveliness. *I wish I could draw her,* she thinks. *Just like this.*

Unaware of her friend's scrutiny, Jinling bites her lip. "Listen," she says. "I want to tell you about something." This is how Jinling begins all her lessons. *Listen,* she'll say. *I want to show you how to make my fat feet look thinner. I want to teach you the difference between silver taels and the fake ones. I want to tell you about Actor Peng; I've found something he'll pay you extra for.* Yuliang sits up dutifully and listens. But what Jinling says this time is, "I've done it. I have enough to buy out."

For a moment the words all but extinguish the world: the coolie's slap-slapping feet, the street's scrambling commerce, the stick-woman left behind in the dust. Yuliang blinks, but sees nothing but her friend's oil-black eyes. *You can't leave,* she thinks.

"I can *leave,*" Jinling says, as if on cue. "I can buy out my contract. Godmother's accounts have me just two hundred taels away. Even if I just sell my diamond ring, it's enough."

They've reached the river; an offshore breeze brushes Yuliang's face with a chilly kiss. She will break, she thinks, if she moves. Even slightly.

Jinling laughs at her expression. "Oh, stop frowning for once!" She takes Yuliang's chin, turns her face. "Come. Come with me."

Her fingers are so cold Yuliang shivers. *"What?"*

"I mean it," Jinling says. "Listen. I'll explain."

The boy runs along, his stride lending quiet percussion to the top girl's words. They pass the temple with its monks robed in orange and saffron, then the market with its wares of clay and fish and human flesh: the lines of shuffling girls being paraded before prospective mothers-in-law and sharp-eyed middlewomen. Jinling continues talking as the market fades from view, and then they're at the docks, where boats strain toward the Yangtze's amber bend. *Slap-slap-slap.* She'll build a Hall of her own. It will be better, more splendid than the Hall of Eternal Splendor. She'll model it on the Shanghai house where she started, the Hall of Heavenly Gates. "I've got enough jewelry now to pay for things while I set up. And Ren Kuanti says he'll invest. He's bringing some of his rich friends, too, to meet with me." She drops her voice. "We're supposed to gather at the teahouse at six."

Yuliang pictures Ren Kuanti, a pale but dapper young man whose "investments" to date have mostly comprised drinking, gambling, and vomiting in the Hall courtyard. But this doesn't seem to bother Jinling. "Yuliang!" she says. "You can be my top girl."

"What?" Yuliang blinks.

"My *top girl*, little fool! We can be together always! I'll help buy you free too. . . Say something!"

"But what about my contract? What about all my debt?"

Jinling strokes her purse, like a cat in her lap. "I told you. There's plenty here. Along with Ren's investment, we'll have more than enough."

Yuliang's head reels with the implications. The rickshaw lurches around a corner that leads to a jeweler-lined street filled with windows winking with gold. The girls are thrown together for a moment, and then reluctantly pull apart. Catching her breath, Yuliang inhales her friend's favorite scent: floral, powdery. Faintly foreign. *It's an important decision,* she tells herself. *I must be sure to use good sense.*

Yet as the rickshaw pulls up to Jinling's shop, senses skip ahead of good sense. Wind takes caution, blows it over the water.

Yuliang shuts her eyes, tips her head back. "Yes," she says with a laugh. "Take me with you."

An hour later they part ways, Jinling to meet Ren Kuanti, Yuliang to cover for her at the Hall. "If the old centipede asks," Jinling instructs, pulling Yuliang's orange shawl around her shoulders, "tell her I've gone to have my hair trimmed. I should be back in time for my nine o'clock call."

Yuliang nods, gleeful at the thought of hiding something beyond tips from the spiteful manager. She will keep this secret under her pillow, like the knife the girl in the old story keeps there to ward off evil ghosts and bad fortune. She will wield the thought of it—a new home! a new role!—through the evening's scheduled visits. And when they're done, she'll carry it down the hallway. She'll creep into Jinling's room and huddle in the top girl's red-draped bed, and they'll stroke and sigh away all scent and sign of those male bodies. They'll fall asleep intertwined, whispering plans for their new life. And in the morning they will will step out and start it.

But Jinling doesn't return—not that night, and not the next. Yuliang covers for her for as long as she can. On the third day, sick with sleeplessness and bruised by Godmother's second beating, she finally confesses at least part of the truth: her friend went not to the hairdresser's but to meet her future financial backer. Clinging fiercely to fading hope, she holds back the other details—the jewelry bag, the escape plans. Her own corner room at the brand-new brothel. In the end, though, neither these things nor the withholding of them matters. The detectives track Ren Kuanti to an opium den in Tongling. There, it is learned, he has been smoking and gambling away Jinling's jewelry for nearly a week.

Two days later they find Jinling herself, bound and abandoned in the trunk of a stolen automobile. The top girl's throat has been slit, her sex mauled and disfigured. Her clothes, including Yuliang's shawl, are gone.

Ten

Y ULIANG IS IN BED. Not her real bed—Xiaochen's loathed bed of lost virtue—but Jinling's bed, with its red silk sheets and gilded headboard. A familiar hand is on her arm, and for a brief moment Yuliang thinks that this too is Jinling's. Taking it in her own hands, though, she quickly sees she is wrong: the fingers aren't the plump, soft digits of her beloved friend. These fingers are almost skeletal. Prayer beads wrap the yellowing palm. They cut into Yuliang's skin like teeth. With a gasp, Yuliang wrenches her own fingers away and turns toward the face next to hers.

"Mama?"

"Don't be afraid, little Xiu," her mama says. Her breath is so ragged it barely seems to carry the words. "I've made arrangements. You'll be safe."

Jerking upright, Yuliang stares wildly around the room. It's still Jinling's room—Jinling's bed, Jinling's armoire. Jinling's phoenix wine cups shine dully from a small shelf on the wall. But the heavy hand on her arm and the dense figure behind her tell her that she's awake now: this isn't a dream clasped in yet another dream.

"Another night-fright?" Merchant Yi says grumpily. "That's the third one this evening. Go to sleep. We've got the banquet tomorrow."

Yuliang lies back down obediently, wrapping her shivering shoulders in Jinling's quilt and her guilt in the waking nightmare of her reality: that in the end, Jinling kept her promise after all. Not by sweeping Yuliang off to a new life, but by leaving her her old one.

FOR ALL OF JINLING'S FABLED JEWELS, her funeral was spare. There were no necromancers, no monks chanting. There wasn't even a coffin. The surviving flowers burned paper trinkets they'd pooled hidden tips to buy: a little dress, a little pair of paper lily shoes that were just a shade too wide. A few false golden ingots. There was no money for anything else; Godmother had claimed the dead girl's belongings as "compensation."

After the ceremony they all trailed home and did what's done when a sister dies: they smoked, gambled, and gossiped. They painted their fingernails. They waited, as they must always wait, for the scandal to break. Yuliang didn't talk to them—she didn't talk to anyone, unless the words were beaten out of her. For the entire mourning period she sat in her room, in near silence.

The resumption of business as usual took more time than expected, in part because of the Ren family's high social status. As the men trickled back, tabloids as far-flung as those in Suzhou followed the court's deliberations, accessorizing the crime with hidden details that their editors claimed to have exclusively unearthed. Some headlines announced that Jinling was a man-hating witch-whore. Others said it was nothing but her own fault—that sex-sickness had driven her young suitor mad. Only one blamed the local police, to whom Godmother paid a monthly sum to turn a blind eye to the Hall's various infractions. "Outrageous," huffed Yi Gan when he read this to Yuliang. "Madame Ping may be sharp-tongued, but she's not a murderess." Still, there was a small note of doubt in his voice.

Even this suspicion, however, barely cut through Yuliang's haze of grief. She trudged through the days with mechanized efficiency, rising, dressing, eating, bedding, and embroidering merely as a means to keep from thinking. At times she almost succeeded. Most times, though, she failed, her legs and arms so heavy she couldn't rise from her bed. She almost welcomed the beatings that inevitably followed. The leather whip felt like justice, hot and pure on her skin. She'd rise up the next morning aching but strangely purged, as though some guilt had been discharged with her blood.

Winter ended. The flowers awoke one afternoon to discover a new doorbell, installed because it was fashionable. No one could get used to the jangling ring, and the fact that it didn't discriminate between honored guests and mere walk-ins. Call-cards resumed their rush in and out, and for some reason many of them requested Yuliang's services. That was when Godmother took the unusual step of skipping naptime, and called Yuliang to her room.

"You've done well this quarter," the madam announced, sliding two last beads of her abacus into place. "Even with your little set-in-stone face."

Yuliang, who hadn't slept in nearly four nights, weathered an urge to take the abacus and slam it down on the fat, smooth chignon. But when the madam beckoned her forward, she obeyed. She let the calculation-callused fingers grasp her chin.

"You miss her," the manager remarked flatly.

You know I do, Yuliang thought. Just the previous night, Godmother had discovered the kitchen crate on which Yuliang had set candles and the few items of Jinling's she'd managed to secret away: a silver hairpin; a lipstick case; the phoenix wine cups. She'd also added the sketch of Jinling she'd obsessively struggled over between clients, as though capturing her on paper might bring her back in the flesh. Jinling's ears were too small, her neck too thin; her delicate nose had come out almost snoutlike. In fact, Yuliang fully expected Godmother to laugh.

To her surprise, though, the madam studied the sketch a moment. Then she pocketed it. "Put those flames out," she'd said as she left. "You know the rules."

Now, though, she smiled coldly. "I know enough, at least, not to get so close to anyone that I'll have to miss her once she's gone." Turning Yuliang's face to and fro in the light, she added reprovingly, "You're as thin as a sesame stalk. Still, you're pretty. And the men seem to associate you with her." Her dimpled chin sank to her chest as she pondered. At last she nodded. "Very well. Get the man to help you move tomorrow."

Yuliang jerked her chin free. "Move? Move where?"

"Into Jinling's room. From now on you'll take her clients."

Yuliang gawked at her. "You mean . . ."

The madam sighed. "Yes, you little idiot. Congratulations. You're the new top girl."

NOW GINGERLY PRYING YI GAN'S FINGERS from her wrist (she can't sleep with a man's touch on her body), Yuliang remembers how the other flowers had muttered about it—Yuliang getting the biggest room and dress budget, the top billing at the gate and at banquets and events. Especially Mingmei, whom everyone had assumed was next in line for Jinling's job. *She's been here barely two years!* Yuliang heard her splutter to Suyin. *She's insufferable, too—won't smoke, won't play cards with us or join our chats. She doesn't appreciate the honor she's receiving!*

Contrary to the gossip, though, Yuliang did appreciate her new post—although not for the reasons the others would have. The heavens themselves couldn't have handed down a worse penance for her: the endless men, the longer hours, the requests of such casual and cultivated abasement that she sometimes wonders how Jinling rose so brightly most afternoons.

And then, of course, there is this: Jinling's bed. The site of such delicious, forbidden memories. Yuliang still can't lie in it without half-expecting Jinling to lie down in it too. She can't wake in it without reaching for Jinling's soft, warm waist—and, upon finding Yi Gan's burly torso instead, being forced to remember. That's her punishment: remembering everything.

Eleven

"Ho-ho!" Merchant Ming shouts in triumph from across the banquet hall: he has just won a round of tiger-stick-insect. "Who is next? Lao Yi! Try me!"

"Not tonight," Yi Gan calls back. "You're invincible. I wouldn't stand a chance."

"That's what your wife says when you put your slippers by her bed," Merchant Ming calls back.

As the hot room resounds with manly chuckles, the guild leader leans past Yuliang with the wine pot. He'd carefully seated his guest of honor, the new customs inspector, between Yuliang and Mingmei at the evening's start. "Essential thing, timing," he says now, pouring. "In drinking as in business. Don't you agree, eminence?"

"I know more about business than I do about drinking, I fear." Pan Zanhua is a handsome young man, though he sits slightly hunched, as though he'd like to pull his head into his shoulders. He eyes his host coolly, as though Yi Gan were a point on some unpleasant horizon.

"Ah. Then clearly our lovely companions have something to teach you." The merchant's voice is light. But the look he gives Yuliang is as weighted as his trading scales. Everyone knows about his agreement with the outgoing inspector: tax abatement on the one side, a well-stocked pantry on the other. It is clear to Yuliang, however, that despite his youth Inspector Pan will not be quite as accommodating: for all their efforts, neither she nor Mingmei has been able to coax so much as a smile from him. He is impeccably civil, utterly unencouraging. He is, she's decided, insufferable. But Merchant Yi has ordered them to give his guest "special attention." So reluctantly, she tries again.

"Have you tried the abalone?" she asks, picking out a plump one for him. "It's a specialty here. It's said the empress dowager had a plate sent out to her barge once. It came back as though it had been licked clean."

Pan Zanhua looks affronted, as though she's suggested they copulate on the table. Without a word, he turns toward the next table. Yuliang stares at his clean profile a moment. Then, affronted herself, she plops the greasy morsel gracelessly onto his plate. She knows this type. Oh, yes. He takes every smile, every female glance as a lure into scandal. But he'll fling his ethics far from his bedside. *One touch,* Jinling used to say. *That's all it takes. They forget everything.*

If only it were as easy for Yuliang.

Sighing, she turns back to her reluctant companion. He is, she must admit, very good-looking. A strong, square jaw. Full, almost womanly lips, though at the moment they are pressed so tightly together they'd have to be pried open for a smile. Yuliang watches him rub his cheek as the merchant leans over with the wine jug, topping his guest's already full cup a second time. Not surprisingly, some wine slops over. *"Aiyoo,"* the host cries, "I missed the mark."

"You did," Pan Zanhua agrees. Yuliang, already sopping up the spilled drink with her handkerchief, looks up at the tartness of his tone. "But really. It's just wine."

"Ah," says Merchant Yi, "there's where you're wrong, if you'll pardon my rudeness. This *shaoxing* is top-grade. From Sheng Huang Fu's shop." He nods meaningfully. "Your predecessor had quite a stockpile, I believe."

"A man of taste," the inspector observes, ignoring the hint. He reaches out for the hot towel that's been left for him, and starts as his fingers knock against Yuliang's.

Yuliang sees him take in the little cloth square in her hand, its floral border, its paired butterflies. When he looks up at her, the pools of his pupils quiver in surprise. She has the strange impression of a great deal of sadness.

"Master Pan!" Merchant Ming has arrived at the table. "How about a little wager?"

"I'm afraid I'm no gambler either."

"I'll go easy on you," Ming promises. "That is, if you will on me. What's the levy on soaps from Shanghai these days? Ho-ho!" Without waiting for a response he holds up his fist, chopstick rising from it like an ivory tusk. The inspector's face stiffens in irritated resignation as his uninvited guest counts: "On three. One . . . two . . ."

"Stick," Inspector Pan says quietly.

"Insect!" shouts Merchant Ming, just a hair after. "Ah-ha!"

"Insect bores stick," pipes Mingmei from behind them, as though no one else would make the connection.

An exasperated look passes over the inspector's face. *He doesn't want to be here any more than I do,* Yuliang realizes in surprise.

That this important man, fawned over by the town's most important names, might feel out of place seems very odd. As does the sight of a hand—her own hand—stretching out to take hold of his cup. "Here," she hears herself saying. "Let me."

A small silence follows as she picks up the cup and downs the wine. It's common for girls to drink for favored clients, but Yuliang does it only rarely. And only for her patron. As she sets the cup back down, Yi Gan sucks his teeth.

"Our honorable guest says he needs more practice drinking," she explains. Even to her own ears, it sounds like a protest.

Pan Zanhua stares at her a moment. Then he excuses himself to step outside. As he leaves, Yuliang feels Yi Gan's hand slide into the high slit of her dress. She clamps her legs shut, mortified at first. But the merchant merely gives her thigh a hard, twisting pinch.

"Your gesture was kind," Pan Zanhua says in a low voice, a little later. He is pulling out a silver cigarette box. "But it wasn't necessary. Why did you do it?"

He's finally addressed her. Leaning forward with her lighter, Yuliang suppresses a small smile of triumph. "I've gathered that your eminence doesn't enjoy drinking games."

"I don't enjoy the *usual* drinking games," he says, watching her keenly through the smoke.

She colors slightly. "I apologize."

"Please don't. Women apologize too much."

Now she gawks at him. No man, not even her eccentric uncle, has ever said anything remotely like this. "I'm sorry," she says—then, despite herself, she breaks into laughter. "I'm a true boar, it seems. It's my destiny to want harmony."

"You let astrologers choose your character?"

"I didn't think it had anything to do with choice."

"You have much to learn."

Insufferable, she thinks again, and she smiles at him sweetly. "May I ask what your eminence's sign might be?"

"I was born in the rat year."

"It seems accurate enough. If you'll pardon my saying so."

"How so?"

She ticks it off on her fingers. "You are clearly very intelligent. You're ambitious and honest. You have an answer for everything." Eyeing him sideways, she adds, "I wouldn't be so surprised if you also secretly enjoyed gambling after all."

He looks startled by the jab. Yuliang hides another smile with a sip of watered wine. "Some say rat and boar are destined to be together," she adds. A small stab of sadness: *Jinling.*

"Certainly." He snorts. "Those who make money out of the union.

I will admit, however, that you are right about the gambling. I simply prefer my wagers to be of a more . . . refined nature."

"How interesting," Yuliang says, though she is thinking, *How pompous.* "Perhaps you'll take the time to teach me one."

He looks at her strangely, trying to assess whether or not she is serious. Then he glances quickly around the room. No one but Mingmei seems to be noting their discussion. "All right."

He explains the rules: She must come up with a theme. It must be something literary, something he can link to a poem or a classic. If he does this quickly and successfully, he wins.

"What happens if you meet my challenge?" she asks him.

"You drink. Though if you insist, I will drink for you."

Now it's her turn to study him. Is it her imagination, or could his tone almost be described as flirtatious?

Two seats over, Mingmei taps her fan in kinetic rhythm on her shoulder, on the button that fashionably secures her handkerchief there. *Click, click.* Her eyes return to the two of them: twice, three times. Ignoring her, Yuliang runs through her stockpile of *ci.* "Swallows," she says at last.

He lifts an eyebrow, and she sees at once that she's made the game far too simple. "Cold Food Festival, swallows," she corrects herself. "And—and catkins."

He blinks at this last clue, frowns. Then he shuts his eyes. His lips move wordlessly, uncertainly. But he starts:

The Cold Food Festival
a quiet and peaceful spring day.
From the jade burner rises the up-curling smoke
of the dying incense.
Dreams came back to me as I slumbered
on the hill-shaped pillow which concealed . . .

His stumbles, stops. Helpfully, she offers another line: " 'My hairpins with flowery ornaments . . .' "

He clears his throat. "'River . . .'" he begins; then stops again. At last he opens his eyes and shrugs. "Your game, my lady."

Smiling, Yuliang finishes it for him as she refills his cup:

Sea swallows have not returned;
people amuse themselves with the game
of vying green herbs.
Plum blooms are withered, willows bear catkins;
Twilight falls, light drops of rain
Wet the swing in the garden.

When he drinks, the fine-stretched cords on his throat tremble like *erhu* strings. When he's done he studies her, his face unreadable.

"Have I offended you?" she asks.

"I wouldn't have expected you to know Li Qingzhao so well."

"I would have expected *you* to know her better."

It comes out more tartly than Yuliang had planned. But he doesn't seem to take offense.

"It's women's verse, in the end. More music than proper poetry, really. We didn't study women's poems. No one I know did."

"That, perhaps, is your loss."

"Perhaps." He finishes off his drink. "Do you know more Li Qingzhao?"

"Almost all, I think." Once more, the words are out before she registers how unseemly it sounds. But the look he gives her isn't one of disdain. It's more one of intense concentration. As though he's struggling to solve a perplexing problem.

"So," he says. "The classics are included in your . . . training."

"No. At least, not those classics. We aren't taught many poems, beyond what we learn to sing."

"So where—"

"My uncle was . . . unusual."

"Unusual in what way?"

Yuliang hesitates, unsure how to proceed. She never talks about

Wu Ding. And yet, looking into this strange man's eyes, she finds herself inexplicably tempted to tell him not just her *jiujiu*'s story, but her own.

She is so conflicted about proceeding that she barely notices Mingmei standing up to trip around to Yi Gan's free side. She does notice, however, when the weary complaint of the musician's *pipa* begins filling the room: as top girl, she is the one who decides when to cue music.

Around them, diners call out their approval: "A song. Yes, let's have a song!"

Mingmei's hand flutters to her neck, a ring-glint of protest: "My throat is sooooo dry tonight," she chirps. "I think I'm getting ill . . . Perhaps my sister will do us the honor. If, that is, the new inspector will share her with the rest of the room."

"Ah," says Yi Gan, smirking. "How about it, eminence—can we borrow her?"

Pan Zanhua blinks at the tipsy crowd, as though he has only just become aware of its presence. "It's not a question of lending," he says stiffly. "I certainly don't own her."

And without further ado he stands and excuses himself.

Stunned, Yuliang watches him make his way to the doors to the courtyard. The cries for a song reach a crescendo. But it's only after he has left that she forces herself to her feet, past the outstretched hands and beery breath of her audience.

LATER, AS WAITERS CLEAR UP the slopped remains of the feast, and guild members stagger home to wives and concubines or to the Hall, Yuliang and Mingmei, friends and colleagues again in the wake of Pan Zanhua's ultimate coldness to them both, shrug themselves back into their padded jackets. Shuffling through her remaining call-cards, Yuliang thinks wearily of the remaining events to which she has been summoned. Then, of course, there is Yi Gan, who will stay the night as he does most Saturday evenings. The thought makes her grimace: she knows all too well how his anger translates in bed.

As she makes her way toward the door, however, he materializes before her. "I won't be seeing you later," he says briskly. "I'm booking you for someone else."

"Someone else?" He's never sent her to another client before.

He's watching her the way a boy might watch an insect in magnified sunlight. "Our new customs inspector. It seems he needs a little more persuasion."

For a moment Yuliang's mind spins, both at the thought of seeing Pan Zanhua again and at the idea of his actually paying for her services. He had struck her as the last man under heaven who would ever place his chop on a brothel chit.

"He is coming to the Hall?" she manages.

"No. You are going to him."

She takes a breath. "When am I expected?"

The merchant smiles. "Ah. That's the beauty of it. You aren't."

Twelve

THE NEW INSPECTOR'S HOUSE is both elegant and impressive, with three full stories, glass windows, a cobbled courtyard. Passing through the moon-shaped gate, Yuliang is forced to admit that it's certainly the nicest house she has visited. Still, outside the doorway there's a sharp, shrill urge to flee. Not just because she is still mortified from their encounter, but because the situation presents her best chance yet. The Hall's sedan chair is needed elsewhere, as is the manservant; the Hall hadn't planned on a last-minute call, and she won't be expected there now until morning. What's more, she has Yi Gan's deposit in her purse.

For a moment—just a moment—Yuliang lets herself consider it: lying. Leaving. She sees herself on a boat, sailing away. When her thoughts delve beneath the water, though, there's the girl in Wuhu Lake.

The Japanese maple tree in the courtyard's center stirs in the wind, and in its whispers Yuliang hears the voice she misses most: *The only way to escape this place is by doing it their way.*

Oh, Jinling.

Yuliang wipes her hands on her jacket. "It's just skin," she reminds herself.

She knocks once. And again.

AS HER EYES ADJUST to the dim light inside, Yuliang surveys the foyer's offerings: a long redwood table. A carved sofa, simple but of superior quality. On top of the table is a Ming vase filled with chrysanthemums. Above that, a large picture-poem. The little image exudes loneliness like a damp aroma. The mountains are black and craggy, wreathed in mist so real she actually feels a chill. The poem is a delicate spider-dance on the right that she can't read. Shadowed pines blanket the peaks, dappled by raindrops so real that Yuliang reaches a finger reflexively toward the wetness. All this from ink. Mere ink! It seems to her an almost godlike act. Like Pangu's eighteen-thousand-year battle to separate the earth from the sky.

Yuliang is still standing there, her nose nearly against the picture's glass, when the amah who'd admitted her reappears. Her seamed face is still tight with barely concealed outrage, and when she sees Yuliang by the painting, she all but crackles. "Don't touch that," she says indignantly. "It's worth more than your whole life, from start to finish."

Reluctantly, Yuliang steps away. "Will—will he see me, auntie?" she asks.

"*Hmmph*" is all she gets in return. Turning on her tiny heel, the old woman starts hobbling back toward the hallway. After a few steps, though, she looks over her bent shoulder. "Come along," she croaks. "He is a busy man."

PAN ZANHUA HAS CHANGED. Instead of his Western suit he wears a Chinese robe, scholar-style. A book lies open on the desk before him, and a notepad. His writing is neat, with disciplined curves, succinct slashes. Yuliang waits in the doorway while he finishes, the amah at her elbow like a stooped jailor.

When he finally looks up, the inspector's eyes widen. He puts down his pen in careful alignment with his inkstone. He has an ink smear on his left cheek.

"Good evening," Yuliang says, and then finds herself fumbling for the remainder of her introduction. "I—that is, the Merchant's Guild, Master Yi . . ."

He picks up his pen, and Yuliang finds herself laughing a laugh that sounds more like a nervous hiccup. "I hope you're not planning to write that down."

He eyes her as though she has just tumbled from the sky and broken his roof. But she has no choice but to continue. "I've been sent by friends," she stammers on. "They know that it's hard being a newcomer in a strange city. And the nights are cold now. So damp and lonely . . ." On the way here the statement had seemed sophisticated and poetic. Uttered, it's unambiguously absurd.

Losing her nerve, she pulls out Yi Gan's wad of cash, sending the inspector's eyebrows flying toward his hairline like alarmed little birds. "What's that?"

"Your deposit. Master Yi paid it on your behalf. He humbly requests that you keep it."

The amah snorts in disgust. The inspector frowns at her. "You can leave, Qian Ma." When the servant doesn't move, he repeats the command. "Out, please."

"*Aiyaaa*," the amah mutters. "I'd rather have died than seen this." But she backs out the door, stepping exaggeratedly around Yuliang as though she is the night-soil man come for pickup.

The inspector watches without expression. After she has disappeared, he beckons to Yuliang. "Come all the way in, please." He indicates the chaise longue with his chin. She sits, feeling like a little girl about to be punished. She even has the urge to swing her feet.

"Do you always work so late?" she asks at last, if only to break the silence.

"It's not work. At least, not the work your friends are so interested in influencing."

"They're not friends." The phrase darts out with the same unplanned impulse with which her hand had darted for his glass. She cringes, expecting her impudence to close him up again: *snap*. But his face reflects just mild surprise. "I'm sorry," he says.

You don't need to apologize, she almost says; *men do that too much.* But that too seems rude. As well as false: in her experience, men never apologize. Which also sets him apart.

"It *is* work, a little bit, I suppose," he goes on, indicating the book with his chin. "After our discussion, I felt the urge to reexplore Li Qingzhao."

"You just don't want to lose another wager."

He smiles slightly. "Maybe so. At any rate, I keep coming back to this line." He points to a sentence. Yuliang just shakes her head, embarrassed. "It's the one called 'Stream,'" he says, understanding quickly. "It begins like this: 'Thousands of light flakes of crushed gold/for its blossoms—'"

"'And of trimmed jade for its layers of leaves,'" she interrupts. Which, again, is unspeakably rude. But for some reason she needs for him to know she knows it. "'Plum flowers are too common,'" she continues. "'Lilacs, too coarse, when compared with it./Yet its penetrating fragrance drives away my fond dreams of faraway places./How merciless!'"

Another short silence. He is watching her again, with that strange look of trying to solve a puzzle. "What do you think that means?" he says finally.

Yuliang thinks a moment. "I'm not a scholar," she says at last. "But I've always thought she was telling us that . . . that no matter how we long for the past, we are rooted in the present." She drops her eyes. "Coarse as it might be."

He picks up his pen, scribbles something on his pad. Blacks it out. "You said you know almost all of her poems."

"Yes," Yuliang says, and feels a small pride in spite of herself. "Though she's only a woman, she is my favorite of the poets. Not just because her works are so lovely, but because she was so strong.

She lived through such hardship—losing her land, her husband. Living in exile." She hesitates. "She bent but did not break. I think that perhaps it was her poetry that helped her survive."

He looks at her curiously. "Why do you say so?"

"It helps *me* survive," she says honestly. "The words are comforting, don't you think?"

"And you—you need comforting. Sometimes."

The thought that he might think otherwise is so disconcerting she can't answer.

"Will you recite another?" he asks quietly. "For me?"

Don't, Yuliang thinks. *Don't, don't, don't.* Nothing's less seductive than a woman pretending to be intelligent. But the poem spills out anyway, almost of its own accord: " 'Who planted the bajiao tree under my windows?' " she begins. " 'Its shade fills the courtyard;/Its shade fills the courtyard . . .' "

The words come faster and freer, liquid from a tipping cup. But Pan Zanhua's expression isn't one of distaste. He is leaning forward, his brow furrowed. And as Yuliang finishes—" 'Lonely for my beloved, grief-stricken,/I cannot endure the mournful sound/of rain' "—his fine hands seem to tremble slightly.

"You said, I believe," he says, "that you learned this from your uncle."

Yuliang nods. "He is—was—a scholar of the classics." Which, given Wu Ding's untutored upbringing and muddled grasp of literature, is as far from the truth as calling the moon's reflection the moon. Still, she finds herself adding, "He was an official too. Back in Zhenjiang." Even less true: her *jiujiu* took the local-level civic exams three times and failed them three times as well, before the halcyon dreams of the den washed away his ambitions.

"What's his position?" the inspector asks. "I go to Zhenjiang on business."

"He died," Yuliang invents quickly, wondering *Why do I keep lying?* "He . . . he fell off a boat. Four years ago. Bringing me here." *Stop talking,* she tells herself. *Just stop.*

There's a small scuffle in the hallway outside. "Hmmph," Yuliang hears.

"Qian Ma!" Inspector Pan calls. "Go to bed!"

The thin voice filters through the door again: "Hmmph. In all my days . . ." But again, the complaint is followed by the stilted patter of retreat.

Pan Zanhua smiles self-consciously. "You'll have to forgive her. She still believes respectable women don't even speak in public if they can help it. Much less visit male friends."

Respectable? Friends? Yuliang looks at him incredulously. But his face and voice both remain blithe. Still, the interruption brings her back to her mission: she looks down at the money stack still clasped in her hand. She thinks of Mingmei, raped and beaten. Of Dai kneeling in the rain. She stands, puts her purse, handkerchief, the money on the table. "Well," she says softly.

As she approaches him she tries to ignore the look of panic on his face, the way he leans back as though to maintain distance between them. As she leans over, she has a fleeting glimpse of his neck. Like his hands, it is white and taut. She'd planned to sit in his lap. Facing him now, though, she sees that this would be as graceful as standing on her head. She kneels instead. "It's late," she whispers. "Aren't you tired?" Taking his palms in hers, she lifts his hands to her cheeks, half worrying that he'll see how they are shaking. After the callused press of Yi Gan's thick fingers, Pan Zanhua's feel as soft as a woman's.

Then, quite suddenly, her cheeks are cold. He is pulling her to her feet. "I'd like," he says, "for you to leave."

"Leave?" She opens her eyes.

"I can't do this."

She stands shakily. "It's all right," she tells him. "Really. It's all taken care of. I am, I mean. Even if you don't want—this. The money." She holds it out. But he strikes her outstretched hand away from him, almost violently. Bills scatter to the floor like debris. Yuliang blinks in surprise. She hadn't thought he'd be a beater.

She steps back warily. But he doesn't touch her again. He just runs his palm down his left cheek. Where the smudge is. "I didn't mean to do that," he says hoarsely. "It's just that you are . . . that I'm not . . ." He covers his eyes. "*Aiyya.* Don't you see? This is just the sort of thing I've come here to fight."

"Love?" she asks, idiotically.

His lips twitch. "Corruption. Exploitation of society's vulnerable elements. You're a beautiful girl . . ." he continues. Then stops. "You see? I don't even know your name."

"It's Yuliang. Zhang Yuliang."

"Of course. Good Jade." A wry smile. "The little jade boar."

She nods numbly. She'd forgotten their brief talk about birth signs.

"You know, don't you, Zhang *xiaojie,*" he continues, "if you stay here, then they've won. Not only will I be in their debt, but they'll be able to hold our—hold whatever would happen over me. That's what they really want."

Her head is spinning, though even through her confusion what he is saying does make a sort of sense. Pan Zanhua will pay if he sleeps with her tonight. The same way she'll pay if she *doesn't* sleep with him. Yuliang snatches desperately at solutions. She could stay with the amah for a few hours. She could go back in the morning, just as though she'd completed her mission. Give them the deposit money, say the rest was coming soon. It could work. For a while, anyway . . .

But really, it couldn't. Yuliang knows that. She imagines the conversation the young inspector would have with Yi Gan later: *Did you enjoy our gift, Master Inspector? Oh yes. She slept on the floor with my amah.*

"I can't just go," she says.

"Why not?"

She kneels, scraping the scattered money toward her. He crouches beside her, hands her two bills that have landed near his feet. "All right, then. Here's what you will tell them. Tell them I wasn't feeling well tonight." He's still frowning, working it out as he speaks. "Tell them that you . . . caught me off guard. That I'm not refusing their gift, I'm just postponing it. I'll take it in a different form. Not as . . ." He gestures awkwardly. "But as something else. As a tour of the town."

"A tour?" Her first thought is that it's one of those rare trade terms she hasn't learned yet, the same way *climbing beneath the warm quilt* is a euphemism for early morning visits to the Hall.

But he means just what he's saying. "We'll take my chair into town. You can show me key landmarks. Help me know what's what. It will be a business-related service." He looks over her shoulder; she follows his gaze to the tall boxed clock by the window. "We'll leave here at nine," he concludes, authoritatively.

"Nine," Yuliang repeats in dismay.

It's sheer madness; the mere idea of leaving now, at three, then coming back just six hours later exhausts her. Then there's the thought of the two of them traipsing about town together. Does he really think that will save him from the gossip? *You don't understand this town,* she wants to tell him. *It's not Shanghai.*

And yet as he helps her up, neatly stacking the bills and folding them warmly into her hand, Yuliang finds herself looking into his eyes, and again, there is that sense of interest. That feeling that he is not just looking back at her but *listening* to her. Even when she isn't speaking at all.

Which, perhaps, is why she finds herself taking the money and nodding obediently. As though this all made all the sense in the world.

IT TAKES MORE THAN AN HOUR for Yuliang to convince Godmother that she hasn't failed her, and another to convince the madam to let her leave again, alone. In the end she gains permission only after swearing that *this* day, at least, will end up in the bed business that was supposed to begin it.

"I'll say this once," Godmother says grudgingly. "Think of this as a test. If you come back without his seed inside you and his money in your hand, you will have a worse time of it than Mingmei did."

When the madam finally dismisses her the sun is already rising. Yuliang flees to her room and paces, too apprehensive to sleep. As the light strengthens, she sits at her toiletry table, doodling aimlessly with a pencil. Images rise and fall: the wispy sorrow of the painting's painted mountain. The feel of his palms on her face. The strange, sharp stirring she'd felt reciting *Bajiao Tree* for him . . . She imagines that things had gone differently. That rather than leaving her face, his hands had done what she'd expected and lingered. And descended. If they had she could sleep now without worry of punishment or humiliation. But then she probably wouldn't be seeing him again, either.

The thought is inexplicably depressing. As she climbs into bed, a vague, leaden sadness seems to coil itself in her chest.

Still, two hours after finally sleeping, she leaps up easily. She even hums a little as she gets ready. She sees for the first time the way morning sun forms rainbows in the glass's edges, surrounding Mirror Girl with all the colors in the world. Yuliang washes and dresses with care, in her soberest clothes. She dusts her face with powder and leaves everything else bare. She even arranges her hair in a virgin's style. *Why not?* she thinks. *Why not?*

And the oddest part is, it works. This time when she knocks, the amah doesn't even recognize her: "Come in," the old woman says, with just a hint of hesitation. Not about Yuliang's identity. Rather, about why a clean-faced young woman would be knocking on her master's door, alone and at this hour. Which is early, but still unmistakably respectable.

Thirteen

A HALF-HOUR INTO "SIGHTSEEING," Yuliang is forced to realize how little she knows of her own town. She knows the restaurants and the teahouses. The opium dens, of course. And she knows the flower-boat brothel on the river, the Hall's main competitor. But she is suddenly struck by how little else she has seen of this bustling city. Standing at the stone tablet touted as the town's most ancient landmark, Yuliang can't tell Pan Zanhua anything about it at all, other than that it is very old. That, and the fact that two coppers will buy materials to make a rubbing of the gritty text. But even this information is superfluous, since she gathers (too late) that it's already scrawled on the charcoal-vendor's sign.

"I think the text tells a story," she concludes weakly, as her companion hands the man his coins. She looks at the little picture etched into the granite: the grainy outline of a beak, a wing. "Something about a bird."

Pan Zanhua studies the delicate tracks, rubbing his cheek. Last night's ink streak, in that precise spot, has disappeared. Yuliang pictures him over his washbasin, water coursing in clear sheets down his face.

"This was written by Mi Fu," he says. "You know about him? One of the great artists of the Song Dynasty." He traces the text with a finger. "It tells the story of the crane and the tortoise. The tortoise got tired of living in mud, so he asked the crane to take him up into the sky. They did it with a bamboo pole. Each animal clamped an end of it in his mouth."

"And that worked?" Yuliang yawns, feeling thick-headed after her long night.

"Apparently." The young official takes the vendor's little roll of thin paper and removes the hemp cord that keeps it tied tight. "Must've been a quiet trip, though. They both knew that if either of them opened their mouth, the tortoise would fall to his death."

Yuliang lets her gaze trace the eggshell-like delicacy of the strokes in the rock. The writing is worn and antiquated in style. She thinks for a moment that perhaps she sees *heaven*, and *mountain*. Then his hand is in front of her, holding the lump of charcoal.

"Here, Zhang *xiaojie*," he says. "Why don't you? I'm sure you're the more talented of us."

"I doubt that," Yuliang replies, laughing. But she takes the lump, strokes it a moment. Then, with a few swift motions that are inexplicably satisfying, she blackens the page, watching the image appear like magic.

As they continue on Pan Zanhua explains his work—what he's been sent here to do, why it is so very important to him. "It's a disgrace," he says. "A calamity. It's the real reason this country is so weak compared to the modern nations of the West."

"That taxes are too high?" Yuliang offers this with some confidence. It's what Yi Gan cites for the nation's problems in general.

But he snorts. "That half the time they aren't paid at all. And half of the half that *are* finally paid end up in the wrong people's pockets." He picks up a small tin of tea from a nearby vendor. "A question: how much will he sell? Probably more than two dozen tins today, wouldn't you say?" He shakes the can, which rustles weakly. It doesn't sound like it's got much inside. "Multiply that by a thousand," he says. "A million. How many versions of this are there nationwide? Then multiply *that* by millions more. Think of all the goods that change hands every day."

Yuliang thinks of clients coming, groaning, leaving. Of tips tossed onto her nightstand. Like everyone else, she hides half of them. The other half gets whittled away by the dues owed the maids, the man-servant, and Godmother herself. She thinks of Godmother's neat account books and the occasional visits of the old customs inspector on feast days. His bills were always sent straight to Merchant Yi: the memory dawns with a new sense of understanding.

Pan Zanhua puts the can back, picks up another. On its label, a willowy woman waves a fan. "Special slimming tea," the vendor offers. "Latest scientific formula."

The inspector smiles. *I wonder what he's like in bed,* Yuliang thinks abruptly. The thought startles her; she's never curious about men and their bedding habits. She simply accommodates them, takes their gifts, tries to forget them. With this one, though, it's somehow different. He speaks politely, warmly. He looks at her not in annoy-ance or lust, but as though he honestly cares that she is listening. He is very, very careful not to touch her.

"Our economy is enormous," he's saying, waving his free hand. "Western and Japanese businesses flock here every day, hoping to sell just one thing—a cheap hat, a bar of soap—to each national. Because if they did, that makes for half a billion—half a *billion*—sales. And yet even with all that commerce, the government has to keep begging abroad for more cursed foreign loans."

"I'll give you a good price," the vendor wheedles. "Even better for two—one for you, one for the pretty little lady." He grins sug-gestively. His prey simply ignores him.

"We can't begin to afford all the new schools we need to catch our people up with the world," the inspector says. "All our major railroads are owned by outsiders. The Japanese are turning our offi-cials into puppets."

"Didn't you live in Japan?"

"I went to university there."

"That must have been exciting."

He shrugs. "It was different from what I expected."

"How was it different?"

"I thought that with all the modern ways and teachings there, I'd feel more at home. But after four years I still felt like a foreigner there as well."

As well? Yuliang pauses, struck suddenly both by the words' implication and the way they unexpectedly sum up her own feelings. She's never thought of herself in such terms: as a foreigner. But it occurs to her that that's precisely what she feels like at the Hall. With its preening, chattering flowers, the petty clients they compete over. With its secret dramas, its tiny tragedies and triumphs. Try as she might, Yuliang has never been able to understand, much less care about, any of it. *It's true,* she thinks, strangely electrified. *They may as well be speaking a foreign language.*

"Do you need to rest, Zhang *xiaojie*?"

Seeing her stop, he has paused too. "What? Oh. No. It's just . . ." Yuliang hurries to catch up.

If he's aware of having said anything unusual, he doesn't show it. "Look at that."

Following the gesture, she sees a skeletal man marched past by constables. "After half a century of trying, we still haven't stamped out the poison smoke that's rotting our core."

"But is that possible? To stamp it out?"

"Anything is possible, with the right leaders and right spirit."

"You don't really believe that."

"Did anyone believe the Japanese could defeat a Russian navy?"

"The Japanese must have, surely."

He blinks, then laughs. "My point exactly."

The old vendor pipes up, sensing he's losing a sale. "Would your eminence like a sample? I can give you a free can. If you like it, you can tell your other lady friends." He glances down the road to where the sedan chair sits in full view, official blue curtains stirring in the wind. Pan Zanhua follows his gaze, then looks back at Yuliang. For the first time today, she sees him waver. *Now he'll do it,* she thinks, stiffening. *He'll realize how bad it looks to be with me. And that will be the end.*

But he simply shakes his head. "No, thank you," he says.

THEY MOVE ON, passing fish stalls, their rainbow-scaled offerings dying and drying in piles, and pause before tumblers tossing and bending as though they had no bones at all. "When I was a child," he tells Yuliang, "I saw a pair of Mongolian twins doing this. One of them gave me the prettiest smile from between her toes." He laughs. "I'd just spent ten hours in a dark study, writing and rewriting classics. The girl looked like heaven. For weeks after that I dreamed of joining the troupe."

"Could you have?"

He shakes his head. "My father was a scholar—a *jinshi,* under the old system. His father had been too. It would have dishonored him immeasurably." He looks at her sidelong. "What was it you said about fate last night? That you didn't think you'd been given a choice?"

It's the first time he's mentioned last night. Suddenly for some reason, Yuliang looks away, toward an old woman at a table that is covered with charts of hands and faces. "Do you think others can read it?" she asks. "My uncle called them tricksters."

Pan Zanhua laughs. "There are women who can do anything, if you pay them enough."

She stops again, feeling herself flush. He looks back, at first surprised and then, registering the gaffe, visibly shaken. "Zhang *xiaojie.* You must—surely you know I didn't mean that."

"Of course not." Yuliang's eyes are glued to the ground.

"Please. You mustn't think—"

"This is foolish," she interrupts harshly. "You must know it only hurts you to be seen with me like this." She drags her gaze back to his. "Why did you bring me?"

To her surprise he looks pensive, as though he's actually pondering her question. "I suppose that also comes back to what you said to me last night," he says at last.

"About fate?"

"About rooting ourselves in the present."

It's such an absurd answer that she almost laughs. But then he steps toward her, his face still somber. For the first time since they've met, he touches her intentionally, placing his hand gently on her forearm. Yuliang flinches. But she doesn't pull away.

"It's always been my belief," he says softly, "that if heaven *does* hand us our fate, it also hands us the tools to shape it."

" 'Man is his own star,' " she murmurs slowly. " 'And the soul that can render an honest and a perfect man commands all light, all influence, all fate.' " The thought of her uncle brings a quick lurch to her stomach.

Pan Zanhua stares at her a moment—again that look, as though trying to grasp something just beyond his reach. Then, shaking his head, he turns to the blacksmith's table they've stopped next to. "I was wondering where these came from. I've received half a dozen as gifts." He picks up one of the wares on it: a small picture of a lotus, forged entirely from black metal.

This, at least, is something she can speak to. "It's a tradition here. They say it began with an argument between a blacksmith and a painter. The painter told the blacksmith that his work wasn't art, that a hammer could never do what a brush does. The blacksmith said he was wrong. He went right to his anvil and created Wuhu's first iron picture."

He picks up one of the palm-sized images: a bulky orchid. It seems to suck in the sunlight. "That painter may have been right."

Yuliang feels a flash of empathy for the artisan, a big-handed young man with resigned eyes. "I don't think they're all bad," she says. "It takes some talent to bend hard metal into something beautiful."

"At the very least, a strong supply of determination." He holds it up. "May I buy this for you?"

Yuliang gazes at the souvenir, recalling suddenly the very first iron picture she ever saw. She sees her uncle staring at it intently while behind his back, a strange woman stares at his niece . . .

"Is something wrong?" the inspector is asking.

Yuliang looks at him. For one inexplicable instant she almost wants to strike him. But she just shakes her head. "No . . . no. It's just . . ." Looking away, she spots another vendor. He is handing a roasted yam to a young monk. The latter's robe, she can't help noticing—for she always notices these things—is almost the exact same shade as his free meal.

"I'd rather you buy me lunch," she says.

THEY GO TO A RIVERSIDE TEAHOUSE Yuliang went to with Jin-ling, on one of her bimonthly consultations with the palm-readers. The inspector orders tea, steamed fish with chilis, shrimp dumplings. He adds bamboo shoots to the list, although they're expensive and out of season. The little hut teeters on the river, just feet from where the town's poor thrust their dirty babies and clothes into the brackish flow. As the proprietor brings the teapot, sounds of laughter and splashing filter through the walls.

"You look thoughtful," the inspector comments.

"I'm sorry."

"Don't apologize. What's in your head?"

A small thrill: it's still such a new question to her. Yuliang pulls out her handkerchief, rubs a charcoal smudge on her nail, then the red crust left behind when she scrubbed off her nail polish last night. "The sounds," she says. "The laughter."

"What about them?" When she looks up, his eyes are like newly turned earth.

"My mother used to do washing like that."

"She did the washing herself?" he asks, cracking open a shrimp.

"We had been well-off at one point. My parents were very skilled at their work—her embroidery was among the best in the whole county. But my *baba* couldn't read, and was tricked in business. We lost everything." She picks up a shrimp and begins peeling it. "He'd hoped for a son who would become a scholar and support him in his old age. My mother said his spirit was broken." She pauses. "I don't remember having any servants until I went to my uncle's house."

"Ah. The scholar who fell from the boat."

"Yes," she says, wiping her hands carefully on her handkerchief.

"And when he died, you came here . . . how?"

"A man whom Uncle knows—knew—arranged it. There were debts."

He just nods, then picks up the handkerchief she's just put down. "Very fancy," he comments, examining the rumpled field of flowers and birds.

Yuliang nods self-deprecatingly. "My mother was much better at it. Although I thought when I came here that I was coming to make a living at it."

"Perhaps you could have," he says, looking at her intently. "Perhaps you still can. Perhaps that's one of your tools."

"No, I couldn't have," she says, with so much vehemence that he blinks. She snatches the bright square from his hand. "Here, look. I made a mistake—see? This petal's too small. I didn't plan them properly. And here, the same problem. And here. And here too. You see? I'm just a woman—so stupid. I keep doing the same things wrong. I can't *learn*." The words keep flying, like bees angered by a shaken nest. "Here I ran out of purple thread, had to finish it in red. It looks *terrible*."

He pulls his hand back. "You're right. It's woman's work," he says quietly. "Men don't understand these things."

They eat for a while, not speaking. Eventually the man comes to clears the dishes. He sets down a plate of pomegranate: soft white wedges jeweled with garnet. The tiny seeds glisten from their wounds. "I'm sorry," Yuliang says quietly, handing Pan Zanhua a section. "It's just . . . I'm very tired. I haven't been sleeping properly."

He takes the fruit, avoiding her fingertips. "I didn't sleep last night myself. Perhaps it was something in the banquet food." He smiles. "The abalone the old Dragon Lady loved so much."

Their eyes meet, part. He spits out a pip. "Where to from here?" he asks.

AS THE AFTERNOON LENGTHENS they leave chair and carriers and walk the last block to the cathedral. For a few moments they simply stand outside, gazing at it. Workmen scramble and holler. A Jesuit shouts in Beijing-accented Chinese to a man sitting sullenly on a barrow. The two-barred Christian symbol rises sternly above neighboring rooftops, a stretched-out number ten pointing at heaven.

Yuliang knows the cross is meant to represent the frame on which the Christian god died. She's received several pamphlets on the subject, both from a Christian client and from streetside evangelists. Most people throw the cheap booklets away, although the very poor use them as winter shoe insulation. Yuliang saves them sometimes, though. Their reproductions of foreign paintings interest her, though Yi Gan maintains they're in bad taste. "All that blood and pain!" he once said, *tsk*ing. "Who wants to see it? A good painting—say, that one—should leave you with a sense of peace, not disgust."

He'd waved at Jinling's old scroll sketch of a lotus and a frog. Yuliang didn't point out that one could find identical works in every room of the Hall, or that she liked the feelings the pamphlet paintings gave her. Their very visceral nature—the blood and bone and blue veins—seemed strangely vital. Almost refreshingly rude.

"Is there only one church here?" the inspector asks now, bringing her back to the moment.

She shakes her head. "But this is the biggest. Actually, it's a replacement. They've been working on it forever."

"What happened to the first one?"

"The Boxers burned it down. They say the government gave the French a hundred and twenty thousand silver taels to rebuild it. Otherwise they'd have declared war."

He gazes up at the steeple. "A hundred and twenty thousand taels. At a time when twenty million of our own were dying of famine." Abruptly he gestures toward the door. "Shall we go see what such riches can buy?"

Yuliang hesitates. She's been inside only one church, in Zhenjiang: the one her uncle went to when trying to break his habit. He did this every few years, resolve gradually capturing him like sleepy net. He'd pace back and forth a little, then take a rickshaw to the church clinic, where he'd take belladonna and something else called *sacrament*. He'd come back with foreign proverbs and a full appetite, and would eat two or three enormous meals. But within weeks, sometimes days, he'd be back at the dens.

Now together, they climb the marble steps and push past the enormous wooden doors. Inside the light is cool and dim, richly stained by Spanish glass windows. Yuliang had half expected to find the church packed with milky-skinned *yangguizi*, but the huge hall is almost empty. A Chinese handyman sweeps around the carved wooden altar. A woman in a gray headdress kneels, her hands bound by wooden beads similar to those Yuliang's mother had held for her prayers. She whispers almost soundlessly, a soft reply to the clanging construction outside.

"Do you know much about him?" Pan Zanhua murmurs, indicating the statue of the foreign god on his cross.

Yuliang shakes her head. She knows his name—Jesus. And that he's very different from Chinese gods like the Jade Emperor and the First Principal. This god looks like a man, died like a man. He is dying in almost all the depictions she's seen—except for those in which he's just been born. The sculptor has tried to capture his pain and humiliation. But with his curled toes and eyes rolled up toward the room's high, arched ceiling, Jesus looks more like he's in ecstasy. "A missionary tried to explain about his being not one god but three."

"A father, a son, and a ghost."

She darts him a glance. "Are you Christian?" The thought, which hadn't dawned on her before, suddenly strikes her as not unlikely. Many forward-thinking, high-up families are these days.

But he shakes his head. "I studied Western religion and thought in Tokyo. It's where I read *Self-Reliance*."

Yuliang nods, eyes dropping absently to the statue's barely covered privates. Sheathed by a chiseled rag, they nevertheless give the impression of a sizable manhood. She stares at them, suddenly fascinated—not by the hidden stalk, but by the way the stone's been shaped into such a delicate semblance of linen. Then she feels his eyes on her and looks away.

"How does a son become his own father?" she asks quickly. "I've heard of fathers who are also grandfathers to their children. This certainly isn't something people should worship, though. Don't you agree?"

He laughs. "I've never thought of it in that way. But I don't think you're supposed to understand it. You're just expected to believe." He points to another sculpture, the mother with the baby. "You're also to believe that she never . . . had relations. Before giving birth."

"He's fatherless?"

"Yes. And no."

Yuliang studies this statue too: the curving maternal arms that seem to exude both delicacy and strength. The pudgy yet strangely adult infant. She finds herself thinking of babies; then, almost too easily, of her mother. Not the mother who lied to her and then left, but the mama who raised her. Who crooned her to sleep. The mama who sang her songs and told her stories. Closing her eyes, Yuliang can almost hear her speaking of the celestial Weaver Girl, of the Heavenly Cowherd. Of the Emperor of Heaven, first joining and then parting them, because their love led them both to cease their duties . . .

A pigeon explodes from a rafter, a flurry of purple and white tail feathers. Then the bell in the half-finished steeple chimes.

The inspector pulls out his watch. "Is it really five o'clock? Astonishing. This must be the fastest day to pass by me in months." He shakes his head. "But I'm afraid I'll have to go. I'm due at the magistrate's."

He's walking toward the door before the words fully settle. When they do, Yuliang feels blood draining from her face. Over the past few hours she hasn't given a second thought to the day's end—to what will happen when it is time to complete their tour. Now she hears Godmother's voice again, as oil-smooth and cruel as ever: *If you come back without his seed inside you* . . . "I—I've enjoyed it as well. Must you go so soon?" It comes out a squeak.

He turns back, surprised. "Believe me. I'd prefer to remain home with my poems. Or with you." Her pulse skips. "Unfortunately, that's not what they sent me here for." He smiles. "Where shall I take you? Back to—to your home?"

It's not home. "No," she says sharply. "That is . . . I can take a carriage." *Think. Think. Think.* "I've heard the magistrate is a very generous host," she blurts. "Would he mind if you—if you brought a guest?"

It's an absurd proposition: him, the incorruptible, showing up at a prominent home with a well-known prostitute. Yuliang knows this even as she hears herself put it forward. When he looks at her, he does no more than shake his head. But she reads his embarrassment on his features. "I'm afraid," he says quietly, "it's a very small gathering."

He begins walking again, more quickly this time. Wretchedly, Yuliang follows. She will, she realizes, simply have to tell them that it can't be done. He's not the type. It was a foolish idea from the start. Still as she passes the grimacing Christ, she is thinking again of Mingmei, the blood soaking her ruined dress.

Eyes fixed on her companion's back, she tries telling herself that this is what she fears most: the punishment. But she knows really that it's much more than that. It is leaving him now, leaving this peerless day. It's going back to her room and bed and bountiful jewelry box, and knowing that the next time she sees him—*if* she sees him—they'll be back to their assigned roles: stiff official, preening whore.

Almost of their own volition, her steps slow as she walks. But not enough to keep her from following him.

Outside, he hails the sedan chair without further comment. Yuliang makes her way toward it, fighting the urge to turn back and beg him for a reprieve. *I'll live through this,* she thinks. *It's just skin. It's no more than I deserve.* Foolish to think there'd be anything else. Ever . . . It's just then, with sickening suddenness, that the sky tilts and the world inverts itself, tossing her to the ground like a sack of rags.

Pan Zanhua turns just in time to catch her. "*Aiyaaaa.* Did you hurt yourself?"

And then somehow she's in his arms and, even more appallingly, crying, even though she's done no more than trip on a piece of lumber. Nor are they the childlike sniffles she's learned to use on stingy clients. These are enormous, heaving sobs. They hurt her as they tear free.

"Here. Come here. Sit down," he says, obviously distressed. "Sit down with me. Here." He instructs the chair to wait.

"I'm sorry," she whispers. "I'm so sorry."

"Do you need a doctor? Are you—are you unwell?" There's real trepidation in his voice, and it occurs to her that he thinks she's with child. For some reason this strikes her as very funny. *Perhaps I am. Perhaps I'm also a virgin*, she pictures herself saying.

"Tell me," he says. "What's wrong? Really. You can tell me."

She's hysterical now, covering her mouth with her hands. "I can't."

"Why not?"

Yuliang takes a deep breath. "I can't . . . just leave." She wipes her eyes. "Not like this."

"Why not?"

"There will be consequences."

"What consequences? Why?" He seems honestly mystified. "You spent time with me. The guild got its wish."

How can a scholar be so stupid? "No, it didn't. They said not to come back if I didn't finish."

"Finish what?"

Suddenly all she wants to do is get away from him, from this place. From the hope she's felt without knowing it, simply by being with him all day. She will walk home if she has to. It will hurt her feet, but that is fine. It will prepare her for the far worse pain she'll face later.

"It doesn't matter," she says, standing.

"No, wait." He jumps up with her. "What are they? What are the consequences?"

The workmen squat as their emptied supper pails are picked up by an old woman, who slings them onto a pole. When Yuliang takes a step toward the street, he follows. "Please," he says quietly. "Please talk to me."

It won't change anything. But again, the novelty of the request—*talk to me*—fills her with a strange gratitude.

"There was a girl," she begins, slowly sitting back down. "At the—at my house. The madam tied her to the bed, facedown." She pauses. "Her back and arms bled for half a day. They had to throw the sheets out."

The foreman puts his thick hands on his haunches and heaves himself to his feet. Yuliang realizes suddenly that until now he hasn't looked at her twice. In her sober clothes, with this sober man, she's looked that decent. That ordinary.

"They *beat* her?" Pan Zanhua is asking.

"Yes," she says dully. "Until she'd all but stopped breathing. Then Papa Gao—that's the owner—and his friends, they went in. They locked the door. They . . ." She pauses, takes a breath. "They said it was compensation."

Yuliang drops her eyes to the marble entrance to the church. The mica flecks embedded in it twinkle deceptively, like little stars. She'd like to stay here and stare at them until the real stars have risen. But when the foreman shouts again, calling the workers back to work, Yuliang stands along with them.

At first the inspector doesn't move. Then he's beside her, touching her arm again. "Zhang *xiaojie*. Please wait. I'd like to help you."

"I'll find a rickshaw," she says, and tries to smile.

"No," he says. "Not that way. I'd like for you to come with me."

She shakes her head. "It'll be worse if they see us like that."

"I don't care what they see. I care what's *right*. Haven't you understood that?" He takes a breath. "I want you to come to my house."

She struggles to keep the relief from cracking her voice. "I can sleep on the floor tonight. Then I'll find some way to explain it to them tomorrow."

"That's not what I meant either," he says, signaling his sedan-chair carriers.

Suddenly she is very tired, almost too tired to care. Still she asks, "What *do* you mean?"

He blinks a few times, as though readying himself. When he finally speaks, his tone is formal, as though making a public proclamation.

"I've decided," he says. "I'm going to take you out."

Part FOUR

The CONCUBINE

At fourteen I married My Lord you
I never laughed, being bashful.
Lowering my head, I looked at the wall.
Called to, a thousand times, I never looked back.

———

Lɪ Bᴀɪ
(Eᴢʀᴀ Pᴏᴜɴᴅ ᴛʀᴀɴsʟᴀᴛɪᴏɴ)

Fourteen

Wuhu, 1916

"IT HAS BEEN A LONG TIME," Godmother says.

It is not a nicety, although the brothel manager's voice is as sweet and oily as ever. She is talking about money: Yuliang is certain that every missed appointment has been entered in the madam's merciless black book.

As though confirming the thought, Godmother flicks her red-tipped fingers against the table. Calculating on an invisible abacus. It's hot. Beads of sweat cling to her inky hairline. Yuliang watches one drip down, tinged lightly with gray.

"Six weeks," retorts the lawyer negotiating Yuliang's release. "No longer than it takes most girls to recover from the clap." He says it easily, inspecting and smoothing the lapels of his heat-wrinkled suit.

The madam sniffs. "Believe me, I'm not complaining. This one's been nothing but trouble from the day I bought her."

In her years at the Hall Yuliang was beaten less than any other flower there, and she draws a sharp breath to say so. Then she feels Zanhua's hand on the small of her back. Following the silent hint, she keeps her lips sealed. Wen had warned them earlier. *She'll try to upset you. Make you lose face, as she has. Whatever you do, don't let her do it.*

"You paid cash?" the attorney asks now blithely, as though referring to the madam's myriad bangles and not the girl seated across from her.

"A turn of phrase," Godmother snaps. "She's my daughter. I have papers."

Wen looks down at his documents, adjusting his spectacles with fingers as thin and dry as twigs. Slavery, they all know, was outlawed since the Republicans took over. Adoption is just one way around the prohibition.

"How old did you say she was?" he asks.

Yuliang awaits the inevitable *sixteen*; everyone at the Hall is always sixteen. To her surprise, though, the madam stays silent.

"My understanding," the lawyer says, easing back in his chair, "is seventeen. Which means she was fourteen when you bought—I'm sorry. Took her in." He smiles, baring a mouthful of smoke-stained teeth. "Which is a bit of a problem, since the law prohibits children under sixteen from living in a brothel."

"I know the law," the madam says sharply. "She's my daughter. Where was she to sleep? In the street? Who was going to protect her?"

Yuliang thinks of the Christian who sank his teeth into her foot. Of the water-dealer, who likes to pay girls to urinate for him and then beat them for being "dirty." She thinks of the dead flower found in Wuhu Lake, and of Jinling bound and mauled in an automobile's trunk. A helpless fury begins to build as the manager-mother's smirk widens.

"Judge Li is a friend," Godmother continues. "He assured me that there are certain . . . exceptions." As the barrister raises an eyebrow, she adds hastily, "He's never had one of my girls, of course." It's also against the law for civil officials to frequent flower houses, a fact Yuliang well knows after smuggling several of them out her windows.

Attorney Wen laces his fingers together and stretches his arms over his head. The room resonates with the soft patter-pop of ligaments cracking beneath the skin.

"Either way," Godmother huffs, "the girl owes. She owes plenty.

Many people—hardworking people—depended on her for their livelihoods. It wasn't just me she robbed."

"No one's robbed anyone," Zanhua snaps, himself forgetting Attorney Wen's injunction.

The madam just smiles indulgently, as at a whining child. "Besides," she continues, "it's costly to take a girl's name down. The censors want fifty taels just to switch her status on the registry."

Yuliang looks at her lawyer: it hasn't occurred to her that her name is still hanging outside the Hall. Although of course, now that she thinks about it, it would be. A brothel's lineup is its official roster. It's the way authorities keep tabs on who has come and left, who has died and who has disappeared. Essentially, in the end, who is taxable. The thought unsettles her more: it is as though the wind-fluttered characters have more truth and substance than the girls whose false names they advertise.

"Then there's her debts," the madam is saying. "Seven weeks of missed appointments."

"Five weeks, six days," Attorney Wen counters.

"And her dressmaker's bills," the madam continues, eyeing Yuliang's dove-gray tunic with disdain. "Gorgeous things. But exorbitant. I know—I paid for most of them. I'd give a bit of that back for the embroidery work she did for us sometimes. But the quality was terrible . . ." Yuliang clenches her fist beneath the table. "And the *smoking!*" Godmother shakes her head.

It's too much. *"I don't smoke!"* Yuliang says shrilly. "You're a liar!"

The outburst is followed by a small, shocked silence. Godmother twists her lips victoriously.

"Please, Zhang *xiaojie*," Attorney Wen says quietly.

"*And* there was damage to her room," the madam continues. "Did you know, eminence, that this girl likes to light fires?"

"How much?" Zanhua says between gritted teeth. "Just a figure."

Godmother waits a beat, an actor delivering a key line. "Two thousand yuan," she says.

Yuliang looks at Zanhua in time to see him wince. *That is it,* she thinks. *It's the end.* She waits for Attorney Wen and Zanhua to stand in outrage. To throw up their hands, stalk out of her life. To her surprise, though, both remain in their seats, although it does seem to her that Zanhua shifts away slightly. Toward the window, the costless cheer of the blue sky.

"You've made your point," Attorney Wen says dryly. "The girl is profitable. Especially since two thirds of her time with you was tax-free." He picks up his abacus and begins flicking beads, his fingers so long they look like they are tangling. "Let me see. Even assuming you paid the proper taxes . . . the fine per day . . . what was it, ten? Twenty?"

"No one pays attention to that rule," the woman protests. "We already pay the police their cursed protection money. If I pay taxes too, how do I compete?"

"That, unfortunately, is not the law's concern," Attorney Wen says. But he's made his point; he sets the abacus back down. "I'd also suggest you take the honorable Master Li's advice with a small grain of caution. There've been complaints about him recently. New China, new morality. All of that. Some say flower houses will be outlawed altogether. But I'm sure he's told you that."

The madam's mouth, a rouge-smeared bud, purses as she turns viciously on Yuliang. "You're such a little fool," she spits. "You think he's *rescuing* you." She flicks her painted eyes toward Zanhua. "You know, don't you, Master Inspector, that these girls never really change? Oh, you can pluck them away from us. But you can't dig up the roots. You can't fight *fate.*"

Zanhua's lips tighten. As his eyes meet Yuliang's, she attempts a small smile. He just looks away.

"Madame Ping," Attorney Wen says coolly, "bear in mind whose protection the plaintiff enjoys. His eminence can still have quite an impact on your customers' fortunes."

"And they on his," she retorts ominously.

"I'll also point out that no court that I know of would send down an order for more than a thousand. Not even"—he sniffs—"the honorable Judge Li's."

"Thievery. Thievery! I'll be driven from business." The madam raps her fan against her shoulder in anger.

"I'm sorry to say that I doubt that." Attorney Wen pushes his chair back and stands. "Still, we're willing to see this to the courthouse, if you insist." He turns, signaling his clients to follow. The madam watches them go with narrowed eyes, fan still tapping in anger. It's a gesture Yuliang knows well. At the Hall it often foretells a beating: even now her back tightens instinctively.

But it's not until she's past the threshold that the brothel manager speaks again. "Eighteen hundred," she barks. "I'm fond of the girl. I want her happiness."

"Fifteen," Attorney Wen says curtly.

"You're heartless," the madam wails. "I'll end up in the pauper's graveyard. No money even for my own coffin." Heaving herself to her feet, she hobbles over to Yuliang. "Like your friend, my dear. You've told your savior here about Jinling?" She beams sweetly. "Such a shame that no one got there in time. Of course, if you'd told the truth to us from the start . . ."

For a moment the world wavers like a heat mirage. Yuliang blinks. Zanhua takes her arm. "Walk," he mutters. "Walk with me."

But Yuliang shakes him off. Without thinking twice, she steps right up to the madam, close enough to smell her old owner's scent: a sick-sweet blend of chrysanthemum and ginseng.

What she wants, more than anything, is to see her dead. She contents herself with finally speaking her true thoughts. "May the heavens forbid," she hisses into the broad, damp face. "May the heavens keep you from ever being anywhere near her. I'll dig you out myself if you do. You ox-skinned old *cunt*."

Shock blots the madam's thick features. She wheezes quickly, then lifts a plump palm. *Do it,* Yuliang dares her. *Give me a reason to strike you back. At last.*

But instead of slapping her the madam snaps open her black fan. For several seconds the only sound is the swish of warm air batted into her crimson mouth. When she recovers herself, she snaps the fan shut again and begins hobbling toward the door.

"Write it up," she snaps. "I'll send for the money in two weeks' time. If it isn't ready, the deal is off."

"The funds will come," the lawyer says shortly. "But regardless of the timing, my client remains under our protection."

The heavy woman stares at him. Then she looks Yuliang over again. A barbed smile spreads across her red mouth. "I wouldn't," she says, "be so sure of that, if I were you."

THAT EVENING THEY MAKE LOVE, with the strange and hesitant intensity that has come to mark the act each of the few times they've performed it. Which is (Yuliang counts quietly on her fingers) now eight.

It seems an absurdly small number given how long she's been under his roof. Even more absurd to be counting at all, now that there's no money involved. No account book to report to. Still, she can't help it. Keeping track of her acts remains an ingrained habit, like staying up until dawn, and checking glands and feet for signs of sex-sickness. Lying here now, her damp back pressed against Zanhua's smooth chest, she wonders if at seventy she will be the same. Still tensing at the sound of heavy feet on a stairwell. Still worrying when a man looks her over, and panicking if he looks away in disinterest.

In her initial weeks here, of course, Yuliang couldn't help but worry. She spent those first meals, walks, and nights alone deep in doubt; not about her "savior's" noble intentions, but about the apparent lack of carnal interest behind them. For all of Zanhua's talk about "natural dignity" and "equality of the sexes," she fully expected him to appear some night in the guest bedroom where he'd installed her. Any other man in his position would certainly have seen this as his right. When Pan Zanhua apparently didn't, she was at first relieved. But as night followed solitary night, her uneasiness grew.

It wasn't that she was eager to get in to bed with him. At that point, she'd have been quite happy never to touch a man again. But in her experience, normal men didn't take whores into their homes—not, that is, unless they planned to really *take* them. And they certainly didn't waste time lecturing them about the world unless they planned on sending them back out into it.

And so she waited, obediently listening when he took it upon himself to talk about his politics or some French or American or Ming Dynasty philosopher. She shared her opinions when asked for them, which was surprisingly often. She smiled and smiled, waiting for some signal or sign that would define what was between them.

Nearly five weeks had passed before such a sign arrived, in a way she'd curse herself for not expecting.

SHE'D BEEN GAZING (as she often does, despite Qian Ma's continuing disapproval) at the mountain poem-picture in the hallway. Drawn to it as always, Yuliang had reached out and unthinkingly touched a finger to the glass.

"Ah," Zanhua said. "You've discovered old Shi Tao." He was standing right behind her—she hadn't heard him come in.

Withdrawing her hand quickly, Yuliang saw that she'd left a faint print on the glass. "I—I've admired it," she stammered, watching the tiny, whorled mark fade.

"It's quite old. More than four centuries."

"It must be very precious," Yuliang said, recalling Qian Ma's first words to her: *It's worth more than your whole life, from start to finish.*

"In value? Yes." Zanhua considered it a moment. "Do you like it?"

"Yes." Yuliang said it firmly, both because his tone seemed somehow to challenge her *not* to like it, and because the word *like* failed to describe her feelings so completely.

Her host ran his finger down the spidery script, reading aloud to her out of habit: " 'Heavy rainfalls and fierce wind blows attend the spring. The door is shut at dusk; the season cannot stay.' " He seemed to contemplate this a moment. Then, abruptly, he turned to face her. "It was a gift. On my wedding day."

For a moment Yuliang found she couldn't breathe. "I'm sure she's very beautiful," she managed finally. The response was reflexive. It was what she always said when men produced their wives from thin air, like magicians.

"My parents chose her. We were children." She felt his eyes on her face. "I argued against it, of course. They'd sent me to Tokyo to learn all the new ways, only to ship me home again and undo it all." He pinched the bridge of his nose, as though the memory were lodged there like a headache, or the beginnings of a cold. "Refusing would have dishonored everyone involved. Also the girl threatened to kill herself. So I married her." He laughed shortly. "Of course, when I joined the secession movement they all but declared me dead anyway. Marrying simply stayed the execution."

"Execution?"

"A turn of phrase," he said shortly.

Yuliang bit her lip. "Are—are there children?"

"Just one."

"A son?"

He nodded. "Born last year. She's remaining in Tongcheng until he's old enough for school. Her parents are there. It makes it easier. But," he went on, "that isn't what matters."

"What matters?" she asked. Not snidely, but with strange urgency: suddenly, she really needed to know.

Zanhua moved his lips silently for a moment. "She doesn't suit me," he said at last.

Yuliang ducked her head, suppressing a smile that had little or no humor in it at all. Out of everything men said to justify what they did or didn't do (or didn't do to their wives but did with vehemence to paid companions), *She doesn't suit me* was by far the most common. She remembered Suyin announcing to lunchtime titters,

"What he really means is *She doesn't* fuck *me!*" And someone else—Xiaochen?—squealing: "No, no! *She doesn't let me release my great jade stalk into her ruby rear portal!*"

For the briefest—just the briefest—moment, Yuliang actually felt a faint surge of something not completely unlike longing. Not for the Hall itself, of course—not for the men, the long hours, the numbing shame of it all. But for the immunity it provided from this particular and peculiar sort of vulnerability. From this tiny voice that now drummed in the back of her head: *He lied. And now he'll leave.*

"The reason I didn't tell you," he said, as though he hears it too, "is that she matters not at all. In my mind, it was never a true marriage."

At this Yuliang couldn't help laughing. "Why not?"

"A true marriage is made through the meeting of minds and hearts. Not of matchmakers and potential in-laws. A true marriage is one where the husband and wife find each other for themselves. A true marriage . . ." He stared at her a moment, his breath fast and his color high. Then, abruptly, he pulled her close.

He's going to kiss me, Yuliang thought breathlessly. *Right here. Right now.* She felt his scholar's hands, surprisingly strong against her waist, and shivered as his lips brushed her ear. She heard his heart, pounding so hard it seemed almost impossible to her that it wasn't inflicting damage in his chest. She also heard the telephone releasing its metallic shriek, causing both of them to jump.

Zanhua groaned, then released her. "I should go," he said, through the second harsh jingle. "We'll talk more later."

"When?" she asked weakly.

"When I return from Shanghai. I'll be back in a week."

And he retreated. She heard him answer the phone in a voice that seemed far too loud ("*Wei!* Inspector Pan here. Yes, operator, put him through . . ."), even given that it had to project itself to some unknown town or city. Yuliang, for her part, walked slowly out to the courtyard, where she sat for several moments in the afternoon's slanting light.

Through the moon-shaped gateway floated calls and clatters of commerce: night-soil men banging tin drums, a tiger-meat vendor with his greasy paper packages ("Cure your asthma! Be fierce and mighty with the girls!"). A dog barked, and she wondered vaguely whether it was a market dog or a pet until a man barked back, "Napoleon! Move it along, you wrinkly whelp!"

Yuliang tilted her head back to feel the sun on her face. She shut her eyes, and watched the light filtering in red through her eyelids. She pictured her, the *da taitai*, the first wife. Dressed in a red dress, riding her red sedan chair to her unseen betrothed's house. She saw her sipping her wine from a cup bound to Zanhua's by a red cord. Exchanging vows, her red-shrouded head bowed demurely. *Never a true marriage,* he'd said. And yet when a strange sensation crept thickly up her throat, it took just a moment to recognize it as jealousy.

Yuliang always thought of envy as a sickness. But for some reason it didn't feel like one in this case. Its vinegary fumes didn't so much turn her stomach as clear her thoughts. And when she opened her eyes, she had made a decision.

LATE THAT NIGHT, after lights had been lowered and Qian Ma had shuffled off to her quarters, Yuliang threw back her quilt. Rising, she combed her hair loose and powdered her face lightly. Then she crept up the creaking stairs to the master bedroom. She presented herself warily, half expecting him to send her away in disgust. Or, worse, for sex to work its peculiar inverse alchemy, turning him from her savior into just another man who lied to her, bedded her, and then left.

And yet Pan Zanhua did none of those things. He stared at her hard, as though she were a poster he was trying to read at a distance, or in rain. He asked her if she was sure. And when Yuliang nodded laying down beside him in silence, he seemed strangely on the verge of tears.

Throughout what followed, he held her eyes in a way no one else had. He seemed aware of her mind, her heart, her pleasure. He asked her questions that, in their newness, left her speechless: *Am I hurting you? Is it too fast?* Most astonishingly of all, though, was the gentle way in which he touched her. As though she were as pure and fragile as the first thin ice of winter.

All in all (Yuliang reflects now, cautiously touching his hair), it was the oddest and most inexplicably gentle way that a man had ever touched her. And while his lips and fingertips didn't coax quite the same delicious quivers that Jinling's had, they did stir up a sensation almost more powerful: a sense of security. An all-enveloping safeness. Yuliang felt it again when he took her to bed twice on his first day back from his trip. Every day since they've made love at least once more, each time conquering more of the stiff distance between them.

Now, though, worry tugs at her like a little anxious dog. At a total of fifteen hundred yuan, that comes out to roughly two hundred yuan a tumble. *Two hundred!*

Don't count, she tells herself. *Don't think. Don't think about it.*

Zanhua shifts against her sleepily. "What's the matter?"

"Nothing."

"Nonsense. You've sighed twice just now."

Yuliang considers her options. If she tells him the truth, she breaks an unspoken rule: that regardless of how openly they discuss China's poor, China's women, and her history (and like many patriots, Pan Zanhua seems to see China as all these things: a poor woman with an ancient, glorious history), Yuliang's own muddy roots are to remain buried. On the few occasions she has even brought up the Hall, he has stiffened, then shifted the subject. Even this morning's meeting, in fact, was announced as dryly as a line read from one of the telegraph tapes with which government runners frequently arrive: "I've found someone to help us finalize your status," Zanhua said. "A barrister. I'll take you to meet him tomorrow." And that was all.

"The truth," Yuliang says now, "is that I worry about the fee. The one we—you—Attorney Wen—set today."

"What of it?"

"It's—it seems too much," she says. Very softly.

Her soul leaps to her mouth as he stares back at her in silence. Then he leans over to retrieve his wristwatch.

"It's nearly six. Dinner will be waiting." He says it indignantly; as though the time has been smuggled past him without proper documentation.

YULIANG DOESN'T ASK AGAIN in coming days. But she can't quite drive it from her mind—*fifteen hundred.* She tells herself that of course he's paying, that he would have told her if he weren't. He's a man of his word. But then she'll stop and realize: even if he does buy her freedom, what has changed? He may still leave. And if he does that, what awaits Yuliang is worse than one simple beating. Beatings (she knows now) are for disobedience. Not betrayal. Payment or no payment, without Zanhua beside her Yuliang doubts she'll last the week.

The deadline is two weeks away. Then ten days. Then one week. *Don't count*, she thinks. *Don't think.* She spends the days as tight-lipped as Mi Fu's turtle, focusing on the vocabulary lists Pan Zanhua has— at her request—prepared for her. *Casualties,* she has written, over and over. *France. France. France. Imperialist expansion. Warlord. Warlord. Bandits.* Then, *Beheadings.*

Despite these bleak teachings, though, she finds that she is happy. She enjoys her studies: the thrill of conquering one new word, then another. Of recognizing it in a formerly incomprehensible poster or essay. She loves the way she and Pan Zanhua talk; the new intimacy between them now that they aren't just housemates, but bedmates. And she loves seeing the city beyond its banquets.

Zanhua takes her out often, at first just on the slow, sidestreet walks they've taken together in the past. Then, increasingly, to more public destinations; like the cathedral, where he wants to see a Sunday service, with its oddly Taoist rituals (rosaries, incense), its swollen-sounding organ music. They go to the new French bakery-café in the Settlement district, where he orders baba and Napoleons and coffee, which arrives in gold-rimmed demitasse cups. Yuliang has had coffee and likes its complex, charred flavor. The baba looks like the Arabian sweets Yi Gan brought her back once from his travels. But as she bites one, she discovers it is soaked not in honey but in some sweet liquor that brings tears to her eyes.

Zanhua laughs at her expression. As the rum beats warm wings within her, he reaches over and picks a pungent crumb from her chin. "You've much to learn, little Yu," he says. At times she's almost tempted to say the same thing right back: his disregard for Wuhu gossip astounds her. And yet despite herself, she doesn't want the outings to stop.

And so they continue: visits to teahouses to eat cakes and sweet, larded rice. Trips to Wuhu Lake for a picnic. They even go to the opera, to see *Escorting Jingniang Home*. It's an afternoon performance, the curtain lifting at a time when most of the Hall's leaves and flowers are burrowed in their dank beds. Still, Yuliang scans the audience between scenes as the stagehands rotate the stage, half afraid she'll see Godmother or Suyin there, glaring at her. The story is familiar, that of a brave warrior who devotes himself to protecting a maiden's chastity. When he fails to do so, of course, she is the one who commits suicide.

Afterward, Zanhua leads her to a restaurant and a table outdoors that is only slightly beyond the light cast by the bobbing overhead lanterns. Yuliang, already giddy from the brilliant backdrops and lush costumes, allows him to fill her wine cup once, then again. Soon she is tipsy and flushed, reveling in the night's colors, scents, even nearby conversations, all so refreshingly different from the spite-filled whispers that fill the Hall. *So I say to him,* she hears, *if you want a modern wedding, go ahead. But damn me if you're going to dress my daughter in white, as though she were mourning someone. Not unless you plan to hang yourself first!* To their left, a group of students are drinking and discussing a Western play that one of them wants their school to put on. *It's by this westerner—I can't recall his name. But the girl in it, Nora, learns that marriage is nothing but slavery.* To their right is a table of well-dressed *taitais.* *The baby was dead already? A mercy, really. After all, it was a girl. The last thing that house needs is more mooncakes . . .*

"Ah," Zanhua murmurs. "*That's* the true evil."

Yuliang looks up. "Mooncakes?" It seems a mild enough tradition to her: after most matches are made, the groom's family sends mooncakes to the bride's house as a gift. Wealthy families send whole cartloads, which perhaps is wasteful. But evil?

"No," he says. "That society still sees women strictly in terms of their ability to serve men, of the fruitfulness of their bellies. It ignores the much more important part of their bodies."

"Which is . . . ?"

"Their minds, of course." He drinks again, the *maotai* tingeing his eyes and cheeks with pink. *He is drunk,* she thinks. "Think, little Yu, about your beloved Lady Li! Look at Joan of Arc! Qiu Jin, the Woman Knight of Mirror Lake!"

"The one they beheaded for plotting to overthrow the Qing?"

He waves this off. "There's Sophia Perovskaya, too."

"Perovskaya . . ." Yuliang twirls a strand of hair, combing her memory.

"The Russian radical," he prompts. "She tried to kill Alexander II."

"Didn't they hang her?"

"Yes, yes. But that's not the point." He indicates the jug with his chin; obediently, she refills their glasses. "The point is, she *did* something. She didn't see herself as some pointless flower, there merely for decoration or fertilization. She didn't fall into a trap of useless beauty."

Don't, the pragmatic part of Yuliang's mind warns. *Don't don't don't don't.* But she is a little drunk as well now, and the *maotai,* sped along by an unexpected swell of outrage, washes right over the warning.

"It's not such an easy trap to escape," She says hotly. "I never had a say in—in the *decoration* I became. And besides—" She's plunging into forbidden territory, but she can't stop. "Besides, beauty's not pointless. It's essential. It's what sustains our minds. It's part of what makes them big in the first place. Men *and* women."

It isn't at all what she'd planned to say, but it comes out so ardently that she knows it's true. Beauty is, at least in part, what sustained her those years, in the Hall's fetid hell. Li Qingzhao's poems. The dull white shine of Jinling's forearm, her graceful ivory hands. The wedding shoes . . . at the thought of the shoes, a sense of loss shoots through her like a physical pain. Like the rest of her belongings, they're still at the Hall. Godmother won't send her things until she's paid.

"I'm not saying that beauty has no place," Zanhua goes on. "Merely that it can be . . . abused. This whole idea of lily feet, for instance. A perfect example of a misguided, even evil misuse of beauty."

"Some might say it's less a way of men controlling women than of women controlling men," Yuliang counters. "There are girls I know who have received everything they ever need from a man. Just by taking their shoes off."

The two matrons at the next table are looking over in disapproval; one simply doesn't discuss such things with men. Yuliang flicks her eyes at them. "Either way, we have no say. My mother bound my feet when I was seven, as her mother did to her. It was simply something that was done." Not looking at him, she adds, "Aren't your wife's feet bound, too?"

For a moment she can hardly believe that she has said it. When she looks up, though, he has a strange look on his face. "Forgive me," she says softly. "I just—I can't help but wonder these things. I have no idea what she looks like."

For once, he doesn't deny her the apology. He takes a long drink, looks down at his hands. "Yes, they're bound. Supposedly, they're the perfect length. But this is one of the things that's wrong. You see, she too said she had no say. Even when I told her there were methods . . ." He sighs. "And remember, it wasn't your feet that drew us together."

"It was my beautiful face."

She says it mockingly. He responds with a vehemence that almost startles her. "It was *you*. Your words. Your mind. Until you used them, you were just another pretty girl to me. When you debated poetry with me, I saw more." He holds her gaze a moment. Despite herself, Yuliang blushes.

"I've been to Anti-Binding League meetings in Shanghai," he goes on. "I have pamphlets on it somewhere. I can help you to unbind them." He leans across the table. "You will still be beautiful," he says softly. "To me, you'll be more beautiful. You'll be free. Free from the oppression of men."

"Free from you, you mean? Will you leave me afterward?"

Again, she means it as a joke. But the look he gives her this time is so hurt she actually catches her breath. "Everyone leaves," she says in a small voice. "They lie. Then they leave."

For a moment neither speaks. Then his hand is on hers. "You must understand something. I'm not like everyone else. I said I'd take care of you. I meant it forever." He squeezes her knuckles, so tightly they hurt. "I'll never lie to you, Yuliang," he says. "I'll never leave you."

To her shock, she sees that his eyes have filled with tears. Apart from the maudlin outbursts of Hall clients who've overdrunk or overspent, it is the first time she's really seen a man cry.

"Say you believe me," he says. "It's essential that you believe me."

It takes a long time to make her mouth shape the word. When she finally does, it comes out in barely a whisper—less a statement than a sighed prayer: "Yes."

She should say far more, she knows. *Thank you. You have saved me.* Still, the look he gives her is one of such vast warmth and relief that Yuliang feels it right down to her littlest broken toe.

TWO DAYS LATER, after Zanhua has left for the day, Yuliang retreats to his office to study. As usual, he's left a page of characters on his desk for her to copy out and learn. On top of the page, though, is something else—a formal photograph in grainy black-and-white. The sort matchmakers give to potential grooms.

Her heart pounding, Yuliang picks up the framed image. The girl in it sits in a lacquer-painted chair. She looks young, no more than fourteen. Her hair is crowned with flowers and pulled back from her slim face. Her eyes are large and strikingly clear, her ears delicate and finely shaped, dripping with jade. She wears a silk jacket with wide matching trousers hiked just high enough to display a perfect set of golden lilies. The feet, bedecked in ornate embroidered slippers with wooden heels, would be dwarfed in an average-sized male hand.

The girl's features, while winsome, seem stiff as a doll's. Nothing hints at what makes them move, to smile or cry. She is simply a product on display at market, like scores of others in a matchmaker's book. The only thing setting her apart, Yuliang realizes, is that Zanhua's parents happened to pick her out.

Her eyes drift to Zanhua's list. *Bind* (紳), he's written. *Cord* (縲). *Oppression* (壓迫). Yuliang traces each with her finger first, absently setting stroke order in her head. Finally, faintly chilled, she pushes the frame to the farthest corner of the desk. She turns it over. Then she picks up her pen, and begins to work.

Fifteen

LATER THAT WEEK Zanhua wakes up and suggests a trip to some gardens a little west of the city.

"Don't you have to go to work?" Yuliang asks him, peeling herself from his arms (where, she realizes with mild shock, she has actually slept. All night).

"They can do without me for one day," Zanhua says, stroking her hip. "Besides, it's time I took a holiday."

Yuliang looks at him in surprise. It's no exaggeration to say that Pan Zanhua is the hardest worker she's ever met. He leaves early each morning to oversee his clerks, arrives home late most nights, drawn and tired. Still, after dinner he works again from his office, in his scholar's robes, reading dispatches and reviewing forms until midnight. In the weeks she has been here he has not taken a full day off yet, and as he pulls her toward him, this thought gives Yuliang some pause. A question hovers lightly as he brings his lips to her neck. A moment later, however, it is gone, fluttering back into the recesses of her mind as his lips flutter against her arched neck.

THE PARK IS THINLY POPULATED when they reach it; as they wander down the dirt paths, they pass children on outings, university students, visitors from various other parts of the country. There are foreigners as well: a khaki-suited man and his wife, a black-robed Jesuit sketching by a pond. As they pass him, Yuliang looks over his shoulder to see a delicate scene depicted in black charcoal. The big man has deftly captured the gentle bend of the willows, the pale bursts blossoming against black waters below.

Zanhua, noting her interest, slows down as well. When the priest glances up, his eyes are as pale as the first chill wash of morning. "*Bonjour, mon père,*" Zanhua says, practicing the French he learned from a Russian tutor in Tokyo.

"I didn't know they drew flowers," Yuliang murmurs, as they continue along the pathway. "I thought they only drew pictures of their god's son. And their virgin."

"They draw and paint many things. They were the first to bring Western art to China. Have you heard of Lang Shining?" Yuliang shakes her head. "His real name was Giuseppe Castiglione. He came from Italy—a priest, like that one back there. Only earlier, about three hundred years ago. He lived in the Forbidden Palace, where he studied *guohua*." He checks his watch, for the third time that morning.

"Are we meeting someone?" Yuliang asks, puzzled.

He shakes his head. "Just habit. I'm not used to taking holidays."

Neither am I, she almost says, but doesn't. Instead she says, "He painted like a Chinese, this Casti—Casti—this Italian?"

"He endowed Chinese art with Western elements. You've heard the saying 'Chinese spirit, Western technology'?" She nods. "He was among the first to apply the idea to art. He understood, you see, that the traditional ways don't have to resist newer ones. That the one might well complement the other, like yin and yang. They don't have to be in opposition." He indicates the receding priest. "The

Jesuits also set up a Western-style art school for boys in Shanghai. It's called—what was it? Siccawei, I think." He strokes his cheek thoughtfully. "My friends in Shanghai say another's been started in the French Concession. Some young fellow who used to paint backgrounds for photo studios—I can't recall his name. But apparently he's set off a furor by bringing in naked girls."

"To the school?" she asks, shocked.

He smiles wryly. "Just so the boys there can draw them."

Yuliang glances at him. "So this school takes only boys?"

"I believe so." He quirks an eyebrow. "Why? Are you thinking of enrolling?"

For some reason she blushes. "Oh, no. Of course not." And yet there's a small thrill at the thought: a school to study art! It seems almost revolutionary, like the goals of Zanhua's beloved Dr. Sun, which he's had her practice writing until she knows them by heart. (One: Expel the Manchus. Two: China to the Chinese. Three: Establish a republic. Four: Equalize landownership.) Yuliang tries to imagine what such a place might be like. But her only schooling has been with her uncle. And after that, at the Hall.

"Speaking of studies," Zanhua is saying, "I'd like to add some political tracts to our reading. Have you heard of the periodical *New Youth*? It promotes developments in science, democracy. It was started by a good friend of mine, Chen Duxiu. He's in Japan now. But we fought together for the republic . . . Little Yu, where are you going?"

"What?" Yuliang pauses. Unwittingly, she's turned back toward the priest.

"Are you tired?" he is asking. "We can go back."

"I'm fine." She resumes walking, but not before giving the artist one last glance. His sketchpad is no more than a tiny white rectangle now, and his robe a black blur against sun-silvered water.

FOR TWO DAYS Zanhua leaves for work each morning and returns at supper as usual. He reads the news to her and writes out relevant terms for her to copy (*Capitalist:* 資本家. *Hegemony:* 霸權. *Freedom:* 自由). When Yuliang finally gathers courage, on the third morning, to stammer her question to him, he cuts her off with a curt "Yes." Both his expression and his tone tell her this is as far as he'll engage with the subject. And so she goes through the next day in a state of suspended relief. She is aware of her freedom (自由). But she is not convinced. And it's not until evening that she understands, at last, how he did it.

On the way to the courtyard to study in her favorite light of the day (the cotton-soft luminescence of early evening), Yuliang stops short in the front hallway. Tucking her copybook beneath her arm, she runs her fingers over the wall, and her entire being thrums in disbelief.

The wall is bare. There is no sign at all that the Shi Tao ever hung there.

"Qian Ma!" she calls. The old servant appears, a pitcher and basin balanced on her tray. "The—the picture," Yuliang says shakily.

"Which picture?"

"*The* picture," Yuliang says, pointing. "The Shi Tao. How long has it been gone?"

Qian Ma sucks tooth. "Why, the man just came for it on Wednesday."

"What man?"

"The man who was sent here to fetch it," Qian Ma says. Quite slowly; as though Yuliang is an idiot. "The man the master said to expect."

Wednesday, Yuliang thinks. *Wednesday.* For a moment her scattered thoughts can't even place the day. Then she remembers: Wednesday was their journey to the gardens. A trip Zanhua had made seem like a last-moment impulse. It's only now that Yuliang realizes he didn't notify anyone else about it. No runner to the docks, no call placed through to his office. He must have notified them in advance.

Stricken, she stares at the wall. "What—what did he look like?"

"The *master?*" Qian Ma says, with exaggerated surprise.

"No, no. The man."

Qian Ma, savoring Yuliang's frustration, ponders a good twenty seconds. "Big," she says finally. "Strange haircut. No queue. But not one of those ocean-devil styles either. More like he'd done it himself."

The Hall manservant. Shaken, Yuliang touches the wall again. The empty space before her is all the evidence she could need that Zanhua has kept his word, that she will stay. And yet, staring at the blank expanse, what she feels is not relief, but grief over the loss of what she now realizes was a little daily miracle for her. A small wonder of ash, water, and brush. *It's worth more than your whole life, from start to finish*, Qian Ma had said, and at this moment Yuliang fully believes this.

"Lady?" The amah's tone deflates the title of all deference.

Yuliang tears her gaze away. "Yes?"

"This tray is heavy on my old arms."

Yuliang holds Qian Ma's rheumy eyes for a moment. And it's in that moment that she senses that something else has changed as well: she has finally moved beyond the scope of the old woman's spite. Not that Qian Ma has stopped feeling it. Simply that now, in this new and Shi Tao–less order, it has ceased to have relevance.

"Yes," Yuliang says cautiously. "I mean, go. Go, but come back immediately. After you've filled those for Master Zanhua, go and heat water for me."

The weathered face furrows further. "What's that?"

"*Water,*" Yuliang says. "Hot water. Lots and lots of it."

She doesn't need to elaborate, not to a mere servant. She does anyway. Just to hear herself say it: "I think," she says, "I shall take a bath."

Sixteen

"SALT GUILD DINNER," Zanhua says with a groan a week later, having arrived home to find an invitation waiting in the hall. "It's bad enough that they all pretend to care for me now that General Sun is back."

"You should go," Yuliang chides from the doorway. "You have a duty."

"To whom?"

"To—to the nation," she says, waving vaguely. "If you won't accept their money, at least don't insult their food."

"It's not their food, Yuliang." He snorts. "It's paid for by funds all but stolen from my own office."

"But how will it look? It's the third trade dinner you've refused."

Which is true: it's the third time in three weeks Zanhua has declined an invitation from one of the groups he polices. And it worries her. For while she welcomes Zanhua's growing attentions—almost as much (it should be said) for their own sake, as for the continued proof they offer of her place here—she is also fully aware of how tenuous his own place is in the porous hierarchy of Wuhu's business world. Yuliang knows these men he's snubbing—all too well, in some cases. She knows how ruthlessly they can act. The Hall has feasted politicians who then fell from grace so fast that a month later they were hiding from Godmother's debt collectors.

"What's the problem, little Yu?" Zanhua is asking. "Want me out of the house already?"

"Of course not."

"Good. I brought you something. This is the periodical I told you about."

Yuliang takes the magazine. "*New Youth?*" she reads slowly.

"Good. Yes."

A small flush of triumph. But Yuliang's attention turns quickly to the artwork on the cover. It shows two strong hands stretching across a giant globe to clasp together. One is slightly darker, callused and muscled like a peasant's. Curious, her eyes home in on the small artist's chop below the logo. Of course she can't yet read it. She contemplates asking Zanhua, but he's already striding to his office.

Sighing, she sets the journal down, giving it one last, faintly envious stroke with her own hand, which (she can't help but notice), looks small, and oddly vulnerable by contrast.

ZANHUA DINES IN THE NEXT NIGHT as well, and breakfasts late both days, displaying an almost rebellious leisure in his meals, his talk, his plans. They live as Yuliang sometimes imagines newly-weds in exotic places like New York, Shanghai, and Paris live: eating, talking, retreating often to his bedroom to make love. He touches her frequently as he reviews her writing, brushes hair from her eyes, dusts lost lashes from her cheek. Yuliang still rarely reciprocates such gestures. But bit by bit, she finds herself sharing with him not only her day's work but the small thoughts that occur in his absence. She talks about Qian Ma's latest super-stitions: "She thinks Western cars have evil spirits in them!" About an etching of an English factory: "Was this what you mean by labor and capital?" About a foreign woman she has seen whose hands and feet seemed almost as small as her own: "Are you *sure* they don't bind them?" He shook his head: "Positive. But some of them do bind their waists."

But there's one observation Yuliang takes pains to hide from him—at least at first: her own, growing fascination with life and its sketched reflections.

Doodlings, she thinks of them. Her little worthless scribbles: tiny fruits, flowers, monkey faces. The occasional dragon topped with Qian Ma's head. These are the figures that almost of their own impetus bud and unfurl in the margins of Yuliang's copybook these days. To her eye, the small pictures are as inexcusably inexpert as was that first grief-stricken sketch of Jinling. More than once, appalled at how her pencil has mauled a plum, she's vowed to stop. And yet the little pictures keep coming, in a process both addictive and mystifying. It's the same need that once drove Yuliang to stay up through the early morning hours, coaxing peonies and fresh-faced peaches onto cloth with her needle. But there is, she is discovering, something liberating about ink and lead. Unfettered by thread, she can bring the whims of her thoughts—whispering trees, wilting flowers—to life. When the images are inept the solution is refreshingly simple: Yuliang simply rips the page out and starts over. And over . . .

As more and more of her study time is devoted to art she starts to worry as she hands Zanhua her "study" sheets; it seems impossible to her that he won't reprimand her for putting so little effort into them. To her astonishment, though, he doesn't even seem to notice the fact that characters she once spent hours on are now dashed off in half that time, in half panic. He still praises her brushwork, the surprising delicacy of her execution. At least, until one afternoon when he is home, working in his office.

Yuliang is lying on his bed upstairs with her writing things. Lulled into a dreamy daze by the rain-patter on the glass, she is thinking about the old French priest from on their outing; about the deft assurance with which those meaty hands captured a flower's frail beauty. The same feeling she'd had then—a thrill, blended with longing—fills her, and almost without thinking about it, she pages past the day's vocabulary in her copybook. Tongue between her lips, she makes soft gray sweeps on the paper. She adds more detail: a faint line there, a smudge here. A dark crease to show the dainty fold of a leaf. The flower's flaws—its unevenness, the unnatural cast of attempted shading—needle her. And yet she keeps on trying.

On her fourth try she takes a different approach. Instead of drawing line by line, she tries to tap into that flash-quick association between image and meaning that is the key to her growing literacy. *Orchid,* she thinks. *Orchid.* And without letting her mind go any further, she puts her lead tip once more to the paper's surface. When she is done, she shuts her eyes, then opens them again.

To Yuliang's surprise, what she has drawn is just that: an orchid. It's still a bit crooked, a little chunky in the stem and stamen. She'd do better if she had one right in front of her. And yet anyone looking at this picture—a schoolboy, a child not yet capable of reading the word even—would know it for what it was.

Flushed with victory, she's just turning a fresh page to try it again when Zanhua flings himself on the bed, almost on top of her. "Ah-ha! Caught you!" he cries, nuzzling her neck. "You didn't hear me come up?" He pulls her, copybook and all, into a rough embrace. "The old sons of turtles are crazy," he complains. "There's no way in hell we're going to be able to check all small craft in the harbor before they reach the docks!"

"No way, certainly," she says into the lime-sweet pomade of his hair, "if you don't ever leave the house."

He pulls back slightly. "Ah. You *do* want me out."

She laughs. "Of course I don't." Snaking her arm out from under his weight, she tries to drop the book over the bed's edge. But he catches her hand.

"Not so quickly. Let's take a look at your work, little scholar." And, still pinning her beneath him, he parts the book's pages.

Yuling feels her face flush again as he looks at her image, then at her. "Did you do this?"

She nods.

Zanhua rolls off her. Bending over the book, he begins paging through it intently. She watches him take it in: the scrawled-off characters, the little pictures that she'd thought good enough to keep. The not-so-bad orchid, and the one that looks like a lion. And the one that looks somehow squashed. But it's the good one he returns to, tracing the black lines with his white fingers. Frowning at it as though it were a puzzle.

"I was having difficulty concentrating," Yuliang mumbles. "The rain . . ."

He doesn't answer. Oddly anxious, Yuliang chews a cuticle. When it stings, she looks down to see that she's bitten too hard again: blood wells.

"This is how you spend your days now?" he says.

"I mostly do them after I study."

"Have you had lessons?"

She laughs. "When would I have had lessons?" Then, realizing he means at the Hall, she bites her lip. "No. Never. I—I just like to try to draw things sometimes. I'm no good at all."

He purses his lips. "Actually, you are. You're very good."

The compliment all but takes her breath away. "I'm no Shi Tao," she manages finally. "You can surely see that—" She breaks off, flustered. They have never discussed the painting's disappearance.

"It's interesting," he goes on, ignoring the comment.

"What?"

"That you decided to do . . . this." He points to where she's tried to show depth with clumsy crosshatching, a technique she'd seen on the cover of a *New Youth* issue. "None of the old masters would pay this much attention to depth."

"I know. It's silly."

"Don't apologize. Artists—modern artists—should paint the world as it is. Not just as some empty exercise in aesthetics." Turning slightly, he waves at the scroll that has hung in the room since before he first led her up to it. "How many versions of that picture hang on people's walls, do you think?"

Yuliang follows the gesture to where the wispily bearded scholar contemplates a barely indicated stream. A carp looks back at him, its goggle-eyes turned up in admiration. Yuliang has contemplated this image often, usually in moments of boredom. It strikes her as skillful, but she has no feelings for it. Zanhua has told her he bought it from a lakeside vendor in Hangzhou. She ventures a guess: "Hundreds?"

"Millions," he retorts, as though he's counted them personally. "But have you ever *seen* that scene? A scholar by a stream? A carp coming up for a little chat?"

"No?" she ventures.

"Of course not!" He rubs his cheek. "Just as no one has ever seen the esteemed Master Tao's mountain covered top to bottom with pine trees."

"But they must have," Yuliang protests, struggling to think back to the shoreline vistas of that long-ago river trip with Uncle Wu. "*I* have, even. Or something like it."

He shakes his head. "No one could get that perspective from the ground. They'd have to be painting from high up. Maybe even from an airship. Not very likely, four hundred years ago." He hands the book back. "You should sign it. All artists sign their work." And as she shakes her head modestly, "You *should*. But you should also keep up with the lessons. I'll always trust words over pretty pictures."

He says this last part sternly, looking so much like a schoolteacher that Yuliang can't help teasing him a little. Stretching back, she folds her arms beneath her neck. "What," she asks, "about pretty women?"

At first he's faintly startled, as he always is when her humor catches him unawares. Then he laughs. "That," he says, reaching for her, "is a completely different story."

TWO DAYS LATER the rain has washed the sky a crisp blue, and the spring sun shines as if it has never done otherwise. Yuliang sits in Zanhua's office, trying her hand at butterflies.

Since their discussion, she's worked more openly on her art.

He's even offered her some supplies: a box of sharp-tipped charcoal, some new brushes, thicker than those used for calligraphy. A sketch-book from a Wuhu art store. The bright white paper is far finer than Yuliang's copybook pages, with their smoothly mashed and faintly discolored surface. It feels different too, not so much absorbing as resisting the brush's damp kiss. It allows a sharper line, with much more sheen.

She is bent over this discovery when the phone in the main hall-way starts to ring. The sound at first makes her leap slightly in her seat. But Zanhua has left strict instructions that no one answer the "electric voice-box" when he's away. It is a welcome directive for the servants, at least, who see the machine as vaguely preternatural. Qian Ma eyes it with open disapproval. "Any people we're meant to talk to, we're meant to meet," she mutters.

Still, for the next half-hour the device continues ringing, on and off, and Yuliang finally shuts the office door against it. Almost at the same moment the front door bursts open. "Why is the floor so damned wet? Can't a man walk in peace even within his own house?" Zanhua bellows.

It's Thursday, the maid's floor-washing day. But Yuliang doesn't note this when he clatters into the study. Instead she stares up at him, taken aback not only by his abrupt presence but by his whiteness, his outraged expression. When the telephone lets loose its shrill call again, he makes no move to answer it. "I'm going to have to work now for a few hours," he says. He waits, tapping his thigh with the rolled tabloid he is holding. Yuliang makes out the banner: the *Crystal*. It's a lowly publication, one Zanhua normally says isn't worth his money. "Singsong girl gossip," he sniffs. "Tissue paper. All rustle." Following her gaze now, he tosses the paper on the chaise. "Please, Yuliang."

With as much grace as she can muster, Yuliang stands and walks past him, butterflies held carefully flat to prevent drips. He shuts the door behind her.

She'd planned to move upstairs. But she finds herself lingering, shuffling her feet just outside her former workspace. Somewhere in her mind a small, shrill chorus begins, like the malevolent hum of summer locusts: *He's leaving you. He is leaving.*

Which, she tells herself, is of course ridiculous. It's probably nothing. Just some ordinance or tax. Another blow to the war-torn new economy. But then, she knows the tabloids, and the *Crystal* in particular. It cares about two things only, sex and gossip about sex. Its coverage of the economy doesn't extend beyond the luxurious lifestyles of local tax collectors. As for war, Yi Gan once read Yuliang two full columns describing how General Fang, the "dog meat" general, once allowed a ranks inspection to be conducted by his concubine's toy chowchow.

Yuliang looks down at her butterflies. She all but feels them fluttering around in her stomach. But she makes herself knock. "I—I forgot something."

When she pushes the door open, he is sitting in the chair, head propped on his hand.

"I—I just wanted this pencil," Yuliang lies, picking up the tool from the desk. "And the *New Youth*." He'd brought her another copy this week. This one shows an enormous Sumo wrestler, Japan's flag wrapped around his loins, preparing to devour all of China with his chopsticks.

"Go ahead," is all Zanhua says.

The magazine is on the shelf right over the chaise. Yuliang makes her way to it slowly, her eyes on the *Crystal*. The paper is folded open to the "Seen in Town" section. She makes out two words: *tax inspector* and *gardens*. Heart in mouth, she bends over to get a better look. "Don't read that," he says, too sharply. "It doesn't concern you."

Yuliang stands up slowly. "That's not true," she says.

He stares balefully at her for a moment. Then he sighs, passes a hand across his cheek. "You're right. I've never lied to you yet. I've promised you I never will."

He heaves himself to his feet, walks slowly past her to the chaise. He retrieves the cheap tabloid. "This came out today." He reads:

Word has it that Master Pan, the new deputy customs inspector, has been spending much time (and, dare we suggest, city monies?) on a young girl from our beloved Hall of Eternal Splendor. The two, said to be living in a "union of the wilds" in Master Pan's home, were spotted last week at Zeshan Wanlu, where the feet of Inspector Pan's lovely companion were said to be even more exquisite— if significantly larger—than any of the blossoms. Inspector Pan, it's well known, prides himself on being one of China's new, "modern" thinkers—too modern, it seems, to avail himself of traditional courtesies extended to him by his many admirers. It is therefore gratifying to know that in some areas he's as old-fashioned as the rest: the Place of Clouds and Dew beckons all men, high and low . . .

A sharp snap. Yuliang looks down to see that she's broken her pencil in half. The sound detonates through the room like a firework.

"I'm so sorry," she whispers. It's all she can think of to say. Other than what she's thinking, which is: *Of course. Of course, it must end.*

"I suppose it was inevitable," Zanhua says, as though once more divining her thoughts. "Yi Gan is a powerful man. And your Madame Ping was quite angry. I knew some brows would lift when I took you in. But I didn't think this would become such a scandal. My intentions from the start were nothing but honorable. I don't understand why they can't see that."

"See what?"

"That I wanted to save you. To . . . to rehabilitate you. That the rest simply wasn't planned."

As Yuliang meets his eye, she realizes with a jolt that he is speaking the absolute truth: his intentions *were* honorable. What's more, she realizes something that he does not: that the *they* he speaks of do see this. All too clearly. And it's this very sight—of his honor, the unstained shine—that makes them hate him as they do.

The thought comes starkly: *This will be your downfall.*

"What's in your mind?" he says.

She feels her ears redden. "That—that you've done more than I can ever thank you for. Or repay you for."

"It's never been a question of payment," he says sharply, even though it's always a question of payment. And this (she thinks) only proves it further. If only he'd let them pay him off, and paid God-mother what she'd asked. If only they'd both paid more attention to the signs; to fate. To how life is lived in Wuhu, rather than how they wanted to live it.

"Yuliang?"

She lowers her eyes. "You shouldn't waste worry on me," she says quietly. "I'll be safe."

He frowns. "Safe? Where?"

"Wherever I end up."

"Don't be foolish," he snaps. "You're not leaving. Where will you go? Back to the Hall?" And, when she shakes her head, "Back to your uncle?"

"He's dead."

"He is not. He's in jail." Yuliang, still fidgeting with her broken pencil, jerks her head up. "The Zhenjiang authorities locked him up last year," Zanhua continues. "He hadn't paid taxes in a decade. Don't look at me like that. You didn't think I wouldn't make inquiries?" He turns away, starts pacing. "I've promised that I won't lie to you, ever. But you also can't lie to me, Yuliang. Not if we're going to do this."

"Do what?"

"Get married." He annunciates it very slowly. "I can't think of anything else to do that will clear your name and shut them up enough for me to get on with my job."

She stares at him, open-mouthed. "Married," she repeats.

"Officially it can't be a real marriage, of course. But a public ceremony. Something symbolic. My friend Chen Duxiu, the one I told you of, is coming back from Japan briefly. He can witness."

A concubine, she thinks. *I will become an official's concubine.* What was it her mother used to say about concubines? *A home's wife is its kitchen, where a home's good things live. A concubine is nothing more than the storage room.*

"It will save face," he is continuing. "It doesn't need to be much—just an exchange of vows in public. We can send an announcement to the *Crystal* and the other papers. Everyone up there has a little wife—or two, or three. Even though they all voted for the monogamy laws." He taps a finger against his chin. "Attorney Wen will draw up the contract."

An image comes: her uncle, Zheng *niangyi.* Yuliang's sale papers in hand. "No," she says, sharply. "No contract."

He gives her an odd look. "But you will do it?"

"Do what?"

"Marry me." And she stares: "You know that I love you."

It's the first time a man—any man—has said it to her; at least, out of bed. The first time anyone has meant it—truly meant it—since her mama. Yet as Yuliang shapes her mouth to say the words back to him, she finds her thoughts drifting to his wife in Tongcheng. *Never a true marriage,* he had said.

What comes out is this: "Will—will we live in Tongcheng?"

For a moment disappointment, and perhaps something more raw, shades his features. "No. Not at first, anyway. But you can't stay here either. I'm sending you to Shanghai."

Shanghai. Yuliang rubs a pencil shard against her arm. It leaves a rough pink line in its wake.

"Tell me," he says stiffly, "does that sound all right to you?" He is organizing his papers now. But she knows without looking that he's still waiting for her to say it: *I love you too. You've made me happier than I ever thought possible.*

So why can't she?

It's true, after all—she does love him. Yuliang knows it with the same detached certainty with which she knows that the sky is black and not blue, that the universe is unlimited and unfathomable. And yet somehow she can't force the words free.

Instead she stands, and holds her arms out to him. Her little sketch is dry now. The paper waves in a draft.

"It sounds wonderful," she says. And then: "Do you like the butterflies? They're for you."

Part FIVE

The HOUSE

The Territorie is an even Playne, and so cultivated that
they seeme a Citie of Gardens, full also of Villages, Hamlets, Towers.
There are many good wits and Students, a good Ayre, and they
live long, eightie, ninetie, and a hundred years.

———

FATHER MATTEO RICCI
(DESCRIBING SHANGHAI, C. 1610)

Seventeen

Shanghai, 1916

YULIANG HAS JUST DRIFTED to sleep when a splash and a shout jolt her back into awareness—just in time for a near-collision with a Shanghai garbage barge.

"Out of the way, dog-face!" their sampan's captain shouts. "Your steering stinks as much as your cargo!" He gestures obscenely, then darts a look at Yuliang. "Sorry, madame. There it is, then." He points. "The great city."

Yuliang shades her eyes. At first Shanghai is little more than twinkling color and tone, a distant blur of smoke and stone and lush green. But as their craft draws closer the horizon melts into clarity, revealing a shoreline so sparklingly alien she draws her breath.

"The Bund," Zanhua pronounces, the word as hard as a piece of metal in his mouth.

"Bund," she repeats obediently. "Is that French?"

"Indian, I think. It means 'gathering place.' "

"That's strange. To name a Chinese place with a foreign word."

He laughs. "Wait until you see the city. Half the street names are French or English. And in some neighborhoods, half the people as well." He smiles. "It will be like living overseas."

The thought is by turns unsettling and thrilling: Yuliang has spoken with only a handful of foreigners in her life. She's trying to summon the few French or English words she knows (*dah-ling,* she mouths; *howareyou, j'taime*) as he points to another building. "That's the British customs house. More money in its coffers than in all of Wuhu's offices put together. And over there—see the bamboo scaffolding?—is the new Russo-Asiatic Bank. They say it will be splendid." He squints, redirects his finger. "Over in that direction are fine hotels. Jews built them. They say scandalous parties take place there."

Yuliang looks at him quickly, wondering both what Jews are and what is considered scandalous in Shanghai. She can only hope the definition is significantly more expansive than the one that led to their subdued nuptials last month.

As a ceremony, it was a far cry from the one Yuliang's mama had dreamed of: there was no red dress, no sedan chair, no stepping over the *an* saddle on the threshold of the groom's house. No "tumult in the bridal room." There was, instead, a simple exchange of vows—written by Zanhua and his friend Duxiu—at the banquet hall at which they'd first met. Chen Duxiu, an elegant young man with sharp features and a quick tongue, provided witness and wrote up the announcement, which was then dutifully sent to every paper in town.

"Is it really all electric now?" Yuliang asks, gazing at the glittering skyline.

"Like broad daylight at sunset."

"They must collect many taxes."

"Not as many as you might think. Foreigners don't have to pay them."

"Really? Why not?"

"Why did the Old Dragon give the French a hundred and twenty million silver taels for a foreign temple?" he asks, shrugging.

The boat bumps over the wake of a linked line of houseboats pulled by a huffing steamer tug. "Ah," the captain says. "Here they come." Clutching the seat for balance, Yuliang sees a horde of shouting beggars wading and poling their way toward them on ragged rafts. They swarm upon the sampan, reaching out, plucking sleeves. One woman, her face less a face than thin copper skin stretched over a skull, thrusts a bundle into Yuliang's face. It takes a moment to make sense of the small, frayed heap. "Please, two cash for my sick child!" the woman cries. "My milk is gone, dried up like dust. Please, two cash, for my daughter!"

The girl's eyes are shut, fly-crusted. Yuliang claps her mouth shut against an overpowering stench—urine, rot, old blood. But something in the sight of it—the thin arms twined so firmly around the tiny body—stirs her. Without a word, she reaches for her purse.

"Don't," Zanhua says.

She turns, startled. "Why not?"

"She'll just give it to her beggar king. Who'll spend it on opium. Or worse."

"But the child . . ."

"Look closer. It's not even alive."

He is right: in an instant sympathy shifts to revulsion. Yuliang almost gags, as much at the sight of it as at the outrage. At least, she thinks weakly, Wuhu beggars are simply honest, poor people: monks, peasants fleeing famine and drought in the north. While this—*this* is something truly scandalous.

Still, while Zanhua tends to the bags, she holds out two coins. Breathing through her nose, Yuliang leans in. "Bury her," she whispers shortly. "If you loved her even slightly, leave her."

The woman's bloodshot eyes fix on Yuliang's briefly. They reflect neither gratitude nor recognition of the act. She merely snatches the coins, tucks them into some hidden, ragged pocket. Then she's off to another approaching sampan, her morbid bundle held aloft.

THE NEW HOME OF PAN YULIANG, the new "little wife" of Pan Zanhua, is on Haiying Li, a shabbily genteel thoroughfare that unrolls just beyond what was once the Walled City's northern gate. The wall is gone now, pulled down by Republican soldiers in an effort to unify the old Shanghai with the new. Still, turning into the warm shadows of the neighborhood, Yuliang feels as though she's found sanctuary. After all the harsh glass, brick, and metal, the endless construction of the new Shanghai, the weathered wood and cool shadows are like a balm. Their rickshaw runners trot past old men smoking long-stemmed pipes, or strolling with elaborately carved birdcages in hand. Grandmothers squat and perch on stools in the shade of their courtyard walls, mending, smoking, exchanging gossip. Students stroll in silk gowns paired with Western trousers, wingtip shoes. A number of them huddle by a dingy doorway covered with posters and lined with stacks of tied newspaper. Yuliang reads the sign over the door with surprise. "*New Youth*? Isn't that your friend's magazine?"

Zanhua nods. "That's the headquarters. Duxiu is back in Japan for the moment. But my friend Meng Qihua—the one who met us at the pier—contributes photographs to it every now and then." He waves an arm at the rickshaw ahead of theirs.

"Does he know the *New Youth* artists?" she asks. At her request, Zanhua now buys her most *New Youth* issues, voicing approval of her interest in current affairs. What he doesn't know is that she rarely makes it through a single article. What she mostly studies is the illustrations— particularly those bearing the still-indecipherable chop she'd first seen, beneath the two hands clasped across the earth.

"I'd assume so," he replies absently. And then: "Ah. We're here."

His friend Qihua's rickshaw has stopped before an old house, its dark wood silvered with years and smoke. "I'm sorry," the photographer calls back. "It's a poor excuse for a home."

And indeed, the little villa is a far cry from Zanhua's Western-influenced house in Wuhu. It's small and worn, and the hallway floorboards squeak sweetly, like small birds. The windows are papered, not glassed. But Yuliang, trailing in after Zanhua while Qihua walks around to check the outhouse, finds this unexpectedly pleasing. She's forgotten how rice paper mutes the light, and eases life's harsher lines and shadows.

Running a finger over a sill, Zanhua examines his fingertip with disapproval. "I'd hoped for something more modern."

"It's more than I require," Yuliang assures him, taking a brief assessment before moving on to inspect the second floor. It is narrow, with two small bedrooms, a bathroom, and a closet. The bathtub has a modern faucet but clearly no pipes attached to it as it doesn't let loose any water when she turns it. The bedroom door sticks at first, but finally relents under her slight weight. Beyond it lies a sunny space with a full-sized bed by the wall.

Hot from her efforts, Yuliang unlatches the shutters and leans out. To the east lies the ornate roof of the Temple of the Wealth God; to the west, the iron cross of the London Mission, its shadow stretched by the pink-ringed sunset over the city.

Breathing deeply, Yuliang thinks: *I'm alone.* It's surprisingly liberating. Not because she doesn't love her new husband, but after three days together in close quarters, she's looking forward to having her own thoughts again. . . .

"Yuliang?" Zanhua calls up to her. "Are you there?"

Sighing, Yuliang pulls herself from the gold-tinged view. "I'm coming."

When she arrives downstairs, he's standing inside a little room she hadn't noticed—a tiny, light-filled space. It takes her a moment to understand what is different: inexplicably, it has the home's only glass window.

"What's this?" she asks, pushing past him.

"Maid's room," Zanhua replies. "As dirty as the rest."

It is dirty: even the window is painted over, with soot inside and bird droppings without. Scattered on the floor, beneath a layer of dust, are clothespins and hemp ropes from someone's laundry, their pale forms embellished by dotted trails left by mice or roaches or some other scuttling creatures. Still, Yuliang's first thought is: *Perfect.* Here she can truly lose herself, not just in the meticulous and increasingly difficult characters she has worked her way up to, but in the work that is slowly becoming as, if not more, important: her sketching.

"There's no *k'ang*," Zanhua is saying. "But the girl should be warm enough. She can stay here as late as the Weeks of the White Dew, or even the autumnal equinox. After that she can move to the kitchen."

"What girl?"

"The servant," he says, as though it should be obvious.

"I don't need a servant."

"You can't plan on managing the house for yourself."

"I've done it before."

Zanhua's jaw tightens. "You did many things *before*. Now you are my wife. And my wife doesn't clean or cook."

"You mean wives," Yuliang snaps back, though seeing him deflate she quickly regrets her words. "It's a small house," she says, more gently.

"It's not just the house. You'll need someone to continue the treatments." He looks meaningfully at her feet. "Unless, of course, you think you don't need those either."

This stings too. Despite all Zanhua's chatter about "emancipation" and "liberation," Yuliang still sees her unbinding as an act of supreme sacrifice, one that has replaced her less-than-elegant lilies with *da jiao*: big, warped feet that are ugly by any standards.

When Zanhua first showed her the Heavenly Foot Society pamphlet two months ago, it seemed like altogether too much work for such unsightly ends: thrice-daily soaks in hot rice wine followed by "brisk rubbing and massage of the emancipated member." Excruciating walks to help the bones settle back in place. Qian Ma, not surprisingly, had thrilled in these painful ministrations, gleefully pounding, rubbing, and banging at Yuliang's unfolded lilies, then yanking her young mistress through the house. On the steamship, though, Zanhua himself did it for her, and at first the sight of him gazing at her naked, battered toes all but made her want to hurl herself overboard. Gradually, though, embarrassment softened into a kind of indebted awe. For what other man on earth would do this—gently rub her warped arches and deformed digits, quietly rinse away pus and callus, without comment?

The memory defuses Yuliang's anger slightly. "I'll have a maidservant, then," she says grudgingly. "But she doesn't stay overnight."

Zanhua turns away from her, jaw working. "I suppose," he says at last, "we can find someone to come in for those times." He sighs. "The solitude at least will be conducive to studying."

IN THE MORNING comes a lone rooster's call, and the plaintive howl of a southbound locomotive. Soon after comes the calm clip-clop of horses making deliveries, and then the irate honks of automobiles and calls of passing vendors. After a week or so, Yuliang has grown accustomed to the four American tenors who serenade her each morning from a nearby Victrola. Their owner (who sings with them while he shaves) provides her first English lessons, after a fashion: *I've got my tickets,* she finds herself humming later. *My train is leaving here at half-past four. Ohhhh, my beautiful doll, goodbye.*

With Zanhua still here, mornings remain much the same as they were in Wuhu. The serving girl Qihua finds comes each day for the first week, creeping in a little after sunrise to prepare breakfast. Zanhua reads the papers to Yuliang, jotting down new words for her copybook. They've agreed upon a system for her to send her work home to him, for him to critique and then send back.

Yuliang enjoys this routine—both the familiarity, and the novelty. It's the hours after breakfast, however, that she cherishes the most. On Ocean Street there is no demanding ring of the telephone, no stream of couriers bearing chits and invitations. They spend every day together, taking rickshaws and carriages across the city. They fill the small house with things to write on, rest in, eat from: wall scrolls from Fouzhou Road, books from Liu and Co. Bookcases and kitchen tables on Nanjing Road. At the Golden Dragon Rug Company they find rugs brought in by loping camels from the desert. Fingering the colors—the rich brown-oranges, the ruby reds—Yuliang finds herself imagining the darkened fingers that made them. The image sparks something like longing.

ON ZANHUA'S LAST NIGHT, they invite Meng Qihua to the house for dinner. After they've eaten, the men lean back and light cigarettes. "Astonishing," Zanhua says, after a few companionable puffs. "The way things went last week in the war."

"At the Somme?" his photographer friend says.

Yuliang looks up. That morning Zanhua had explained to her about the latest bloody battle covered by the *Echo de Chine*: twenty thousand men killed in less than an hour. Yuliang, who has seen death in ways many could never imagine, still has a hard time imagining this horrible scene. As Zanhua read the news, she'd been able to summon only its colors: a nauseating palette of grass green, mud black, vermilion blood. Now, unsettled, she stands and pours more of the French table wine Qihua brought to dinner. "It's unthinkable," Zanhua is saying, "that technology has given man such power. Not only to better life, but to wreak such havoc on it." He stares up at the old ceiling beams. "They'll have to enter it at some point now. They'll have to."

"The Americans?" Qihua leans back, his glasses glinting in the candlelight. He's a slim man, and always quite fashionably dressed. He's a good deal younger than Zanhua's writer friend, Duxiu, and yet Yuliang finds him the more intimidating of the two. He somehow makes her feel both unschooled and low-class—a bit, in fact, the way the Hall's men always made her feel.

"Wilson can't just stand by and watch this mess get worse," Zanhua says.

"Perhaps. Perhaps not." His old friend shrugs. "At least the war keeps the *yangguizi* out of our hair. Let them fight over their own damned land for once."

"But there are still the Japanese," Yuliang points out.

Meng Qihua looks at her, faintly amused. "A good point, Madame Pan. What troubles me is how easily they dominate us. We're the biggest nation on earth. We've thousands more years of battle experience."

"The problem lies in spirit," Zanhua says. "We need to think of ourselves that way. As a nation. As General Sun has been saying from the start." His eyes brighten a little, as they always do when he speaks of Sun Yat-sen, who even in exile remains his hero. "First, military rule. Expel the imperialists. Second, political tutelage. Teach the people to rule themselves. And then . . ."

"And then—ah, yes. The grand dream of self-rule," says Qihua, waving his cigarette holder theatrically.

Zanhua looks at him levelly. "Of course. Just as we always said back in Tokyo. You did too. You no longer believe in the Three Stages?"

"Perhaps I'm too old now to believe in easy answers of any sort." The photographer looks up contemplatively, blowing a series of rings that float up slowly in the damp, hot air. "Or perhaps it's this city. Perhaps," he says, indicating the pooling custard his Napoleon has left on his plate, "all this Western decadence has addled my thinking. But one thing strikes me: China is not England. It is not America. It's not even France. It has a vastly different past and problems."

"What's the answer, then?" Zanhua challenges.

"It may be a lost cause."

"I never saw you as a pessimist."

"A pessimist would say China had no spirit in the first place. I say China has spirit. I just don't think her leaders do. Or perhaps any leaders at all." He leans back. "Perhaps that's the answer: no leaders."

Zanhua studies him in surprise. "You're advocating anarchism?"

His friend just smiles. "I don't believe in *isms*. Have you forgotten that already?"

"I have not. Just as I haven't forgotten about the hundred yen you still owe me."

"From what?" Qihua laughs.

"From that wager you lost in Tokyo, over Marx. . . ."

The men talk into the night, discussing the old days in Japan and their high hopes for China when the New Republic was born. When Qihua leaves at last, it is late. Dishes lie scattered on the table like lard-layered pieces of some chaotic mosaic. But when Yuliang stands to clear them, Zanhua stops her. "The girl can do it."

"I sent her home at midnight."

"In the morning, then."

She starts to protest. But he cuts her off gently, merely saying "Come," and leading her to the staircase.

Upstairs, his lovemaking is almost like an attack: he touches every inch of skin with his lips, hands, and tongue. Later, he covers her body like a blanket or a net, pressing down on her torso, her legs and arms and even fingers, his ring cutting into her slim knuckles. Afterward they lie together, staring up at the ceiling and the drifting smoke from his last cigarette of the day.

"I don't know how to do this," he says, at last.

"Do what?" She traces the one black curl that falls onto his smooth brow.

"Leave. Live. Without you." He sighs. "I feel like I need you with me to breathe."

Yuliang opens her mouth, then closes it again, unsure of what she wants to say. What she feels for him is not the sort of visceral and thick dependence of which he speaks. She hasn't felt that for anyone except her mama. Turning over on her back, though, she realizes too that he is right—it is a little like the need for air, such love. You aren't aware of it until the air is removed. And suddenly, you realize you are suffocating.

She takes a deep breath. "Six months is no time at all, really. You lived far longer by yourself before we met."

"I wasn't myself before we met." He interlaces their fingers again. "What—what I'm trying to say is that I don't want to go back to 'before we met'. . ." His voice cracks slightly. "Promise me. Promise me you won't leave."

"Leave?" She laughs. "Where would I go?"

"I've had terrible dreams of waking up one morning and find-ing you gone." He smiles self-consciously. "I know it's foolish. But the city's dangerous. There are gangs here that grow more powerful every day. Even the police are corrupt. Little Yu . . ." He turns his eyes. "Promise me that you will stay safe."

Safe, she thinks. She recalls her first night with Yi Gan. She thinks of the Hall, the beatings and "discipline sessions." And the men—night after night after bleak night. These things are now a part of her, so hopelessly ingrained that even in her happiest moments she knows she will never forget them. She may be able to deny them, even to wipe them out—at least, from the spoken story of her life. But they will always mark her spirit. Like scars.

"Yuliang?"

When at last she turns to face him, she still can't say the words he so clearly wants to hear, and the shame over this shakes her voice. She comes as close to it as she can manage without betraying herself:

"I promise," she says. "I'll stay safe."

Eighteen

THE WET SHANGHAI SUMMER dries into a slightly crisper autumn, before sliding down in fits and starts to the cooler moistness of the Jiangsu winter. Yuliang unpacks her warm things, shutters the windows against the cold. She marks Zanhua's next visit on the calendar she has hung in her study, and settles in as a woman alone.

In the beginning, life seems disorientingly loose, as unspun as the silk ticking in her comforter. She wakes at night in a vague but forceful panic, certain she's lost or forgotten something valuable—her wedding ring, her purse, her copybook. It takes several minutes of lying there, her heart tapping its frantic beat, before it dawns on her that what is missing is her husband.

The pain inflicted by the lack of him almost startles her sometimes. When he writes, after three months, that his next planned visit has been delayed, she at first is uncertain that she's read the note properly. When Qihua confirms it for her—"You're making good progress!" he says, condescendingly—she returns home and goes directly to bed. She remains there through the afternoon and the evening, reciting Li Qingzhao's poetry to herself.

One of the few things that helps to distract her is work; Yuliang crafts a study schedule from breakfast straight through until lunch, staunchly writing out row after row of radicals and character combinations. At week's end she surveys the pages and tears them out, tucking them into prepared envelopes she seals with Zanhua's official seal. Ahying runs them out to the mail courier, who passes at noon and at three, surrounded by his "red-headed rascals" or Sikh guards. Yuliang studies as scrupulously as ever. But she also finds herself drifting more and more to her little scribblings, sometimes even drifting from pictograph to picture without realizing she has made the transition. The character for *imperial* (帝國), with its regal-looking crown radical, is unthinkingly transformed into a regal head. The three trees of *forest* (森) give way to a dead leaf, its crinkled skeleton drifting on a lake. Fengtai (鳳台), the site of the famed battle between the Qin and Jin kingdoms, becomes phoenix (鳳), which in turn gives way to a dreamy sketch of Jinling's phoenix wine cups, which perch on Yuliang's bookshelf, bone dry.

After studying some and sketching more, on most afternoons Yuliang ventures out to explore her new city. In the beginning she walks merely to try to strengthen her feet, which are slowly adjusting to their reknitting bones. Gradually, though, she becomes entranced by the city's myriad cultures, and soon she's walking with the determination of an explorer. She wants to see it—all of it. And for the first time in her life, there is no reason to be home by dinner.

She explores from the silvered antiquity of Ocean Street to the glossy offerings of Nanjing Road—which, as Zanhua predicted, twinkle even more brightly after dark. She strolls through coffee-scented alleyways in the French Concession, and the Japanese colony in Hongkou, with its hushed shops smelling of barley and green tea. She paces the Bund, breathing in its heady scent of gasoline, fish, and sweat-slicked cash. She shades her eyes and watches steamers inch their way out of sight, trailing seagulls like white beads on windblown thread. The sight always moves her for some reason—something she considers one of her own peculiarities, until the day an entire art class arrives to sketch the scene.

The students—young men dressed in dusty robes and paint-splattered shoes—arrange themselves at the base of the bridge, around an older man wearing a cravat and a felt beret. They watch intently as he holds up his pencil, squints, and drops it back down to his page. "If you'll note," he says, "that small steamer tug to the east takes up no more space than a third of my pencil. And now"—a brief pause as he drops the pencil again—"I calculate it to scale on this paper. A third, gentlemen. No more."

Continuing to sketch, he adds, "There are those, even at the academy, who believe this is too technical a method to use in art. Believe me, it is not. A painting lacking in perspective is a painting lacking in persuasion. Take the time to get size and distance right." The students nod and follow, lifting their pencils and sketching in unison like an awkward, silent orchestra.

The academy, Yuliang thinks. The Shanghai Art Academy. And for some reason, she shivers.

She has passed the school often on her excursions to Bubbling Well Road, sometimes even going out of her way to wander by its gates. She studies the announcement board that stands outside. *Western Painting Lecture Postponed,* said one notice recently. *Life Study to Reschedule Due to Model Cancelation,* said another (*Is she knocked up?* someone had scrawled beneath). There was also a list of materials for incoming students to obtain: plywood, hide glue, brushes and paints that could be purchased at a store two blocks down. Yuliang copied the shop's name, meaning to go back and explore it, although in the past weeks this small goal was forgotten.

Now, creeping closer, she peers over the shoulder of one of the students, a strong young man with thick, long hair. He sits stooped, as though apologizing in posture for what Yuliang can tell, even when he is seated, is an unusually tall frame. His wrists and fingers are as strong as a farmer's. But they hold the pencil with a delicacy that strikes Yuliang as oddly poignant. His big hand curls back and forth across his page, leaving an impressive billow of clouds in its wake.

"Xudun," the teacher calls to him. "Draw with your arm, not your fingers. If you focus too tightly it constricts your image."

The boy lengthens his strokes, deftly capturing a junk that waits just past the dock. As Yuliang watches, he embellishes the day's weather, adding a black-bellied thunderhead (nowhere on the true horizon) and an underlying shadow of approaching rainfall. Apparently unhappy with this last bit, he bends down for his eraser. Then his eyes catch Yuliang's, and widen slightly. He smiles a large, easy smile.

The boy seated next to him sees his face and looks up as well. "Hey, sister," he calls. "Come closer. One thing we always need here is a model!"

His friend elbows him hard enough to dislodge his dusty fedora. "Bastard," he says affably. "Clamp it."

Yuliang colors. There is little doubt as to the boy's meaning: editorial sections are still seething over the Shanghai Art Academy's continued use of nudes. Vocabulary permitting, Yuliang has followed the debate as intently as she does any news about the school, which has fascinated her ever since Zanhua first mentioned its existence. She has even fantasized sometimes about walking through those green French doors, along with the fashionably bohemian students she sees chatting and smoking outside. But never, obviously, to take her clothes off for them.

They're all looking at her now, twenty blank male gazes. Yuliang's throat tightens. In her mind's distance she hears a thick voice: *Smile! Smile!*

But Yuliang doesn't smile. What she does is spit—something she's rarely done before, and certainly not in front of a group of men. The globule flies from her lips and lands with a small splat near the iron railing. She stares at it for a moment, in disbelief and self-horror.

Then, heart pounding, she turns on her heel and walks as quickly as her beaten feet will permit. Away from the men with their pencils and the departing steamships and gulls. Toward the gleaming safety of the nearest shopping street.

Nineteen

ZANHUA ARRIVES, AT LAST, in March. Over the weeklong span of his visit, Yuliang lets him lead her through the international settlement, lecturing her on trade policy and extraterritoriality. They dine to the music of a flower-bedecked choir billed as the "best Hawaiian singers who ever left the islands." At night they delve deeper into memory and skin.

On their last day together, Zanhua takes Yuliang to one of the cinema houses that have sprung up around the city in the past two years. The film is American—*The Hazards of Helen*. Its blond heroine proceeds from feat to death-defying feat—commandeering a motorcycle, foiling a train robbery, and finally leaping lithely from a bridge. Not to kill herself (as a Chinese heroine would do) but to save the baby in her arms. Each act is lauded by the cinema's narrator: "The hero sees Helen! He too rushes onto the bridge. Can he possibly reach her and the child before the train comes?"

Unlike some in the audience, Yuliang doesn't leap to her feet in protest when the last reel runs to its end. But she too feels strangely desolate; as though the velvet curtains have closed not just on Helen's life, but on her own.

She finds herself unusually quiet, both at dinner and later on. Even when she and Zanhua make love she feels distant; as if part of her has remained in the gray America of the screen. Afterward, Zanhua pulls away and leans over her, staring down searchingly.

"What's in your head?" Yuliang asks him, half teasing.

He doesn't smile back. "I'm just wondering whether this . . . arrangement was a wise one. Wondering if there would be some better place for you elsewhere."

"I won't stay in one of those women's lodges. They're like—prisons," she says (though she almost said, *like the Hall*).

"I'm thinking of somewhere else. Where you wouldn't be alone so much."

"I *like* being alone," Yuliang says, before realizing how it sounds. "That is—I miss you. Certainly. Terribly. But I—I fill the time."

"That," he says, "is partly what worries me." His lips tighten. "This is a dangerous city, little Yu. There are many ways in which a young girl could be pulled into trouble. I'm wondering if we should perhaps move you back home."

"To Wuhu?" she asks carefully.

If he hears her ambivalence, he doesn't acknowledge it. He simply looks at her and says, "No. To Tongcheng."

"With . . . your wife."

He nods. "That way I wouldn't have to divide my time. I'd actually see more of you. Both."

A short silence follows. Closing her eyes, Yuliang tries to picture it: scurrying out after his first wife, carrying a parasol to protect the flawless skin she'd seen in the matchmaker's picture. But the worst by far would be nighttime. Yuliang imagines such a life, sleeping not in a master bedroom but in a smaller room off the same hall. She imagines lying there alone, waiting for her lord's footsteps. Then, perhaps, hearing them make their way not to her door but past it.

"I can't do that," she says softly.

"Don't you want to be with me? With your husband?"

"Yes. But . . ."

"But what?"

She feels his eyes on her, still deep in thought. After a moment he sighs and rolls onto his back. "If you only knew how you confuse me."

She opens her own eyes. "How?"

"Everything I've ever wanted in a marriage, I've found with you. No—more. I can talk with you openly, without fear or pretense. I am more myself with you than I've ever been with a woman. At times I believe that you are like me in that. That we're the same. But then . . ."

Yuliang finds herself holding her breath. At last he continues. "You remember the city I told you of, in Italy? The one covered by the volcano centuries ago? Sometimes—tonight, for instance—you feel less like my wife than one of the bodies they've found. I feel as if I must chisel through layers of rock to reach you."

Yuliang bites her lower lip. She remembers talking about this city, seeing pictures of the bodies that had been uncovered. The faceless forms of women and children who'd been caught by death, only to be redelivered into the world centuries later—as contorted white ghosts. She'd been both repelled and intrigued by how these sad sculptures had been created: the scientists had drilled through the hardened rock, filled the hole with plaster of Paris. The casts worked because the bodies themselves had long been vaporized by heat and time: they existed only because of that wrenching, tragic emptiness.

"Are you saying I'm empty?" she asks now, softly. She is surprised at just how much the thought hurts her.

"Not empty. Just . . . distant. Sealed off from me sometimes. And when I feel this, I feel unspeakably lonely."

For an instant she can't respond; she is too overcome by guilt. For how could she let him feel this, after all he's done? "I'm not sealed off. Not from you, at least. You know me better than anyone." Yuliang curls herself around his stiff form. Putting her lips close to his ear, she adds, almost without thinking about it, "And I don't have to be empty."

He looks at her. "What do you mean?"

"We could have a child. A son. For you."

She doesn't know why she says it—she certainly hasn't been thinking of childbearing. In fact, unbeknown to him, she's continued the few preventative practices she can manage outside the Hall. She doesn't dare ask Ahying to find her tadpoles. But she still uses coins tucked into secret places, and furtive, heavily salted douchings. She marks the bated-breath wait for blood every month. Not as good wives do, in hope, but in anxiety.

And yet at this moment, seeing his misery, having him all but hand her his heart, Yuliang vows she will be better. She reminds herself again that he deserves it: if not the dozen sons that the old blessing prescribes, at least one. Just one. She knows it is something he wants. And if in her own mind a spark of doubt flickers (*What about what I want?*), she quickly suppresses it, kissing his nose, his chin, his ear. Reveling in the strange sensation of, for once, giving him something of value too.

Twenty

Ayear after Yuan Shikai dies (from heartbreak, some say, over the collapse of his imperial dreams), a northern warlord charges into the Forbidden Palace and reinstates Puyi, the boy emperor, on the throne.

The news sends shock waves through Shanghai: special editions materialize on every newsstand, in Chinese, French, Russian, German, English, Yiddish. Students take to the streets with mixed déjà vu and disgust. On Ocean Street, the neighborhood grandmothers smoke their pipes and debate the new monarchy, while the *New Youth* staff scrambles a crisis issue to press. Setting out on her daily walk one day, Yuliang almost bumps into a tall young man bustling past with a carton of cartoon-embossed leaflets, several of which slide off the top as he stops short. Looking up, she recognizes the boy she'd watched at the academy's sketching outing to the Bund.

Yuliang blanches. But the boy just smiles at her. "Excuse me," he says, and steps back.

Yuliang kneels to gather the dropped leaflets, hoping desperately he hasn't identified her. But as she stands to hand them back, his large eyes light up. "Say," he says, in his deep, sleepy voice. "You're that girl from the Bund—I *thought* I'd seen you before."

"I . . ." On top of being one of the few that has ever seen her hawk like a fisherwoman at the market, he has to be the tallest man she's ever met. Looking up at him requires her to tilt her head back, almost uncomfortably.

"I must apologize for that day," she begins.

"No. *I* should apologize," he interrupts. "My friend was unpardonably rude. I'm afraid he doesn't see many pretty girls at the academy."

Not according to the papers, she thinks, recalling the latest anti-nude essay to appear in the *Shenbao*'s editorials. But what she says is, "Don't you go to the academy?"

"I did. And I still tag along for the *plein air* sessions sometimes. But I've decided to put my efforts into more important causes."

"What's more important than art?"

The question comes out unprompted. Yuliang drops her eyes in embarrassment. The boy's heavy brows lift in surprise. Then he gives another grin. "That's a very good question," he says. "Here's another I've been thinking about: what, in the end, *is* art?"

Yuliang stares back for a moment. Then, despite herself, she laughs.

A call comes from the *New Youth* office: "Hey, Lao Xing! Are you here to work or to impress girls?"

"Your friends here aren't much more polite than those at the academy," she notes.

"I suppose not. But manners don't get you far in politics. Yesterday's news more than proves that, doesn't it?" Still smiling, he turns away. Then he turns back again. "Wait. I still don't know your name."

"Yuliang," says Yuliang. For some reason she hesitates before adding, "Pan Yuliang. My—my husband knows your editor well, I think."

She sees the information register in his dark eyes. "Master Chen," he says. "Yes. He's in Tokyo at the moment." He grins again—that big, open grin. "Anyway, I'm Xing Xudun. It was nice to run into you again. I'll hope to see you soon, Pan Yuliang."

As he hurries to the doorway Yuliang realizes, too late, that she's still holding the leaflets she's picked up. She takes a step forward, then stops and studies them, surprised. One, a caricature of a toddler in split pants staggering under a hefty crown, she has never seen before. But the other she recognizes instantly. It's the *New Youth* cover from a little over a year ago. The one showing two hands clasped across a globe.

And for the first time, she also knows how to read the tiny artist's chop beneath the black-and-white world: Xing Xudun.

OVER THE NEXT FEW WEEKS Yuliang throws herself into her sketches as never before, rising sometimes as early as five or six to work in morning's first light. She ponders breakfast peaches, with their velvet skin and dripping flesh. She lingers over fish with glassy eyes and paper-thin scales. She spends hours on a durian, its porcupine silhouette, and no easier to draw than to eat with its stink and spines. Her interest fired by the debate over models, she even tries her hand again at a real person, choosing as her subject the one female body she's sure she still knows by heart: Jinling's.

Sequestering herself in her little room one morning a little after sunrise, Yuliang draws, her tongue clamped hard between her lips. She summons her late friend and mentor, not bloated and bruised and wrapped in sackcloth, but as she'd looked at the very start of a big evening: hair sleek and bound with pearls. Eyes and lips deftly defined. The eyes, Yuliang thinks, go . . . there. No, no, lower. There. *There.* She draws the nose men so adored, its delicate nostrils slightly flared. A nose fortunetellers had said foretold a life of money and ease. Although (only now does Yuliang realize) no one said anything about its length.

After working for an hour, she pauses and takes in her progress. The neck looks squat, the eyes beadlike, suspicious. She sweeps the page away and starts over. *Head, hair, neck. Think willow,* she wills her-self. *Fine, slim, straight. A dimpled hallow. A tiny lake at its base. Draw with your arm, not your fingers.* She sketches two high breasts beneath a simple silk robe, hints at the tiny furrow that runs to the navel like a small river. The world outside gossips and bustles as always. But Yuliang hears nothing but the soft scritch of her pencil tip and, almost as often, the reproving rub of her eraser.

And then suddenly, it's ten o'clock.

Exhausted, she sits back, her spine and her eyes aching. She surveys. And once more whatever small hope she's been harbor-ing withers. She has drawn a girl, certainly. Even a pretty girl. The hair's the right length and style, the eyes the right size. The body is slim and graceful. Yuliang has captured one lily foot, fetchingly short and pointed but just a shade too wide on the sides. Despite all this, though, it isn't Jinling. The girl she's drawn is a complete stranger.

Dispirited, Yuliang rips the picture from her sketchbook and crumples it into a ball. She slumps back in her chair, sketchpad in her lap and eyes fixed numbly on the previous page. It's a sketch she did last week, the day after she met Xing Xudun. For the first time she'd actually mastered her own hands. She did several versions: one hold-ing a wineglass, another resting against Zanhua's picture. In this last one, she clasps a silk chrysanthemum she'd bought on a whim from a street vendor. Yuliang studies it listlessly. Why is it, she wonders, that she can draw her own hands so well and yet fail to capture even Jinling's littlest finger?

She stretches her hands toward the morning light, flexes them, makes fists. The answer comes in a rush of clarity: she can draw her hands because she *has* her hands. She can draw them from life. That, of course, is why it's called "life study." Whereas she has nothing of Jinling's life but her wine cups.

For just an instant Jinling's light voice seems to circle the little room. *In Shanghai, it was more than just beds and money. We danced, wrote poems. Even drew, if we could . . . Back in Shanghai . . . When I worked in Shanghai . . .*

Yuliang picks up the little ball and throws it in the dustbin. Then, barely letting herself contemplate what she is doing, she picks up her shawl and purse and goes out.

Fouzhou Road begins, broad and tree-lined, on the Bund's western side. Its first mile is lined with the looming Western-style buildings of commerce that give Shanghai its European patina. But that austere architecture is soon replaced by a more suggestive sort of structure, the clubs by teahouses, the banks by brothels with their red lanterns and elaborately carved exteriors.

For those seeking more refined pleasures, there are used-book stores crowding the little cobbled alley. But there's no mistaking the real trade here. Even now, in late morning, there are still girls in the street, although most are simply returning from their evenings out on call. They come from all provinces, and nearly every country as well—there are even "saltwater sisters" catering to Shanghai's shifting tides of foreign sailors. Taken together, though, the whores' worn faces and weary walks strike a startling chord of familiarity—and revulsion. Listening to an exchange she herself has had a hundred times, Yuliang finds herself fighting back a wave of panic:

"Good night, Ling Ma?"

"Ah, not so good, not so good!"

"Eat well, at least?"

"Ha! No time for food with an old dog like him!"

There's an inexplicable fear that at any moment one of the women will spot her and, if not actually recognize her, see some unseen aura or subtle clue of what she was. *Good night?* they will ask her. *How's your tax man holding up? How much jewelry, how many dresses has he bought you?*

I can't do it, she thinks as the faded flowers part ways. *I don't know why I'm here.*

And in truth the trip was less plan than impulse, a wild, sudden hope that if she found Jinling's first hall, she might also find some lingering remnant—a calendar portrait, a cameo cutout. A picture from some other lover's locket. Now, though, the idea strikes her as foolish. For what on earth would be left to find? Everyone knows what happens after a flower dies or leaves: her belongings are sold, stolen, or burned. And while madams may call their workers "daughters," the term is legal, not sentimental. They'd certainly never hold on to a keepsake of a flower who'd fled.

As with most tasks she sets for herself, though—and as with most boars—Yuliang can't bring herself to simply give up. So when the runner stops the rickshaw in front of a row of green-painted shutters, she doesn't say *Take me home*. Instead, she gives him the name of the flower house Jinling had said she got her start in: "Do you know the Hall of Heavenly Gates?"

"Never heard of it," he says. "And I would have—I've connections with most houses here. I direct many a gentleman to their gates." He scans the street thoughtfully before nodding toward the biggest establishment in sight. "You might try there."

He says it respectfully, without a hint of suspicion or implication. As he gallops off, Yuliang stares after him a moment, slightly ashamed of her own lingering demons.

The house he'd indicated has walls covered with climbing geraniums. A swinging sign pronounces it the Palace of Eternal Joy and Pleasure. Except for the Sikh guard in the doorway, it seems deserted. But as Yuliang approaches, she sees two women on the other side of the street hurrying toward the same building. One, burdened with parasol, purse, and some greasy-looking packages (banquet leftovers, Yuliang guesses) is clearly a servant. The other's profession is easily identifiable by her uniform: a tight yellow dress, Western style, that reveals half her bosom through the white fur coiled limply around her shoulders. "For the love of heaven, Meimei," she calls, looking back at the maid, "hurry up, will you? I could die, I'm so tired!"

Yuliang squares her shoulders. "Pardon my rudeness," she calls, quickly crossing the street. She has to call twice before the girl turns around.

"Are you talking to me?" The prostitute speaks with the coveted sibilance of a Souzhou native. But her eyes belie her voice's softness.

Yuliang swallows. "Yes," she says. "I must speak to you."

The girl signals her maid to stop. "Is this about your husband?"

"What?" Yuliang stops short.

"Some advice for you, elder sister." The woman is already turning away. "You want him, work for him. Keep him happy and he'll stop straying. But either way, leave me out of it."

She starts for the door again, maid scurrying behind. Yuliang stares after her blankly. For an instant she actually tries to picture Zanhua with this tart-mouthed beauty. Then she shakes herself. Of course the girl would assume that. As she's already noted, Yuliang is obviously no whore. The clear alternative is that she's an angry wife.

"No," she says, more loudly than she intends. "I'm here because I'm looking for someone else. A girl."

"We don't do that." The girl sniffs, unwinding her stole. "There's only one place in Shanghai that does. Madame Lou's, on Rue du Père Froc. You'll never get past the guards, though. White devil women only."

"No, no, not like that," Yuliang says hastily, not even allowing herself to blink at this startling information. "A girl I knew. Know. I—my sister." She steps closer, fabricating as fast as she can and praying that she sounds compelling. "We were separated as children. Our father sold her here. Now he's dead—drowned. In the river . . ."

The girl heaves a bored sigh. Yuliang, sensing a gate closing, holds out both her hands. "Please. My—our mother is very sick. She must see her before she dies, to apologize. She sent me to find her. She said she'd been sold to the Hall of Heavenly Gates . . ."

It sounds patently untrue, even to her own ears. But at the broth-el's name the girl looks up, her pink tongue touching her lips. To Yuliang's amazement, she breaks into a peal of laughter. The maid, who has now caught up, joins in with a small titter until her mistress whirls on her fiercely. "Don't laugh at the lady," she barks. "Have you no feelings? Her mother's dying!"

She turns back to Yuliang. "Hall of Heavenly Gates, you say? Unless your sister's a ghost, it's not possible." She wearily pulls out a hatpin. "There was once a place like that further down, near Nanlu Lane." Carelessly, she places her bonnet on the maid's precarious pile. "But it fell into ruin long ago. While the empress dowager still reigned." Seeing Yuliang's shoulders slump, she adds, not unkindly, "Tell me more. Where are you and your sister from?"

"We were born in Hefei. Though I've heard rumors she left here for Wuhu."

"Wuhu!" The girl wrinkles her nose, as though the mere name releases a provincial stink. "Why don't you go there, then?"

"I—I did. They told me she'd disappeared. I thought maybe she came back here . . ." She breaks off again, certain that she sounds as foolish as she feels. When she looks up the Suzhou beauty is yawning so widely Yuliang can see straight through to the back of her throat. "Her name was Yuhai," she finishes quickly, fighting the urge to step back. "Zhou Yuhai." She can only hope that this is right. Jinling had several versions of her origins, and several family names that went with them.

"Traits? Skills?"

"She sang and danced and played *pipa*. She had lily feet, many dresses. In Wuhu she was famous for her jewelry."

The girl shrugs. "She didn't work with us, anyway. Our men go for modern girls." She tosses the fur to her servant. "You could try one of the smaller residence houses down that way. A lot of the Anhui girls end up there." And in the same breath, neither changing her tone nor addressing anyone in particular, she adds, "I must go to bed this very instant."

And with that, she is gone. The maidservant follows once more. She hands the greasy leftovers to the guard as she slouches through the doorway. The latter grins, then slaps her backside in thanks.

YULIANG SPENDS THE NEXT TWO HOURS combing the smaller brothels and teahouses. Remembering that brothel life hides a soft and sisterly belly, she directs most of her questions to the girls: the younger maids, the little servants. She pleads with kitchen help, with "leaves" hanging laundry in the back courtyards as she and Suyin once did. She reweaves her story until all its holes and gaps are covered, and it flows as smoothly as a sad ballad. Oddly, with each retelling the tale also feels more true, until by noon she almost feels it might just happen: if she finds the right person and strikes just the right note, she actually might find Jinling again. Here, whole. Singing out in her giggling voice, "Yuliang! Where on earth have you been?"

Still, at the first six houses she learns nothing new, apart from confirming that the Hall of Heavenly Gates hasn't existed for many decades. Her questions are met with universal headshakes and shrugs, except when one bitter-looking madam answers her fabrication with her own malicious lie ("She was here, yes. But she died of Guangzhou sickness. Very sad!").

It's well past noon—and well into the formal start of the day at most brothels—when Yuliang reaches the third-to-last establishment on the Lane of Lingering Happiness. A tiny, tumbledown house, it declares itself the Palace of Shining Opulence despite several broken shutters and a balcony that sags. So ramshackle is its appearance, in fact, that Yuliang almost passes it by. But the servant Yuliang calls to returns her greeting willingly enough.

"I'm sorry, auntie," Yuliang says, picking her way over crumpled, yellowing call-cards and cigarettes. The courtyard looks ancient, as if no one has been through in weeks. Upon closer inspection, the servant proves older as well: her hair is ink-black, but her face is deeply carved with wrinkles. Her complexion is a strange and almost opalescent pearlish color, the legacy of years of skin-stripping whitening treatments. But she listens as Yuliang rattles off her story one last time. "Beautiful Moon," she says, thoughtfully scratching her scalp. "I know that name. Let me think. She was a young one, wasn't she?"

Yuliang's heart leaps. "Yes," she says, trying to calculate how old Jinling must have been when she left Shanghai. At the Hall, of course, she was always sixteen. But Suyin, who always knew these things, claimed that she was twenty-four the year Yuliang arrived.

"I might have known her," the woman is musing. "I might have. But it takes something to jolt an old memory like mine." She stares pointedly at Yuliang's little silver purse.

Yuliang hesitates. If she succumbs to bribery, she'll have to walk home—something still not easy on her healing feet. Moreover, this woman and her shambling "palace" unsettle her. Yuliang wavers a moment, fingering her purse's snap. The woman shuffles her tiny feet. "Well, missy?" she croaks.

Yuliang snaps her purse open and extracts her coins. She hands them to the woman, who holds each to the light before tucking it into her pocket. "Crooked teeth. Big lanternlike eyes," she says cheerfully. "Feet not quite right—a shade too wide. In my day they called them 'silk with linen sides.' " She eyes Yuliang's feet sternly. But her disapproval is lost in Yuliang's burst of excitement: she has just described Jinling's feet to perfection.

"And something on her leg," she goes on. "A black mark. This big, wasn't it?" She holds up her hand, forefinger and thumb making a crabbed circle approximately the size of Jinling's mole. "Like a big black eye, guarding the jade gates."

"Yes," Yuliang whispers, blinking back the tears that suddenly smart against her eyelids.

"We called her Little Black Moon for that circle," the woman says, nodding. "How she hated it."

"The name?"

"The mark."

Yuliang frowns. Jinling had always said her mole was lucky. "Oh, yes." The woman chuckles. "The girls were always catching her stealing tooth powder and skin whiteners. She wanted to bleach it away."

The idea of Jinling stealing anything is as beyond Yuliang as the idea of her working in this grimy place at all. Still, the woman's description connects with something. She steps closer, ignoring the sharp whiff of rotting teeth. "Please, auntie," she says. "Are there photographs of her here? Pictures? Did anyone paint her portrait?"

The woman peers at Yuliang for a moment, as though gauging whether she is serious. Then she laughs, a coughlike fit that weakens her enough to lean against her broomstick. "Photographs!" she says at last. "Who under heaven would want to photograph *her!* Even if I allowed them here. And mind you, I don't. Those foreign-devil fire boxes snatch the soul straight from your body." She taps Yuliang on the sternum, as though reprimanding her for a bad joke. "But even if I did, why spend the money? She was barely a slave girl here. She's half river-dweller, you know. Sometimes a gentleman would take her if the others weren't available. But I'll guarantee you, none would think to *photograph* her."

"You must be mistaken," Yuliang says when she finds her voice again. "Jinling—I mean, Yuhai was top girl. She was the most requested of all the flowers in Wuhu. She had dozens of dresses and jewels. She was wooed by a prince. The *Crystal* followed her every move."

"Wuhu?" The woman scratches her head again. "Is that where she went? I always wondered. Didn't bother tracking her down, though. Wasn't worth it." She turns back to her sweeping. "I suppose that makes sense. Wuhu. Yes, that would."

"Why?"

"Why, she was with child when she left here," the old woman says, as though this were common knowledge. "Obviously Cook couldn't keep her in the kitchen. And the girls all thought she'd done it on purpose, to try to steal herself a husband." She squints, as though trying to see the memory more clearly. "Xiumei was the angriest. Her best customer was a Wuhu merchant. She told Black Moon to stay away—even whipped her once, if I recall. But she always said that Black Moon made eyes at him. I never believed it myself. But perhaps I was wrong. She probably stole those dresses you talk of too." She sighs. "Poor Xiumei." She surveys the little courtyard again before lifting her eyes to the balcony. "You haven't told me what you think of our banner," she adds reprovingly.

Yuliang follows her gaze to a tattered yellow triangle hanging limply from the second story. Barely discernible on it is the five-toed blue dragon of the Qing Empire. "Dug it up from the pantry yesterday," the old woman says proudly. "As soon as I heard the good news. I always said this New Republic nonsense wouldn't last. Maybe now they'll stop these wretched inspections." Leaning her broom against a tree, she nods to Yuliang. "Well, they'll sleep all day if I don't wake them."

As she turns away, Yuliang steps after her quickly. "Wait! Can—can I speak to Xiumei? Or the cook?"

The woman keeps hobbling, shaking her head. "Cook's dumb as a log. The societies cut out his tongue a few years back. And Xiumei . . ." She shakes her head again. "She died two years ago. Went out one night, turned up the next morning, her throat cut neat as you like. They're careless with themselves, these girls. Not like *we* were."

She shrugs dispassionately. A moment later Yuliang hears her, voice dry as bark, threatening her sleepy flowers to their feet.

It's several moments more before Yuliang can pry her feet from the ground. Slowly, painfully, she forces them to walk.

With child. A river-dweller. Barely a slave girl. She's always known that Jinling embellished things. But was everything she'd said—to Yuliang, her acolyte, her sister of the soul—was every single thing she said untrue?

"Hai!" someone behind her grumbles, practically right in her ear. "Are you a horse, that you sleep standing up?"

Looking down, Yuliang sees that she's stepped into the gutter. But she doesn't step out of it. Staring down at the mud, she pictures Jinling at her elegant toilette. She sees her tasting her pearl paste and grimacing: *More sugar, Yuliang!* She feels Jinling taking her hand after a particularly rough night: *Listen, Yuliang. I want to tell you something I learned in Shanghai. Listen, Yuliang. You're different from them—from all of them. You're like me. You were not meant for this place* . . . Was she lying then as well? And where *did* she get it all—her finery, her fancy stories? Were they stolen, as the old woman had said? Well, why wouldn't they be? After all, the top girl clearly had stolen her own past. And in the end she robbed Yuliang too, of the one beautiful truth she'd had in that harsh world. And of the chance to comfort someone who surely needed comforting, too. *She could have told me,* Yuliang thinks. *She could have cried to me about her losses, her wounds. . . . her child . . .*

People keep pushing past her. "Are you all right, miss?" someone asks. Yuliang doesn't answer. Nausea sweeps her, a bile-green flood.

They lie. And then they leave.

And then she is retching into the gutter, watching, helplessly, as everything within her joins the flowing refuse of the Lane of Lingering Happiness.

Twenty-one

Puyi's second reign lasts less than two full weeks, until another warlord ingloriously pulls him from his throne. Across China's northern borders another monarchy has been toppled too; Yuliang now puzzles over character combinations barely older than the developments in Russia (*Bolshevik, Kremlin*). She is walking slowly home one day, *Shenbao* in hand, when she's stopped by a sudden strain of foreign music. It is nothing like the reedy warblings from the neighbor's Victrola; these are sweeping orchestrations, a sobbing soprano. Almost unconsciously, she follows the sounds to their origin, a nearby open window.

The room inside is almost unfathomably messy. Chairs and table are littered with scraps of paper and paint-stained rags. Jars of murky liquid and brushes abound. Canvases lean haphazardly against every vertical surface, dazzling her after the day's grayness: jewel-toned oils, swirling fruits. Impossibly vivid stars and flowers. Less images than riotous dreams in paint. Yuliang is so absorbed by them that at first she barely notices the two men in the back of the room. It's only after she blinks a few more times that she sees it's not two men at all, but one. He is studying himself in an enormous mirror.

Humming along with the music, the man draws a huge black cross on a small sheet of paper clipped to his easel. He deftly sketches a figure in each of the four resulting squares, adding shade and depth with quick, skilled strokes. In an astonishingly brief time he's created four figures, each a perfect rendition of himself.

The whole process takes perhaps five minutes. But it's the most timeless five minutes Yuliang has ever experienced. Watching this man re-create himself—out of nothing, out of coal—she has no sense of the impropriety of the situation. There is, rather, a strange and giddy emotion that's part recognition, part elation.

She leans further into the window frame. She doesn't want to miss a single stroke.

The man squeezes a dollop of paint onto a wooden tray, which he lifts expertly in his left hand. He works the paint with a flat knife. Then, touching brush to palette, he quickly begins to create. To Yuliang's faint disappointment, he uses not the brilliant spectrum of his other paintings but a muted brown. Still, she follows breathlessly, concentrating so hard that after a while her eyes actually begin to ache, and she pauses reluctantly to rub them.

When she looks up again, the man is gazing at her in his mirror. "You must be tired by now," he says. And, when Yuliang jumps back, "Oh, please. Don't scurry off again."

Again?

It is only as he swivels his stool around to face her that it all falls into place: she *has* seen him before. He was teaching the tall *New Youth* illustrator she's just met, Xing Xudun, and all those other students that day on the Bund. Yuliang flushes as red as a cherry.

"I believe I owe you an apology," the man says. "I'm afraid my boys can get unruly."

"No," Yuliang stammers, "I'm the one who is sorry. I really didn't mean to stare. That day. I mean—now."

Mortified, she stops. The soprano's voice soars. He waves. "Verdi. Lovely, isn't it? I find it very conducive to concentrating. In part, I'm afraid, because my Italian is so poor. I don't get distracted by the lyrics." He looks at his wristwatch. "But it's been nearly an hour. Your legs must be tired. Why don't you come in for a break?"

An hour? She had no idea so much time has passed. "Oh, no," she says. "I couldn't . . . I really should be on my way home."

He indicates his painting. "Well, at least give me your opinion."

At first she's unsure she's heard correctly. "My opinion?"

"I hope no one would study any work that closely, let alone mine, without forming some thought or idea." He taps his fingers together, waiting, his expression faintly amused. As though they are old friends. As though he's honestly interested.

"I think," she says carefully, finally, "it's the best Western-style painting I've ever seen up close." Which is true: before today, she's never seen one up close. "Except . . ." Yuliang bites her lip. She's uncertain how to proceed without seeming unspeakably disrespectful.

"Perhaps," he prods, "you question the perspective. Did you like one of the other studies more?"

"No," she says, with an ease that surprises her. "That one was the most natural. There's less empty space in the background."

He removes his spectacles, polishing them with his spattered apron. "And this, you believe, is a good thing."

Yuliang nods. "If there's too much space, then the eye gets confused. The viewer doesn't know where to look."

"Ah. A fellow artist."

Yuliang blushes. "I scribble. I'm not any good yet."

"Few of us are qualified to assess our own skills," he says sternly, redonning his glasses. "But I apologize—you still haven't told me what your question was."

"I just wonder why you use that color. Why do the whole painting in brown? Surely it would be more realistic to paint the picture in something other than . . . than mud?"

Mud? Immediately she wants to clap the word back into her mouth. But the man just nods. "Excellent question. You haven't had much exposure to oil work. Am I right?" Yuliang shakes her head. "There's no shame in that, of course," he continues. "Very few have yet. At least, not here. The thing is, oil painting works quite differently from water-based painting. Rather than leaving the canvas or paper blank, one covers every inch of it with paint. Some of us like to block out the shapes and shades beforehand."

He holds up the paint tube he used. "A neutral tone is best. Like this one. Which is not mud, but"—he squints at the tube's tiny label—"burnt sienna. After Sienna." He pauses, staring ruminatively at the ceiling as the music swells in the background. "Sienna. Lovely city. Have you been?" Yuliang shakes her head, faintly flattered he'd assume she'd even know where Sienna was (which, in fact, she does not). "This underpainting serves two purposes," he continues. "First as a buffer. Then as a blueprint. Not only does paint take to paint better than to linen or pasteboard—we all express ourselves most naturally with our own kind, don't we?— but it gives one a map. The truth, miss, is that paintings are a bit like dogs. Give them too long a leash and they end up walking you." He grins. "That's good, isn't it? I must remember it for my next lecture." He jots something on the corner of one of his sketches. "But it's rude of me to babble on about myself and my dreary work. I still don't know about you. Apart, that is, from your apparent interest in *plein air* art outings."

Yuliang flushes again. "I'm afraid I acted unforgivably that day. I—I wasn't feeling very well . . ."

His eyes twinkle. "I might forgive you if you tell me your name."

"I am Pan Yuliang. A wife of Pan Zanhua. I live just around the corner."

He bows slightly. "And I am Hong Ye, a painter of little or no consequence in this huge city." He smiles broadly, and though there's nothing insinuating at all in the expression, the situation's impropriety rushes back to her. And yet his gaze, as he sits down again, remains so matter-of-fact and friendly that Yuliang can't help but return it. This, she suddenly senses, is a man who wouldn't blink at the fact that she recently spent an hour simply staring at the Japanese maple in her courtyard. Or that she sometimes spends her allowance on expensive magazines from the French Concession, just to copy the doe-eyed models on to her sketchpad.

Yuliang hasn't told these things to anyone—not even Zanhua. For all his encouragement of her drawing, she's still afraid he'd think it odd. A waste of her time. But this man, this complete stranger: *he* would understand.

What was it he'd said? *We all express ourselves most naturally with our own kind.*

She touches a hand to her cheek. "I—I should go now."

Teacher Hong eyes her mildly. "It was a pleasure. Please feel free to come again."

"Oh no, I shouldn't impose," she says, though what she's thinking is: *When?* She wants to shout it over the soaring music. *When can I come back?*

Instead, of course, she bows politely, murmuring, "Thank you so much for your kindness," before hurrying off toward her street. Leaving Verdi, whoever she is, to sing sadly in her wake.

TWO WEEKS LATER Ahying appears in the study, drying her chapped hands on her pants. "Madame, a gentleman has come to see you."

Yuliang looks up from her sketchbook, surprised: apart from the occasional jewelry or fabric vendor, the only "gentleman" who visits her is Qihua. But he checked in on her just two days ago. "Who is it?"

Ahying shakes her head. "An older gentleman. With a funny hat."

Yuliang frowns.

"Like a blackened pancake, sitting on his head," the girl adds helpfully. "Shall I show him in?"

Yuliang hesitates, then puts her charcoal down. For all she knows, it might be one of Qihua's friends. Or a courier from the Shanghai Customs Office—they were the ones who arrived with word that Zanhua's last visit was postponed. "I'll meet him in the courtyard. Please offer him some tea."

A few moments later, apron off, she steps into the courtyard—

and freezes. Her guest, who sits with his legs crossed on the court-yard's one small stone bench, sipping tea, is none other than Teacher Hong.

The artist wears baggy trousers such as construction workers wear, although they're spattered with paint instead of dust. These he's paired with a blue work shirt like the ones Yuliang has seen on French foreign nationals. On his head, looking as though it might slide off at any moment, is the black beret he'd worn on the Bund.

"Good morning," he says cheerfully, lowering his cup. "I trust I don't arrive at a bad moment."

"I wasn't doing anything important."

"Work isn't important?"

Yuliang stares at him. Hong Ye grins. "Charcoal on your forehead."

"Oh," she says, and pats her brow helplessly. "It's very kind of you to visit."

"Not at all. I'm enjoying your very fine tea."

"Oh, it's nothing, really. My husband buys it from Hangzhou."

"He's not here now, I gather." Yuliang shakes her head, uncertain as to how much to elaborate. Ocean Street, like most old neigh-borhoods, is an open harbor of information, filled with whispered cross-currents of other people's business. The last thing she wants, for Zanhua's sake, is more scandal.

Seeming to sense this, Teacher Hong clears his throat. "Autumn," he announces, "is my favorite season. Easier to work once the fans are set aside and the humidity lifts. Don't you think?"

Yuliang nods. "I do hope my rudeness the other day didn't inter-fere very much with your work."

Teacher Hong shakes his head. "Art is a lonely profession. In fact, it was your visit that encouraged me to intrude upon you at this early hour." Setting his cup down, he reaches for the canvas she's only just noticed leaning against his seat. "Words don't paint a picture, as they say. I thought it might be helpful to illustrate a few of my points."

He turns the canvas toward her, and she finds herself looking at the portrait he'd been working on in his studio. At least, she assumes it's the same one. For the work is very different now. The painted Hong Ye has been infused with color, fleshed out with brilliance and depth. His trimmed beard and mustache glisten with gray and silver. The eyes that peer through the glinting lenses (*How,* Yuliang wonders, *does one do that—paint what one barely sees?*) look just as they do now: sympathetic, warm with interest. As she stares into them, a strange feeling washes through her. It's a little like longing. A little, too, like love. But not the kind of love the poets write of. It's more a fierce yearning to *be* this man, to inhabit his weathered skin. She'd give anything, anything at all, to be able to paint like he does.

"You see," he is saying, "the sienna undertones do nothing to dampen the brightness. They merely give the image depth." He looks up at her. "I take it you approve?"

"Is it dry? Can I touch it?" After she says it, the request strikes her as outrageously intimate. Like asking to run her hands through his hair.

But Teacher Hong simply nods. "That's part of the appeal of oils, isn't it? Texture. So much richer and more interesting than water-based paints. The first time I saw Monet's *Japanese Bridge*, I found myself reaching toward it as a boy reaches for candy." He chuckles. "The guards almost wrestled me from the room."

He waves her closer. Yuliang, too intrigued to bother asking who *Mo-nay* is, cautiously traces his brush's lines with her fingertips. At first glance the paint seemed almost sculptural—thick and layered. Following shifts in light and shape with her fingertips, however, she realizes it's less the physical dimensions of the paint itself than its color that throws the image into relief.

"It's my belief," Teacher Hong says as she explores, "that brushwork is the key aspect of painting. Principal Liu from *l'école* where I teach agrees. You know of him?"

Yuliang nods, although in truth she knows only what she can make out in the newspapers, or hears from Ahying and the scandalized grandmothers on the street. "Isn't he the one who's been paying the models . . ." She drifts off, faintly embarrassed.

"To undress, yes," he says pleasantly. "One editorial last week also called him a 'traitor to art.' He liked the title so much he's had it carved into a chop. He signs all his documents with it now." He turns back to the painting. "But as I was saying, brushwork is the foundation of any good painting. Many of these Western artists have impressive perspective and color schemes but little grasp of how crucial the actual application is." He strokes his upper lip contemplatively. "It's really much as in embroidery. Your strokes are the stitches. Without them, everything falls to pieces."

Yuliang looks up, struck by this unexpected reference to her first and most familiar form of art. For all of Zanhua's teachings on fate, it seems almost like a sign. It may even be what prompts her to ask what she asks next, since she certainly had no intention of asking it:

"Teacher Hong. It's very forward of me . . . but may I show you something?"

FINGER TO LIPS ONCE MORE, the gentle-faced artist contemplates Yuliang's latest sketch—a bowl of chrysanthemums, inspired in part (though of course he doesn't know it) by Hong Ye's own brilliant florals. Outside, Ahying is beating a rug. To distract herself from her clamoring nerves, Yuliang counts the blows: *one, two, three* . . . At *twenty-seven* she finds herself mildly irritated: does it really take so much beating to get such a small rug clean?

After what seems days, Hong Ye finally turns to her. "You have further pieces," he says. An assertion, not a question.

Obediently, Yuliang retrieves her sketchbook from behind Zou Rong's *Revolutionary Army* in the bookcase, then watches as Teacher Hong leafs through the images. His face is impassive. But he taps some of them decisively, much as he'd tapped the study of himself he finally chose to paint. He spends several moments on the image of a little doll which she'd found lying abandoned on the street. "Disturbing," he notes.

Yuliang drops her eyes, uncertain whether this is praise or condemnation.

"Do you have a tutor?" And when she shakes her head: "Not in a formal manner, you mean."

"Not at all. My mother taught me some embroidery. Sometimes we'd sketch patterns together, to decide designs. And my husband has worked with me on calligraphy. But this"—she waves at the chrysanthemums, the coal-dusted book—"this I've done on my own."

Another short silence. "And your esteemed husband encourages this?"

"Yes. But . . ." Yuliang hesitates. "He's afraid it will detract from my other studies."

HongYe's lips lift into a brief, grave smile. "I hear this frequently. Although not often from women, I must say. Your husband must be an unusual man."

If he's aware of her anxiety, he doesn't reveal it. He sighs, removes his spectacles again, probes an ear with an earpiece. "What I'm going to say," he begins at last, "isn't something I say easily, or often. By no means take it as an excuse to fall back from your work."

Yuliang holds her breath, barely daring to move.

"Only a few times in my career," Teacher Hong continues, "have I seen someone so unformed show such promise. I might add that my career has been long and has taken me many places. Japan, Italy, France . . . Happily, though, talent knows no nationality."

"You—you like them," Yuliang interrupts, barely trusting her ears.

He nods. "The images are simple. The perspective is often off. More disturbing is the intense romanticism here. Some are so feminine it's almost intrusive. As a woman artist, you'll want to guard against that. Let the art speak for itself."

For some reason his use of *woman*—or perhaps the way he emphasizes it over *artist*—annoys her slightly. "It doesn't now?"

"The little doll adds a nicely jarring note," he concedes. He resettles his glasses on his nose. "But true art must contain an emotional range that speaks to the viewer. Speaks—and I know many of our traditional masters wouldn't agree—not by lulling them into a false sense of complacency, but by probing. Challenging. Even hurting, if need be. Anything to force us beyond life's easier thoughts. I believe you will learn this with us in coming days."

"With—with *us*?"

The hope in her voice is so raw he must hear it too. But he just smiles. "What would you say to standing for the academy's entrance exams in January?"

Yuliang's hands fly to her throat. *"What?"*

He nods, the action sending his beret slipping slightly back on his head. He slaps it absently back into place. "I should warn you, we haven't had many women yet. Actually, just one who stayed the full two-year term. But my sense is that you could hold your own with our young men." Seeing her expression, he quickly qualifies: "I mean only that I have sensed in you, almost from the start, a certain . . . shall we say strength? You trust your instincts. You aren't afraid to stand up for yourself. You don't let paltry boundaries of custom or etiquette stand in the way of self-expression. May I ask what year you were born?"

Yuliang blinks again. "The year of the boar."

He nods. "Interesting. I'd have said sheep."

But Yuliang is still processing the first astonishing part of Hong Ye's pronouncement. "You want *me*," she says slowly, "to enter the Shanghai Art Academy."

He holds up a finger. "I want you to stand for the academy examination. Our school is selective. Particularly when it comes to women artists."

Again the emphasis is on *women*. Even so, it's as though the room has turned to pure gold. Yuliang sees herself: an academy student! Sitting with *plein air* sketchers on the Bund. Striding through the school's French doors, sketchbook under her arm . . . Then her gaze falls to the bookshelf behind him, filled with books Zanhua has given or sent her. Yuliang drops her head. "I'm overwhelmed," she says slowly, "by the honor you are offering me. But I'm—I'm afraid I'll have to ask my husband first."

"He seems a modern-thinking man, from the way you describe him."

"Oh, he is. He's been very, very kind. He—he just wants me to focus on my learning. Some art, perhaps. But mostly useful things—history, politics. The classics." She smiles wryly. "He trusts words over pretty pictures."

Teacher Hong digests this for a moment. "I'm sorry to inquire so inelegantly. But your husband—he doesn't live in this household?"

"No," says Yuliang, feeling herself blush yet again. "Well, he does sometimes. But he's posted in Wuhu."

"And might I ask, equally rudely, when he comes next?"

"Just after the New Year." It's an unspoken agreement that Zanhua spends the Chinese New Year, that most important of holidays, with his official family.

Teacher Hong claps his hands. "Well, then. We're in luck. The examinations for the next term were supposed to be next week, but they've now been rescheduled for January twelfth. You can certainly take them without committing to anything. And eight weeks, I believe, is time enough for me to help you prepare." He looks up at the ceiling. "I'd suggest three study sessions with me weekly, between now and then. Monday, Wednesday, and Friday evenings work well with my schedule."

He doesn't understand, she thinks. "Sir," she says breathlessly. "I'm sorry, but perhaps I haven't explained myself. I'm not at all sure I can even go to the school. It's—it's not just the art." She hesitates; it's bad form to discuss the family finances in public. But she blunders on. "There's the issue of money too. Not that we're poor. But I'm just not sure—you see, he has three households to maintain already."

Teacher Hong stands up, tucking his cravat into his padded jacket. "My dear, one of the first things you must learn, if you are to enter this terrible field, is to ration out your anxieties—and there will be many—to where they're truly needed. It isn't yet a question of paying or even going to the school. For the next two months it's a question of creating opportunity." Standing, he sets the sketchbook down on Yuliang's little desk. "Happily, Education Minister Cai is a great friend of the arts. If you are accepted—*if*—I believe there is some scholarship money left. If that is the case—and again, *if* you gain entrance—why, then we can worry about the rest."

"The rest?" Yuliang asks faintly.

He winks. "How best to approach the esteemed Master Pan."

Twenty-two

"Y ou will," Teacher Hong announces, "refrain from picking up your pencil until I give the order."

He frowns at the crammed but silent classroom, briefly meeting Yuliang's eye. Embarrassed, she looks away. "The examination will run for exactly two hours. Any scribbling beyond that will disqualify the offending applicant. Am I understood?"

A chorus of voices, seventy strong and overwhelmingly male, shouts back, "Yes, teacher!"

"Good." Stepping around the young men who sit cross-legged on the floor (there aren't enough seats for all the applicants), he picks up a large hourglass from the windowsill. "Three . . . Two . . . One . . . *begin.*"

The air fills with the tap of pencils hitting paper. Yuliang stares down at her blank page, her mouth as dry as the sand trickling lazily through the timepiece. *I can't do this,* she thinks miserably. *What under the heavens was I thinking?*

She finds herself surreptitiously studying the other applicants in the room: slick-haired boys, a haughty handful of well-dressed girls. They're all rich—she can tell. And of course this makes sense. For while a poor family might spare a son for scholarship, who'd spare one for something as frivolous as Western painting? And what poor family would send their daughter to school to start with?

"It's all *shit*."

Abruptly her deskmate flings down his pencil and crumples his first attempt. The room chuckles, but Yuliang feels a ray of gratitude: at least she's not the only one facing an empty page.

Sighing again, she turns her gaze back to the still life. *Don't think of it as a whole at first*, Teacher Hong told her yesterday. *Break it up. Use one object as a road into the next.* But what if all the roads seem blocked?

Her deskmate is now well into his second attempt. His face no longer reflects frustration but intent focus. *Just draw*, she commands herself, fighting back a wave of panic. *Just draw something.*

Obediently, she sketches something: a square. It is an approximation of the red table's surface. The shape isn't quite right. But it's always easier to start over than it is to start from nothing at all.

Tearing off the sheet, she tries again, this time with better results. *Use each object as a road into the next.* She proceeds to the easiest object on the table, the orange . . . And in the space of a moment that neither registers nor matters, she is no longer outside the still life but working within it, running her mind's hand over nubbly fruit skin. Pressing her face against the smooth tang of bottle glass. Exploring a vase's crevices with both finger and pencil tip, each item part of a visual sentence she is translating. It seems a mere five minutes later that Teacher Hong raps his desk and says mildly, "Time." And then more crisply, "*Time*. Pencils down."

A swell of groans. Yuliang has just enough time to scribble her name down the left margin. She hands over her paper, averting her eyes. She's come to realize this about her work: that no matter how she feels while she's sketching, her first sense upon finishing will be one of failure: they all fall so short of her initial hopes for them. She sometimes wonders—particularly since Zanhua's last visit— whether this is the way new mothers feel about their babies, sliding wet and puckered from the womb. Her mother, of course, claimed otherwise. *You?* Yuliang recalls her saying. *You were the prettiest baby in the world.*

Was I really? Yuliang had asked, fascinated—like all small children —by the improbable idea of her own infancy.

Of course, her mama had laughed, moistening sky-blue thread with her tongue.

WHEN SHE REACHES OCEAN STREET Yuliang's mind is still on her test, reexamining each twist and pass of her pencil tip. The cut-glass vase in particular had been hard—all clear corners, reflected shadows. She is undoing her frog buttons, pondering her choice to use her eraser to create glints, when she hears it: a low, unarguably male murmur in the parlor.

Burglars! is her first thought; there has been a rash of gang-related robberies in the neighborhood. Her satchel crashes to the floor. She is just backing toward the door when Zanhua materializes in the hallway. "Where on earth have you been?"

He starts toward her, then stops as a pencil rolls underfoot. Yuliang looks down at her spilled art supplies. "I'm sorry," she stammers, although whether the apology is for the mess or her tardiness she doesn't know. Belatedly, she adds, "You're home."

"Yes," he concurs.

Yuliang swallows. "Your letter said you'd in Tongcheng for the holidays."

"My plans changed." He smiles grimly. "I wanted to surprise you."

"You did," she says weakly. Her heart seems somewhere in the vicinity of her eardrums. "Zanhua, I—"

There's a quick, light tap of additional steps in the hallway. For a petrified moment Yuliang pictures First Lady Pan, here to approve her new subservient fellow wife. Thankfully, though, it's just Qihua. "Ah," he says. "You see. I told you she'd come back. Welcome home, Madame Pan. I trust you had a pleasant afternoon." His gaze drops casually to the floor. "Charcoal," he observes, poking a piece with the tip of his shoe. "What a coincidence. I was just telling your husband of your new pursuits."

"My pursuits?" Yuliang quavers.

"Your private study program at Master Hong's." He grins. "It's been quite the topic among our elderly neighbors."

Yuliang's heart sinks. "I wanted to tell you," she says to Zanhua. "Really. I just—I didn't know how to write it."

"I've no doubt," he interrupts coldly. "Between traipsing around in other men's homes and doodling away the hours, you can't have had much time left for your studies."

"Zanhua," she says, "it's not at all what it seems. I *have* been studying. I've just—" She drifts off under the ferocity of his glare.

Unasked, Qihua begins gathering up her sketches. He hands them, not to her, but to Zanhua. "My congratulations," he says to Yuliang. "I've heard much of your progress."

"Progress?" Yuliang repeats blankly.

"The academy's founder, Liu Haisu, mentioned you last week. We ran into each other at a photography lecture at the French Consul."

"Liu Haisu?"

"It's not often they're faced with a serious woman candidate."

For an instant Yuliang can only gawk. She'd entirely forgotten that Qihua knew the artist, who used to paint photography sets. She turns giddily back to Zanhua. "He knows about me. Liu Haisu knows about me!"

"No doubt the whole city knows about you," Zanhua says, with asperity. "You're paying visits to a man who pays women to strip."

Yuliang's ears sting as though he's boxed them. But she struggles to keep her tone even. "He's been giving me lessons," she says. "Painting and drawing lessons. He thinks I can get in. As a *student*."

"I don't suppose these lessons are chaperoned at all, are they?"

In fact, they are not. To Yuliang's surprise, though, Qihua again comes to her rescue. "To be fair," he says, fishing a pack of 555s from his vest pocket, "anyone who knows Madame Hong couldn't doubt that they've been appropriately supervised. I've dealt with her over her daughter's engagement portrait. The woman is a tigress." He shudders theatrically, strikes a match. "And for what it's worth, the academy is highly respected. Haisu told me they offer courses in anatomy, history, and even political painting."

Zanhua is studying Yuliang's sketches. On top is the little broken doll. For some reason Yuliang wishes it were something else—a bamboo forest. A picture-poem. "This Hong Ye," he says, still not looking up, "he really thinks you have talent."

A tendril of hope—pearl green, vulnerable—unfurls. "More than almost anyone he has seen." She says it not in arrogance, but in desperation.

"And one gets into the school—how?"

"There's—there's an examination."

"And when is this examination?"

She swallows. "This afternoon," she whispers. "Between three and five o'clock."

He stares at her, stunned.

"Zanhua," she says. "I was going to tell you if I got in. I wasn't trying to deceive you. Please—"

But it's too late: with a single motion he crumples the doll sketch and throws it at the wall.

"You had no right to do that," she cries. "That's my *work*!"

"That's a *lie!*" he shouts back, just as furious. "You have lied to me! After all your talk of honesty. *Honesty!*" His laughter is cold, utterly without humor. The step he takes toward her is so quick she actually cowers. But he just kicks the paper ball viciously across the floor before turning and striding toward the door. At the threshold, though, he pauses and turns back. For just the barest of moments, his lips twist into a bitter smile. "And I thought," he says, "I was surprising *you*."

He stalks into the frosted courtyard, his footsteps fading onto the street. Sobbing in frustration, Yuliang hurls her charcoal against the wall. It leaves a dot-dash, a black streak against whitewash. She makes no move to try to clean it off. Instead she kneels, picking up the little drawing and smoothing it against her knee.

Yuliang doesn't weep. But her shoulders heave—his anger, sparked by nothing more than her own cowardice. For he's right—her silence was as good as a falsehood. Why on earth didn't she write to him? Is her distrust still so deep that she can't share her real hopes with him, untainted by shame?

She stares down at the ruined sketch. The doll's blank face is now as wrinkled as an old woman's. Yuliang shreds it into small, smudged bits. She lets them slip between her fingers, like dirty snow.

"Madame Pan." Behind her, Qihua's voice is uncharacteristically stripped of sarcasm. Starting, Yuliang twists toward him. She'd forgotten he was here.

"I'm very sorry," she murmurs, rising to her feet. "I'm behaving shamefully."

"To be honest, so is he." He hands her back her charcoal. Very gently, as though returning a toy to a child. "But I'll talk to him. We artists should stand up for one another."

Yuliang gazes at him in surprise: it is the first time he's addressed her almost as an equal. "He's in the right," she says dully. "I'm a poor excuse for a wife."

"You underestimate both yourself and your husband." Brushing off his hands, Meng Qihua walks unhurriedly to the doorway, pausing to light another cigarette. Looking back at her, he winks. Then, flicking his match into the darkening courtyard, he follows its arcing ember outside.

WHEN ZANHUA RETURNS, it's nearly midnight. Yuliang is hunched in her study, sketching flowers in sputtering gaslight. As he enters the room, the smell of *maotai* drifts in with him like an excuse.

But Zanhua doesn't make any excuses. He moves toward her, his step unsteady, his eyes red with fatigue and drink. He sinks to the floor and hugs his bent legs to his chest, resting his head on his knees.

He remains this way until Yuliang finally goes to him and kneels by him. Touching first his cheek, then his hair. Both are wet. "Is it raining?" she asks.

"Snowing."

Surprised, she looks out the window, something that, in her absorption in her work, she hasn't done for at least an hour. Sure enough, cold flakes tap against the glass. It's not the heavy, gentle snow one expects here, fattened by ever-present moisture and falling with the grace and softness Shanghai itself lacks. This is a vengeful snow. It hurtles in harsh lines and slashes. Somehow, the sight of it disturbs her.

"I didn't mean to deceive you," she tells him. "I was so afraid you wouldn't let me go."

He lifts his head and stares at her for a moment. "I came home this afternoon half believing you'd be gone. And when you were, I feared it was for good."

"Why would you think that?"

"You hadn't answered my letters. Even the telegram I sent two weeks ago went unanswered."

Yuliang drops her eyes guiltily: it's true. In her frantic race toward today's exam, she hasn't written to him in over five weeks. The telegram—one line drawn from one of Li Qingzhao's poems (*Her possessions are here, but her essence is gone: everything has ceased*)—she had placed beneath her pillow, then forgotten. *I'm so selfish,* she thinks—but less with shame than a dawning kind of wonder.

"And then you did come back," he goes on. "But Qihua had already told me how you'd been spending your hours. Perhaps I reacted badly. But the thought of you with another man . . ." His voice cracks. "I'm so afraid you'll leave me."

She just stares at him at first, stunned as always by this fear, so precisely the opposite of her own. *Boar and rat,* she finds herself thinking. *Perfectly matched.*

"I'll never leave you," she tells him. Turning, she picks up the sketch of the flowers. "Please look at this. There's something I want to show you."

He stands, lifting the picture to the dim light. "It's good," he says simply.

"It's not that. Look at the left border. At the name."

"Pan Yuliang," he reads as Yuliang stands and steps behind him.

"Do you remember," she murmurs, her lips right by his ear, "when you told me to sign my work?"

He nods, shutting his eyes.

"I do now. And there you are. You are a part of every picture. Even the ones that take me away from you."

Leaning into her, he traces their name with one, white finger. Then he sets the picture down and, pulling her into his arms, rests his lips on her hair. "Promise me one thing."

"What?"

"Promise you'll always come back."

She parts her lips to answer, but her tongue seems frozen. Instead she drops her face onto his damp shirt. Apparently taking this as a nod, her husband doesn't press her. Lifting her into his arms, he carries her through the doorway. Then up the stairs, and into the darkened bedroom.

Twenty-three

THE DAY THE RESULTS ARE POSTED, Zanhua himself takes her to the academy.

On the drive over, Yuliang looks at her husband just twice. Throughout the holiday they've feasted, shopped. They've bought new clothes for the New Year, dined with friends, played their poetry drinking game (again she beat him). Lovemaking has been frequent, tender. Throughout it all, though, it's felt as though some part of her has been tautly waiting. Now that the moment is here, her nerves feel as brittle as the ice that crunches beneath the horse's clipped hooves.

As they pull up to the academy, Yuliang warily scans the swarm of youth there, chatting, blowing steam and tobacco into the chill. She sees three young men toss their caps in the air. A moment later they're striding past, arms linked, singing a tune popularized by the cinema. "You're certain you don't want me to go look for you?" Zanhua asks as the carriage slows to a stop.

"No." It comes out starkly; chagrined, she takes his arm. "I'm sorry. I just—I think I should do this myself."

"Don't apologize." He pats her elbow. "I felt the same way when

I received Todai's acceptance letter. I all but snatched it from my mother's hand." Sadness shadows his face briefly, as it always does when he speaks of home. Then he brightens. "Anyway, I got this for you." Reaching into his pocket, he pulls out something tiny and green. Taking it in her hand, Yuliang sees that it's a tiny boar carved out of jade. "Your sign," he says. "For good luck."

She looks up. "But you don't believe in luck."

"In times of crisis I do. As long as it's good." He gives her hand a squeeze, then nods toward the waiting bulletin board. "Can I at least come with you?"

She removes his hand from her sleeve gently, shaking her head. Then, taking a deep breath, she steps down from her seat.

For a moment she's back in Zhenjiang, approaching a crowd of fellow passengers on their way to Wuhu. What was it that Wu had said then? *A good woman is not afraid of people* . . . Yuliang sets her jaw. The crowd, seeming to sense her resolve, makes way for her. She soon finds herself at the board's base, facing the list.

The names are posted in no clear order. *Zhang Diwa,* she reads. *Wong Zhihou.* In the rear someone curses: "Fucking sons of slave girls!"

"Bad luck, brother," says someone else. And then: "Bull's balls. I'm not here either."

Yuliang reads on: *Ho Shenwan. Li Renju.* Each name that's not hers is a small weight added to her chest. *Yong Reji. Sen Lishang,* she reads, without blinking.

And the last one: *Yi Leishe.*

Three more boys hoot in victory, "See you in September!"

I must have missed it, Yuliang thinks numbly, and pretends to read the list again.

"Yuliang." Zanhua is standing behind her.

She turns to him. "It's not here."

"It's all right."

"It's not here."

"A mistake," he says, taking her arm. "The principal himself wants you here."

She shakes her head. "He lied." She starts pushing back toward the car. Thinking: *Little idiot. Stupid whore.* The truth is, Zanhua was right in the argument about her candidacy: the whole city must know of her. And who on earth would want a street chicken in their art school?

Blinking back tears, she glances at her husband.

But he has stopped again. "Wait, Yuliang. You dropped . . ." He bends down, stands up. Holds out the little green boar.

Yuliang takes it back, though she's tempted to throw it in the gutter. "Let's go. *Please.*"

The crowd around the announcement board is now clearing, but still Zanhua stands there. And when he does finally start walking, it's not toward the car. It's in the other direction entirely—toward the school's entrance.

"Where are you going?"

"To make inquiries." He strides toward the French doors. Several students look after him, bemused.

Yuliang blinks at them, at their smug, smooth faces, and then hurries after him. "We should just go home. We shouldn't create a stir." And when he continues: "*Zanhua.* That's why we left Wuhu, isn't it? Not to cause a stir?"

He pauses. "No," he says. "We left Wuhu so that we—*you*—would be happy."

And having made this astonishing statement, he turns back toward the doors. At that precise moment, though, they burst open from the inside.

Two men emerge, walking very rapidly. The first is in his sixties and wears a merchant's robe. The other looks young enough to be one of the students, although he's dressed far more elegantly than any of them. Yuliang forms a quick impression: a well-proportioned, amused-seeming face; a strong, square chin; sharp eyes beneath high, well-shaped eyebrows. His voice carries a calm confidence as he shouts after the merchant, who's now heading for a Bentley parked across the street. "The point, Master Chu, is just that. Contrary to your assertions, our school is not a whorehouse. And yes, it would be a most shameful waste of time and money if your son were simply ogling naked women in public. But that is not what he or anyone else at my school is doing."

The older man turns back, incredulous. "Then you're as blind as you are impudent. In case you didn't notice, that girl had no clothes on—none at all! And not only has he been staring at her openly for days at a time, but he's been displaying his pictures of the little chicken to everyone! Including, may I inform you, his future *mother-in-law*!" He signals to the waiting chauffeur to open the car's passenger door. "Or perhaps I should say now his *former* future mother-in-law."

He barks to the driver, who hops to the front to crank the engine. Hands cupped to mouth, the younger man shouts over the loud grinding: "Within our hallowed walls, the human form is sacred. Nudity is that form's most natural, pure state. As an artist, your son has the task—no, I'll say it, the *duty*—of studying it. As a scholar studies the Analects, the Doctrine of the Mean!"

The merchant pokes his face out the window. "Now you compare yourself to Confucius!"

"There is nothing dishonorable in what I'm saying!" Principal Liu retorts. "Western artists have been performing life studies for centuries! In fact, it's not just artists but all people who should strive to appreciate the body. As Robert Henri said, 'When we respect the nude, we will no longer have any shame about it.'"

"At which point," the man barks back, "I'll be leaving China. Along with every respectable person here." As the chauffeur guns the engine, he puts his head out of the window again. "I'll send my steward to discuss the bill. Athough I'm not convinced, Master Liu, that either you or your school deserves a single dog-fuck yuan of my money."

The Bentley leaps forward, nearly hitting an old woman who is passing. Cursing, she fumbles in her pockets and pulls out a small mirror. This she flashes at the retreating vehicle, presumably to deflect evil spirits.

Liu Haisu, for his part, drops his gaze to the ground. He fishes a cigar from his pocket and lights it. A few students hurry up to him with sketches to show, questions to ask. Most, however, have already turned away. Apparently the spectacle is nothing new to them.

Yuliang glances at Zanhua, fully expecting the scene to have weakened his resolve. But he just straightens his hat. "Master Liu!" he calls. "A moment, if I may . . ." And in a few short steps he's joined the small crowd gathered around the artist.

Yuliang watches, stunned, as her husband and Principal Liu fall into conversation. Zanhua's back is to her, his voice low. But she reads the surprise on Principal Liu's face easily enough. "That's very odd, Inspector Pan," she hears him say, and she is struck by how easily his quiet voice carries. "At our last meeting we agreed upon your wife's acceptance." His eyes flick thoughtfully toward Yuliang. His gaze this time is long and leisurely, and not without male inflection. It certainly doesn't leave Yuliang feeling "sacred" or "pure." She makes herself look right back at him, holding his gaze.

Liu Haisu smiles slightly. Then, nodding to Zanhua, he walks slowly over to where she's standing. "Madame Pan. I've heard so much about you. I'm only sorry to meet under these"—he flicks a glance at the board—"unfortunate circumstances."

What she really wants to do is throw herself before him. *Please,* she wants to cry. *Please take me. I'll cause no scandals. I'll work hard. I'll . . .* But even as she pictures doing this, she knows it isn't the solution. She knows Principal Liu. Or at least has known men who are like him. He may revel in scandal, as everyone says. But a weeping woman at his feet would simply bore him.

Instead, on an impulse, Yuliang lifts her chin. "Unfortunate," she says, "for whom?"

Principal Liu blinks. "I'm sorry?"

"Forgive me, but I can't help thinking that my rejection is less unfortunate for me than for your school."

Two young women students, overhearing her, stop in disbelief. One titters, elbowing the other.

Principal Liu, however, is looking at her with renewed interest. "You do," he says.

"I know I'm being forward. But I was so encouraged by all I'd read and heard of you and your famous academy. And impressed by how in the past you've stood up to narrow minds—minds like those of the man who just left. You made it so clear that his mode of thinking is outdated, and that your goals are indeed noble. And modern."

Yuliang can hardly believe herself as she goes on. And yet she stands firm: there is too much at stake. Besides—she's rarely known flattery not to work on large egos. Particularly on large male egos.

"I'm glad to hear it," he says. He is actually beaming. "This school was founded largely for that. Modernity. Art in its truest sense, clothed or unclothed. Male or female."

"So I'd thought. Which is why I'm surprised that when a qualified woman presents herself at your doors, you turn her away. Not on the basis of skill, it seems. But on . . . other things." She hears Zanhua take in his breath sharply. "If I'm not mistaken, I believe you were quoted as saying that women should play a key role in China's art revolution. Just as they should in the social revolution that's to come." As Principal Liu frowns, she clarifies: "The *Shenbao.* Two weeks ago, I believe."

"I may have said that," he says, clearly pleased by this evidence of the weight of his own words. "Although this city's reporters are often even greater fabricators than its painters." He tosses his cigar to the ground. "The truth, though, is that today's results aren't about revolution. They're about history. There are those on my staff who claim that women students are more distraction than boon here. They take criticism badly and drop out the minute they marry or decide to have a baby. In fact, the last one here left for no better reason than that she was upset by the nude models. Even more than the boys were." He snorts. "Which is saying quite a lot."

Yuliang pulls herself up stiffly. "I'm not like that."

He looks at her closely. "Tell me how you're different."

Because, she thinks, *it will take more than a pair of bare breasts or a*

jade gate to make me weep. And because I've seen more nudes, in more posi-
tions and indignities imaginable, than you or your precious boys will see in
their whole lives. Even if they are lucky.

But what she says is simply, "I'm better."

Is she imagining it, or do his eyes take on a keener gleam? "Better than the women who've come before you?"

"Better than most students. Men or women."

It is an indefensible show of arrogance. But as Yuliang watches Liu Haisu react—thinking, looking her over, then finally nodding— she knows again that she has played the moment correctly. Tapping his chin, the principal glances back at the bulletin board, then at the place where the Bentley was parked. "We certainly have space for one more now," he says at last, a little ruefully. "And though I'm younger than many here, I *am* still principal."

"So . . ." Yuliang hardly dares push her luck further. But he still hasn't answered her question. "So I'm in?"

He looks her in the eye, then bows a sweeping, theatrical bow. "You are welcome, Madame Pan, at my poor little school. May you not live to regret it."

Part SIX

The ACADEMY

Renoir is vulgar, Cézanne is shallow, Matisse is inferior.

———

Xu Beihong

Twenty-four

THE WOMEN RECLINE in postures of rest and gossip, bodies gleaming with scented oils and soaps. Yuliang, huddled behind a bath bench, surveys them tensely, a huntress stalking her quarry.

She sizes up the young girl who stands as slimly straight as a sapling, as well as the stooped grandmother scrubbing her skin six shades of pink. She examines the two middle-aged women who chat in the corner, rubbing rough spots on their heels and elbows with rice cloth. One is thin and sinewy. The other's twice as broad. Her thighs, breasts, and belly are textured with accumulated fat. Put together and divided evenly (Yuliang ungenerously thinks), they'd both be of average size and weight. Then there's the girl with the slim wrists and the serious gaze who smiled at Yuliang in the dressing room. She seems young, and has brought a book in with her despite what the steamy air must do to the pages.

Trying to choose just one suddenly seems harder than doing the drawing itself. *Why?* Yuliang wonders, pulling her pencil out from its hiding place. They're all women, after all. So what makes them seem so different? And why does she automatically think of one version as *pretty* and the others *plain* or even *ugly*? And does she—in the end, merely another woman—really have the power to change that perception, with little more than her bare, damp hands?

Liu Haisu clearly thinks so. "It's your job," he told students during his commencement speech for this, Yuliang's second year at the Shanghai Art Academy, "to challenge the assumptions of your viewers. To take a dead flower and show us its hidden life. To take an ugly woman and show us the beauty in her ugliness." He neglected to talk about painting men—presumably because he, like everyone else, seems to think it's somehow even more scandalous to paint them naked than women. At least *for* women. Male-study classes, therefore, are open to male students only. As annoyed by this as Yuliang is (though she can hardly say so in public—they whisper enough about her as it is), she knows that it's not purely an Eastern phenomenon. Caillebotte's *Man at His Bath*, after all, shows just the barest dangle of scrotum, yet was considered so shocking in Belgium that it was first exhibited in its very own closet.

Now, keeping her motions quiet, Yuliang unwraps the rest of her materials from the towel in which she's smuggled them. Then she turns, surveying the women again. The easy thing, of course, would be simply to pick someone randomly and draw her—quickly, accurately, coldly. The way she always draws her nudes. But today she's after more than mere accuracy and form. She's here to capture something Teacher Hong calls *the life force*—which, for all her skill, seems to elude Yuliang in the classroom. Session after session, she has thrown herself into her nude sketches. But while her nudes are anatomically correct, something is missing.

"Stop thinking of them as just skin," Teacher Hong suggested last week, in a turn of phrase that brought Jinling suddenly and stingingly to Yuliang's mind. And Yuliang has tried to stop. And yet even her best nudes seem to come out as just that—skin. Stiff, flat forms, devoid of spirit and life.

The thought of the bathhouse struck last week, when Teacher Hong brought in a sketch to show the room. "I found this in Paris last year," he told them. "Note the lines, both strong and alive. Always remember that it's lines, not detail, that are the key. The great Spaniard Picasso once spent months sketching just one cow. Not embellishing it, mind you, but stripping away. In the end the cow was no more than three or four strokes. But it was far more striking than it would have been were it drawn in the detailed style of, say, the Victorian animal artist Landseer."

"Is this a Picasso?" someone asked.

"Do you think I could afford Picasso? On the dogshit they pay me here?" Teacher Hong retorted. As the chuckles subsided, he added, "No. It's a woman's work. A Valadon. I found it at a little gallery in Montmartre. Was there a question, or were you ladies just exchanging cooking tips?"

He looked pointedly at the two other girls in the classroom, who as usual were whispering together. One of them rolled her eyes. The daughter of a wealthy comprador, she frequently boasts about her Western travels. She also makes pointed comments about "decent women."

"Apologies, teacher," she said now. "But isn't it true that Valadon was a whore?"

"It is true that she is untutored and was once very poor. But these things don't make her a whore."

"Then she was just a pretty woman who used her wiles to seduce her teachers. And salon judges."

Around the room, a chorus of smothered laughter. Yuliang felt eyes dart to her, then back. She has no idea how many here know anything of her past. But it seems clear that rumors about it abound.

The teacher, however, frowned. "On the contrary. In many ways she shows us the truth of Lao Tzu's philosophy: she turned her weaknesses into strength. She used the one asset she could to enter the art world—her beauty. In modeling, she earned the friendship of Toulouse-Lautrec and Degas, who saw past her body to her significant talent. She also worked extremely hard—something some at this school clearly don't put much stock in . . . Madame Pan."

He'd reached Yuliang's desk by this point. Much to her surprise, he put the Valadon squarely before her. "You in particular might benefit from a closer look at this. Go ahead," he prompted as Yuliang hesitated. "Take a good look."

Yuliang looked. The Frenchwoman's charcoal had captured a young girl in a tin tub, half kneeling, as Christians do in prayer. But in this case the pose seemed openly sensual: the curve of the girl's shoulder, the wet tendrils of her hair seemed to beckon the viewer to come closer, to touch her. Tracing the strong lines with her finger, Yuliang realized Teacher Hong was right. The portrait's strength wasn't its physical accuracy; it was something more elusive. The way the artist had created not a picture, but a girl. A girl utterly unaware of her portraitist or viewers.

A girl simply . . . taking a bath.

"You'll have to lift your head. I'll never get this horse's mane clean otherwise."

The girl obeys, squeezing her eyes shut as the grandmother ladles water over her head. The liquid transforms the hair into a shining sheet of black, reaching smoothly to the backs of the young woman's knees. She waits quietly through the subsequent lather and rinse, one hand draped over her bare breasts.

Watching from her hiding spot, Yuliang feels her breath catch. It's not just that the girl is lovely, or that her slender shoulders remind one of Jinling. It's that as a subject, she is perfect. Perfect. Her skin is smooth, her pose natural and youthfully assured. She's like Botticelli's *Birth of Venus*. In a bathhouse.

The sketchbook paper is now pulpy with steam. Still, Yuliang draws quickly, her lines as simple and firm as they are in her calligraphy. She works for perhaps a half-hour, oblivious of the women's chatter and banter, eventually even of her own location, so that when water splashes her pad she ignores it at first.

Then another drop falls, and another. She finally looks up to see that a muscular woman with deep frown lines is standing over her.

"Hey!" the woman says loudly. "What the hell do you think you're doing?"

Behind her, the chatter stops abruptly. "What is it, sister?" someone asks.

"This steaming ox vagina is drawing us, is what!" the woman retorts. "Naked!"

Pulling Yuliang up roughly by her arm, she snatches the sketchbook away. The other women clamber from their baths. "Where?" they cry. "Who is it?"

"Here!" The woman thrusts the sketchbook forward, tightening her grip on Yuliang's arm with the other hand. "She was probably planning to sell it down the block."

Yuliang tries to shake herself free. "I wasn't—" she starts. She doesn't get further before the women congregate around her. With their bath brushes and prunelike fingers, they point and scrabble. "Take her towel!" shrieks one. "She's probably a man in disguise!"

"Or a white ant," hisses the grandmother, thrusting her pretty granddaughter behind her. "That's how it starts. Dirty pictures first. Then the brothel! I've seen it happen myself."

"This is crazy." Pulling her towel around herself more tightly, Yuliang begins edging toward the changing quarters. But the women block her, jostling her instead toward the reception area.

"Lao Chen!" calls the mannish woman. "Help! An attacker!"

"Please," Yuliang says, watching her precious sketchbook pass from hand to dripping hand. "I'm a student at the art academy. I was just trying to practice—"

"The art academy!" The first woman reaches for her towel, tugs it. "Tell me, should I draw *you* naked now?"

"No—no! Take her photograph! We could sell *that* for a pretty cent!" shrills another.

Most of the women fall back as they approach the beaded curtain that marks off the front entrance. But the short-haired woman, now Yuliang's self-appointed warden, marches right on and hustles Yuliang out into the front room. "Lao Chen!" she calls again. "If you please! I've got her!"

"What? What's this now?" The clerk, a burly man, stands up.

"Dirty pictures!" the woman crows, thrusting Yuliang's sketchbook at him. "Look! She drew Sumei without a stitch of clothing!"

"I didn't! Or at least . . ." Yuliang clutches her towel as it slips. "Please, sir. I keep telling them. I meant no harm. I'm a student at the art academy. I was just trying—"

The man looks Yuliang up and down suspiciously. "I thought it was just boys there," he says darkly.

"There are three girls now," Yuliang mumbles (thinking, *Unless they expel me*.) "Please. I—I didn't think anyone would mind."

"I think perhaps the constable would mind," snaps the woman. "Don't you?"

"Shall I fetch him?" asks the clerk eagerly. "You're—you're not quite dressed for it, Chung Ma. If you'll pardon my saying this."

"No!" Yuliang blanches. She can already see Zanhua, reading the headlines. "Please," she says, her voice climbing now, "you can't do this. I meant no harm . . ."

The beaded curtains part again, this time for the young girl Yuliang had noticed earlier. Like the others, she has a towel wrapped around her slight form now. But she still holds her damp red book in one hand. "Hold on a moment, Chung Ma," she says to the older woman. "I'd like to speak with her first."

The short-haired woman hesitates. "What do you know about it?"

"I was a student there too. At the academy. So I'll know if she's telling the truth." The girl puts a hand on the woman's shoulder. Her towel slips precariously. But if she notices this, she doesn't care. "Chung Ma, don't you recognize me? I was the one who helped you last month. With the *constable*."

"I don't know what you mean," the woman says stiffly.

"When your boy was almost arrested for stealing?" the girl

prompts. "And you needed someone to read the charges against him? The New People's Society sent me."

"He didn't steal!" the older woman says hotly. "That coal dropped from the cart, fair and square. It was ours to sell."

"I know, I know," the girl says soothingly. "And we told the police that together, didn't we?" The woman nods grudgingly. "Just think," the girl goes on. "What if you call the constable now and our sister here is telling the truth as well? What if she truly meant no harm and you have her sent to jail? You know what that feels like. To be wrongly accused."

For a moment the woman hesitates. Then she nods. "All right. She can go back in with you. But I go too. And if she's lying . . ."

"I'm not lying!" Yuliang protests, as the woman takes her arm and marches her back in (as if that had been her plan all along).

Back inside the bathhouse, the other bathers form a small ring around the trio: Yuliang, her accuser, her unexpected defender. "You say you're from the academy," the latter starts, picking up the sketch-book. "Who are your teachers?"

"Teacher Hong has been my adviser. I've had Teacher Li for land-scapes, Teacher Jiang for still life. This term I'm studying with Pro-fessor Hong for life study."

The girl's eyes narrow. "Life study," she repeats. "And Teacher Hong. He told you to come here and draw naked women?"

"He told me I needed practice."

The girl waves her sketchbook. "Practice in this sort of exploit-ative, bourgeois art form."

Behind them, Sumei whispers in a frightened voice, "What's *bour-geois*, Nainai?"

Yuliang blinks. "It's not exploitative."

But the girl shakes her head. "Of course it is. Real art shouldn't just be about soothing the senses, or heating the blood with images of pretty naked girls. It should further the plight of the poor. The oppressed." She eyes Yuliang skeptically. "Something I doubt you know much about."

"I know more than you think," Yuliang says coldly.

"This misses the point!" someone shouts. "Why not just draw at the school?"

"I do. But there are just not enough models."

"So why not sneak into the *men's* bathhouse?" A small wave of titters.

"Anyway, she is being truthful." The former academy student turns to the group, sketchbook in hand. "Although she certainly isn't being clever. Sisters, how about a deal? If she tears up the drawing, will you let her go?"

"What if there are more?" the grandmother asks. "She was over there long enough."

"She didn't get a chance to do more." The girl holds up the sketchbook.

"She could have," Chung Ma insists. "She could have drawings of all of us."

"Where?" Yuliang cries. "Under my towel?"

The woman just juts her chin. With an apologetic shrug, the girl turns back to Yuliang. "You'll have to show them."

Sighing, Yuliang parts her towel, subjecting herself to their scrutiny until they're satisfied. The girl hands Yuliang her sketchbook. "Just the one page," she murmurs. "Rip it up so they can all see it."

"Wait!" It's Sumei. Timidly, the young girl steps forward. "Can I . . ."

"Little Su!" the grandmother hisses.

But Yuliang has already handed the book over. She waits with odd anxiety as subject studies image. A vision comes: herself, shivering nude in another bathing room. But when the girl looks up again, she seems less frightened than awed.

"I look like that?"

"You look even better," Yuliang says gently. "That's why I need more practice."

The girl's eyes widen. "If you need practice, I could—"

"Enough," the short-haired woman bellows. "Sumei, seal your

lips. And give me that filth." She twitches the sketch away and hands it to Yuliang. "Get rid of it. Now."

I'm sorry, Yuliang tells the girl silently. And without looking away, she rips the smudged paper in half. Then into quarters.

A short, damp silence follows. Then the former art student nods. "That's it," she says. "Let's all get back to our business, shall we?"

The women disperse to their buckets and benches. Before leaving, however, the short-haired one leans over. "Fortune was with you today," she hisses. "But if you ever come back here, you'll be sorry your mother—whom you've so unspeakably shamed—went through the misery of having you at all."

"I CAN'T IMAGINE WHAT you were thinking."

Back in the changing room, the girl unfolds her high-necked jacket and trousers. "They're good women. And honest. The short-haired one was a farmer. Prosperous once, too. Since the famine hit, though, she's made her living begging and selling coal her sons sneak away from the railroad companies."

"So they did steal!"

"So what? Those foreigners steal from us every day. They take our jobs. Our money. Our *pride*." Glancing at Yuliang, she adds, "For some people, you know, bathing here isn't just a wash. It's a special event. It's no wonder they were angry." Her voice is muffled as she pulls her blouse over her head. "Your work is really good, though. Much better than mine ever was."

"When were you at the academy?" Yuliang asks, slowly toweling off her hair.

"Two years ago. There weren't enough models then either. Luckily, I never thought to try the bathhouse." She smiles wryly.

"Why did you leave?"

The girl shrugs again. "Some friends convinced me that there are more important ways to be spending my time and my parents' money." Lifting her wet book, she adds, "This is the first complete translation of Marx's *Communist Manifesto*. It just came out. My discussion group leader, Teacher Chen, arranged for it. He even got us all an advance copy."

"Chen Duxiu is your teacher?" Yuliang asks in surprise. "Isn't he in Beijing now?" She's read about her husband's old friend in the papers—his return from Japan to lead Beijing University, his influence in the so-called May Fourth anti-imperialist movement, his recent founding of China's first Communist Party. Since he's been in Shanghai, however, she's seen him only in passing—once coming out of the *New Youth* office, once leading a protest against the recently signed Treaty of Versailles, which ceded Germany's former landholdings in China—not back to China—but to the Japanese instead.

"He's been back and forth a lot since they released him," the girl says. "They imprisoned him after the riots, you know." Gently blotting the book's cover with her towel, she adds, "Listen—just listen to this."

Opening the book, she runs her finger down to a section outlined and starred in red ink, which is already running into the page's border. "'The world will be for the common people, and the sounds of Happiness will reach even the deepest springs. Ah, come! People of every land, how can you not be roused?'" Looking up, the girl adds dreamily, "I never knew Marx was so poetic. Did you?" She straps herself into a pair of Louis-heeled two-toned slippers that are surprisingly chic for someone with such seemingly stern views. "Anyway, you don't really need to come to the bathhouse, do you?"

"Not really. No," says Yuliang, feeling oddly defensive.

"Then, to be frank with you, I don't think you should return." The girl slips her book into her satchel. "I was here this time, but I might not be the next. Find some other way to solve your problem at school." Walking Yuliang to the door, she adds, "If you're ever interested, come to one of our woodcutting classes. Tuesday evenings. We meet on the second floor of the Uchiyama Shoten, on Bubbling Well Road. I'm Guifei, by the way."

Yuliang suppresses a smile. Her new friend is named after one of China's famed "four beauties"—the one who so enchanted an eighth-century emperor that he left the nation vulnerable to a devastating rebellion. The Japanese bookshop, on the other hand, is well known as the meeting spot of the more rebellious youth in the city. Yuliang can't help wondering whether Guifei's parents know of their daughter's new pastime.

"I'm Pan Yuliang," she says. Then, on a whim: "Does a boy named Xing Xudun ever come to your meetings?"

"From *New Youth*? He and other staff members come often. Are you friends?"

"We've—we've met," Yuliang says quickly. "I was just curious."

She leaves the bathhouse with Guifei's address jotted down on the same sheet as her last aborted sketch. Her forearm is bruised from the farmer's grip, and her brilliant solution has been literally ripped into pieces. What's worse, she's no closer to Teacher Hong's *life force* than before.

But, she consoles herself (as she trudges slowly home), at least she's done something that is nearly as difficult: she seems to have made a new friend.

Twenty-five

Wagner's Post Office Savings Bank, completed seven years ago in Vienna and gloriously interweaving Teutonic [something] and classic concepts of [something] is both a [something] manifestation of modernist [something] and, to the outsider, quite easily accessible . . .

Which, Yuliang decides glumly, is more than can be said for this text. For all her studying, she grasps barely half the terms. She'll have to have Zanhua read it to her next week.

Annoyed, she shuts the book with a snap. Then, glancing at the clock—3:15; as usual, Principal Liu is late—she lights a cigarette, and shifts her attention to the painting over Liu Haisu's desk.

The painting is of an enormous monster consuming a man, or what was once most likely a man. The corpse's head is gone, and so is one arm. The remaining arm is lifted in a sort of bloody salute. The monster's eyes are wild, his mouth stretched in such gory ecstasy that Yuliang is actually feeling slightly queasy as Liu Haisu bursts into the room, papers flapping.

"Apologies!" he cries breathlessly. "Damn staff meeting. Don't ever get yourself on a staff, madame. You'll rue it." He seats himself before his cluttered desk. "I haven't made you late again, have I?"

"I have no class today," Yuliang lies.

"How fortunate for you." Plumping into his seat, the principal pulls out his cigars. Yuliang watches him, slightly uneasy. The truth is, she has anatomy. She is skipping it—the thought of staring at pictures of bones and muscles for two hours straight was simply too unappetizing for her this morning.

Puffing on his cigar, Liu Haisu follows Yuliang's gaze to the monster.

"It's very . . . striking," she offers.

He laughs. "That's one way of putting it. One wonders what Goya was thinking."

"This is Goya?" Yuliang looks at the work with renewed interest. Liu Haisu considers himself an impressionist. But he idolizes the Spanish master, whom he considers to be the first truly modern artist.

"A copy of a reproduction of his work," he says now. "I made it years ago, when I first became drawn to his work—in the beginning, because it struck me as so uniquely Chinese."

"Really?"

He nods. "Same color schemes, same attention to brushstroke. I'm always intrigued when art reaches across cultural boundaries. I can't recall why I chose that particular work to copy, though. I think I was having trouble working on my own."

"*You* have trouble?" Yuliang asks, astonished. Liu Haisu is the most prolific painter she's ever met. Despite his frantic school schedule and his apparent quest to get his name in every paper and art journal in China, he still produces more—and more exquisite —work than Yuliang would have imagined humanly possible. The paintings at his last show at the Shanghai Exhibition Space had literally taken her breath away: lush yet impeccably elegant still lifes; misty, impressionistic landscapes built, when one looked closely, on brushwork that would have passed muster with Shi Tao. The blending of these two styles—of East and West, of old and new— had affected Yuliang profoundly.

"We all have trouble sometimes," he is saying now. "The muse visits. She rarely moves in." He strokes his upper lip. "But this isn't what I wanted to talk about today."

Yuliang stubs out her cigarette, wondering uneasily if he's going to bring up the bathhouse incident. He must have heard of it. She still hears her new, whispered nickname here: *Bathing Beauty*.

"I trust you're entering the student-faculty contest this year," he says instead.

"I—I hadn't thought of it." Again, Yuliang it's a lie. In past weeks she has thought of little else. It doesn't help that the whole school is buzzing about this year's prize: a full scholarship to the new Sino-French Friendship Program, at Lyon University.

When Teacher Hong first mentioned it to Yuliang, she'd felt her pulse leap. She'd thought of Rubens's soft-hued castles, Gentileschi's lush green fields and crisp folds of fabric. She'd pictured walking cobbled streets alongside Leonardo's limp gods and smoky women—perhaps even running into Suzanne Valadon. About a week ago, however, Yuliang finally resigned herself to the fact that the dream would remain just that—a dream. The truth is, she has no work to enter this year. And even if she did—even if she *won*—Zanhua certainly wouldn't welcome the thought of her traipsing off to France.

"I've nothing worth entering right now," she tells him. "The muse seems to be avoiding me. Perhaps she's been listening to all the gossip."

"Gossip," he pronounces, "is little more than envy in disguise. You should have heard what they said of Leonardo."

"I'm no Leonardo."

"That's not what you once led me to believe."

He selects a cigar, nearly trims off its top. As he lights it, Yuliang finds herself dangerously close to crying for some reason. "I just . . . I can't make them work," she blurts, dropping her eyes.

"Your paintings?"

"My nudes. Teacher Hong says my coloration is good. It's just— I can't seem to get the figures right." She sighs. "To be truthful, I don't think that I *can* do bodies. I think that perhaps that part of me is just . . ."

He puffs, pensively. "What?"

"Damaged," she says at last. "When it comes to such things."

It is the closest she's come yet to confessing her past, to anyone other than Zanhua. Strangely, though, the confession of her artistic failing almost shames her more.

Yuliang hears Liu Haisu's chair creak as he leans forward to tap his cigar in the old inkstone that is his ashtray. "Goya once said that the dream of reason produces monsters." He pauses. "Sometimes I wonder if our monsters produce art."

She looks up. "What?"

"Has it ever occurred to you that our wounds are what drive us to create?" He looks thoughtfully back at Goya's *Saturn*. "After all, loss in one arena compels us to compensate in others. Think about the senses. The way loss of sight leads to heightened senses of smell, touch, and hearing for the blind. What if the same is true of the creative process? What if those who've lost something compensate for it in their work? In that case their damage helps them. It's what compels them to create." He turns back to her. "And it might explain why the best artists tend also to be the poorest."

"Really?"

"Name one rich painter worth his salt."

She eyes him warily. "Is that an exam question?"

"Not yet." He grins.

Yuliang crosses her legs, still unsmiling. "It's not just that, though. I also need more models. Ten hours a month simply isn't enough."

He sighs. "I'm well aware."

"And I know nothing at all about drawing male bodies. Why is it that the male students get to sketch both female and male nudes while we women are given access only to other women?"

Like the tears, the outburst comes out unexpectedly. But Liu just smiles broadly. "Now *there's* the girl I broke ranks for. Welcome back."

And despite herself, Yuliang can't help but finally smile in return.

"But," he continues, "I'm afraid that's one rule I can't break. It's hard enough to draw the women without causing a ruckus. If we put the precious wives and daughters of China's elite near naked men, they won't just shut me down. They'll shoot me." He grins affably. "Wonderful publicity, of course. But my painting career would be at its end."

Outside, a bell rings. Liu Haisu looks at his wristwatch. "*Aiya!* I'm due in Takeshita's class. I'm to lecture on fauvism. What the hell will I talk about? Matisse? Derain?"

"I like Matisse."

He frowns, giving the distinct impression that this is the wrong answer. "I suppose it doesn't matter. To most of them it's all the same anyway." He pushes his chair back and strides toward the door, turning at the threshold to beckon her to follow.

They cross the swaybacked floors, past peeling, painted walls. To Yuliang's relief, the door to Teacher Lin's anatomy class is shut, although she hears him expounding inside ("What bone is this? Can anyone name it?"). Liu Haisu hurries on ahead, papers flapping from his half-clasped satchel, mouth moving in silence as he patches together his lecture. When he stops, it's so abruptly they almost collide.

"You must work through it, my girl," he says sternly, as though they've been talking all the way here. "The days of rich scholar-painters are long gone. Your work may very well one day be your rice bowl."

Yuliang swallows. "I—thank you for your guidance. I will try."

"A final note: I'd strongly urge you to compete for the Lyon prize. We all agree that your skills would benefit from further guidance abroad."

She stares at him, stunned. "But how can I compete if I've nothing to enter? The contest is less than three months away!"

"You must jolt yourself back to work," the principal snaps. "Some of the best paintings on earth were done in a matter of days. Three months is quite enough, *if* you stop indulging your doubts." The words, delivered in the artist's characteristically calm but buoyant voice, ring through the halls like a shouted speech. "Find a model any way you can. A servant. A friend. Someone too stupid, doddering, or shameless to care if you turn her inside out and draw her that way. You must just *paint*. That is all."

He puts his hand up to the door to knock, then turns back. "And don't look for friends in a roomful of insecure artists," he adds, at last lowering his voice. "It's like looking for an honest face at Versailles."

A WEEK LATER Yuliang still hasn't been to a class. But she is, at least, finally working. Inspired (or shamed) by Liu Haisu, she has racked her brain and her contacts and finally found a model to meet her requirements. It took nerve, determination, and two mortifying refusals. But when the solution came, it seemed at once both pure genius and sheer insanity. She started that very same afternoon.

Now she chews a cuticle, studying her subject. "I'm supposed to live in you," she tells the girl. "That's what Teacher Hong said."

Her model stares back balefully. Goose bumps sprinkle her bare thighs. Yuliang rubs her own arms—it *is* chilly. The dorm she's moved into (both because it's close to school and because it allows her to avoid Qihua and Ahying while she works) prohibits charcoal braziers. For good reason: last year more than thirty girls in a similar dorm died in a midnight fire, pounding on a door bolted to keep them "safe."

Setting her teeth, Yuliang mixes her flesh tones: violet, yellow, earth red, vine black, Venetian red. She creates a quick and expert outline of the body's shape on her canvas. Then she loads her brush and begins to fill it in.

As she works, she doesn't let herself think or question. She just paints; stolidly, methodically. Modeling in the peach-tinged curves, the beige shadows. When she reaches the breasts, she hears God-mother's voice: *If they touch the breasts directly, charge seven extra. Ten for the feet.* "Hush, you old bitch," she mutters, and moves on to the hips. The belly. The puckered kiss of the navel.

She is just brushing back up to fill out the hair some more when a clamor erupts outside. A funeral is in progress on the street. At first Yuliang tries to work through it, but it's no use. The mood is broken.

She sets her brush in her jar and throws on her shawl against the cold. Walking to her desk, she uncorks the wine she has taken to sipping as she works. She pours a glass. Then she walks to the open window.

The coffin is set out just outside the house across the street—the deceased must have died away from home. But there is no shortage of mourners. The daughters are dressed in black, grandchildren and great-grandchildren in blue. The sons-in-law wear stark white and bright yellow. Underscoring this colorful chorus of bereavement is the clicking of the *pat-cha* dice. The mourning gong, hung to the right of the house's doorway, signifies that the departed is a woman. The presence of great-grandchildren means she was probably quite old. But Yuliang is too far away to make out the portrait propped on a stool by the coffin, amid layers of flowers and other offerings. She tries to recall the grandmothers who greet her sometimes when she comes home. One has a face like a withered pumpkin and a sweet and oddly young voice. She sometimes calls to Yuliang: "Going to your school, little daughter? When are you going to paint my picture?"

Yuliang imagines the same woman now, lying still in her coffin with her face and body covered by yellow and blue cloth. What would it be like to paint *that* in life study—a body that has no life in it at all? Her anatomy class works from textbooks and an old medical skeleton, donated by the mission clinic because it is missing two ribs. But Leonardo is said to have learned from the actual dead, spending hours in darkened morgues, dissecting, peeling back. Sketching. Her classmates, raised to see death as the ultimate contaminant, were openly horrified by this. Yuliang, though, merely shrugged—at least inwardly. She couldn't help but think that if the Italian master had taken up the flesh trade, he'd have gained just as firm a sense of human physiology.

Now she studies her model again—the hardened nipples, the goose-bumped skin. The sight of her like that—stripped, alone—hurts her heart. Yuliang shuts her eyes, then berates herself in silence: *Stupid whore. You can't paint her if you can't see her.*

And then, just like that, it hits her: *I can't see her.*

Electrified, she opens her eyes, Teacher Hong's words coming back with new meaning. *Try to see the skin as more than simply skin,* he had said.

As advice, it is directly and fully at odds with that Jinling once gave her: *It's just skin.* And yet studying her model again now, Yuliang suddenly realizes that her troubles, then and now, arise from her own failure to see skin as either more or less than itself; to see it outside a spectrum of pain. In her old life it was a liability, a soft surface waiting for wounds. As such at the academy it inspires not creative passion but a wave of remembered revulsion. And in both places she's been unable—hard as she might try—to see it as beautiful. As somthing *worth* painting . . . Outside the mourners wail: "Aiiiiiiiii. Come back, Mother. Come back!" Heart racing, Yuliang shuts her eyes once more. She thinks of Jinling, not in death, as she was the last time Yuliang saw her, but in those impossibly early days when Yuliang first began to attend to her. Before she fully understood a body's worth in monetary terms, and could value it only in the currency of beauty. She thinks of the way Jinling's skin had looked in the early morning. Sheened in perspiration, stretched out in sheer joy. Limned in the early light of a sunrise.

Beauty, she thinks. She looks again into the mirror.

And perhaps it's the timing. The sun is finally setting, touching everything in the room with orange and gold. But at that moment Mirror Girl strikes her as almost ethereal—as far from mere skin as a rainbow is from mere rain.

Yuliang stares at herself: her thin thigh, her curving hip. And for the first time in years, she truly *sees* herself. She sees herself as finally free of the white ant's probing fingers, of strange men's hands. Of jewelry that binds it, chainlike, to debt . . .

Picking up her palette, she hurriedly paints over the stiff first image. She cocks her head, takes a breath, and starts anew. She paints until the light outside has seeped away into the black sky; until the monks go home, and the mourners leave, and all that's left is the soft click of the gamblers' ivory.

Twenty-six

"FRANCE," ZANHUA REPEATS, setting his cup down. His voice is incredulous, humorless.

"It would just be for two years." Yuliang is careful to keep her own voice casual. "But if I won, the scholarship would pay for everything. I truly think it would be easier . . ."

His tension thickens the air between them. "Easier to live thirty days away by steamship, instead of three? Easier never to see your husband at all, instead of rarely?"

"Easier for me to do my . . . work," Yuliang says. Which, of course, is precisely the wrong thing to say. She can see it in his face. *Work?* He is thinking. *What work?*

She bites her lip. It isn't (she reminds herself) that he's not proud of her achievements. He sent her a telegram when she placed second in last year's student-teacher exhibition. He's visited her dorm space, her school studio, several teachers. He protested when one credited him with discovering Yuliang's talent. "All I did was fall in love," he'd said, charmingly.

Now he shifts his gaze back to his paper. Yuliang drops her eyes to her own reading, an article about a popular young modern artist named Xu Beihong. What she is thinking about, however, is Zanhua's homecoming last night, the warm embrace he gave her. Followed by an announcement: "I'm being transferred back to Tongcheng." The news shocked Yuliang into a silence that completely overrode, for the moment, the subject of her own hope to travel.

"Speaking of Paris"—Zanhua rattles his paper—"there have been more demonstrations outside the Chinese legation there this week."

She doesn't look up. "What about?"

"The usual things. Conditions and pay for Chinese laborers." He snorts. "I'm beginning to think this is their idea of democracy—treating us all equally like cow dung."

"The laborers are on strike?"

He shakes his head. "It's those work-study students—the ones on that so-called government program."

"Is that the one where students work in French factories to pay for schooling?"

The question is somewhat disingenuous, since Yuliang has several friends (including Xing Xudun) who have applied for the "Diligent Work/Frugal Study" program. But she also senses that Zanhua wouldn't approve of these friendships. It's an impression confirmed by his next statement:

"In theory. But everyone knows the program was founded by anarchists." He turns the page crisply. "By this point I'll wager that this New People's Society is behind it."

"Someone needs to defend Chinese interests abroad," Yuliang points out.

He lifts a brow. "I see you're thinking more about these things. That's good." And then: "What is it?"

She looks up. "Nothing."

"You keep sighing. Something's in your head."

Yuliang opens her mouth to say "Of course not." Then she shuts it again. As usual, he knows her too well. "It's just . . . Principal Liu really thinks I have a good chance at winning that Lyon scholarship. He says I'm one of the most promising students he's seen."

"So we're back to that." Zanhua shuts his eyes briefly. "This is what comes from marrying a boar. You dig your tusks in. You don't let go."

"You don't believe in astrology," she reminds him. "And it isn't just me. The truth is, all my teachers think the program would be good for me."

Now it's his turn to sigh. "The program might be good for you if you were a man. Or if it were in Shanghai—say, at the French consulate. But the truth is, you've studied for two years here already. It's enough."

"Plenty of men study here first and then go abroad to finish. You yourself told me that foreign study is an essential part of China's new culture. And you've always said that women have the same capabilities as men."

"They do. And you've shown that admirably." He's beginning to sound impatient. "But there are also some *capabilities* women have that men don't. Particularly inside the home."

"But someone needs to represent Chinese interests *outside* the home." Despite herself, Yuliang's voice is rising now, too. "What would have happened at Versailles, if those students hadn't barred the Chinese delegation from going to sign the treaty?"

"Exactly what happened regardless," he says dryly. "They would have objected. Quite eloquently, I'm sure. And then our so-called allies would have given our land to Japan anyway." He jabs the paper with his finger again. "If you'd pay the same attention to national events as you do to your 'work,' you'd know no one gives a dog's fart about what we think. All they want is to suck more money out of us."

"We've a better chance of being heard, at least, over there."

He laughs shortly. "Heard on what subject? Your still lifes? Your country landscapes? Your thoughts on the color gradations in a peony?"

Yuliang looks away, stung.

"Face the truth, my Lady Guan," he continues. It's a new nickname for her: Guan Daoshen is China's most famous woman painter, best known for her renditions of bamboo and evening mist. "You don't paint for politics. You don't even read the newspapers unless they're covering your beloved Principal Liu."

Yuliang shuts her magazine, coloring slightly. "I love my country as much as the next person. More, in fact, than most men I know. And besides, you can't separate it like that. Kang Youwei himself wrote that everything—industry, commerce, money—is intertwined with art. That modernizing art is as essential to China's future as modernizing the economy. Or the navy."

He looks taken aback. "Did I read you that?"

Yuliang stifles a dry smile. "I read it myself. For our class on political painting."

"And you, of course, are taking it upon yourself to further this great cause." He waves at Ahying to clear. "Very well. Tell me more about this new development. Your newfound sacrifice. Painting pretty pictures in the name of your country."

Ahying slips Yuliang's bowl from her place, eyes dutifully downcast. But her ears are flushed like those of Sargent's buxom white-skinned ladies. Yuliang feels her own cheeks flush too. Not with embarrassment, but with outrage.

"You know nothing of my work," she tells Zanhua angrily. "Or my life. *Nothing!*"

He slams his fist on the table. "Precisely! Which is why I want you in Tongcheng, with your husband and your family."

"*Your* family! Not mine!"

"My family, therefore yours," he counters harshly. "We're all the family you will ever have."

The words hit like a blow to bruised skin. Startled by their sting, Yuliang shuts her eyes. *We're your family now,* Godmother whispers within her head. *We're all our own family. We're all that any of us need.*

When she opens her eyes again, it's as though Lady Guan's delicately depicted mist has cleared from her own vision. For the first time she sees how little the titanic changes Zanhua himself set in motion have registered with him until now. How everything—her hard-won literacy, the burgeoning political awareness fed by friends like Guifei, the unanticipated success at school, even her newly bobbed hair and chic strappy shoes (with the latest leather-covered French heel)—is as invisible to Zanhua as the emperor's fabled clothing. As far as he is concerned, she's the same girl he rescued. Ingénue. Protégée. Presumed bearer of his next son.

Zanhua nods. *That's settled,* the gesture says. He returns complacently to his paper. Yuliang finishes off her wine, still fuming. "I—I want to show you something," she says, when she at last summons her voice.

He still doesn't look up. "What?"

She rises to her feet. "Come and see."

Zanhua frowns. But he folds his paper, and follows.

At the threshold to her studio, Yuliang watches him take in its state: the paint-splattered tarp that protects the floor from splashes, the bookshelves filled with thinner and varnish, a variety of glass mullers gleaming dully by the window. The smell of turpentine is all but overpowering: for a moment, Yuliang almost feels faint. But she regains her balance and walks wordlessly over to the easel. Slowly she turns it toward him.

Zanhua approaches the painting cautiously, as if it's some animal he's never seen. "What is this?" he asks stiffly.

"My submission for the student-faculty exhibit in May." She smiles dryly. "I call it *Bathing Beauty.*"

She follows what he is seeing: the rippling hair, the wet limbs and features that have taken up hours and appetite. Yuliang has shown herself stepping from her morning bath, captured in a shaft of yellow-white sunlight. Her thighs glisten with heat and steam. Her breasts are fully exposed, as is the belly rounding whitely below them. Below it, she has outlined the faint patch of her pubic hair with almost calligraphic brushwork.

When Zanhua finally tears his gaze back to the real Yuliang, dry and clothed before him, his face is startlingly devoid of color. "It looks unfinished."

"I still have two weeks left to work on it before submitting it to the panel."

"What—what must you do, to finish?"

She ticks it off on her fingers. "The legs are off. The shading around the tub's base isn't quite right. And the background is incomplete. I want to put more into it—a small red table, perhaps. Or another towel. In the corner."

He says nothing.

"In brown," she adds, as though this matters.

"And the face?"

She looks at him blankly. The face is nearly complete. It's all she's worked on these past several days. She has gone to sleep dreaming of her own eyes, lips, and cheekbones.

"The face," Zanhua presses. "You are keeping it."

Only then does she understand: he expects her, quite literally, to save her face. To replace it with someone else's.

For it is her face, after all—her *own* face, untouched by shame or makeup—that makes the painting so outright revolutionary. Yuliang has taken Manet and outdone him by a step: she stares down the tabloids, the whispers, the academy, dressed only in the nude truth of her talent. "Yes," Yuliang says.

Zanhua repeats it slowly, as though she hasn't understood the question. "*Your* face. Staring out at everyone with . . . that look."

"It's a self-portrait."

"It's a *naked* self-portrait."

"A *nude* self-portrait."

The look he gives her is so pained her heart almost hurts for him. "Zanhua," she starts, stepping toward him. "When Yuan Shikai betrayed the republic, many people were too cowed and old-fashioned to protest. But you picked up your sword. It's part of why I admire you so. Don't you see that this is like that—that this is my battle?"

"Don't you *dare* compare that to this." He jerks away. "And don't *touch* me."

Stunned, she drops her hand. Outside, a dog bursts into a furious round of barking, then quiets just as abruptly.

Zanhua's jaw is working in silent fury. He doesn't move until Ahying, stuttering abashedly through the closed door, asks if she may leave. "Yes," he says, far too sharply.

Several moments pass before he speaks again. "I cannot," he says at last, "comprehend why you have done this. After all the opportunities I've given you. All the chances to better yourself."

"I have bettered myself!" Yuliang cries. "I'm the top student in my class!"

"If this is your idea of bettering yourself, you're more misguided than—" His voice breaks. He shuts his eyes. "Get rid of it."

Yuliang jerks her head up. "*What?*"

"Get rid of it. Or I will. I will not permit you to—to do this to yourself. Again."

That one word, *again*, has the weight of a slap. Very quietly, she asks, "Do what again?"

Zanhua opens his eyes. "Make a whore of yourself."

It's what she knew he'd say—perhaps, even, all he *could* say. Still, she barely manages to whisper the words: "You shouldn't have said that."

"*You!*" Zanhua shouts. "You have the impertinence now to tell me what *I* shouldn't do! *You!* Who . . ." He steps toward her, his fists clenched, and Yuliang wonders if he'll finally strike her now. There's an odd satisfaction in the thought: if he does, it will almost certainly hurt him far more than her.

But instead, he lunges the other way, and does the one thing that hurts her more at this moment: lifting his arm, he strikes the painting from the easel.

"*Stop!*" Yuliang leaps forward.

Zanhua pushes her away with enough force to send her spinning toward the wall. When she launches herself back at him, he shoves her again. Then he sweeps up the jade letter-opener from her desk. Blade in hand, he whirls back toward her painted image, his face so contorted that it looks like a stranger's. "*Don't*, Zanhua," she cries, terrified now. "*Please . . .*"

"I won't have it," he hisses. "You're my *wife*. I order you to stop this." Holding her off with one hand he lifts the green blade over the canvas. "*Stay there*."

But Yuliang doesn't. Instead, using a Hall-taught technique she has no recollection of learning, she aims a flat-palmed punch at her husband's neck. When he staggers back, she hurls herself to the floor, shielding her painting.

Zanhua recovers. An awkward dance ensues as he tries to stab past the clothed body to the undressed one. "*Stop.*" She claws at his hand. "You don't know. You don't know what you're doing."

"I'm doing something I should have done long ago. I'm putting a stop to this insanity."

"You're hurting our *child*."

He laughs harshly. "You dare to compare this—this *filth* to a child?"

"I'm not talking about the painting!"

A stunned silence. Slowly he rocks back on his heels. "What did you say?"

Yuliang blinks at him, squeezing her belly with her arms.

"This is true?" he asks, quietly.

And the astonishing thing is, it is.

Yuliang nods numbly, checking off the telltale symptoms as dispassionately as she'd checked off her remaining work for him: the mood swings, extreme even for someone of her extreme nature. The bloating and belly twinges. The nausea and indigestion, which she'd attributed to the fact that she always eats badly when she's working. The soreness in her breasts that came and went two weeks ago. And then, more obviously—and how in heaven could she have ignored this?—the menses that simply did not come.

As if that weren't plain enough, there is the abrupt way that paint and turpentine and even coffee have become noxious to her. There are the frequent trips to the outhouse, which until this very moment she'd told herself were from drinking extra tea in an attempt to fend off her growing fatigue.

Over the past week Yuliang has attributed all these symptoms to nerves. It's only now, with him here, with her naked image behind her and her clothed body tingling with fear, that Yuliang finally allows the colossal truth to dawn on her.

Moving very carefully, Zanhua puts the opener back on the desk. "How far along is it?"

"Nearly—nearly three months, I think."

"It's almost rooted, then," he says. His voice barely contains his excitement. "It happened on my last visit."

She nods bleakly. She vaguely recalls an empty box of the Six Fairies tea she buys from Lin's apothecary on Fouzhou Road ("Ideal for cleansing the system of unwanted seeds"). And thinking, *Just one day. And I probably can't conceive anyway.* She made the classic mistake Jinling often warned against: putting faith in her flailing cycles.

"You shouldn't be on the floor." He is holding out his hand. Hesitantly, Yuliang lets him pull her to her feet. Once there, she immediately bends to study the painting.

Behind her he's pacing, planning. "You'll go to Tongcheng when the term ends. I see no point, in fact, in staying on."

She looks up at him. "I have exams!"

"All the more reason to leave," he counters. "You should be somewhere safer, quieter. Healthier for the child." He moves toward the door. "You can tell Principal Liu tomorrow. Do you have much to pack?"

Yuliang bends down again, dazedly retrieving her work. She locks gazes with herself. "No," she says softly.

"Good." He begins walking toward the door. "We'll find some movers before I leave. I'll put a call through to Qihua."

"*No,*" Yuliang repeats.

"You don't want movers?"

"I am not moving."

He frowns. "But you just said . . ."

"I am staying through the student-teacher contest."

He lets out a short laugh. "You're not serious. What's the point?"

She turns to him slowly. "I can't just leave. What would Principal Liu say?"

"What about me? What about what *I* say?" His face is honestly puzzled. "Yuliang," he says. "Do you really think that by doing this— by *undressing* for them all—you'll finally win their respect?"

"They do respect me."

He snorts. "They do not."

"How do you know?" She almost shouts it.

"Because you're a woman," Zanhua says. "Because, you're an orphan, and a concubine. And your past . . ." He waves a hand at her painting. "There are a thousand reasons why they'll never respect you. This only gives them one more."

"This isn't my past," she says furiously. "It's my future."

"It's *my* future too. You know they'll use this against me. You do recall that your reputation nearly cost me my position in Wuhu."

What she recalls is his arrogance—his ridiculously naive faith that he could parade her around town without consequence. But what she says is this: "Is it possible for you to recall that I, too, now have a position?"

He laughs. "Position? You're a *student*. Of an art no one in China understands."

"I'm a *painter*," she counters stubbornly. "A painter of Shanghai. And this"—she touches her canvas—"this is my *painting*."

For a long moment he just stares at her. Then he drops his head. When he speaks again, his voice is flat, and very careful. "Very well. Here's a choice for the painter of Shanghai. You can keep your picture. Your *position*." He takes a breath. "Or, you keep your position as my wife."

For a moment, Yuliang isn't sure that she's heard correctly. But the look on his face leaves no doubt. *He would*, she thinks, thunderstruck. He'd abandon her to the streets, carrying his child. And not a court in Shanghai would deny him the right. After all, she is not even a wife. She's a concubine. A slave, really. Nothing more.

For an instant the world stands still. Then, slowly, she turns to the door, tucking *Bathing Beauty* beneath her arm. He doesn't move as she walks, then pauses, then walks again. At the threshold she stops again. He doesn't even blink.

Out in the hallway she sets the canvas down long enough to lift her padded jacket from the hook. She listens again: still no sound. She feels as pale and empty as a cast corpse after Vesuvius. But she continues: past the Japanese maple in the courtyard, through the gate. Into the forgiving shadows of Ocean Street.

FOR ALMOST TWO HOURS Yuliang wanders in the Old City, her breath forming cloudlike puffs against the evening chill. She's barely cognizant of crossing Suzhou Creek, and of following the greening lines of Bubbling Well Road's willows. She passes the deserted racecourse, St. John's University. The Tudor homes of the taipans and compradors, Russian doormen standing staunchly at attention. Eventually she swings onto a northbound streetcar. Staring blankly out the window, she makes two, perhaps three runs before the conductor gently informs her that the tram is going out of service. When she alights, she has no idea at all where she is. Not, that is, until she sees the red lanterns of Fouzhou Road.

It's early Tuesday evening in the brothel district, but the evening is already in full swing. Tipsy sailors pass, joking in Cantonese. Red-faced Japanese businessmen follow libidos and a young guide who lisps at them in pidgin: "Can do go topside that girly house, chop-chop, two, maybe three dollar? That b'long much better than street chicken."

Yuliang finds a bench and sits down. A few of the men look Yuliang over speculatively as they pass. She ignores them, staring instead at the padded swell of her stomach. How well it's hidden, this unwanted guest. She presses her hands there, half expecting to feel it. She can't, of course. And yet the way her flesh gives—it's just that, after all; just flesh, *just skin*—is strangely reassuring. She kneads herself absently, as though her abdomen were a lump of clay. After a few moments she becomes aware of a dull ache. Rather than stopping, though, she presses harder. Soon she is driving her elbows into her stomach.

Some French sailors pass in boyish striped and collared uniforms. "Hey, mademoiselle," one calls. "You lookee-see good time like that *avec moi?*" But what is ringing in her head is her husband's earlier command: *Get rid of it.* The words circle Yuliang's mind as she escalates her attack: *Get rid of it. Get rid of it . . .*

Oblivious of the gathering crowd, Yuliang strips off her coat, then stands to slam herself against the bench's back. She batters herself for a full five minutes, her mouth filling with bile. "She is mad," someone says. "Call the constable." The voice drifts to her, dreamlike.

And yet Yuliang has never felt more sane. Each lunge is a leap toward her future, each throb a harbinger of victory. Her belly's on fire now, her ribs little more than bony bruises. She is as focused and determined as she's ever been in her life. When strong hands land on her shoulders, she struggles wildly. "Leave me. Leave me *be.*"

When they don't, she goes limp, just until they release her. Then she whirls back to the bench.

"*Aiya,*" one says, heaving her over his shoulder.

"*My painting!*" Yuliang cries.

"How can they let them out on the street like this?"

"*Please,*" she sobs. "Get my painting!"

"She doesn't look like the others," says the other. "You sure she's salt pork?"

"They'll know at the Hope Clinic," says the first. "Let's just take her there. What's that, miss? Paint? Your make-up? Oh. Your painting." He swings around. "She must mean that."

His partner picks up *Bathing Beauty* gingerly. A slow smile spreads on his face. "Sure," he says. "She's salt pork, all right."

Twenty-seven

THE CROWD SWARMS TOWARD HER like locusts to new crops. There are dozens of them, their eyes glittering, their lips moist. The women are heavily painted, the men burly and loud. They are not the sorts of viewers she normally sees at exhibitions. They are more like spectators at an execution. They are raucous, overwrought. Some are already drunk, on the atrocious wine Liu Haisu offers at these occasions. Standing by her painting, Yuliang can make out their condemnatory hum from across the room. "Shameless," she hears. "Pornography." "Disgraceful."

Her first urge is to run. Instead, she smiles. (*Smile, smile.*) It is, after all, what Principal Liu would tell her to do. "Artists are sinners," he said, in one of his recent interviews. "We're late, self-centered. We sleep with one another's wives. But the one sin a true artist never commits is to apologize for his work."

And yet it's clear that this crowd wants far more from Yuliang than an apology. "Little slut!" one man shouts. "Smiling while showing her teats like a sow. There's only one place for a low woman like that."

"And those *feet*," cries a woman. "Like big, floppy fish! Why bother taking off your shoes?"

"How old did you say she was?"

"Not a day over sixteen!"

Cruel laughter. Panic rising, Yuliang backs away. She's almost directly against her canvas when another voice breaks through, familiar. Oversweet and insidious. "Please, gentlemen. Let me pass."

The crowd falls back for a fat woman in a red dress. Fanning herself rapidly, she trots to where Yuliang stands. Hands on hips, she studies her. "You're too thin," Godmother pronounces. "You'll blow away at the first wind."

Yuliang follows the hated gaze down to her body—which (she sees with shock) is suddenly as naked as in her painting. And yes, she is thin. As thin as a great-smoke addict. As thin as the famine victims from the north. Her skin stretches over the bony frame of her womb, sheer as silk. Aghast, she shields her belly with her palms. "It's the child," she pleads. "He eats everything."

The bells on the madam's little purse jingle with false cheer as she steps forward. "Don't lie," she says. "You know what happens to girls who betray me."

The crowd, smelling violence, closes in. "Give her what she deserves!" they shout. "Pass her back when you're through! I'll pay twenty!"

"I'll pay thirty!"

Yuliang curls her body against the first blow. She's just sinking to the ground when she hears another voice: "Xiuqing."

The cold air tastes suddenly of ash and citrus, of old cedar.

Yuliang drops her hands from her eyes. The sight of the slender form gliding toward her seems to release something clenched in her chest. "Mama?" she murmurs. "Mama. You came back."

Her mother sweeps forward, dressed in her finest brocade. A shawl of silver hides her face. But Yuliang would know her anywhere —the fine, soft hands, the perfect posture. Joyfully, she leaps up to greet her.

But then, abruptly, the slim form drops her arms. She looks at *Bathing Beauty,* then back at Yuliang. "Daughter," she says, pushing back her headdress. "Xiuqing. What have you done?"

Icy water seems to trickle down Yuliang's scalp. Because while the body—clothes, fingers, the perfect posture—are undeniably her mama's, the eyes aren't. These eyes have no pupils. They have no color at all. They are as white and as soulless as snow.

YULIANG JERKS HERSELF UP, her breath coming in shallow gasps. She presses her fingers to her chest. She feels the sweaty closeness of her cotton shift, her undergarments. When she finally rouses herself enough to scrabble for her wristwatch, she sees it only reads 2:30. She has slept for less than an hour.

Mouth still dry, she flops back on the cot, hands reflexively fluttering to her belly. The skin there is smooth and tight, unmarked by her visit to the Russian abortionist Zanhua found for her in the French Concession. For an instant there's an empty ache, more emotional than physical—an echo of the strange sadness that descended after the procedure. Sitting up, she shakes it off, forcing her thoughts to a pleasanter place: last night's pre-exhibit "varnishing party." She reminds herself of Liu Haisu's clear excitement over her submission: upon seeing it, he promptly put *Bathing Beauty* first in the order of exhibition. "It's the one they'll be talking about," he said gleefully. "We'll make it easy to gawk."

And even Yuliang, jittery with nerves and lack of sleep, half terrified of what she was about to do, had to admit he was right. Alongside the other works—landscapes, still lifes, a few traditional portraits—*Bathing Beauty* was little less than a phenomenon. Its crimsons, oranges, pinks, and purples seared one's eye against the smoky grays of the neighboring watercolor. Yuliang's naked gaze commandeered the room; defiantly facing down both admirers and opponents. Daring them to order her to redress.

The work also unquestionably fueled the resentment that many of Yuliang's classmates felt for her already. Hanging herself in place, Yuliang heard the whispers; she saw the smirks. She felt envy fill the room, more astringent than the stink of the veneer. It came as no surprise when her nemesis, the comprador's daughter, strolled over, her face as tight and painted as her (fully clothed) self-portrait, which Principal Liu had hung in a corner alcove.

"Madame Pan," she said sweetly. "You have my congratulations. Such a prominent spot—I expect plenty of men will want to buy you." Glancing at *Beauty*, she added, "And I'm certain, of course, that your *husband* will be very proud. Will his first lady be coming too?"

Boar or no boar, Yuliang very nearly slapped the girl's face; nothing more than the prospect of certain expulsion kept her hand by her side. But that didn't mean that she wasn't still fuming when Liu Haisu came by *Beauty*'s new spot.

The young principal's visit, however, was far more encouraging. Liu Haisu handed her a full wineglass that smelled faintly of sewage, then cocked his head in thought. Yuliang assumed he was giving her painting a second going-over. But when she looked up from her drink, his amused eyes were on her.

"Courage, my friend," he said. "Think of how Manet must have felt before showing *Le déjeuner sur l'herbe* at the Salon des Refusés. Or Sargent, with *Portrait of Madame X*."

"And look what happened after." Fresh from European art history exams, Yuliang knew how much scorn was initially heaped on both works.

"Look indeed," Liu Haisu retorted. "The paintings woke a sleeping public. They're now studied by every art devotee in the world." Lowering his voice, he added, " 'The deathly white of Madame X's complexion, so disturbing forty years ago, in today's light can be seen as nothing short of pure genius.' "

"You read my essay?"

"It ended up in my portion of this year's exams." He swirled his wine expertly, as though this might somehow improve it. "Your writing has certainly progressed."

Yuliang grimaced as she recalled her first essay two years earlier —the one she'd finally had Zanhua finish for her, after stubbornly resisting help until two hours before class. It was a humiliation she'd promised never to repeat; within a term she'd conquered five hundred new characters.

"Does that mean I passed?" she asked now.

"I pass people based on work, not words." He drained his glass. "For me, you passed the day you sat for the entrance examinations. Why else do you think I overruled those conservative old ox-farts who wanted to keep you out?" He nodded at Yuliang's wineglass. "Finish that. It will help."

Yuliang did—and it did.

Still, seven hours later, she now feels it all over again: the damp-palmed cramp of raw terror. Not for the first time, she finds herself wondering whether she is making a fatal mistake. She expects controversy, of course. But what if her work is met with complete outrage . . . and nothing more? What if her career ends before it's even begun? Zanhua (she suspects) would be relieved, at least—though of course he'd never be ungentlemanly enough to say so. It is one of the unspoken terms of their reconciliation: they don't discuss her painting. Just as they don't discuss her aborted child.

THE DOOR OF HOPE, where the French Concession constables took Yuliang that night, is a Nanjing Road refuge for prostitutes. Inside the whitewashed clinic, a stern German doctor probed Yuliang and asked questions through his Chinese nurse. "Were you drinking?" the nurse murmured. "Do you smoke? Take white powder?" And a moment later, frowning, "Are you aware that you're with child?"

Yuliang turned her face away. "Get rid of it," she whispered.

The woman crossed herself and shook her head.

Later, they gave her a sedative, opened a file. They asked more, endless questions: "Do you know what day it is?" "Do you know where you are?" "Can you give us the name of someone we can send for?" Guifei came to mind first, but she was away, visiting relatives for the upcoming holiday. Chen Duxiu was in Beijing, and Ahying and Qihua would both simply turn to Zanhua.

And so Yuliang said nothing. Through her laudanum-induced haze, she simply waited, and watched the room fill with girls.

Some straggled in bleeding, their cheap dresses ripped. Others sashayed in in false fur and satin. Some were older, their faces hard beneath the harsh lines and bluish bruises. Others were young enough to carry dolls. One girl, thirteen or fourteen at the most, said she had been tied to a bed and fed on table scraps, like a dog. When the German doctor tried to touch her she flung herself across the room. Sickened by the familiarity of it all, Yuliang fixed her eyes on the atrocious painting that hung on the wall: Jesus Christ, having his feet washed.

The washer girl's eyes were almond-shaped, her modeling clumsy, her color flat. The work's perspective was almost laughably skewed. And yet for all her scorn, Yuliang couldn't help but remember another pair of feet, bruised and broken in a small tin tub. She remembered Zanhua's white hands massaging corrupted tissue and shattered joints. The hours spent encouraging her ("Take a deep breath; walk with me") as, step by agonizing step, Yuliang hobbled around the house, relearning how to walk.

Eventually she drifted into a bruised half-sleep, one filled with floating images of the past. She thought she saw Jinling smiling at her, whispering, "Listen, Yuliang. *Listen* . . ." She saw Wu Ding in an opium haze. "You see?" he slurred. "You're very smart. You could be just about anything . . ." She shut her eyes against him, only to feel his soft grasp on her wrist. "Yuliang. Yuliang, my beloved. Wake up."

"Don't *touch* me." Jerking away, Yuliang opened her tired eyes again—this time to the sight of her husband.

Zanhua stood before her, his face drawn and pale, his left cheek smudged again by ink. His hair was uncombed, pointing stiffly in three directions. Confused, she tried to sit up. "How . . . ?"

He put a finger to her lips. "The painting. You wrote your name and address on the back."

She stared at him a moment, struggling to comprehend both the words and the evening's astonishing reversal—the fact that the very work that had driven them apart earlier had somehow brought them back together.

"The baby," she said at last. "They won't take it out. But I don't want . . . I can't . . ."

"Shhh," he said again. "It's all right. We'll have more."

Yuliang doesn't remember speaking another word. She just remembers the way he wrapped his arms around her. And his warmth: the way it covered her in safety. Allowing her to slip back into her stonelike sleep.

Twenty-eight

THE NEXT DAY'S TURNOUT is the best mix of wealthy Shanghainese and art-savvy Chinese. The men wear slim suits, understated ties. The women are powdered and pouting, their dresses bedecked with the braids and buckles still popular in the wake of the Great War. Altogether, they're about as far from Yuliang's loutish dream mob as could be. Still, for the first hour her heart leaps to her mouth each time anyone views her work.

The reactions fall mostly into the expected range: there are guffaws and giggles, double-takes and outright blushes. "You should be ashamed of yourself," snaps one matron. "Not even your husband should see so much of you at once." Another man studies the portrait with bulging eyes, then invites Yuliang on a holiday in Hongzhou. Far more offensive, though, is the first offer Yuliang ever receives for her work. It comes not from a man (as her nemisis predicted) but from a young couple flush with new Shanghai money.

"*Dah-ling!*" gushes the wife, using the Anglicized endearment that's now fashionable in chic social circles. "It's perfect for the parlor—it matches the chaise wonderfully."

"I don't know—the browns might not work with the ottoman."

Her husband narrows his eyes in thought. "We could try it in the billiards room."

"Or the third-floor powder room," the woman offers, already reaching for her purse. "Over the bath? Once they finish the plumbing? It might be amusing . . ."

"I'm sorry," Yuliang interrupts, unable to bear any more. "It isn't for sale."

"Not for sale?" The woman turns to her husband in confusion.

"Of course it's for sale," he says. "This is Shanghai. Everything is for sale."

"Not this," says Yuliang (though what she almost says is, *Not me*).

The woman points at *Bathing Beauty*, like a child denied a toy. "But then, why paint it at all?"

Yuliang takes her in—the impeccable bob, the tasteful nails, the Paris-perfect suit of summer wool. Her outfit and grooming for today alone likely cost more than Yuliang's entire wardrobe. Oddly enough, though, what Yuliang feels for her isn't envy but pity. *You're bored to death,* she thinks suddenly. *And you don't even know it.*

She says it gently: "I paint because I am a painter."

The majority of her viewers, however, are appreciative in far more affirming ways. "*Charmante! Une belle image—très post-impressioniste!*" exclaims one Frenchwoman, whom Yuliang only later realizes is a juror. An American in pongee pumps her hand like a well handle. Uchiyama Kanzo, the young Japanese who runs the bookstore where Guifei and Xing Xudun attend their meetings, offers to hang her work on his shop walls. Perhaps most encouraging is the French consul, also one of the day's three central judges. A florid man with a shining flap of hair combed carefully from one ear to the other, Monsieur Delafleur spends nearly five minutes before *Bathing Beauty,* blinking as though something's caught in his eye.

"You've studied abroad?" he asks Yuliang at last, through his translator.

"No, monsieur."

"You did this—how? With mirrors?"

"A combination of mirrors and memory." She drops her eyes rather than see him trying to picture her painting this way.

"Quite surprising," he offers finally, and looks her up and down once more.

There are warm responses from Chinese attendees as well. When Lo Jialiang—Silas Hardoon's wife and a well-known patron of Shanghai artists—stops by, Yuliang stands up a little straighter. The flicker in the older woman's eye as she appraises Yuliang's clothes and person evokes an uncomfortable recollection of Godmother. In the end, however, the famed socialite pronounces Yuliang (or perhaps her painting) "promising," a comment duly noted by the *Shenbao* reporter who is tailing her.

The latter photographs *Bathing Beauty,* then inquires into Yuliang's thoughts on women's suffrage and free love. When she pronounces herself in favor of the former and against the latter, he smiles skeptically, and scribbles extensively. "I'll look forward to seeing more of your work in the future," he says as he leaves. "I have a feeling Shanghai will want more of Madame Pan."

As hours pass and attention mounts, Yuliang's anxiety softens into jittery excitement. The only thing dampening her mood, in fact, is Zanhua's continuing absence.

Her husband had telegraphed her to say he'd be coming in from Guangzhou, where Sun Yat-sen is being sworn in as provisional president. His train was supposed to have arrived at one. But it is now nearly four o'clock, and Yuliang is just wondering whether he will finally fail her when she spies a slight figure striding purposefully across the room.

Joyfully, she turns to greet him, only to see not Zanhua but a dour-looking man of about his build. Three others follow forcefully in his steps.

The men march through the crowded room, ignoring the other works and artists, stopping aggressively close to her station. "This is your painting?" the leader demands.

Yuliang scans the room for Liu Haisu. But the young principal is nowhere in sight. Neither are the Russian guards he's hired for the occasion.

"Answer me! You're with the academy?" the man barks.

"What else would I be?"

Turning his head, the man spits straight onto the polished wood floor. The mucus lands, green and glittering, by Yuliang's shoetip. "You missed," she murmurs.

"*You*, miss," he retorts, "are a disgrace to your sex, your ancestors, and your nation. And this"—he waves at *Bathing Beauty*—"is a filthy excuse for art. You should be expelled, exiled and thrown into jail like a common whore. You should be beaten until you learn some respect."

The words, projected loudly enough to fill the room, have their desired impact: heads turn, eyebrows lift. The comprador's daughter breaks into one of her smuggest smiles. Out of the corner of her eye, Yuliang sees Teachers Hong and Chin whispering. *Come*, she wills them. *Come help me.*

But Teacher Hong turns on his heel and hurries off toward the gallery doors.

"You're a disgrace," her accuser continues. "You should be tried and beaten for pornography." His breath comes in short, sour bursts. Yuliang takes a step back, experiencing a chilling sense of déjà vu: she half expects Godmother to materialize by the man's taut left shoulder. Instead, to her immense relief, she spies Teacher Hong again, this time hurrying toward her. Liu Haisu strides behind him. Pushing through the gathering crowd, the school's young founder puts a heavy hand on the man's shoulder.

"Today's event is open to friends of art, progress, and the academy only, Master Jiang," he says crisply. "I don't recall extending you an invitation."

"I've come as a friend of the city," the man retorts. "And the governor. And, hopefully, to see that you've come to your senses. Which, clearly, you have not." He jabs a finger at *Bathing Beauty*. "Instead I find that things are worse than last year. Now you're corrupting young women."

"At least I'm not attacking them." Liu Haisu smiles thinly. "Does she seem such a threat to you, and your *governor*, that you need to bring his gangsters along?" His voice drips with sarcasm: Chen Jiongming may call himself governor, but in reality he's no more than the latest warlord strong enough to control the raucous city.

"She's a threat to public decency," the man continues. "So, yes. You should know we plan a full report. To Governor Chen, the Education Ministry, the provincial government authorities. If necessary, to the president as well." Reaching into his pocket, he pulls out a pamphlet. "This outlines our plans for a new law. One that will ban this filth for good."

Principal Liu scans the little paper before tossing it to the ground. "We will see," he says shortly. "To be honest, I don't think your 'law' stands much of a chance in Shanghai. Our true leaders are still more interested in modernizing than in backtracking." He turns pointedly to the door. "For now, though, I've a school to run. And you, sir, are officially unwelcome in it. As I believe I've made clear in the past."

The guards have mysteriously reappeared behind the young principal. They loom there with a comforting animosity. The interloper gives Yuliang's painting once last glare. But it's to Liu Haisu that he addresses his parting words. "Prepare yourself," he warns. "I will see you shut down."

"I'll see you on a steamship sinking down to hell first," the young artist calls after him affably.

After the man is safely through the doors, he stoops and picks up the leaflet from the ground. Crumpling it neatly, he hands it to a guard. "Burn that." He turns to Yuliang. "They didn't hurt anything, did they?"

She shakes her head, although her legs are still quivering. "Who are they?"

"Self-righteous thugs. It's not the first time they've put on a show like this." He nods toward Teacher Hong, who has drifted off to the judges' table. "At least they didn't break things. Last year they picked on Teacher Yang—made a stink over *Young Girl by a Mirror*. Smashed a few of the sculpting students' busts as well. Don't you remember?"

Yuliang nods, although in truth she'd all but forgotten. At the time she'd assumed that the protesters were just drunks. Now, shaking her head, she glances again at the double doors, hoping to see Zanhua. Instead she sees Tang Leiyi, the *Shenbao* reporter, raptly writing in his notebook. She blanches. "*Aiya*. It will be in the papers now!"

Principal Liu follows her gaze. "Of course," he says cheerily. "This is wonderful." And off he scurries again, hand outstretched.

Yuliang stares after him a moment, then presses her fingertips against her eyelids. Perhaps, she thinks tiredly, it's best Zanhua doesn't come. The last thing he would want would be to be a part of all this. And even she must admit that any wife who puts her husband through what she has is just what that man called her: a disgrace.

"Madame Pan?"

Yuliang blinks up, registering the warm gaze of Xing Xudun, her neighbor and fellow artist.

"I'm sorry," she says distractedly. "I didn't see you come in."

"Apparently I'm too late for the fireworks." He grins.

She smiles back sheepishly. "I made a spectacle of myself. In front of my superiors, no less."

"*Les grands ne nous paraissent grands que parce que nous sommes à genoux. Levons-nous!*" he declares. " 'Our superiors only appear powerful because we are on our knees. Let us get up!' " He grins. "It's what the Bonapartists said while storming the Bastille." He has, she knows, been studying French, mathematics, history, and rudimentary factory skills at the new Sino-French Educational Association school in the French Concession.

"You must be earning high marks," she tells him.

"I do well only at the things that interest me."

"Such as French?"

"Such as revolution."

Yuliang blinks at him, wondering if he is joking. But he just grins again. "Did you hear that I received my visa?"

"No! You're going, then?"

"In August." He scuffs the floor with his foot. "Perhaps we'll meet in France."

He says it tentatively, which for some reason she finds touching. "I doubt they'll want me after today," she says, fingering the little jade boar in her pocket. "You'll be in Montargis, won't you? That's far from Lyon . . . or is it? You see how little I know."

"I hope to be in Lyon as well. I'm hearing the Montargis work-study program is now too full for us. A student from my province wrote me that there's hardly any work—or even beds—for the students still there. Apparently he and dozens of others are sleeping in the administration office. Some are even in tents on its grounds."

"Why on earth do they keep sending students?"

Xudun laughs. "The problem would be if they tried to keep us from going. The chance to live in France is worth more than a few nights' bad sleep." Looking into her eyes, he adds, "Especially if the company is good."

Yuliang turns away from him, feeling her face flush slightly. Her eyes land on *Bathing Beauty*, and on impulse, she gestures. "But you still haven't told me what you think of my painting."

His eyes sweep the work without a hint of embarrassment. When he turns to her, his smile has disappeared from his face. "It's almost the most beautiful thing here," he says quietly.

For a moment neither speaks. Then he glances at the clock. "I must go. Metal-working class." His grin reappears. "I'm sorry I won't be here to see you win."

"I won't win," she says breathlessly.

"Yes, you will. I can feel it. And we'll have coffee. *Un café, s'il vous plaît.*"

Turning smartly, he doffs an imaginary bowler in a gesture taken from the latest Chaplin moving picture. As he strides out, she sees him loping across some green and Cézannesque campus. The image sparks a mild amusement—that is, until Yuliang recalls her former train of thought.

Her smile fading, she scans the room for Zanhua again. *Please come,* she prays, with a strange desperation, as though his arrival were some sort of celestial sign.

And then, just like that, he is there.

Zanhua stands in the doorway, his travel satchel in hand. Looking flustered, he nods and starts toward her. As he approaches, there's an odd urge to step in front of *Bathing Beauty*. To block it from his harried gaze. Yuliang doesn't do this, of course. She waits for him, as still as stone. And in the end he keeps his eyes on her anyway, looking neither left nor right, but directly into her eyes.

"I almost didn't make it," he says, giving her hand a hurried clasp. "The trains to Shanghai were packed after the celebrations. They had to put half of us on a later one."

He looks tense, tired. She can't tell if he's heard about the protesters. "I'm glad you're here," she tells him. "They're about to say whether we have won."

Yuliang doesn't know why she says *we* instead of *I*. Nor does she know why she then turns, and points to her painting. It's a different urge from the one that made her turn Xudun's attention to her image, and her emotions are also different at this moment: her heart beats as though Zanhua were not merely her husband, but one of the day's judges. And when his eyes don't—or won't—leave her face, a small part of her suddenly feels as though she has already lost.

Thankfully, though, the feeling lasts just a moment. Then Liu Haisu's clear voice rings out across the room. "Ladies and gentlemen! *Mesdames et messieurs!*" He is looking right at her, a broad smile on his face.

"May I please have your attention," the principal continues. "We're delighted to announce today's results."

Across the room, faces turn to stare—not in contempt or avarice, but in anticipation and encouragement.

I can't do it, Yuliang thinks giddily, in sheer terror. *I will never move again.* It's as though iron nails pin her feet to the floor.

But then Zanhua is beside her, taking her arm. "Come," he murmurs. "Walk with me." And, step by step, he helps her walk across the room. Away from *Beauty*. Toward the judges' decision.

Part SEVEN

L'ÉCOLE

The waters are blue, the plants pink; the evening is sweet to look on;

One goes for a walk; the grandes dames go for a walk; behind
them stroll the petites dames.

———

NGUYEN TRONG HIEP,
PARIS, CAPITALE DE LA FRANCE:
RECUEIL DE VERS (HANOI, 1897)

Twenty-nine

France, 1923

IN JULY SHE LEAVES LYON and its staid streets of finance and industry and boards a northbound train for the capital. She answers the conductor's queries politely, in her still-stilted French, and ignores the offended gaze of her carriagemate, an elderly matron with buttercream hair. One of the things Yuliang has learned, over these past two years, is to use unwanted notice as an excuse to cocoon herself in her own thoughts. Pulling her book from her purse, she opens it, screening herself from view and taking some satisfaction in the thought of the title (which, unlike herself, is clearly French).

The book is Tolstoy's *What Is Art?*, a new edition sent back to her by Xing Xudun after he arrived here. Though Yuliang's French has improved vastly reading it is still laborious, and in the end she rarely gets past the Chinese inscription: *I thought of our first conversation when I found this, and am overjoyed at the thought of you holding it in your beautiful artist's hands. I look forward, still, to that long-awaited cup of coffee. S'il vous plaît.*

What Yuliang is looking for, however, isn't this somewhat audacious note, or even the book itself. It's what lies sandwiched between the pages: a letter, postmarked Paris but written in Chinese. Yuliang slides it out, appreciatively eyeing the graceful characters. Apart from Liu Haisu's characterization of him as an overdressed windbag, she doesn't know much about Xu Beihong. But if the old proverb about painting and calligraphy flowing from the same brush is true, his work must be truly impressive.

She scans the note again, double-checking the details for the meeting the young artist has proposed for tomorrow. It's at eleven-thirty; if she's lucky, she thinks, perhaps he will buy her some lunch. Her mouth waters at the thought of croque-monsieur: since the Anhui government cut her stipend six months ago, she's had meat only a handful of times.

Sliding the note back between the uncut pages of *What Is Art?*, Yuliang gazes hungrily at the cover for a moment. Then, sensing the old woman's eyes again, she turns her attention to the scenery outside.

It's the kind of vista so loved by Millet: green pines forming the darkest point of summer's spectrum; the bright, blurred forms of peasants working the wheat-brown fields; houses of toasted crimson flashing past in chortling rhythm, beneath clouds as clean and white as combed cotton. The landscape is as lovely as any ever imagined from a cramped, smoky classroom in Shanghai. Nearly three years after she arrived here, though, it also strikes her as ordinary. Uninterpreted by paint, it's not a landscape—just land. Far more interesting is her own reflection against it: a sober-eyed young woman, her image melting into tracks that lead steadily westwards.

XU BEIHONG IS NEARLY a full hour late for their appointment the next day, but he makes no pretense of apology. Instead, in a regal motion (oddly in keeping with his red velvet coat) he waves down a passing waiter. He requests *café noisette* for himself and adds half a pitcher of milk to the coffee. He plunks in several sugar cubes.

Observing him, Yuliang notes his soft chin and full lips, both at odds with a broad, strong nose. Jinling, she thinks, would have liked this man's face. She would have said his nose predicted strength in finance, his lips and chin a weakness for pleasure. A fortuitous combination, at the Hall.

"So," the artist says, sipping his milky beverage. "You want to study here. But your letter implied a complication."

"These explain it better than I could." Yuliang removes the other two notes she has stored in her Tolstoy. One is her curt Beaux Arts rejection notice. The other is even curter; the communiqué from the Anhui government notifying her that both her scholarships have been withdrawn.

The young artist scans first one, then the other. Yuliang settles back to study Parisian café culture, something that on her last brief trip here she had no time for. It is indeed a far cry from Lyon. As she watches, a man dressed in a harlequin costume prances past, delivering a note to a girl who is sitting across the room. The girl reads it and blows a languid kiss to the note's sender. She herself is dressed in what looks like a man's military uniform, her poodle tucked like a purse beneath one arm. Between its golden hairclips and monkey-fur-trimmed little sweater, the dog is decidedly better dressed than its owner. Or (Yuliang thinks dryly) than Yuliang herself.

"You were with the new Sino-French Institute?" Xu Beihong is asking.

Yuliang forces her attention back to her own table. "Just for six months. Before I transferred to the art academy in Lyon."

"Long enough to tire of grammar drills and endless lessons on table manners." He drums his fingers. "Were you there for the demonstrations?"

"Yes."

"You participated?"

"No. But I supported them." And, as he lifts an eyebrow: "They were in the right. The Chinese consul told them he'd guarantee their admission."

"From what I've read that's not his story."

She sets her cup down. "Then he's a coward and a liar."

Her companion looks amused. "Shouldn't you be careful? For all you know, he might have friends in this café."

"If he does, they're not friends of mine." Still, Yuliang casts another glance around. The dark young woman is now feeding her poodle almond pastry, shredding it with gold-painted fingernails before pushing the bits between the dog's black gums.

"Do you ever honey your words?" Xu Beihong asks, reaching again for the sugar.

"I did at one time. But I've learned you can't paint with honey."

He smiles, a slow, warm grin that seems to illuminate the air around him. "Bravo! You'll do well here, mademoiselle."

"Madame," Yuliang corrects him.

"That's right," he says, without interest. Patting his pockets, he pulls out a tarnished cigarette case. "This stuff about the consul," he says, flicking a Gauloise into his mouth and putting the case back, without offering it. "You heard it directly?"

Yuliang nods. "A friend of mine from the academy came to Lyon from the Montargis faction."

"And he said he'd been lied to."

"They all did. I believed them." She laughs, remembering. "Although at that point I barely believed I was in France."

"And this friend—he was one of the radicals?"

"A student, like me. Or—anyone else." Yuliang had been going to say *like you*. But even though the young artist graduated from the Beaux Arts just last year, she senses that he'd bridle at the suggestion they're contemporaries. Xu Beihong has, after all, already shown with two salons. He is a protégé of the realist Dagnan-Bouveret.

"It's just that the government had taken away his stipend," she continues. "His job—he worked in an auto factory in Montargis— paid less than a living wage, let alone enough for schooling. It left no time to study, in any case."

She stares into her coffee. It's excellent—cleanly bitter, far stronger than the black-tinged brew she's allowed herself since her funds were cut off. But what she sees, staring down, is not this potent and precious liquid, but Xing Xudun's warm eyes staring back without shame or reserve.

THE DAY SHE'D LAST SEEN HIM, Yuliang had been racing to class, her head filled with half-learned phrases and faces. Her taste buds felt flattened by all the butter she'd been eating, and at night Zanhua's absence felt like a fresh bruise. Against the empty ache of her home-sickness, the abrupt descent of a crowd of shouting Chinese students almost felt like a small homecoming. Pushing her way through them, she even found herself smiling at their high spirits. They greeted her in a flurry of dialects, French, and even a little German. They offered her a beer, a chocolate. A placard. "I have class," she'd laughed. "Please let me pass."

But then she'd paused, registering for the first time the image on the signboard she'd just rejected: two strong hands. Reaching across a giant globe to clasp each other.

And suddenly there was Xing Xudun, as large as a statue before her.

"*Levons-nous!*" he boomed, and spread his arms in welcome.

Her shocked hesitation stranded him for a moment, like some enormous bird. He dropped his arms, but not his smile. "Wh—when did you get here?" Yuliang stammered.

"Just this morning. Consul Chen paid our way. He's supporting our fight to find placement here." Someone shouted his name from across the crowded student green. Xing Xudun waved back, his long arm reaching into the brilliant autumn sky. "Loosen your belt, will you?" he called back. "The others aren't even here yet." He turned back to Yuliang. "Where have they put you?"

"In the girls' dorm." She grimaced. "With five other girls. And you?"

"That," he said cheerfully, "is what we're here to settle." Another grin. "But if all goes according to our plan, perhaps we can finally go and get that coffee."

"*Xudun!*" his friends called again. "We need that banner, comrade!"

He touched Yuliang's elbow. "Listen. Are you free tomorrow, at, say, four?"

Yuliang had a seminar at four, on French culture and etiquette. She considered this. Then she said, "Yes."

"Good." Xudun smiled again—or perhaps he simply hadn't stopped. "I usually need a coffee at four. Meet me here, then. *S'il vous plaît.*" And off he loped across the trim green campus.

Yuliang went on to class in a state of pleased anticipation. By nightfall, though, she couldn't shake that vague sense of guilt she always felt when she saw him, though she told herself there was no reason for it. *It's just Xudun. We're just meeting to discuss art.* To soothe herself, she recited Li Qingzhao's "Red Plum Blossom" three times, then composed a list of scholarly subjects to discuss.

She spent the next morning and early afternoon at the Lyon Fine Arts Museum, copying Van Goghs she wanted to show him at their meeting. At three o'clock—somewhat early—she packed her satchel and hurried back, reaching their meeting spot a little before four.

Xudun, however, was nowhere to be seen. Nor were any of the other protesters. Grass was uprooted; placards lay crumpled, stripped, and smudged. Cigarette butts littered the site. When Yuliang asked what had happened, the old janitor who was cleaning up the mess just pointed toward the men's dormitories. It was then that she saw the line of police wagons parked in front of them. When she tried to push through the crowd, an officer blocked her. "Go home, little Chinagirl," he said. "Stay away from these lemon-faced troublemakers."

It wasn't until much later that Yuliang read the story in the French papers: how, threatened with expulsion from the university, Xudun and sixty others locked themselves in the men's dormitories, chanted slogans, and sang "La Marseillaise," eventually unrolling a banner Xudun had drawn of a blindfolded figure captioned both *La Justice* and 正义, its Chinese counterpart. How most were trundled off to holding pens in Marseille, and from there shipped home on French postal steamers. How one hung himself, in shame, on the way.

For several months, proceeding numbly from grammar to history to etiquette class, she'd assumed that Xudun too had shared in this fate. It wasn't until his note came that she learned that he and several others were still in Marseille. They'd been helped by Le Parti Communiste Francais, with whom they'd formed a European branch of the Chinese Communist Youth Corps.

"I wouldn't really have considered myself a radical before," he concluded in his neat, dark script. "But if that's what they want of me, then *par Dieu,* that is what they'll get."

Now Yuliang stirs her coffee, smiling as she almost always smiles when she thinks of this earnest pronouncement, which even now strikes her less as "radical" than as unaccountably sweet. For in the end, for all his impertinence and his talk of "revolution," this is the impression Xudun always seems to leave with her: *sweet boy.*

"It's hard for all of us," Xu Beihong is saying, sipping his sugared sludge. "We didn't come like rich Americans, to drink and eat and dance *le Charleston* all night." He nods toward a table of them, speaking loudly in their twanging voices. "We have to make our own way. We have to work."

"He was trying to get into a course that would let him both live and study," Yuliang protests.

"And he failed."

"The system failed *him.* It failed all of us." Yuliang eyes him evenly. It is clear that he is bored now by this subject. She picks another, which she expects he will like more. "Is it true that you've been accepted into the next salon?"

Predictably, the artist's frown inverts into a small, smug smile. "Four paintings so far. And five more that they're deliberating on."

He leans back expansively. "But I want to hear more of you. How did you manage to transfer to the Lyon Beaux Arts so quickly?"

"Principal Liu Haisu helped set up the arrangement. He had an acquaintance there."

"Liu Haisu." He pronounces the name as though it rings a distant bell, and Yuliang suppresses a small smile. In Shanghai, Xu Beihong and Liu Haisu are now almost as famous as rivals as Picasso and Matisse are here in Europe. It's even said that when Liu Haisu started his Heavenly Horse painting society in Shanghai, Xu Beihong counter-launched his own painting society here: the Heavenly Dog Society. So named because dog eats horse. Having met Xu Beihong, Yuliang now fully believes this story. It's about the level of hubris she'd expect from a man wearing red velvet.

"So Monsieur Liu pulled some strings to get you in at Lyon," he's saying now. "But I take it they don't reach to Paris." He sounds distinctly pleased by this fact as he picks up the other letter: Yuliang's Beaux Arts rejection. " 'Respectable performance, particularly in coloration,'" he translates, with an ease that makes her envious. "That's not so bad. Many people don't even survive the entrance *concours*. Is it still three days of exercises—perspective, portraiture, architectural drawing, et cetera?"

Yuliang nods. "I think I did all right until the oral part." Grilled in Renaissance art history by a man who might have sat with Marat on the revolutionary tribunals, she'd felt her French disintegrate, hard-won word by hard-won word. Everything she had memorized—phrases, dates, architectural jargon—vanished like so much candied rice paper on her tongue.

"Which old fart was it?" he asks.

"Lambour. Or Lambourelle. Something like that."

"*Ah, oui.* Claude Lambourdière." He rolls his eyes. "A negligible talent. He got his job because he exhibited with Pissarro in the old days. Which is somewhat ironic, since Pissarro didn't even go to the BA." He glances at the portfolio that has been leaning against her leg throughout their talk. Yuliang lugged it here from her *pen-*

sion this morning, despite a fear that this would seem forward. "May I . . . ?"

Yuliang nods, her mouth suddenly as dry as the cardboard folder itself as Xu Beihong leafs through its contents, cigarette dangling from pursed lips. "The problem," she tells him, suppressing a surge of anxiety, "is that even if the Beaux Arts had accepted me, I'd still need a scholarship. The government cut off my stipend too. They're cutting everyone's. I guess they need every bit of gold to fight the warlords."

Pausing over a Cézannesque landscape, the young artist chuckles. Thankfully, it is not over her work. "No one born abroad will ever get a centime from the Beaux Arts," he says. *"It's like trying to pull ivory from a dog's mouth."*

He shifts through several more pieces, staring at each with practiced intensity before finally stubbing out his second, half-smoked cigarette. "Very impressive," he says at last, sliding the folder back toward her legs. "Though I'd urge you to take yourself to the Louvre immediately for a healthy dose of Prud'hon, Delacroix, and Rembrandt. What you must focus on is form. That's the meat of art. You paint with honey after all, Madame Pan."

He waves at another waiter, one carrying a tray of small tarts. "Speaking of food, how important is it?"

"Excuse me?"

"You're about to move to the culinary capital of Europe. Some say the world. Although I have to say I wish they'd use more salt." Lifting the pitcher, he dumps what's left into his cup. A bit splashes, less a drip by now than a milky shadow of one. "By the way," he adds, lowering his voice conspiratorially, "never salt foie gras. No matter how bland it tastes. It's rude. Like taking the last dumpling." He conveys the sloshing cup to his lips, sips. Then adds, "You think I'm joking."

"About the foie gras?"

"About the food."

"*Are* you?" Yuliang says it with a hint of annoyance. She hasn't the faintest idea where this conversation is leading. And for all her hopes of a free meal, her celebrated host hasn't even looked at the menu.

"Think about it," he says. "What's more important, a good painting or a good slab of beef? Or, for that matter, one of those loud Poiret dresses my wife is always pointing out to me?"

The answer comes without hesitation: "A painting. Of course."

He grins again: that slow and liquid beam, and again Yuliang feels an absurd flush of pleasure. He is, she suddenly realizes, a man who flashes his charm like a swordmaster: it is his secret weapon.

"*Justement,*" he says. "The steak fills you for a day. The dress will win you compliments, at least from my wife, for a week. But in ten years' time, or a hundred, what you've made here"—he indicates the portfolio—"will remain. Your children, your children's children will see it. You have children?"

The waiter arrives. Xu Beihong hands him the creamer, although Yuliang wonders why—by this point he barely has any coffee left. "Not yet." She looks away. "But I do need a little food to live on. Don't I?"

"A little," Xu Beihong concedes as the waiter materializes again, to replace the tiny pitcher with a flourish. "And as you'll discover, a little in Paris costs much more than a little elsewhere. Biwei and I moved to Berlin for a while last year, thinking it would be cheaper." He pops a sugar cube into his mouth. "Of course prices were rising *there* at a rate beyond comprehension. You've heard how it is?" He crunches, swallows audibly. "Bread cost a mark or two at war's end. It cost two hundred *billion* marks—or more—by the time we left. Our friends with jobs were getting paid two or three times daily, just to keep up with inflation. But even then they had to race to buy things—basic things." He shakes his head fondly, as though this recollection were one of the happier ones of the trip. "Things are better now. *If* you have talent, and if you know a few tricks—no bonbons, no fancy hats or shoes. On some days, even many, no dinner. Do all this and you'll get along, as I have." Here he breaks into a hacking, chest-deep cough that for some might have undermined his point. The waiter appears like a genie, a glass of water on his tray.

"As for the school," Xu Beihong goes on, after a sip or two, "at heart they still don't want anyone who's not born here. When they do accept them, they give them *postes extraordinaires*. Not full student status. Those they leave for the full-blooded Frenchmen. Those few who are left after the war, of course." He finishes his water. "And you know, of course, that even if you win the school's highest competition, the Prix de Rome, you won't get the prize. Or the purse."

Finishing off his coffee, he signals to the waiter and, in French as virtually free of shame as it is of accent, requests *un petit pot* of hot water. Then he turns back to Yuliang. "So don't build that into your budget," he adds in Chinese.

The waiter returns with a steaming teapot. "Anything else, monsieur?"

"No. Thank you, André." The young artist produces from his jacket pocket a hard roll that looks suspiciously like those Yuliang had seen outside, left on tables by paying customers. As he dips it into the milky mixture she stares at her place setting, remembering those first dreary weeks in Lyon. *Small fork for salads. Big fork for meat. Knife for cutting meat, not butter. Spoon for soup or ices, never for the dinner plate. But don't lick it when you use it. And don't touch any of the utensils before you unless you plan to use them.* Somewhat defiantly, she picks up her soupspoon, studies it. What she sees is her own face, clouded. Upside down.

"My husband wants me to come home," she says abruptly.

"My wife wants me to stop buying paintings," he replies affably. "My gallery wants me to pay its commission. The world will always want us to spend differently, think differently." He jabs his finger at her. "What is it *you* want?"

"To stay." The answer wells up fully, a small part of her soul. "I want to live here. To paint here. I want nothing more. But if the Beaux Arts won't take me . . ."

"They'll take you."

She stares at him. "How? I didn't pass the entrance examination."

"There is more than one entrance to the rabbit's burrow. If you know where to look. Have you heard of the *étudiants libres*? They're alternates, effectively. But if you're disciplined, and if you form a good relationship with the *maître de session*, you can get every bit as good an education as any Frenchman." He finishes the bread, wipes his slim fingers on his napkin. "And while I can't get you a scholarship, I can help find you cheap lodging. You wouldn't need to pay much." He looks at her thoughtfully. "Do you embroider?"

She blinks. "A little."

"Biwei does some work for the Magasins du Louvre. You know, handkerchiefs, scarves, ties. That sort of thing. It's manual labor, of course. But it pays well enough."

Despite herself Yuliang stiffens, thinking of her mother. Her long, artful fingers, her glorious threaded gardens. *It isn't like assembling a Renault,* she wants to tell him.

"Of course," he says, misinterpreting her expression, "if that's not what you want—"

"No!" Yuliang forces a smile. "It's—it's so much more than I deserve. I'd be so grateful . . ."

He nods beneficently. "All I'd ask in return is that you keep me in mind if you happen to meet anyone useful."

"Useful?"

"Oh, critics. Important painters. No picture dealers, though. If you ask me, their goal's to squeeze the life from art as we all know it." Scanning the room, his face suddenly brightens. "*Allo!* Fujita!" he shouts at a couple that's just been seated. The darker and more diminutive of the women turns to face them, and it's only then that Yuliang sees that it isn't a woman at all. It is, rather, an Oriental with a severe haircut, owlish glasses, and glittering golden hoops in each ear. He waves back at Xu Beihong, then turns back to his companion. "Fujita Tsuguharu," Beihong offers, turning back to face her.

"*That's* Fujita?" The man, Yuliang notes, is also wearing lipstick. Expensive lipstick, from the look of it.

"In the flesh, as they say. He calls himself Leonard Foujita here." Xu signals the waiter. "His painting's a bit bland for me. Lots of skinny girls and cats. But his lines are lovely. And of course he's very well connected."

He is also clearly successful. As Yuliang watches enviously, the Japanese artist picks several tarts from a passing pastry cart. To her horror her own stomach growls. She crosses her arms over it quickly.

"Are you all right?" Xu Beihong is watching her with amusement.

"What? Oh. Of course." She fights back a flush. "I was thinking about that old saying. About not being able to draw a cake and eat it too."

He grunts. "One of Biwei's favorites. I heard it often in Berlin."

"And what did you tell her?"

Xu Beihong pulls his fragile frame slightly straighter. "That if I give up my art, I'll end up eating my dreams. And dead dreams are worse than hunger. They're poison."

He holds her gaze for a moment. Then he licks his teaspoon, crunching its last granules of sugar with clear relish.

Thirty

IT IS NOT QUITE EIGHT-THIRTY, and the door to the Ampitheatre d'Honneur has been left very slightly ajar. Sounds of morning setup echo into the Cour Vitrée: easels clatter, stools shriek across the warped wooden floor. *"Alors,"* someone scoffs. "That's the boy? Looks more like a monkey."

"More like your sweetheart, you mean." The second voice is deep, full of soft consonants and silky vowels. Yuliang recognizes an Italian whom she often works beside in session.

"Which sweetheart?" says the Frenchman. "Your mother?"

"Vaffuncuolo! Vai in culo!"

Yuliang, standing outside with the other alternates, stifles a tired smile. She doesn't know what the Roman said, of course. But it sounded quite satisfyingly like a curse. She senses that she would like Italy.

"Gentlemen!" A third voice now: it's Vincent, the professor's assistant, charged with collecting the monthly fees, calling out the rest and pose times for the models, and in general maintaining the atelier's order. "If you insist on fisticuffs, please go over to Julian's," he says, referring to the cheaper—and famously rowdier—atelier across town. "Otherwise, please shake hands and resume painting." He returns to roll call: "Baudin!"

"*Oui.*" Coins clink. The fee, three hundred francs, is a full three quarters of the allowance Zanhua sends her: paying it, Yuliang always feels a swell of frustration at how little it leaves her for the next four weeks. Even more frustrating is the fact that, as dear as the money is, it's no guarantee that she'll get into session—even though she's usually first in the alternate line. Which is no easy task in itself: faced with reading assignments that often take her days to translate, as well as the embroidery assignments Xu Beihong's wife passes over to her every few weeks, Yuliang frequently doesn't sleep until three or four in the morning.

Worse than sleeplessness, though, is hunger. She survives on a pauper's diet: coffee, day-old bread, the occasional bruised, discounted fruit. Thanks to soaring postwar inflation and the weakening yuan against the franc, Yuliang has even had to sacrifice her monthly Métropolitain rides. Now she walks to the Chinese legation, on shoes with soles that have given way to holes and patches made of cut-up canvases. It comes as little surprise, then, that exhaustion, like hunger, is mated to her; that she paints in a kind of giddy fog. Still, walking gives her time to look about her. And hunger adds a poignant glow to the city's already ethereal beauty. The sheer number of styles and schools and eras of Paris's famed architecture baffled her at the start. But at the same time it charmed her; the way each architectural thought seemed perfectly harmonized with its surroundings. It's a marked contrast to Lyon's low-lying urban sprawl. Or Shanghai's Bund, where old and the new clash against the shoreline, bickering members of some enormous concrete clan.

But most of all, of course, there is art.

Art is everywhere here: sedately hung in the city's *musées*, blaring in crowded color in galleries and exhibitions. It beckons from cathedral alcoves and dangles from café walls, its tones darkened by smoke and kitchen grease. In her first week in Paris Yuliang all but lived at the Louvre, sketching until her neck ached and her eyes smarted. Her feet and legs throbbed from all the walking and standing. But she tackled each style in turn: classic, Renaissance, realist. Romantic. She stared for hours at the brilliant blues and gilded ochers of Fra Angelico's *Coronation of the Virgin*; at Corot's frayed and tender *Woman with a Pearl*. In China, she wrote to Zanhua, *such works would be locked away in the mansions and palaces. Here they are strung up like peppers drying for the winter! Anyone with five centimes can come see them, sketch them. Do anything, in fact, but touch them.*

She can see, too, how Teacher Hong was so tempted, as he'd told her, to reach out and connect with such wonders. And yet Yuliang doesn't need to touch them. Just as she doesn't need guides or teachers to articulate dryly why these works matter so supremely. Every time she copies from Raphael's *Portrait of Baldassare Castiglione* (admired by Cézanne, Matisse, and Titian) she comes away more in awe of the Umbrian's skills, of his controlled lines, his expert shadows and blending. At two paces, the work embraces her as powerfully as any living man.

Although of course she doesn't write *this* to Zanhua. Not just because it would seem hurtful, but because she's given up trying to communicate in writing the way such works make her feel. It's like trying to define the undefinable: infinity, enlightenment. It's like trying to put true words to love.

Instead, she sketches him little pictures of vistas and monuments: the Arc de Triomphe, Sacré Coeur, the Luxembourg Gardens. She writes that she misses him, and this of course is true. *There is no one here,* she writes, *who knows me as you do . . . I missed you at sunset last night, walking home. You would have enjoyed the sights . . . I spent last night reading the book of poetry you gave me and drinking wine. I very much miss playing our poetry game together . . .* But even as she writes these things, and addresses the letters in two different languages, and carries them to the legation for expedited posting, another hangnail of guilt snags. For the bigger truth, the *overriding* truth, is that she's not merely happy here.

It is that she has never been happier.

"Are you all right?"

Yuliang drops her gaze from the courtyard's iron and glass rooftop. Her friend Fan Junbi is peering at her with concern. "I'm fine," she says. "Why?"

"You were swaying again. And your eyes look . . . odd. Red."

"I think I'm tired. I had to embroider until nearly two last night, and then translate that piece for art history."

"Oh, Yuliang. You know you could have read my translation. It takes me half the time it takes you."

This is true. And yet Yuliang shakes her head. "I need to do it myself."

"You," Junbi pronounces, "are as stubborn as a water buffalo." She reaches into her bag. "What were you embroidering?"

"Men's silk cravats. *Le Louvre, Paris, 1924.*" Yuliang holds up her fingers morosely: they are dotted with tiny sores. "I lost my thimble, too. I practically sewed it into my own skin."

"Eat this." Junbi pulls out a small package. Inside the folded newsprint is a croissant: the scent hits Yuliang like a waft from heaven. It is every bit as rich and light as one of Van Gogh's glowing wheatfields. "The baker gave us a dozen of them at closing yesterday," her friend says.

"But you should keep it," Yuliang protests. "You have more mouths to feed."

Junbi, who has been in France for nearly a decade, lives with her husband (a rising star in the Republican Party) as well as her young son and one surviving sister. The other, an early anti-Qing revolutionary, was beheaded during the first rebellion. "We have too many," she says. "I'll bring another for you tomorrow."

Gratefully, Yuliang rewraps the little parcel. She's hungry enough to eat it now, but food isn't allowed in session. And she certainly doesn't want to jeopardize her hard-earned position in line by greeting Vincent with a mouthful of crumbs.

At 8:45, Vincent appears with his clipboard and his hat. "*Alors,*" he says. "Many people are under the weather again today, it seems. Pay November's *masse,* and you all get to work." To Yuliang, he says, "Ahead of the crowd again, Mademoiselle Pan."

"Madame," Yuliang reminds him. "I get up early out of habit," she adds, trying both to summon and to translate that old saying about rice fields and dawn, before deciding that she's too tired. Instead she hands over her handful of mixed bills and coins.

To her surprise, however, Vincent pulls the tin away. "*Vous savez*," he says quietly, "if you need the money you can hold off. Pay me later."

Yuliang looks at him warily, wondering whether he's taunting her—or, worse, trying to seduce her, as he tried to once last term. This time, though, his gray eyes reflect only honest sympathy. "Maître Simon gives me license to help those who need it. But don't worry. We keep a record." He grins. "You can repay us when you become rich and famous."

For a moment, Yuliang actually lets herself consider it. Three hundred francs would mean the new tube of cadmium green she's been putting off buying. She could replace her easel, which has lost several screws and totters slightly when she strokes too heavily on the right. And of course there's the new winter hat she's wanted. Perhaps a felt derby with a feather or sparkling brooch. She would wear it low, to accent her self-trimmed fringe, and to keep her ears warm in the winter wind . . .

But even as she weighs the option, a thick and oversweet voice seems to breathe into her inner ear: *Pretty, isn't it? You can buy it. I'll just add it to the black book.*

"I'm fine," she says curtly. And drops the money in the tin.

INSIDE THE AMPHITHEATER the mood has settled. Students work in an absorbed semicircle around the nude's block, their easels lined up against worn tape marks on the floor. Sunlight spills through the high windows, illuminating tin cans of brushes and flat glass palettes as well as the impressive frescoes on the walls—life-sized portraits of seventy-five of the West's greatest figures in art. All (Yuliang noted immediately) are men; the only females are those depicted by Delaroche as the four great art periods: Greek, Roman, Gothic, and

Renaissance. There is also *la Génie des Art,* buxom and bare-breasted, distributing laurel crowns to the men who flank her. The painting, rendered in wax, still bears the mark of a fire eighty years earlier, which melted the *genie*'s navel and streaked Renaissance's face with glutinous, soot-toned tears.

Still, as always when setting up, Yuliang finds her spirits rising. She devours these hours as she once devoured the sweets her uncle splurged on, usually after an unexplained absence. "Your veins must be filled with sweet bean paste instead of blood," her *jiujiu* would joke. "I've never seen such a greedy little demon." She never told him, of course, that such bingeing stemmed not from greed but practicality: too many of Wu Ding's gifts vanished, once sobriety and debt cast their long shadows in the daylight.

Now, using her brush, Yuliang checks her angle against the model, whom Vincent pokes and prods so his member falls as it did yesterday. In the beginning, such sights so mortified one other Chinese student that she actually fled the room. Yuliang, though, feels less discomposure than sheer sympathy for the boy. He can't, she reflects, be here by choice. He's no more than fourteen, an age at which (as Yuliang knows only too well) offering up one's body for inspection isn't easy. His slumped form, the shoulders newly broad but the chest still bare of manly hair, strikes her as a study in conflict; like the full lips shadowed with the mocking down of adolescence. It is these contrasts, she decides now, that she wants to capture in her painting: the battling forces of vulnerability and manhood. The simultaneous dread of and longing for adulthood.

Unsheeting her palette, Yuliang takes a moment—only one—to reflect on the fact that she herself never harbored such conflict. That her childhood was stripped away with such brutal efficacy that she barely noticed that her wounds had left her a woman. She doesn't, however, linger on this. As she once told her husband, we are rooted in the present. And at this particular present, for better or for worse, there is no place she would rather be.

She dips her brush in Venetian red, and begins.

Thirty-One

Paris, 1925

MAY ARRIVES OVERNIGHT, touching the Luxembourg Gardens with soft shades of pink and violet and green. But while fresh blooms materialize, Yuliang's monthly allowance does not.

The last she'd heard from Zanhua was a telegram in late March, sent shortly after Sun Yat-sen's sudden death: *The loss of the general is a disaster. Am being reassigned to Nanjing. Will send details and monies when settled.*

But that was more than five weeks ago. There has been nothing since. And there have been no further notes from Xu Beihong's wife, offering work. Down to her last few centimes, Yuliang waits—and worries: she has only one month left in the Beaux Arts program, but even if Zanhua's allowance arrives, she'll barely make *masse*. The heel on her Mary Janes has broken, forcing her to buy cheap new shoes. At twenty francs, they all but clean out her grocery budget.

She eats the last of her canned sardines and peaches, her boiled eggs and dried macaroni, before resorting to a stealthier subsistence: secreting away hors d'oeuvres at art openings. Collecting bruised apples left behind by the vendors at day's end. Sometimes, even rescuing brioches left for pigeons in the parks. Yuliang has always been a selective eater, if for no other reason than that she's had so little choice in other matters. Now, though, sheer hunger drives her to eat anything. Her mouth even waters at the crumbling gray cheese that looks like plaster and smells of used foot-bindings.

Happily, the warming weather makes at least a few things easier. It nullifies the need for charcoal at night, and graces her easel with longer, richer light. The outdoor diners who flock to the Rues Montparnasse and Vavin often leave bread and scraps on their tables. Following Xu Beihong's example, Yuliang spirits these away, always keeping a sharp eye out for waiters. She still rebuffs Vincent's offer to defer paying *masse*. But she does allow him to give her food left over from the still-life displays. She makes the orange an appetizer. The pear is the main dish; she cuts into sheer slices with her palette knife.

As the days drag by, the hunger worsens. But she tries to tell herself that it's no worse than a cold or a headache. That there will be plenty of time to eat later, when she's back home. She reminds herself of her mama's tales of eating bark, and dust. She tries to treat the sensations of starvation—the dull ache replacing her gut, the blurred vision, the starlike sparks that perpetually seem to orbit its periphery—as a luxury: as sensations, after all, they are far preferable to many she was forced to live through at the Hall. And besides, there are so many other things to fill her attention: her slow mastery of painting with the tip of her knife, and of pointillism. Of fauvist coloration. The endless array of masters waiting at the Louvre. Most encouragingly, there is Lucien Simon's recent and unexpected encouragement for her to submit to the Salon d'Automne.

The *maître*, a known champion of both women and foreign students, stopped by her easel recently on one of his leisurely ambles around the room, during which he critiques each student's work in turn. With most he corrects and counters; picking up a paintbrush or a maulstick to highlight an eye or a dark pleat. But when he arrived at Yuliang's painting, a sober-toned Mary Magdalene based on a plaster cast of the Michelangelo sculpture, Lucien Simon simply watched, his long fingers stroking his carefully trimmed goatee.

"What is that?" he asked at last, pointing to one of Yuliang's three central colors.

"Cadmium yellow, mixed with white and phthalo green."

He nodded. "Not so far off. And where will the cheekbone be?"

She indicated a slanting line just beneath one of Mary's sad eyes.

"Excellent. You must always be looking for the bone."

With a nod, the *maître* moved on to the next student. After class, however, he pulled Yuliang aside. "Your work is quite distinctive. Have you considered submitting it to the salon?"

"Me?" she asked, astounded.

"You shouldn't be so surprised. Your paintings have exoticism, a fresh face. They are looking for such things these days."

Yuliang left the seminar that day in an even greater haze than usual. But despite his encouragement, she can't settle on a subject. Every idea that comes seems neither exotic nor fresh enough to satisfy her, let alone the salon judges. More disturbingly, her mind and eyes are beginning to betray her. In class, she has difficulty distinguishing between the simple tones on her palette. Her productivity drops. She can't concentrate in session. She sits through lectures and seminars in a fog, penciling in notes—*sensibilité moderne, le fruit defendu dans le paradis, les ouvriers se font passer pour des bourgeoises*—in a blurring mélange of French and Chinese which later confounds her completely.

Finally, one day, while she is working on a still life in class—a teal vase filled with velvet-petaled roses—the room starts to reel in concert around her. When Yuliang drops her gaze the worn pine floorboards lurch toward her. Their age-old tape marks and splatters of ink black, Canton rose, Egyptian violet bleed and recede, then abruptly rush forward again, to blanket her in a rainbow of darkness.

SHE WAKES SLICK WITH SWEAT, in her own small bed. A metal pot of some sort has been left on her painting table. So has some wine, some bread and cheese, and a short note in French:

The doctor said you simply need nutrition and rest. Please stay home
Monday. I promise that you can make up the time later.

Vincent

Yuliang rises and lifts the lid on the pot. Fat has congealed like wax over the beans. But the mere smell of it—salt and meat, lard and garlic—cramps her stomach in anticipation.

It's not until she replaces the lid that she spots the letter lying next to it, in the familiar yellow envelope sealed with an Anhui Prefecture seal. A note is jotted directly on the envelope: *Have sent your allowance,* it reads. *Check with funds manager at legation.*

For several moments she just stares at it. Then she picks up her jade letter opener and breaks the red wax of the seal. Carefully, she slides free Zanhua's note.

Its contents are nothing unusual: complaints about incompetent superiors, delayed paychecks and office intrigue; updates on the ongoing antiwarlord campaigns; musings over the power struggle between right and left that has emerged following Sun Yat-sen's death. The latter, Zanhua writes, is largely the reason he was passed over for another promotion. *Which was just as well*, he adds. *The supervisor is both corrupt and inept. And at least now I can focus on our new home and on Guanyin's health.*

At the characters for *Guanyin*, Yuliang catches her breath: it's the first time Zanhua has mentioned his first wife by name in two years. It is also the first concrete confirmation of something Yuliang has long suspected: that they are finally living together.

Stunned, she traces the characters with her fingertip, remembering the expressionless girl in the matchmaker's photograph. When Yuliang had first heard her name (Guanyin! Goddess of Mercy!), she'd actually laughed. Now, though, an emptiness seems to spread through her, bleak and damp-fingered, and utterly unrelated to her hunger.

She fully realizes that the insertion of Guanyin's name is far from casual. It is, rather, the iceberg's tip; a tiny, deliberate hint of the enormous and icy discontent that lies just below the short letter's blithe surface. And the picture it paints could not be clearer. Zanhua's attempts to advance himself are being rebuffed. He can no longer afford a big house. The wife who doesn't suit him is sick—apparently sick enough for clinic visits—which must be why he has finally moved her into his home. Moreover, Yuliang knows his son is attending an elite private school, adding yet more financial pressure. The note's true message might just as well be scrawled on her own wall in large red characters: *I need you, Little Yu. Come home.*

Yuliang reaches for the wine. Using the same jade opener, she breaks the red wax at its neck and uncorks the bottle. As she drinks, she thinks of her husband's long fingers, his lush-lashed eyes. She feels the force of his longing—a husband's longing. A *reasonable* longing. And she is deeply, unspeakably ashamed. For what she feels in return is not a reciprocal love or gratitude. It is something entirely different: apprehension.

The sun is setting now. Outside shops are shuttered. Bells toll. A whore barters harshly with a client. Two of the unlikely foursome who live a floor up—a red-faced Russian who maintains two wives and one infant—burst into their nightly battle. The words, as usual, are unintelligible to Yuliang, but for a few French signposts: *francs* and *vin, café* and *bébé.* Eventually, the door slams, and the man's feet pound heavily down the stairs. The woman weeps, her sobs harmonizing sourly with her child's.

After a long while and a full glass of wine, Yuliang replaces Zanhua's letter, in its envelope. She allows herself a bite of stew, then another, straight from the pot. The salt and fat and spices merge so richly on her dried tongue that for a moment she almost thinks she'll faint again.

Forcing herself to pause, Yuliang refills her glass, watching Mirror Girl do the same. For an instant, that framed image seems inexplicably shocking. As though she were pouring herself a glassful of blood. And yet lifting the glass again, she can't help but think that she'd like to fill a canvas with this color. With *precisely* this color, which is not cadmium or terra rose or even manganese violet but some uncapturable combination of them all—a tone both illicit and essential.

Thirty-two

A MONTH LATER classes at the École des Beaux Arts have ended, and Yuliang sits in a Latin Quarter café. Studies are scattered on the marble tabletop; poses charcoaled, considered, and then rejected as themes for her submission painting to the salon. In fact, Yuliang has just decided that she despises them all. But when a breeze skates one off to a neighboring table, she leaps after it in a panic.

The man who retrieves it, however, gives it little more than a glance. *"Vous êtes étudiante?"* he asks, and when Yuliang nods, he says, *"C'est très bien."*

Sitting down again, she finds herself smiling. In Shanghai, the picture (which of course shows her own, nude form) would at minimum raise a few eyebrows. In more conservative Nanjing, where she's expected by summer's end, it could quite possibly get her arrested.

Anchoring the errant sketch beneath her saucer, Yuliang tips her chair back and lights a fresh cigarette. She scans the insipid urban stars for the celestial lovers of Mama's stories: Weaver Girl, her Heavenly Shepherd. As usual, though, they remain overwhelmed by the battling neon of Montparnasse, or else disguised in new and foreign positions. The only constellation she vaguely recognizes is the

Celestial Mansion of Emptiness, although she's used to seeing it in the north. Everything else is out of place.

Then again, she muses, perhaps it is *she* who is out of place. Perhaps Zanhua is right; she should go home. At the very least she should finish the letter she started to him two weeks earlier, which still hasn't progressed beyond 心爱的丈夫: *Beloved husband*.

Dispiritedly, she begins gathering up her sketches, glancing around for a waiter. Spotting a tall figure in dark clothes, she lifts her hand. Then she drops it again, stunned.

Xing Xudun stands just outside the *terrasse* area. Seeing her at almost the same moment she spots him, he breaks into a broad smile; that beloved, beaming smile that seems to touch every feature on his large face.

"Madame Pan!" he calls.

He makes his long-limbed way toward her table, bumping and apologizing, finally beaming down at her from what seems an almost unearthly height. The café lights are behind him, and for a moment he looks to Yuliang the way Klimt might have rendered him: silk-skinned. A limpid body, outlined in gold.

Without preamble he leans over and, grasping her shoulders, plants kisses on each of her cheeks. *That's new,* Yuliang thinks blurrily, and, almost simultaneously, *He still loves me.* The thought passes through with as little surprise as a note on the weather (*the sun is out*) before she throws it away.

"Sit!" she says breathlessly.

"You aren't waiting for someone?"

She shakes her head. "I come here to work."

"Lucky for me. May I?" He folds himself onto a seat and, setting down the journal he's carrying, reaches for Yuliang's sheath of papers.

"No!" she exclaims, hastily sweeping them into her purse. "They're all just awful."

He looks her in the eyes again. "I doubt that anything from your pencil could ever be awful."

Smiling again, he turns toward the group of Chinese and Indochinese students who often gather here by the window. He waves at one, mouthing something. Studying his profile, Yuliang finds herself thinking, *He's changed.* But she can't quite put her finger on what exactly is different. His gaze seems steadier, perhaps; his lips a little harder. She spots a dozen or so white hairs as well: They look like sleet cutting through a tousled night.

"You look well," he says, picking up the menu. "A bit skin-and-bones. But that's what's in fashion here, I hear."

She lifts an eyebrow. "I can't afford many chocolates."

"It suits you. When I first saw you, I thought you were a French girl."

"You didn't!" She laughs; it feels like the first time in weeks.

"I did. I thought, 'How on earth does that chic French girl know my name?'"

Yuliang assesses herself mentally. Her scarf is frayed; her hemline pinned and pinned again to hit the ever-moving mark of Parisian fashion. The only truly chic thing about her is her lipstick: she recently bought a gleaming tube of Arden's Scarlet Sauvage from a Gypsy vendor, a block from the Rue de la Paix salon from which it was very likely stolen, and applies it in a pouty bow at her lipline's center. Suitable, perhaps (she thinks skeptically). But chic?

Still, like everything Xudun says, he appears to mean it—emphatically. Even perusing the menu, he still strikes her as so pure in purpose that she can all but see him standing heroically at the helm of some great ship. "I wanted to see you sooner," he is saying, wistfully eyeing the café's offerings. "But I had no idea at all where you were living." He looks at her reproachfully. "You didn't write to anyone with your new address."

"I—I was a little overwhelmed," she tells him. Which is true. What she can't bring herself to tell him is that since coming to Paris, she's had an almost superstitious fear of writing home. As though reminders of the past might somehow break the magic spell of her life here.

"Overwhelmed by school?"

"Yes. It's been very busy." She finishes her *noisette*.

Xudun watches her a moment, his eyes as warm and rich as she remembers. "Well," he says, "we're finally doing it."

"Doing what?" she asks, faintly alarmed.

"Having that coffee. *S'il vous plaît*." He puts the menu down. "Although actually what I'd really like is beer."

He thrusts his arm up for a waiter. No one takes any notice but a bushy-browed southerner just inside the door. "Comrade Xing!" the boy shouts. "I heard you'd come back. Come over here! Catch us up on Moscow!"

"In a moment," Xudun calls back. "I've got a prior engagement."

"Don't waste much time, do you?" The boy hoots.

Xudun turns back to Yuliang. "Don't mind him."

"Why do you always choose such rude friends?" she asks dryly.

He laughs. "That one's Zhou Enlai. He's our minister of mimeography. Does most of our printing."

Yuliang throws the boy a stiff smile before turning back to Xudun. "Were you really in Moscow?"

"Stalin's set up a school there. You haven't heard of it? The University of the Toilers of the East." He says it both in Chinese and in Russian, the words rolling from his tongue in rich mystery.

"You speak Russian now?"

"More now than I did at the start, anyway."

Yuliang sets down her cup, genuinely impressed. She herself recently attempted an exchange of language lessons with Perelli, the Italian painter in her class. She stopped after their third session, when he pulled her into his lap. "Is it much harder than French?" she asks, honestly curious.

"It won't be when they come out with a Sino-Russian dictionary. We had to make do with a Japanese *jiten*." He frowns. "Which, I might add, caused a problem at first."

"Because no one spoke Japanese?"

"Because the only one available is put out by a Japanese publisher. No one wanted to put money into their pockets."

Yuliang laughs. "Surely a publisher isn't to blame for Hirohito's crimes."

For once he doesn't return her smile. "You can't blame the fox's head and not its legs, Madame Pan. They're all part of the same enemy."

She looks at him, curious. "You say *enemy* as though we were already at war."

"It will come soon enough. And don't let China's greater size lead to complacency. If we don't rid ourselves of old ways, we will lose."

Yuliang ponders this. She can't help recalling one of Xu Beihong's recent comments: with typical bravado, he declared that no art painted after 1880 was worth emulating. She remembers, too, Zanhua, on that long-ago day in the Lotus Gardens: *The traditional ways don't have to resist newer ones.*

"Can't the old and the new exist together sometimes?" she asks. "In harmony?"

"Perhaps. But don't forget that we lost Formosa to Japan twenty-five years ago because the empress built up her summer palace instead of her navy. Sometimes you must strip off the old in order to rebuild a sounder structure."

"I'm not saying we shouldn't modernize, or strip away corruption," Yuliang says. She'd forgotten how she enjoys arguing with Xudun. The way he hears her out—not indulgently, as Zanhua sometimes does, but as though she might actually have something to teach *him*. "If you carve away all of China's old ways, then what do you have left?"

"You still have the roots. Land. People."

"Yes, but at what point do you stop? What's to keep you from continuing to change and change until there's nothing of your true self left inside?"

Xudun digests this for a moment, his big thumbs tapping the table. "There will always be something," he says at last. "You choose to wear French lipstick and French dresses."

Yuliang purses her lips. "Actually, the lipstick is American."

He waves impatiently. "Either way. Does the fact that you wear it make you less Chinese?"

"No," Yuliang says immediately. "It's obvious that I'm Chinese." *Too obvious, sometimes*, she notes wryly. She thinks of all the schoolboy taunts she's endured here, of the old man who, mistaking her for Indochinese, harassed her recently at the Louvre. *Dirty native*, he'd sputtered. *Go back to Hanoi!*

"Whether I like it or not," she goes on, "my skin will always tell the truth. And unlike my clothes, I can't take it off."

She fights back a blush at the unintended implication. But Xing Xudun just presses on. "Say you could. Say you were dead, soon to be buried. The dress you wear into your coffin will be your outfit for eternity. Would a French dress make you any less Chinese?"

Yuliang chews a thumbnail: the thought is surprisingly compli-cated. On the one hand, it would seem hypocritical to say yes, given that she's worn nothing but Western clothes these past few years. At the same time it is faintly disturbing; the idea of the coffin door clos-ing on her own form. Resplendent in her short skirt, silk stockings, and sheer blouse. "I don't know," she says at last, honestly.

He grins as though he's won a point for himself. "All right, then. Listen. Say this is China." He holds up his journal. "By peeling back a few layers"—he bends back one page, then another—"you're not changing its true nature. What remains in my hands is still land."

"No, it's not. It's a journal."

Yuliang smiles again, to show him that she's teasing. But the look he gives her is unexpectedly sober. "I have missed you," he says, simply.

Another silence unrolls between them. Inside the café, the min-ister of mimeography curses his bridge partner. When Xudun speaks again it's an enormous relief for some reason. "And when," he says, "are you going home?"

Yuliang clears her throat. "I—I haven't quite decided. There's a scholarship that would pay for me to study in Rome. I want to study sculpture there, too." She scrapes at the small heap of sugar crystals at the bottom of her cup. "It may be nothing but a dream. In any event, I'm not done here. I have to finish up one last painting."

"Self-portrait?"

Yuliang nods.

"Nude?"

She nods again, though she can't meet his eyes. Thankfully, at that moment the waiter finally chooses to notice them, and Xudun orders his beer.

"So," he says as the man saunters away, "Paris in the past, Italy in the future. Where is it you are living now?"

"A place a friend found. It's not much." Which, of course, is an understatement. The alley Xu Beihong found for her, off the rue St. Denis, is actually a small brothel district, though it's fine for Yuliang's purposes. During daylight, in fact, it may well be one of the quietest streets in the city. Still, anxious to change the subject, she reaches for his journal—though seeing the title, she grimaces. *Red Light.*

"What's ECCO?" she asks, pointing at the acronym at the bottom of the page.

"European branch of the Chinese Communist Organization."

"Do you write for this, then?"

"I do the artwork. But Zhou over there wrote the piece about the labor corps. That is, the workers the British brought over to dig trenches and graves during the war." He nods. "Page fifteen."

Yuliang flips through to see a striking woodblock print: a band of stick-thin men crammed into a barred box. "Were they really kept in cages?"

"Technically, they were 'camps.' But the men were locked in at night. Many did not live to see their real homes again." He leans back, stretching his long, long legs before him. "They were shot at the front or died from disease. The governments that paid their way here wouldn't even ship the bodies back. Around two thousand of them are still buried in France." His beer comes. He lifts it grimly: *"Ganbei."*

Yuliang toasts back, suddenly sheepish about her own goals in this country: a few tubes of paint, meat, a more fashionable hat. She skims ahead a few more pages, stopping at a grainy photograph of a familiar scene these days: Chinese youth, marching. "This is Shanghai?"

"Paris. We occupied the legation. You didn't hear?"

Yuliang shakes her head—she still doesn't read the papers regularly. "I would have thought you learned your lesson."

He snorts. "What we learned in Lyon is that we need to fight harder. And that we can't trust old dogs who hold hands with imperialists." Reaching over, he points at a small black dot in a ground-floor window. "That's me," he adds proudly. "We took over the whole of the first and second floors."

Yuliang squints. "But if you were inside, who is that marching *outside?*"

"The PJC."

"Le Parti des . . . what? Jeunes Communistes?"

Xudun snorts. "They're as Communist as the old Dragon Lady was."

She tries again: "Jeunes . . . Chinois?" She says it hesitantly: the blizzard of factional acronyms into which China's two thousand students here divide and subdivide themselves continues to daunt her.

But Xudun nods. "Although *jeunes fascistes* is more like it. They've attacked us more than once, even shooting into one of our meetings. We've all bought guns since. For protection."

"You have a gun?" she asks in disbelief.

Xudun waves dismissively; as though pocketing arms were no more alarming than putting on a tie. "They weren't even protesting the May 30 massacre. One of their idiot chemists blew himself up in Billancourt." He runs the back of his hand across his wet lips, a rough gesture that Yuliang can't help thinking Zanhua would never make. And yet, oddly, it makes her warm to him even more. "They wanted the legation to pay to send the body back to China. And for once in his life, that motherless bastard Chen did the right thing and refused them."

"Not that you've forgiven him."

"Not in this life. Or the next." He stretches. "The massacre made the major papers here, I assume?"

Silently, Yuliang vows to start following the news more carefully. "The one I read blamed radical student elements," she says cautiously.

"That's dogshit," Xudun says angrily. "It started with the Japanese. They locked their Chinese workers out of one of their factories. When the workers tried to break in, the guards shot them point-blank. One fellow was killed."

"A friend of yours?"

"Does it matter?"

Chastised, she drops her gaze to her hands.

"Some of my friends are still in jail, though," he goes on. "The ones who protested his murder. So there was nothing 'radical' about the May 30 march. It was simply to protest the hypocrisy of it all: our leaders letting the Brits and radish-heads not only exploit our workers but *shoot* them. With no consequences."

"It was a peaceful demonstration."

He nods. "In the beginning. You've marched, haven't you?"

"Not much," Yuliang admits. Actually, she has never marched at all. Somehow, her own crises have always seemed more pressing than her nation's.

To her relief, though, Xudun lets this pass. "The march," he continues, "went past police headquarters in the British Concession. The constables there shot them."

"I read that it was warning shots."

"Eleven people died. If that was from warning shots, I'm the son of a slave girl." Draining his beer, Xudun sets down his glass. "Guifei was wounded too."

Yuliang looks up, shocked. "She *was?*"

"Along with twenty others," Xudun nods, grimly. "I'd have written you if I'd known where to send the letter. The bullet shattered her shoulder. Last I heard, she wasn't allowed out of bed."

Yuliang stares at the marble tabletop. For an instant, all she can think of is the famed Han-era beauty after whom her friend was named. The thought brings a chill. For in the end Yang Guifei, not her infatuated imperial husband, paid for her nation's defeat—by hanging herself.

I'm so selfish, she thinks miserably. On another day, perhaps, this thought would sink Yuliang into one of the dark, dense moods that sometimes close over her here like an icy pool. But when Xudun's foot brushes hers briefly beneath the table, it startles her from her gloom. Blushing, she tucks her legs primly beneath her seat.

"My husband," she says, twisting her wedding band, "writes that even more conservative Republicans will ally with the CCP now. For the nation's sake."

"If anything, it's a marriage of convenience." Now he looks straight into her eyes. "And one I doubt will last."

This time it is impossible to misinterpret his meaning, and Yuliang's heart all but stops. *I should leave,* she thinks. But she does not.

"How about another coffee?"

"Too much makes me jumpy," she snaps. "It interferes with my brush-strokes." Tensely, she transfers the the last of the milk to her cup.

"At least tell me about your work these days."

She takes a deep breath. "It's changed a bit."

"May I come and see it sometime? Or, better yet, watch you paint? I've always wanted to."

The image that comes to Yuliang (herself, naked, painting herself naked; him, fully clothed, watching her) feels like such a transgression that her heart seems to pound in her ears. And yet part of what disturbs her is its illicit appeal. The thick streak of excitement that, like crimson swirled into black, only makes the black seem blacker.

"What time is it?" she asks, intensely aware of his gaze.

When he glances at his watch it's an almost physical relief. "Nearly twelve."

"I—I really should leave now. I have work."

"I thought you work here."

"I'm not getting much done, though, am I?"

This, too, emerges more tartly than she'd planned. Flustered, Yuliang stands. She doesn't realize she is holding her breath until he stands as well, rising to his full and shocking height. "I'll walk out with you. I have an appointment."

"I thought you were meeting your friends."

"I'll come back. They're here every day. As you must have noticed." Seeing her fumble with her bag for her change purse, Xundun reaches out and catches her hand. The warmth of his fingers travel, directly to her stomach. "I'll get this."

"Oh, no!"

"I consider it an investment."

"In what? Slow waiters?" She pulls away, trying uncomfortably to smile.

"In one of China's greatest new artists." He says it without a hint of irony. "Actually, is your deadline so pressing that you can't spare an hour or so?"

"No," Yuliang says, though this couldn't be less true. *What am I doing?*

"Come with me."

"At *midnight?*"

But by this point even she recognizes the words as purely symbolic. And when he offers her his arm, the gesture doesn't seem alien or forward so much as simply inevitable.

As does her response: linking her own arm right through it.

Thirty-three

THEY STROLL BY THE RIVER, arms still linked, the warm wind smelling of summer. As they walk, Yuliang ponders this unexpected meeting, this odd moment. This intimate silence between them, so easy to maintain and yet more complicit, somehow, with each languid step. *He's just Xudun,* she tells herself. *There's no reason to worry.* And yet what she is feeling isn't worry—not quite. It's a low-lying, tingling tension somewhere just below her belly. And if she's truthful, it's not entirely unpleasant.

They walk on southward, in silence. Eventually Yuliang realizes he is steering her toward the Petit Pont and the cathedral, though of course the massive church must be closed.

"Where are we going?" she asks. But Xudun just puts a broad finger to his lips.

He leads her through Notre Dame's courtyard, across the square. They pass the enormous rose windows that Yuliang has sketched and painted several times, and are just reaching the tower's entrance when a diminutive figure peels itself free from the shadows. It solidifies, step by step, into a short Frenchman in thick glasses.

"Monsieur Xing?"

"Monsieur Barton," Xudun replies in French. "I'm sorry I'm late. I hope you don't mind—I brought a friend, Mademoiselle Pan."

Madame, thinks Yuliang. But what she says is, "*Enchantée.*"

"Monsieur Barton controls admissions here," Xudun explains, still in French. "We met at a workers' rally two weeks ago."

"What a coincidence." She smiles. And in Chinese: "Why are we here?"

"We're going up."

"Can we do that?" Yuliang glances at Barton, for the first time noticing the impressive ring of brass keys slung at his hip.

Barton intuits her meaning, or else is unexpectedly conversant in Chinese (and knowing Xudun's friends, she would be surprised by neither). "Well," he says, "in truth it's against the law. But the sight at night is magnificent. This trip is a gift I give to only a few good friends." He beams. "Like your young man here."

"He's not—" Yuliang starts.

"*Alors,*" the Frenchman continues. "We shouldn't stand here much longer. If we're seen, my job—" He draws a line across his neck with his thumb and makes a sound like a gagging cat. "Also, from this point on, no cigarettes. No fires, no light. Not a match. Not a spark." He winks. "Follow me."

He unlocks the great doors, cracks them open. When he steps in, the damp darkness of the church seems to swallows him whole.

Yuliang looks at Xudun uneasily. "Should we really be breaking laws?"

"Some laws are meant to be broken," he whispers, and takes her hand.

Crouched like thieves, the three of them creep through the sanctuary, passing hulking shadows of pews and pulpit, the looming Mary, a wall of angels. The enormous stained glass rose, so vivid by day, now appears closed against the night. Stripped of color by the darkness, it makes its splendor known only by its subdued, jewel-like glints. But when they reach the Western Tower even that meager light is snuffed out as Barton quietly shuts the doors behind them.

"*Allons-y*," he says. "Be careful where you step."

They begin the climb in near-total darkness and Yuliang combats a surge of panic by silently reciting Li Qingzhao's "Like a Dream": *I always recall the sunset / over the pavilion by the river / so tipsy, we could not find our way home . . .* Each step is echoed by Xudun's, right behind her.

"Doing all right?" He whispers it, though the closest set of hostile ears couldn't be any nearer than sixty meters below them.

Too winded to answer, Yuliang simply nods. She wordlessly chants her way to the top, where they break through the arches and onto the first level.

A blast of warm and rain-scented air greets them. Stepping toward the platform's edge Yuliang surveys the Île de la Cité, her eyes tearing in the wind. Leaning over the balustrade, she takes in the glimmering city below: the misty play of the shadows and the light. The looming façades of the great buildings—the Hôtel-Dieu, the Tour St.-Jacques—look as if they're sculpted from black paper. Testing her own terror, she leans out a little over the railing until her feet lift slightly from the ground. If she squints, the harsh lines and angles blur, and she can almost—*almost*—imagine she is looking not at the Seine, but at the Yangtze.

How did he die? she mouths into the starry darkness.

The answer comes so clearly she almost can see him: her uncle, standing merrily at the prow of *The Crying Loon. He died the same way you very well might*, he says, *if you're not careful.* Where is he now, she wonders, her ageless trickster of an uncle? Rotting in prison? Sprung free by one of his opium allies? And what on earth would he think if he could see her here now?

Yuliang pushes herself a tiny bit more forward. A little further, really, is all that it would take. She can picture so naturally what would come next: the stomach-tumbling chaos, the soft gray sky at her feet. The moon a sideways smile, encouraging her down. *Any farther and you'll fall right over . . .*

"*Attention!*" Barton exclaims.

"She's just taking in the view," she hears Xudun say. But he leans down to her. "A bit too far, don't you think?"

Tilting her head, Yuliang meets his gaze. Like the man himself it is strong and solid, without a wisp of pretense.

"Come here," he says quietly, and reaches for her. She studies his big hand a moment—the same hand she first saw on *New Youth*. The fingers are improbably thick, the knuckles raw. With an odd sense of portent she finally accepts it, and he pulls her from the edge to the center of the viewing platform. As they stare at each other, there's a sudden giddy sense that he has seen something no one else ever has. Or perhaps, more astonishingly, that she has let him.

Xudun smiles again, as though to seal in their secret. *"On peut?"* He indicates the next staircase.

The Frenchman puffs out his cheeks. *"Moi, non . . .* I climb to this spot and back three times every day as it is. You go, though." He winks again. "Take your time."

"He thinks we're sweethearts," Yuliang whispers, mortified, as Xudun steers her toward the next landing.

"Mais oui," he replies smoothly. "He is French."

"But . . ." For an absurd instant she is convinced that she has to set the record straight, with this odd little man she's just met. Step by step, however, the impulse dwindles, until once more there is just the sound of their climb together: leather soles, stepping lightly and in rhythm.

Now that Barton is no longer with them, they climb side by side. Xudun's closeness is initially distracting. Counting her steps, Yuliang holds on tight to the small boar in her pocket, although she has no idea what she is wishing for.

"Voilà," Xudun says at last. "La Galerie des Chimeres."

The Seine curves below, limned in reflected light. Yuliang, awed, lets out her breath. "Oh, I wish I'd brought my sketch pad!" She traces the arching line of the river with the tip of her index finger.

"Sketch it up there." He taps his head.

"I can't paint life from memory. Or from a postcard, like Utrillo."

"I agree with that. Pictures from pictures . . . I far prefer his mother's work."

"Valadon," Yuliang murmurs. Another small thrill, at how easily they understand each other.

"Are you too cold?" He is reaching into his jacket pocket—for a lighter, she assumes.

"No flames," she reminds him. "Or guns."

"This'll only put fire in your belly." He pulls out a little silver flask. "Smirnoff."

He looks so proud of himself she can't help but laugh again. "Didn't they ban liquor in Russia?"

"I bought it here. They've just opened a factory." He twists off the cap. "I had to line up behind a dozen Americans to get this. They can't drink there now either, you know."

Yuliang nods. Actually, she knows little about Americans. But she certainly remembers the Russians who'd poured into Shanghai after the czar was overthrown. Many ended up indigent, playing cards on the street outside the China Inland Mission, waiting for handouts of rice and drinking water. Passing the line was like passing through a liquored cloudbank. "Imagine Russians not drinking," she says.

"I don't think *they* can imagine it. It's the one area where their revolution might not succeed." He takes a swig, grimaces appreciatively, and hands over the flask. When Yuliang hesitates—she's never had vodka before—he says, "Go on—it's very pure. It won't slow you down tomorrow, even if we drink a lot."

"Are we drinking a lot?" she asks warily.

"Not if you don't care to."

For some reason, it sounds like a challenge. "I do care to," she says defiantly. And drinks.

The liquid simmers in her nose and eyes, swells her throat. The second swig goes down more smoothly, although she still feels her gut convulse as she hands it back. She coughs lightly. "Are you certain this isn't paint thinner?"

He laughs. "Positive. I haven't picked up a paintbrush in nearly a year."

She eyes him curiously. It's like hearing him admit that he hasn't eaten bread, hasn't sipped water. "You're only drawing, then?"

"The occasional cartoon. And woodcutting." He stretches his long arms up above him, rolls his neck.

"You like woodcutting?"

He nods. "There are those who claim it's not real art at all. But of all I've done, I find it the most satisfying. It's a challenge, combining sculpting with drawing. Deciding where shadows fall with an awl."

"How did you start?" she asks.

"Woodcutting?"

"No. Painting. Art." It strikes her suddenly as odd that she doesn't know this.

"I fell into it," he says. "My father was a farmer. He sent me to a tutor so I could read for him and do the accounts." He laughs. "I did learn to read. But I spent most of my time copying the images and engravings I found in his almanacs. And you?"

"My mother embroidered for a living. Before she died."

It is all she offers. He doesn't press her. When he hands the flask back, Yuliang takes it, her fingertips sensing the warmth left on the metal by his own. Her head swims from the unaccustomed strength of the drink. But it also eases that anxious tingling in her gut. Yuliang drinks again and holds out the flask to him, barely conscious that she is shifting not just her hand, but her whole body toward him.

Above, the stars are coming out again in full force now, sapped by the city's lights, but still plentiful. "Xu Beihong—you know him?" She is slurring slightly now, she realizes. "He hates Van Gogh, calls him a fool. He says *Starry Night* could have been painted by a child in primary school. I think he's a genius."

"Xu Beihong?"

Yuliang giggles; then is faintly shocked by the sound. "In his own mind, certainly. But I meant Vincent."

"Maybe all artists are both fools and geniuses."

"Are you saying I'm a fool?" she asks, with unaccustomed playfulness. (*I am getting drunk*, she thinks hazily.)

"You are the last woman I'd call a fool."

Looking into his dark eyes she senses something tightening between them. "Tell me," she manages, indicating the glittering river. "How—how could you carve something this dark and rich, this complex?"

He squints toward the Sorbonne, thinks a moment. "I'd center it around that dome. And have that gargoyle over there positioned on the left, as though it were about to fly over and shadow the whole city." He frowns. "Although getting those shadows in at night, in wood—that would be very difficult."

"So why not just paint it?" Yuliang asks, honestly baffled. "Wouldn't that be easier—and really more beautiful, in the end?"

"That's the point," he says firmly. "Beauty in art can be used to mask truth. False but beautiful images are too often used to distract us from dangerous realities."

Again Wu Ding's voice drifts into her thoughts: *Artists are after life's reflections, not life itself.*

"Have I offended you?" Xudun asks, misinterpreting her silence.

"I—I was just thinking of Li Bai. He died chasing beautiful but false images."

He smiles. "The moon's reflection."

"He truly thought the moon was underwater," she says, a little defensively. "At least, that's what my uncle told me."

"And China lost its greatest poet. You've just illustrated my point." He toasts the moon, then hands back the flask. Yuliang takes it.

"What if Li Bai was a great poet *because* he chased life's reflections?" she asks slowly. "If he'd spent all his days writing only about ugly truths, perhaps no one would have wanted to read him."

"What people want to read isn't always what's best for them."

"But can you make them read what they don't want to read?"

"You explain to them that it's for the greater good."

"And if that fails?"

Xudun sweeps the flask back, in a movement both abrupt and unexpected. "You take away other options."

His face seems suddenly hard, as though he—like the Gothic hawks and taloned serpents of the great naves—were chiseled from stone. He drinks again, his strong neck etched against the darkness. "Your turn, Mademoiselle Pan. Paint this for me." He waves a hand at the view.

Madame, Yuliang thinks reflexively. But the thought's like a little fish that leaps once and is gone. "I'd use thick swatches of vine black, ultramarine. Phthalo blue. Maybe a little like Monet's paintings of that English river—what is it? The Thames. But my Seine would be different, I think."

"How?"

"A silver swirl down the center. The color of the moon."

He lifts a brow. "The moon underwater."

"Yes," she says defiantly. "But I'd lay it on thickly. Perhaps even knife it."

"Knifing," he says admiringly. "I like the sound of that."

His approval sparks a small burst of pleasure. "A fauvist technique, really. But I've used it a lot recently. It adds texture. In this case I'd knife from that building to . . . there." She runs her palm over the scenery, smoothing it like some vast, windblown sheet. Inadvertently—because she's too close; because of the vodka; certainly not because she plans to (*does she?*)—she ends up brushing his shoulder. It's an innocuous enough contact at first. But as her hand remains, white and limp against his shoulder, the gesture sheds any resemblance to chance or accident. And by the time he's covered it with his own, it is something else entirely.

Yuliang stands completely still for a moment, feeling not only his warm fingers but the moment's vast significance through its shimmering strangeness. Tentatively, she strokes his lip, where the beer foam had been earlier. *I cannot do this,* she thinks. *I must . . .*

But by that point she's already on her toes, reaching up. And when she kisses him it's with as little hesitation as she'd felt taking his arm, sharing her table. Calling his name: "Xudun," she says, against his lips.

And then his big arms are around her.

Yuliang tastes his tongue, feels the vast land of his back. She strains toward him; she would pour herself into him if she could. It's just his skin, his warm skin, keeping her out . . .

Only when the cathedral's great bell chimes does she pull back.

"What—" he begins.

"Wait." She claps a hand over his mouth, loath to have the moment broken.

"What will we do?" he asks through her fingers, at last.

"Wait," she repeats. (*I can't I can't.*) "Let me think." But her mind feels as dense and heavy as the sound still reverberating through the old stones. *Don't think.*

"We'll go home," she says at last.

He blinks again. "To China?"

"No. Home to my studio."

THEY MAKE THE TRIP to rue St. Denis in half the time it normally would take, their steps quick and matched, tight with purpose. They don't touch on the street. But he is hard behind her as they take the four flights to her room, and his hands are on her hips as they reach her floor. He's kissing her neck as she turns the key in the lock. When the door opens they fall inside together, landing half sitting, half kneeling on the paint-splotched floor.

He is frantic at first, and shy, and touchingly unschooled. He fumbles with her blouse; she furiously strips it off. When he cautiously runs his fingers over the sheer fabric of her undershirt, Yuliang yanks the garment up to her chin. It's only when he pulls her skirt up that she stops him, for it is her only one. "Wait," she tells him again. And with unfailing fingers she frees the four hooks from their blind eyelets.

They clamber out of their underthings, and then at last they are naked, and he leans over and takes her face in his hands. "I want you to know," he says, very seriously, "it is all right. If you tell me you can't."

Sweet boy, she thinks. "All right."

His face falls. "You—you don't want to?"

"No," she says, and wraps her arms around his neck. "I know that it is all right."

Though she doesn't know it's all right—she doesn't know it at all. (*Don't think.*) There is no trace, in fact, amid the aching turmoil that now fills her, of right or wrong. Of caution, or duty, or regret. There is simply a need—entirely new to her, and searing, and—like painting—far, far too true to deny.

Yuliang takes Xudun's hand, strokes the strong, hard fingers for a moment. Then she leads him across the room.

ON THE COT, unexpectedly, comes a tremulous confusion. Not because Yuliang doesn't know what to do, but because the things she's always done—all those small acts and moves and murmurs—fail her. Because every bed act she's ever learned seems so utterly insufficient. She could, she thinks (kissing his lips, his big chin, the pulsing point in his neck), swallow him. Bit by bit. She could sap him of his life, like the voracious Fifth Wife in *The Golden Plum Vase*. For the first time she understands some of the things done to her in the past, the bitings and the bindings. The occasional, dreaded burns. It isn't always cruelty, she suddenly realizes. Sometimes true desire bears a semblance to cruelty. Sometimes it's too strong even for skin . . . She pulls away for a moment, disturbed by her own longings.

"What's wrong?"

Propping herself on an elbow, she tries to smile.

"Come here," he breathes, warmly. And finally, in that moment, the last of her hesitations melts away.

She lies still as he traces the whorl of her ear with his tongue, letting the lush agony wash over her until she can no longer stand it. She traces each of his eyelids, runs her lips from his neck to the small mouth of his navel, and then down further as he groans again. She studies it, this strange, stiff stalk that she has catered to, slaved for, and feared for so many years, and yet—astonishingly—hasn't really known at all. Or rather, she knows the obvious things; things taught by nuns and books and diagrams. She knows it well enough to pleasure it, to paint it. But no matter what her various teachers have said about it, and no matter how abstractly Yuliang has considered it, she has never before seen it this way. Not even (she realizes, flinching slightly) with Zanhua.

Guilt, however, lingers only for a moment, until she looks up once more at Xudun. She waits until his breathing slows again. Then, slowly, she moves back over him. "Open your eyes," she commands, reveling in her strange and new sense of power. "Look at me."

She lowers herself onto him gently, taking stock of the sensations. Of the sheer novelty of the way they meet *here*, then *here*, then *here*. As they begin to move together joy just nips at her at first, barely noticed. But then somehow it's bigger than she is; she is gritting her teeth against it. *It can't,* she thinks as he arches and gasps beneath her. *There can't be more.*

But there is. There's a moment of shivering silence—an enormous inner breath—not unlike the emptiness she'd felt atop Notre Dame. And then she's falling, tumbling down to him, Washing Silk Woman hurling herself into a surge of skin and fluid and rippling muscle. There are waves and then more waves. She is washed onto his chest, astonished. And when the tears fall, she doesn't question them. She barely feels them at all.

Thirty-four

THE NEXT DAY BREAKS with the bright vengeance of early summer. Sun pours through the small, square window overlooking black rooftops and pink chimney pots, bouncing off the cracked red tiles of the floor. It pounds Yuliang's eyelids open; and groggily, she takes in her tiny, top-floor alcove: the little stove, the chipped washbasin and pitcher. The piles of books, papers, and sketches. The untouched canvas against the wall. It is the latter that sparks the first wave of panic. *The salon,* she thinks. *I still haven't even started.*

Then a leg moves against her thigh, and the rest of it comes back. Bolting upright, she sees Xudun in bed beside her. For an instant there is there nothing other than a sheer and shocked horror. Then he opens his eyes. Smiling sleepily, he rolls over and wraps her in his arms.

And for one of the very few times in Yuliang's life, her mind goes almost as blank as her waiting canvas.

IT IS LATE AFTERNOON by the time Yuliang finally manages to push him out the door. Afterwards she straightens up distractedly; making the tiny bed, sweeping crumbs from their lunch off the floor. When she at last sits down between her easel and her mirror—still naked, in her brightly patterned old armchair—the light coming through the window is tinged with garnet. Taking stock of her image, Yuliang sees she is too: she looks pink and dreamy, touched by the day's reflections. Her eyes ache from lack of sleep, her muscles from stairs and new exertions. There is a familiar and yet entirely new soreness between her legs, and even noticing it is enough to tempt her to race into the street after him. And yet this, she knows, would be disastrous. Almost as disastrous, in fact, as allowing herself to truly contemplate what's just happened. (*Don't think.*)

Instead, she forces her focus to the canvas before her. She lets all her unmade decisions, her confused affections, her unfinished letter (*Beloved husband*) hover beyond her thoughts, like white moths tapping at her happiness. She will think about it all later. After the painting's painted. And after it's dried, wrapped, delivered to the salon. After she meets Xudun again in one week, back at the Café de Cluny, and has had a chance to think away from these paint-thinner fumes.

For today, there is just this: her new-old skin. Her blank canvas. Mirror Girl, watching her with languid interest. Arms folded behind her head, Yuliang takes in the lazy eyes, the flushed cheeks. The sated flesh. Humming to herself, she reaches for her palette. She will, she decides, paint herself just like this: in her lush chair, her skin the color of a summer sunset. A triad of color: peach and gold and rose pink. A neutral violet for unity and control—qualities she'll examine, for today, on the canvas alone.

Part EIGHT

The *WIVES*

To yield, I have learned, is to come back again.

———

TAOIST PROVERB

Thirty-five

Nanjing, 1936

"**B**EFORE WE BEGIN," Xu Beihong announces, "I'd like to remind everyone that Teacher Pan's seventh solo exhibition is in two weeks." He turns to Yuliang. "It's at the Shanghai Exhibition Space again, isn't it?"

Yuliang nods. Her old friend and mentor takes a sip of his coffee before setting it down with a grimace. He drinks it like a rich man now: as black as pitch, as black as crow, made fresh each morning by a fetching young secretary. Despite his attentive tutelage, however, the girl (at least, according to Beihong) still doesn't make it strong enough for his liking.

"Please mark the date in your calendars," he concludes.

Yuliang surveys her fellow teachers. Only one, a fellow oils instructor, has actually written down the date. Other reactions reflect a familiar spectrum of emotions, from indifference to barely stifled insecurity. All, that is, but that of the calligraphy instructor, Shu Meiyi: her broad face reveals something close to outright malice. It's a look Yuliang encounters fairly often from Teacher Shu and others of her plain, disgruntled colleagues. *I don't like you,* it says. And: *It's not fair.* And as intended, it hurt her—at least in the beginning. When Yuliang was still naive enough to believe things might change. She knows better now.

Vaffanculo, she thinks, and even considers accompanying the insult with its peculiarly gratifying hand gesture. She satisfies herself instead with snapping open her sterling silver cigarette case, a farewell gift from fellow students when she left Rome.

"Ah, excellent. May I?" Xu Beihong extends his hand. As dean of arts at National Central University the diminutive artist can easily afford his own smokes these days. As the old saying goes, though, rivers and mountains may be malleable; only man's nature is eternally hard to overcome. It's a lesson, Yuliang thinks (extending both cigarettes and her lighter) that she seems destined to keep learning. And relearning.

Bending toward the flame, Xu Beihong puffs appreciatively. "Now, for the first item . . ."

The meeting begins with the usual lineup of trivia and complaints: the tardy relinquishment of a classroom by the one o'clock seminar for the two o'clock. The dire need for easels, paints, and models. Xu Beihong uses this opportunity to point out proudly that the plaster *David* he brought from France has been refurbished and will be on display in the Fine Arts Library for students to sketch. "Should the current outcry over his loins continue," he adds delicately, "we'll consider covering them. Perhaps." He clears his throat. "Is that all?"

"As long as we're on coverage," interjects the classics teacher, "I was wondering if anyone else would consider a dress code."

"A dress code," Xu Beihong repeats.

"At least for the female students. You must have noticed how girls in the art school dress far less"—he glances at Yuliang—"*appropriately* than those in other departments. Hardly any of them wear *qipao* anymore. And yesterday we saw three skirts that were not only absurdly tight but actually showed the knees."

"Really."

"Well, when the girls sat down."

Dean Xu directs a wry glance at Yuliang. She crosses her trousered legs, blows a smoke ring at the ceiling. Her own fondness for pants—not loose-flowing Chinese trousers, but the trim style favored by Dietrich—is another source of much muttered resentment.

"I see," the dean says. "And you believe, no doubt, that we should require our young women to adhere more strictly to the standards suggested by Madame Chiang. Skirts safely at shin length, slits no higher than three inches. Ah, and let's not forget—shirts that cover the entire buttocks. Isn't that right?"

"The other disciplines do all that," Teacher Shu chimes in staunchly. "We stand apart."

"We're *artists*," Dean Xu snaps back. "No one expects us to dress like damn accountants." He takes a swig of his coffee. "No dress code. Next item?"

Teacher Shu, undeterred, lifts her plump hand. "We were wondering whether the dean has considered our petition yet."

"The one on classroom morality?" he asks. "No."

"But we gave it to you—"

"Last month." He cuts her off. "I know."

"Did you read the item on staffing standards?" she persists.

"The one on 'not permitting persons of dubious backgrounds and questionable histories to come in excessive contact with our students'? Not a word," Dean Xu replies smoothly. "And if you ask me why I did not, the answer will remain just the same. It is still my position that no person in this department fits that particular description."

No one looks at Yuliang. But she still feels the grip of their attention like some vast vise.

"But . . ." Teacher Shu splutters.

"*That*," the dean snaps, "is my final word on the subject. If you wish to take it further, you will have to do so with the university president. Or, better yet, Madame Chiang."

The calligraphy instructor's round face takes on the approximate color of a ripe eggplant. To celebrate, Yuliang sketches one in her notebook's margin.

She spends the rest of the meeting as she almost always does: doodling. A cobbled street. The Ponte Vecchio. An orchid. When she looks up, the room is filling with paper rustle and scraping chairs: the staff has been dismissed.

Xu Beihong leans toward her as he pulls his folders together. "Ignore them," he says quietly. "They're just jealous of your success."

"I know," she tells him.

And she does. Still, Yuliang throws him a grateful look as she gathers her things. How many times has this man now come to her rescue? He set her up in Paris, wrote her Rome Art Academy recommendation. Over the four years she was there he introduced her to numerous contacts, and secured her participation in several salons and exhibitions. Not least of all, he offered her this job after her much-publicized split with the Shanghai Art Academy.

Much to Liu Haisu's delight, the tabloids ran various versions of the story for weeks. How the painter Madame Pan attacked a fellow teacher at the school, how the victim wore a French scarf wrapped around her face for two days afterward (although in Yuliang's opinion, this was more for dramatic impact than because of injury). What the papers didn't mention, of course, was that the Hermès-draped instructor (the same woman, in fact, who had made Yuliang's life a misery as a student) had called Yuliang a whore to her face, in front of students. "She's had that slap coming for twenty years," Yuliang fumed when Liu Haisu called her into his office. "That woman is a snake."

In the end, despite a small movement to have Yuliang terminated, Principal Liu asked only that she apologize. But by then Yuliang had had enough. Enough of politics, of tabloids. Enough of the endless scandal. Enough of sleeping alone every night. She'd even had enough of Shanghai: its ever-increasing construction, the tireless scream of the latest everything—cocktail, salon, Negro band. Not to mention the growing signs of Japan's grim intentions.

Thanks to the League of Nations, Hirohito's soldiers patrolled the same foreign concessions they'd abruptly attacked in 1932, while China's troops (which had fought them off for over two months) were barred from their own city. All in all, she'd decided, it was time to leave. And when the invitation came from Xu Beihong, the staid, broad streets of Nanjing seemed a welcome respite.

Still, making her way across campus now, Yuliang can't brush off a vaguely soiled and sticky feeling. Hurrying past the university's athletic fields—filled now not with athletes, but with civilians maneuvering in obligatory combat training—she still feels it; as though she's just pushed through a roomful of spiderwebs. Shutting her eyes briefly, she can all but see them: circular ladders of lethal silken strands. Studded with the crisp carcasses of insects.

AT HOME, SHE WORKS in the room she's staked out as both studio and second bedroom on nights when sleeplessness makes her a poor partner in bed. The large window offers glimpses of Nanjing's tree-lined boulevards. In the east looms Purple Mountain, the resting site of both Sun Yat-sen and the "beggar king" Zhu Yuanzhang, who rose from poverty to found the Ming Dynasty. To the south lies Yuhuatai Shan, Rain of Flowers Mountain. There, the story goes, a monk once chanted sutras so sweetly that the Buddha showered him with flowers. The heavenly blossoms transformed as they fell, into the rainbow-toned stones that now lie scattered across the summit.

Since Chiang Kai-shek assumed the mantle of China's leadership, however, the mountain has become famous for something else: it is (people whisper) where Communists and other radicals are taken and disposed of. The luckier ones, like Zanhua's old friend Chen Duxiu, languish in Nationalist prisons. The luckiest of all, like Meng Qihua, have fled to the north with the few Communists whom the government has not yet purged.

Still, despite such dark murmurings, Yuliang has painted prolifically in this bright little space, producing more than enough work for the two dozen exhibitions she's been in since returning home nearly eight years ago. The last one, in Nanjing, included her very first political painting, inspired by the National 19th Route Army that fought so bravely against Hirohito's troops.

Yuliang is intensely proud of *Our Heroes*. She can't look at it without remembering the shock of those first few weeks—the shriek of Japanese planes, the whistling mortars and roaring bombs. Entire buildings collapsed, as if Shanghai's perpetual building boom has sudenly gone into reverse. After the all-clear sounded, Yuliang slipped outside, defying curfew to survey her wounded city. Outside, all was eerily quiet; the streets stripped of chatter and motor-purr and the jangle of worldly wealth. It smelled not of cash and coffee but of rubble and soot—and, somewhere behind that, seared flesh.

Amid the temporary quiet, the Red Cross workers helped soldiers pull the corpses into the street. Survivors lined up on the sidewalks, awaiting the attention of foreign doctors. Pausing in the street, Yuliang stepped toward a wounded child who appeared to be lying in a patch of gasoline. The child, however, turned out to be the legless corpse of a small man, the gasoline his dust-darkened blood. It was an image that refused to leave Yuliang, even after she'd finished the painting—a mere twelve hours after she'd fled back to her little house.

Her current project, *Strong Man,* was likewise launched in fury—though as much against her critics as against the Japanese. Five years ago, when Yuliang first returned from Europe, her work was greeted by critics as "fresh" and "deftly Western," "rivaling Manet," and even "exuding the air of the Old Masters." Later, though, as the Generalissimo's "New Life" program cast its shadow, the tone began to change. "Why French countryside, Venetian bridges, and bare-breasted Negroes?" asked *Shenbao,* in its review of her last show. "Is Madame Pan ashamed to paint things that suit Chinese taste and culture?" The right-leaning *China World* went even further, calling her work "pure pornography": "Come to see it if you must. But treat it as you'd treat a flower house: leave your wife and your daughter at home."

Gazing up at *Strong Man* now, Yuliang reassures herself that even the staunchest neo-Confucianist couldn't find anything to malign in this painting. Granted, the subject is shirtless. But so are most of the fieldhands she has spent past weeks sketching as they drive their buffalo through the fields for spring seeding. And surely— surely no one will miss the significance of the rich earth the man carries in his hands. Yuliang has put hours into those hands, struggling to make them both broad and gentle. Hands that, on the one side, will allow China to flourish, and on the other keep it from crumbling apart.

She holds her filbert brush vertically against the figure, then loads it with newly mixed brown ocher. For twenty minutes she scrapes and mixes, dabs and brushes and paints, allowing no thoughts beyond the buttery blending of one tone into the next. She is just wetting her bright brush when she hears a distinctive *creaketty-creak* of wood-soled shoes, followed by the banging of the studio door.

Guanyin appears, her face half covered by dark glasses. She scans the room with vague fury, blind Justice seeking a fugitive. Which, Yuliang reflects, in some ways she is: the law, after all, still prohibits concubines.

"Xiao taitai!" Guanyin shouts, using the term Zanhua loathes. "Second lady!"

"Yes," Yuliang answers quietly. Guanyin's doctors claim that her eyesight is failing rapidly; in a year or two, she might be blind. Yuliang suspects it's partially a front: the first lady's eyes were sharp enough, after all, to spot the delicate gold earrings Zanhua bought Yuliang for her birthday this past year.

"Did you need something, elder sister?" she asks now, setting down her brush.

"I came to see if you've preferences for dinner. I'm sending Cook to market." Guanyin steps in. "I was thinking of snapper with mushrooms. But the price of both has gone up. And he needs a new pan, too—the one he's using now has cracked."

Yuliang suppresses a smile. The last time Cook "needed" a new pan was a month back, and Yuliang dutifully handed over the requested sum. Two weeks later, the pan on the stove remained cracked and tarnished. Guanyin, however, sported a new *qipao* of Nanjing silk.

But the last thing Yuliang wants now, with so much work ahead of her, is to argue. Besides, she's promised Zanhua she'll try her best to keep the peace. "I have no preferences," she says shortly. Picking up her purse, she counts out three crisp new Nationalist bills.

Guanyin accepts them with a nod, tucking them into her waistband. Instead of leaving, though, she wanders around the room. She lifts books to the sunlight. She leafs through Yuliang's sketchbooks. Eventually she makes her way over to Yuliang's canvas.

"This is for the Shanghai show?" She squints over Yuliang's shoulder.

"Yes."

"When do you leave?"

"In a week and a half."

"All this shuttling about." Guanyin sighs, as though she honestly would prefer to have Yuliang stay at home. "And it's such a long trip."

"The government has laid down new tracks to the north. It's smoother even than a motorcar nowadays."

"Still. You'll have to settle down at some point, if you truly want to be with child." Guanyin sucks her teeth portentously. "It's hard enough to coax a pearl from an old oyster." She steps back on the tiny feet she still refuses to let Zanhua liberate, and squints behind her glasses. "Is it a boy?"

"A man."

"Naked?"

"Dressed." And then—defensively—"Mostly."

"So you didn't need to sneak in anywhere to paint him."

"No," Yuliang replies shortly. She recently made the papers by dressing up in men's clothing to slip into one of the men-only male-figure-study seminars. As she did this mostly to make a point (about the university's rules on decency) it didn't bother her that she was recognized. Zanhua, however, seemed less than amused. Particularly when the incident appeared in the *Nanjing Daily* ("Famous Woman Painter Turns Brush on Nude Male").

"Western or Chinese?" Guanyin persists, now.

"What?"

"The clothes he will be wearing. Will they be Western or Chinese?"

Yuliang rolls her eyes. "Truly, *da taitai*, what does it matter?"

"People pay attention to such things these days." The older woman shakes out a newspaper she's picked up on her stroll around the room. "When a newsman writes that your paintings lack national spirit or womanly decency, it reflects on the honor of us all."

"Your eyesight certainly seems to be improving," Yuliang observes dryly.

Guanyin just shrugs. "Of course, I don't know if that's *exactly* what it says."

"What newsmen know of art could be inscribed on a grain of rice," Yuliang says, turning back to her painting. "Some of them," she adds pointedly, "might as well be blind."

"Some of those blessed with sight can't see past their noses," Guanyin snaps back. "They paint things no good or decent person wants to buy."

It's not a new insult—and not even particularly unfair. Yuliang can't argue that both sales and commissions have dropped these past months. Still, she swivels angrily on her stool. "You seem, first lady, to forget that my work pays for Weiyi's university fees. It's what keeps our social position in Nanjing intact. Lately, it even keeps us in this house. "

Guanyin's eyes narrow. "What I remember," she says malevolently, "is that you have worked in many houses. In many *positions*."

You old ox-fart. For an instant Yuliang actually lifts her arm to strike the woman. It takes tooth-gritting will to redirect it to her paintbox: *keep the peace.* Jaw clenched, she sweeps up her painting knife. "I'm very sorry, *taitai*," she says, as levelly as she can manage. "Thank you for your concern about me. But have Cook make whatever you think is best." She stabs the knife into a pot of obsidian, then layers it roughly on her background.

Guanyin, however, is not quite through. "Was he the one, then?" She jerks her head toward the huge canvas.

Sighing, Yuliang turns around again. "Who?"

"The one whose face you drew in your fancy books."

"I don't understand your meaning."

Guanyin smiles—a slow, crocodile smile, which reveals the two gold teeth with which she replaced her last two incisors. "And yet they call you a professor."

Her unfocused eyes gleam for a moment behind the dark glasses. Then she turns on her heel, and creaks off down the hallway.

Thirty-six

Aꜰᴛᴇʀ Gᴜᴀɴʏɪɴ ʜᴀs ʟᴇꜰᴛ Yuliang remains motionless, her eyes glued to her newly blended palette. *It can't be*, she thinks. *She is even madder than I thought.*

But even as this thought's completed she is already on her feet, making her way to the small bookcase beneath the window. She runs her fingertip across the neat row of textured spines, with their titles in myriad languages and shades of ink: Baudelaire's *The Painter of Modern Life*; Colette's *Chéri*. Her own two-book set, a limited edition of her prints published at the height of her public acclaim. Wedged in at the end are a few copies of *L'Gazette du Bon Ton,* still warped and spotted with dried seawater.

At first, whether by accident or some protective sleight of her subconscious, Yuliang skips over the text she wants. She finds it on the second run—the soft green spine and flaked gold paint of *What Is Art?* Pulling it out gently, she passes her thumb over the inscription that so embarrassed her a decade ago: *I thought of our first conversation when I found this, and am overjoyed at the thought of you holding it in your beautiful artist's hands.* The characters swim before her for a moment. Blinking, Yuliang pushes past them to the once-blank inserts in the back.

It's all there: the large, square jaw; the hand-raked hair; the boy-ishly round cheeks. All reproduced a dozen or more times, in a style more tentative and overtly Western than the way she would paint him now. Still, it is inarguable that it's all her work. Even Guanyin—near-blind Guanyin—can see that.

Sinking to the floor, Yuliang studies the images. In the first one Xudun is sleeping, his face free of lines, his lips slightly parted. In the next he sits, a sheet draped across his waist. In another sketch he stretches his arms toward a night sky. Then he's against the Seine, his hair dark against the water.

The last image, drawn while she waited for Xing Xudun at the Cluny, shows Yuliang's one lover in a simple upright pose. Devoid of detail, he's composed primarily of smudged crosshatch; it is impos-sible to tell whether he is approaching the viewer, or leaving. Coming to her now, the thought makes her shiver slightly. For the fact is that as she waited on the appointed day of their reunion, and the next, and the one after that, this was precisely how she came to see Xudun; as a vague and dreamlike figure who was either racing through Paris to meet her or who had already lied to her, and then left.

Sitting there, that day, at their appointed meeting place, Yuliang had had no way of knowing that Xing Xudun was not in Paris but in Mar-seille; betrayed to the police by the same PJC he'd once ridiculed. He and a dozen other CCP members would soon be marched aboard an overcrowded steamship and carried east, where, simmering in ever-mounting resentment, they would only bring their revolution home that much more vehemently.

Yuliang, both wounded and vaguely relieved, eventually moved to Rome. There she lost herself in her own revolution—the one she and Mirror Girl had started together. She took no more lovers. But over the next four years she gave herself to the Vatican, to Leonardo and Rembrandt, to the Gentileschis. Her hurt she treated simply much like a sculpting mistake—something to smooth over, to chip away at.

Yuliang takes one last look at the book. Then, bracing herself, she turns her face to her easel. Confirmation of her suspicions crashes down on her, all but emptying the room of air: the man she'd sketched then and the man she's just painted are identical.

Winded, Yuliang drops her head into her hands. *How did this happen?* She hasn't thought of Xing Xudun in months. Like other painful parts of her life, she keeps him locked in a black box, in her memory's deepest recess. And the model for *Strong Man* was someone else entirely—a beefy first-year student she tutors sometimes. It's true she made some alterations to the face, but only because the boy had risked enough to pose for her.

Furious with herself, she throws the book to the ground. As she does, two notes flutter from its pages. One is a news article, torn jaggedly along the edges. The other is a letter, yellowed and curling at the edges.

Yuliang smoothes them each out in turn against her knee. But she doesn't read them; she doesn't need to. She knows them word for word:

MOBSTERS LAUNCH PREDAWN ATTACK ON UNIONISTS; SOVIET SYMPATHIZERS
Hundreds killed, scores jailed. Death toll still rising, officials say.

Shanghai, April 13, 1927: The city was rocked yesterday by word that hundreds of union organizers and leftists were rounded up before sunrise and summarily executed.

The news comes in advance of the long-awaited arrival in the city of General Chiang Kai-shek with his Northern Expedition forces, which until now have been allied with the Communists. The surprise crackdown—supposedly organized by the city's notorious "Green Gang" crime syndicate—also interrupts a widely advertised general strike being planned by unionists and Communist sympathizers around the city.

Sources close to the attacks claim that Shanghai's own law enforcement agencies were aware of the planned purge. A government spokesman, however, denied this charge, calling it "absurd."

The letter is dated September 1929.

My dear friend:

It is with great grief that I confirm that our friend Xing Xudun was indeed lost on the night of April 13. He was staying at the Lucky Chan Boarding House in Hongkou, and that house was raided by the Green Gang. Only two of my colleagues are known to have survived. Everyone else was executed in the street.

I am very sorry to greet your return from Europe with such terrible news. But as you are no doubt aware, these have been hard times for those in our party. We lost more than five thousand members during that one week alone. I consider myself lucky I wasn't injured again—or worse.

I will give this note to my mother to pass along to you. Perhaps, if things improve, we'll have a chance to meet again in happier circumstances—both for ourselves and for our poor and abused nation.

Guifei

FOR A LONG TIME YULIANG SITS, the notes and book in her lap. It's not until the sun's rays are slanting dangerously close to the floor that she realizes how late it has become: there's barely enough time and light left to remix her face tones. The truth is, the last thing she wants to do is paint. She wants nothing more at this moment than to allow herself the luxury of despair.

As she is thinking this, however, a door slams shut downstairs. She hears two voices in the small courtyard outside. One is Guanyin's. The other belongs to the amah she takes with her to go shopping sometimes—not Qian Ma (who has long since died) but an equally crotchety niece.

Yuliang sits back on her heels, listening dully as the two secure a rickshaw, which then trundles off toward Beijing Road. Then, carefully, she folds and tucks the yellowed papers back in place in the book, which she carries back to her easel with her. Clearly she'll need to find a new hiding spot.

Still all but in a trance, she picks up the paper Guanyin dropped. She pages past the incriminating review, perusing and dismissing photograph after grainy photograph before stopping in front of one that vaguely catches her interest. It is of Chiang Kai-shek, commending a KMT general who seems both suitably strong and anonymous. Yuliang taps it with her finger, then slices it free with her box knife. She tapes it to the top of her canvas.

Don't think, she thinks. But as she lays on the first wet strokes, a soft grief returns. For a moment Xing Xudun stands before her as he did on that last morning. She feels the broad, warm muscles of his back against her palms. She sees him turn to her, exhausted. Overjoyed. *Meet me in one week,* he tells her. *I'll be waiting at the Cluny again, at noon.*

Yuliang sits very still. *Don't think*, she thinks again. Instead, she reloads her paintbrush. She hesitates for just a moment. Then, with a small, tight breath, she paints him out of her frame.

Thirty-seven

TWO DAYS BEFORE THE EXHIBIT Yuliang enters the dining room to find Guanyin at the breakfast table. "Good morning, elder sister," she says politely.

Guanyin merely inclines her head. But Yuliang, sensing watchfulness in those near-sightless eyes, is immediately suspicious. *She's planning something.*

At first glance, nothing appears amiss. The food looks unappealing —most food does when she is nervous, and Yuliang is always nervous before shows. Her teacup and spoon are in their proper places, as is the herbal supplement (a blend of ginseng, tang-kuei, and peony) prescribed by the doctor she and Zanhua visited last week. Zanhua has also left the *Shenbao* for her to read in its usual place, squarely in front of her chair.

It isn't until Yuliang picks up the paper that she sees it: the conservative *China World* has been placed neatly underneath. Opened to the arts section, it is folded to the lead story: " *'NOVA' Exhibit Seen as Travesty; Lack of Ticket Sales Forces Early Closure.*"

Ah, she thinks.

She pretends to skim the article casually while emptying the wax-paper packet into the water and stirring. Secretly, though, she homes in on every word.

The show, which was promoted by her own gallery, was made up primarily of Tokyo-trained painters, working in schools that baffled even some Westerners: neo-fauvism, magic surrealism, neo-plasticism. The exhibition's goal, as voiced by its curator, was "to do away with the manacles of figurative form and representation and set viewers' minds free to follow their dreams." According to this article, though, the result was more of a nightmare. "I've never understood futurism," one attendee was quoted as saying. "If anything, these works make me nostalgic for the old art of the past." Another man was more straightforward: "My dog could have done better with his ass, his tail, and some paint."

Even more disturbingly, two paintings were apparently defaced. *Defaced?* Yuliang thinks, grimacing as she tosses back the glass's bitter contents. Setting the cup down, she pulls the paper over and reads the piece again more thoroughly.

Across the table, Guanyin smiles triumphantly. "I had the master read that to me yesterday. I thought perhaps you'd be interested."

"The NOVA exhibit was based on a different style of painting from mine," Yuliang says coldly, swirling her teapot.

"Aren't you a futurist?"

"That term means nothing. The uneducated use it to describe anything they don't immediately understand."

Guanyin tightens her lips. Though she's never displayed an interest in learning beyond Confucian classics like *Xiao Xue,* the *Book of Moral Training,* she bitterly resents Yuliang's extensive schooling. Or, perhaps more accurately, their shared husband's spending on these things. "Education," she says now, with a sniff, "is given too much importance these days. Even the most learned woman in the world is useless if she's unable to bear her husband sons."

She watches Yuliang through her dark lenses, clearly expecting her to protest. But Yuliang has made this mistake before. All it has done is given Guanyin an excuse to note the scores of barren months that have passed since Yuliang moved in, marked by menstrual rags that Guanyin somehow always contrives to have seen. It's a tense and bloody vigil, eerily evocative of the Hall, and of Godmother's dreaded red book.

Yuliang reaches for the hot water. "I would be happy with a girl," she says.

"I had a dream you had one."

"Really?" Yuliang glances at her again. For all of her and Zanhua's banter about "fate," she's increasingly superstitious about her womb. When she'd first returned to China, her barrenness had seemed a kind of reprieve, a period to rediscover her husband, her nation. Herself, here. As the years have passed, though, what has taken root—in lieu of a child, it seems—is a dense sense of culpability. As though her own flesh is punishing her for all the years she's abused and deprived it.

"It was a girl," Guanyin says slowly. "But she wasn't Chinese. Or at least she didn't look fully Chinese. She looked . . ."

"Looked what?"

"Well, older, for one thing. I can't remember it exactly. It was just a dream, after all." She laughs self-consciously. "And either way, it doesn't matter, does it? Girls are girls. You bear and raise them for others."

"I wouldn't."

Guanyin blinks behind her glasses. "Surely you're not too modern to let your daughter marry?" she says indignantly, as though Yuliang has proposed not letting her daughter eat.

"If she chose to, of course. But I'd have no complaints if she decided to do something more with her life."

"What more could she do?"

"Anything at all. Look at what I do."

Guanyin makes a dismissive gesture, underscoring how little she knows or cares about what Yuliang does. "I suppose you'd waste thousands of yuan to send her here and there. To fill her head with frivolous things for which she has no need."

"I'd give her as much schooling as any boy," Yuliang returns.

"And yes, perhaps we'd take her to Paris and Rome. Weiyi too. Someday."

Guanyin wrinkles her nose. "Whatever for?"

Yuliang smiles. "We wouldn't force you to go along, if you didn't care to."

For a moment she can almost see it: herself and her daughter, together at the Louvre. Yuliang would reveal the secrets she'd discovered in those gilded halls: Solario's morose self-portrait, embedded like a bleak gem in the tray's stem in *Salome with the Head of St. John the Baptist*. The ghostly customer in Manet's *A Bar at the Folies-Bergères*. The artful array of tricks and jokes in *Le déjeuner sur l'herbe*. Its nonsensical picnic, with its mismatched fruits and muddy bread loaf . . . "She should know about the world," she says quietly. "To teach her wifely ways alone will bind her soul. It's like blinding her."

For once, the slight is unintended. Still, Guanyin's shoulders droop a little. "It's probably pointless to discuss it anyway," she snaps, swallowing the last bit of her breakfast. "What time does your train depart?"

"Six," Yuliang says. She looks at her watch. It's only eleven, but she hasn't picked out her outfit or begun packing. *Strong Man* still needs to be wrapped and taped for his journey. There are those papers, too, she'd intended to pick up in order to read and grade them on the train . . .

"A shame the master can't join you," Guanyin says.

Yuliang merely nods. Zanhua, in fact, is meeting her in Shanghai, as he almost always does when she has an exhibit. The last time they informed Guanyin of a similar plan, however, Yuliang returned to a subtly destroyed studio. Some of her brushes had been snapped in half, the others plucked free of their boar and fox hairs. Her oil tubes had been opened and squeezed into a monochromatic mess. Now they make up cover stories. This time Zanhua has supposedly been sent to a Wuxi Merchant's Guild meeting.

"You're traveling second class, I hope," Guanyin goes on.

"Third," Yuliang says accommodatingly, although in fact she is traveling first—Zanhua insisted that she needs the rest. "Do you have anything you'd like me to take to Weiyi?" she adds, eyeing her first lady from the corners of her eyes.

Predictably, Guanyin's face closes up like a book. "Don't bother him. He's written that he is very busy right now."

Which is doubtless true. Yuliang knows from her own letters (for Weiyi writes her regularly too) that her stepson belongs to both the Society for China Reconstruction and, partly at her urging, the Society for the Resistance of the Japanese. Recently he has also explored an Ibsen reading group. If he didn't have his father's intellect, Yuliang might find it a minor miracle that he has any time for his studies at all.

And yet she knows Guanyin well enough to know that the warning wasn't made out of concern for her son's study habits. As her health has declined, what was once mere possessiveness of Weiyi has become a kind of vicious territorialism. It is, Yuliang suspects, at least part of the reason Guanyin won't let Zanhua bring him home from Shanghai, as many other families did after the Japanese attacked. "He's no safer here than he is there," Guanyin said staunchly. "Who says the island dwarves won't attack the capital as well?" In truth, though, she's less worried about a Japanese attack on the city than a concubinal attack on her son's loyalties.

Now as if to underscore just this point, she turns suspiciously to Yuliang. "He's not coming to your exhibit tomorrow, is he?"

"Of course not," Yuliang says, standing. "You know I wouldn't go against your wishes."

"You've never cared about my wishes." Guanyin turns her vague gaze to the plate before her. "Neither of you have," she adds.

Something in her tone makes Yuliang turn to face her—this woman who would be only too contented to see her die. Who has waged a continual war against her since the very day Yuliang arrived here, insisting she perform the traditional kowtow of subservience. Not wanting to begin things badly, Yuliang complied with that demand, touching her forehead three times to the dusty front hall floor. Inwardly, however, she'd imagined poking out those bitter, shielded eyes with her sculpting awl.

Looking at Guanyin now, though, what Yuliang remembers most clearly is Zanhua's first words about her: *It is not a true marriage.* And what she feels is a stab of sympathy—not just for this ill, aging, and unloved wife, but for a world seemingly structured to pit its weakest members against one another. Perhaps for no better reason than to keep them weak.

"You're right," she says softly. "We haven't."

Guanyin stares at her. For the first time in recent memory, she actually removes her glasses. "What?"

Her eyes, in the late morning light, are wide and dark, and just as lovely as they were in the matchmaker's photo Yuliang saw long ago. They are also wet, though whether this is from sadness or the illness there is no way of knowing. Still, Yuliang has the urge to step over. To offer her Louvre '24 handkerchief, or her shoulder, almost the same way she sometimes offered her fellow flowers solace after a particularly bad night. Or a beating.

The feeling lasts just a minute, though. Until Guanyin covers her eyes again.

"You'd better leave soon. You can't afford to be late." She holds out the newspaper, smirking again. "You can take this for the train."

Thirty-eight

THE BLUE STEEL EXPRESS pulls into Shanghai the next morning with an efficient chorus of clangs and sighs. Yuliang, dressed and, while not particularly rested (she never sleeps well before shows), fueled by two cups of excellent coffee, descends its metal steps, kicking her carpet bag before her. *Strong Man*, however, she holds, swaddled in blankets and brown paper. Once on the platform, she looks for a porter. Instead her gaze runs straight into two young Japanese soldiers. The pair is standing off to the track's side as though they have every right to be here.

For the barest of instances there's an urge to step right back on the train. At least Nanjing, for all its stuffiness and screeching Nationalist planes overhead, is still free of those hated khaki uniforms.

When she reaches Tianmu Street a few minutes later, however, Yuliang's mood brightens. She always forgets just how much she misses her life here, the color and chaos that are so completely lacking in the orderly capital. After paying the porter she takes a moment to simply stand still, in the city she still thinks of as her true home. It is (Yuliang thinks) like a shot of good whiskey: the noise and glitter, the endless energy. A rickshaw passes, its bony runner pulling a priest easily three times his own weight. As they reach the intersection a Duesenberg leaps toward them, causing the boy to stop short. Runner and rider join in a chorus of salty insults. These are promptly returned by the sedan's driver, a peroxide-blond *taitai*.

Observing the exchange, Yuliang has to laugh. *Heaven help Hirohito,* she thinks, hailing her own rickshaw. If the Japanese do attack Shanghai again, they will be in for a far worse fight than they expect.

SHE ARRIVES AT THE EXHIBITION SPACE a little before noon, just as the workmen finish installing her name on the marquee. Shading her eyes, Yuliang reads over their shoulders: PAN YULIANG: FAMOUS WESTERN-STYLE WOMAN PAINTER. "Idiots," she mutters. No matter how often she requests otherwise, they insist on inserting that word: *woman*. Though as Liu Haisu has reminded her on countless occasions, "Be happy they stop at *woman*. They'd put up *naked* too, if they thought it'd sell tickets." And grinned. "Which wouldn't necessarily be a bad thing."

Inside the main gallery all signs of the disastrous NOVA show have vanished. The walls are clean and whitewashed, studded with new hooks and nails. The gallery director stands amid a cluster of assistants. As Yuliang's heels click across the room his face breaks into a wide grin, and Yuliang reluctantly inclines her head. In terms of facial expression, the little curator is completely and fully her opposite: a compulsive smiler. Matching him tooth for tooth hurts her face.

"Ah, Madame Pan," he says now, beaming. "You look very well indeed. Have you by any chance put on some weight?"

"I don't believe so," she replies (musing that in France this would be the height of insults). "But thank you. I must say, by the way, that I noticed the marquee on my way in."

"New characters!" he announces brightly. "Multicolored, as you doubtless observed. And a full six millimeters larger than the ones from last year."

She nods. "But I couldn't help but notice that you've done it again."

His brow creases very slightly. "Done what?"

"Called me a 'famous woman painter.' "

He beams. "So you are."

Yuliang stifles a sigh. "May I ask—again—why it's necessary to insert 'woman'? Does anyone honestly think at this point that I'm a man?"

He appears to ponder this, teeth still bared. "I wouldn't think so."

"Is it too late to remove it?"

"Unfortunately, I'm afraid it is. You see, we've already printed it on the posters and programs." Reaching into his pocket, he hands one over. "I truly am sorry. I completely forgot our conversation on the topic. The unfortunate truth is, there have been a number of things on my plate recently."

He is still smiling. But Yuliang also detects—or thinks she does—a note of uncertainty in his voice. She waits a moment. But when he doesn't elaborate, she changes the subject. "Is that the hanging order I sent you?" she asks, pointing to the list. "May I?"

She studies the hastily scribbled little chart, then turns back to study the wall. "I'm going to make some changes," she announces.

"Ah," he says. "Of course." Well accustomed to Yuliang's obsessive involvement in her exhibitions, he normally gives her free rein. Today, though, is different. Still grinning staunchly, he trails after her, smoking with quick, fraught puffs. He wrings his hands as she unwraps *Strong Man*, taps his foot when she puts it on the central wall. But it isn't until Yuliang has turned to leave that he makes his move.

"Madame Pan."

"Yes?"

"A word, please?" Inevitably, he's still smiling. Only a twitching

eyelid betrays his agitation. "I was just wondering about the position-
ing of that—that one." He points at *Dreaming Nude*.

Yuliang looks at the work. "Is there a problem?"

"No, no, of course not. It's just, I wonder if it might work a bit
better elsewhere. For instance, there." He points toward an alcove
that is more or less hidden behind the western wall. It is where
Yuliang has placed her recent *guohua* pieces, traditional watercolors
she's completed to strengthen her Chinese lines. She's less happy
with the results than she might have been—which, of course, is precisely why she put them there.

She frowns. "But it would have no visibility there."

"Well, yes. I merely think it . . . that is, that we perhaps . . ." He
chuckles mournfully. "It might be safer."

"Safer than what?"

He wrings his hands together. "I'm sure you've read of the NOVA
show. The reaction was, shall we say, somewhat more volatile than
we'd expected. The incident prompted the board to consider the
need to adhere more firmly to certain . . . ah, standards."

She tries to suppress her irritation. "Surely my work still meets
your artistic standards."

"Oh, undoubtedly, madame. You are, after all, China's famous
Western-style woman painter." He chuckles again.

Yuliang stares back, unamused. "What standards do I now not
meet?"

"Well—and this isn't *my* thought, of course—but there are certain new breezes, that is to say, new moods in Shanghai. Even among
its more modern gallery goers. In light of what happened, we are
simply wondering whether we should make the more . . . ah, shall
we say *forceful* pieces a little less, ah, salient . . ."

"Wait." When she holds her hand up he actually flinches: the tabloids must be running that old story about her slapping the landscapes instructor again. Yuliang can't help but take a small, spiteful
satisfaction in his terror.

"You realize," she says quietly, "that I've exhibited to fund the anti-Japanese movement. And that I've showed with the Silent Society."

He nods, looking slightly uncomfortable. Yuliang's anti-Japan statements (and open scorn for those who do not take a stand) have been amply covered in the papers. As was the Silent Society show, a collection of modern, Western-style paintings held in defiance of the nation's newfound conservatism.

"So you must realize," Yuliang continues, "that I really have no interest in hiding my work. If people dislike it, they may leave."

"In principle I agree. Of course. It's just——" The curator hesitates, then lowers his voice. "It's been suggested to me that we highlight only the works that fall within the bounds of . . ."

To his credit, he can't bring himself to say the word. Yuliang says it for him: "Decency."

He just grins.

"You are saying," Yuliang continues slowly, "that after profiting from my work these past five years, you have just now decided it's pornographic?"

"Not *pornographic,* of course. Only . . ." Though still smiling, he throws a desperate glance at the door; quite possibly he is plotting escape. "Only one can't argue with the fact that you—that your nude—shows all."

Yuliang suppresses a sigh. How often must this discussion be had? "Isn't that the *point* of nudes?" she asks dully.

"Perhaps in Paris."

"They do call Shanghai the 'Paris of the East.' "

"The *laowai* do, yes." Again, that apologetic little chuckle. As though Yuliang were a foreigner herself. "But, madame, that is just the point. Our audience is one under foreign attack. Not just its borders, but its very culture. Its way of life. It seems to me that our job now, as artists, is to make them feel safe. To remind them of the strength and purity of their own heritage."

For a long moment Yuliang simply stares at the floor. When she looks up again, she speaks slowly. "Master Ma. You studied in Germany, didn't you?"

"That is where I first met Master Xu."

"Then surely you, of all people, must understand that art isn't about shutting down borders. It's about expanding them. It's about encouraging new techniques, fresh viewpoints. Not censoring them."

The little man bridles. "I am not endorsing censorship. I am simply stressing the need for sensitivity. And not just for the sake of our viewers." His smile turns almost supplicating. "I have, as you also know, a wife and two small children. And you—you have a husband, of course—"

"My husband supports me fully," she interjects. For some reason, it comes out sounding like a protest.

The curator smiles sympathetically. "I'm sure he does," he says. "But—and I don't mean to be rude—have you considered whether you support your husband?"

For a long moment there's no sound but the scrape of a worker sweeping plaster from the floor. Yuliang crosses her arms and turns away. She gazes at *Dreaming Nude,* its calligraphic lines, its jewel-like colors. Mirror Girl gazes back, flushed and secretive.

She'd painted the self-portrait six months ago, when she suspected that at last she might be pregnant. For all her reservations, there'd been a small thrill in the thought. As the idea took hold, she'd even included subtle hints: a white cloth draped in the background that might be mistaken for a swaddling cloth; a bottle of wine for the post-birth celebration, festooned with childish ribbons; a Cézannesque peach, recalling the peach-wood arrows traditionally put by a cradle to keep away the demons. When she was done, Yuliang had even placed her red chop extra-gently. Like the lipsticked kiss a mother might place on the face of her newborn child.

Two days later, however, her cycle reasserted itself with a vengeance. Racked by cramps and nausea, Yuliang berated herself for allowing herself even to hope. In the days that followed, when the bleeding seemed to go on and on, she even wondered whether she'd brought a curse upon herself. After all, Guanyin holds that saying the very word *baby* invites bad luck into a pregnancy. What must painting one—even a hidden one—do?

"We might move *Negress* as well," Curator Ma is saying behind her now, cheerfully. "Actually, we could put some of the oil landscapes there too. The one of the Parthenon, for example. That's old, isn't it? Most people have seen it. And *Nursing Mother*, though lovely, does deserve a bit more privacy. I would love to see the watercolor of pigs moved more to center view."

"What about that one?" Yuliang asks, indicating *Strong Man*. "You can't argue, at least, that he is dressed."

He studies the canvas, chin in palm, oblivious to her sarcasm. "Well," he says, "half dressed."

For an instant Yuliang really does want to hit him; her fingers actually curl into a fist. Digit by digit, she forces them to relax. "I don't want them moved," she says tightly.

He swivels to face her. "Not even the nudes?"

She shakes her head.

"But if you've understood me—"

"All too well," she interrupts him. "It stays as I directed. In fact"— she eyes the wall—"call the workmen back."

He swallows. "May I ask—"

"No. Just listen." She begins scribbling on her notepad—plans for a revamped display. "Put the European landscapes here, closer to the doorway. The watercolors—*Pigs, Lotus Lake*, and *Suzhou Bridge*—can be moved back here, to the alcove."

"And the nudes?"

"On the center wall. All of them. *Dreaming Nude* in the middle. Move *Strong Man* over if you have to." She hesitates. "But not too far from the center. I want him to be one of the first three works people see."

The curator takes off his glasses. He has finally stopped smiling.

His face, stripped of its veneer of cheer, suddenly strikes Yuliang as almost menacing. "You truly want this."

"Yes," she says firmly. "I truly do."

The little man parts his lips, then clamps them shut again. He rubs his bald head, his thin neck. When he looks up again, his smile is neatly back in place, as mechanical and meaningless as ever. "It shall be so," he says smoothly. "After all, you are the artist."

"The *woman* artist," Yuliang reminds him.

And smiling at last, she turns to leave.

Thirty-nine

"**Y**ou did the right thing," Zanhua says an hour later.

He reaches over, pats her hand. Yuliang clasps his fingers briefly, then sets them free to travel back to the plate of pastries that has just arrived. They are sitting windowside at La Maison de Patisserie, a favorite meeting place of theirs from the old days. "You don't think I behaved badly?"

He plunges his fork into a mini-Napoleon. "The important thing is to hold on to your principles."

It's on the tip of Yuliang's tongue to remind him that he doesn't always approve of her principles, but she contents herself with dabbing sugar from her lips. The last thing she wants to do is to upset the careful balance they've worked so hard to maintain these past years.

And in truth, she reminds herself, reaching for a small, glossy ramekin of *crème brulée,* she doesn't *know* that Zanhua disapproves of her principles. They don't discuss her nude paintings. Just as they don't discuss his slow fall from political grace, prompted—or so Yuliang thought until today—by his close friendships with known Communists like Chen Duxiu and Meng Qihua. Their respective careers have come to occupy the same silent space in conversation as does her history at the Hall. Yuliang still can't help reflecting at times, however, on the role reversal that has transpired since the day she was rescued from that place by Zanhua—a dashing young firebrand who seemed to know everyone and everything. Who had traveled abroad. Who was able to support her . . .

"What's in your head?"

"It—it was an interesting morning." She smiles uneasily.

"These are interesting times, as they say." He brushes his mustache free of lingering crumbs. "When a nation goes to war, even the most mundane things can seem threatening. Some might even see this, for example, as a weapon." He waves at the English cane he'd appeared with earlier, which now leans against the wall by his chair.

"I meant to ask about that. Where on earth did you pick it up?"

"I found it on the way over here from the train station. At the Shanghai Second Hand Shop on Nanjing Road."

"Are you becoming so lame in your old age?" she teases.

"I simply decided it's high time I looked as smart and international as you do. So you see, I really bought it for you." He smiles. "You see how much I'll sacrifice on your behalf."

Yuliang laughs along with him, but there's a strange density to her mood. She scrapes gold flakes from the top of the little cake. "I sometimes wonder if I should sacrifice more for you."

He looks startled. "What does that mean?"

She hesitates. "Does my work . . . worry you?"

"Only when you suggest painting me without my clothes on."

Of course, this too is a joke. Yuliang has never suggested painting Zanhua nude, although over the past years she has done some affectionate, clothed sketches of him and Weiyi. "No, really," she says. "Has it hurt you? At the ministry?"

"No," Zanhua says firmly. "Other associations have, perhaps. And of course there is my well-known 'arrogance,' as they call it. Which in truth is simply old-fashioned honor—a concept as alien to them as it ever was." He bites into an éclair. "Why?"

"I've heard rumors. And after today's exchange with Master Ma,

I'm wondering whether there's any truth to them." Yuliang traces a circle in the snowlike dusting of sugar on her plate. Blue porcelain shines through: a small, hard lake. "Some say there's a blacklist of artists and writers. Those whose work is seen as reactionary."

"What does your Dean Xu say to this?"

"That it's just wind. But he's said to be on it too. As is Liu Haisu." Yuliang forces a stiff smile. "It might just be the one society in which they'd have to agree to share membership."

Zanhua is studying his hands. "There have been discussions," he says at length.

Yuliang's finger stops circling. "About the list?"

"There's no list. At least, I don't think so. But my superior has implied in past discussions that the Culture Ministry has been, ah, *aware* of your works."

"Aware," Yuliang repeats.

"Of the nudes, in particular." He smiles wryly. "And of course, of your views on the Generalissimo's appeasement policy toward Japan."

"That's all they said? That they're 'aware'?"

"There was some discussion as to whether I have any . . . influence. Over you."

Yuliang drops her hands into her lap. It's not the first time it's occurred to her that she—her controversial work, her dubious background, her foreign connections and fashions—might hurt him. There are moments, in fact, when his bleak silences fill their little house. He'll quietly turn from her in bed, turning their bond into a barrier. Yuliang is torn at these times between wanting to ask what is wrong, and wanting to stop her own ears against the answer. Now, though, she plows forward, prompted by a growing sense of unease. "What did you tell them?"

"That I'd have more influence over an earthquake." He grins. And for just an instant, he's the dashing young man who swept her to safety twenty years ago. But as the smile fades the image ages back into that of an older man. He looks paler, thinner. Less a victorious soldier of General Sun's than an embattled bureaucrat. Almost, in fact, like someone who needs a cane. She can't help wondering: *Have I done this to him?*

Yuliang takes a deep breath. "Zanhua. Dean Xu has offered me a raise to take on a new seminar. If it's just a matter of money, I could get an advance."

He looks at her fiercely. "I've never stooped to that kind of corruption."

"I know you haven't. But if it's a question of honor . . ."

"Don't you see, it doesn't *matter*." He almost shouts the words. "Even if we pay them a small fortune, it will just make me seem like a hypocrite. It won't change the fact that they all laugh at me behind my back. The fact that every report I write is stacked up somewhere, unread. The fact that—" He catches himself, shakes his head.

"The fact that what?" Yuliang asks. "What?"

"It doesn't matter." He tightens his lips.

After a moment, Yuliang sits back heavily in her chair. Nearby, a waiter drops a tray, unleashing exclamations from surrounding tables in French, Yiddish, and Cantonese.

Yuliang leans over again. "Zanhua," she says quietly, "I need to know the truth."

He passes a hand across his eyes. "You always do. I never lie to you, Yuliang. I promised I wouldn't." Another wan smile. "Just like I promised I'd never leave you."

For a moment she's so overwhelmed that she can't do anything but blink. Seeing her face, he clasps her hand once more, and is about to speak when a smooth voice interjects from behind her: "I hope I'm not interrupting at a bad time."

Startled, Yuliang looks up—straight into the amused gaze of Meng Qihua.

"Qihua!" She leaps to her feet.

Like Zanhua, the photographer is older, and thinner. But he's still as dapper as ever, his hair combed back, his suit crisp and London-cut. He bows slightly. "A pleasure, as it always is." He indicates the young man standing by his side. "I don't believe you know my colleague, Master Zhou."

"Ah. The famous Madame Pan," the latter says.

Meeting his gaze, Yuliang gasps again. Because she actually does know him—or at least she has seen him before. The slender figure in the drab suit is in fact none other than Xing Xudun's friend, the bushy-browed boy from the Café de Cluny.

"You're—you're the minister of mimeography!" she stutters, astonished.

"So I was, in Paris." Zhou Enlai laughs. "My title is somewhat different now."

For a moment she just gazes at him, the room spinning slightly. Then, for some reason she won't later understand, she leans over and kisses him. French-style. On each cheek.

She's just leaning back when there is a flash of light. Blinking, she turns to see yet another newcomer—this one in a newsman's suit. "Madame Pan," he says, lowering his Kodak, "do you remember me? Tang Leiyi."

Yuliang takes his card dazedly, afterflashes bobbing before her like tiny planets.

"I heard you had a show here," the reporter's saying. "What luck to find you."

"Thank you."

Yuliang says it coldly; her warmth toward reporters has more or less dried up, along with her good reviews. She's about to turn away when, somewhat to her surprise, Zanhua steps in front of her. "Why did you take that?" he demands fiercely.

"Social pages," the reporter says cheerfully. "You're familiar with our 'Seen in Town' section?"

"I'm not," says Zanhua. "Moreover, I find it rude to take a picture without asking permission. We were simply having coffee."

"Many famous people have coffee here." The journalist is already slinging his camera over his shoulder. "Yesterday I got Butterfly Hu, sitting right there." He points to a corner table, occupied now not by the svelte starlet but by two Japanese businessmen.

"It's an invasion of our rights. I could take you to court."

The reporter shrugs. "I'm no lawyer. I just shoot what my editor tells me to."

"Tell your editor you can't put my wife in your paper."

"Why?" Tang Leiyi asks, smirking. "It's not as if people don't know what she looks like."

For an instant, Zanhua looks as though he's been slapped. "How dare you," he hisses. And to Yuliang's horror, he actually swings at the man's camera with his cane.

"Zanhua! Stop it!" she shouts, reaching out to pull him back. Qihua, however, gets there first. "Easy, old friend," he murmurs.

Zanhua shakes them both off, breathing heavily. Tang Leiyi chuckles. "I was hoping for a brief interview. But I think I've gotten more than I needed." Straightening his fedora, he adds, "Good luck with your exhibit, Madame Pan. I'll look forward to seeing you both tomorrow."

As he saunters out, Yuliang turns again to Zanhua. "Why did you do that? He was just a photographer!"

"Ah, but they're a dirty bunch, those photographers." Qihua offers Zanhua his hand. "Please accept my apologies. For all of us."

Yuliang glances at Zhou Enlai. Not surprisingly, he looks distinctly uncomfortable: he avoids her eyes, scanning the room. Then he brightens slightly. "There are some comrades I should catch up with. If you'll excuse me, I'll come right back . . ." And off he hurries.

Mortified, Yuliang turns back to her husband. Qihua is addressing him earnestly. "Why so cold, old friend? Surely our different paths haven't taken us so far apart."

"If they had, you wouldn't be here. You, of all people, should know that." He turns to Yuliang. "We should go. You need to rest."

Yuliang, still mystified by his behavior, brushes him off. "I'd like to catch up a little first."

"Suit yourself." Turning away, her husband picks up the bill. Yuliang gazes at him for a moment before turning back to Qihua. "Where have you been? We haven't heard from you since I came back from Europe!"

"I'm more or less settled up north now."

"Yan'an?"

He nods.

"Did you go on the march?" The CCP's flight last year from its former base in Jiangsu is already almost legendary. Caught in a stranglehold by Chiang Kai-shek's forces, the Communists initiated an almost impossible escape plan: a yearlong trek stretched through mountains, marshes, and hostile tribal and warlord territories, encompassing some nine thousand kilometers in total. By some accounts the Red Army forces, ninety thousand strong at the march's start, were stripped down to a mere ten thousand over its course. "Was it as bad as they say?" Yuliang asks, a little awed.

He just shrugs. "Against the odds, I am alive. Although since I want to stay that way, I'm in Shanghai just until morning." He glances at Zanhua, who is assiduously ignoring them both. "And you?"

Yuliang attempts a smile. "As the newsman said, I have a show tomorrow."

"Ah, yes." Qihua grins. "I've followed your rise to fame and fortune."

Yuliang feels her cheeks heat. "It's all just a lot of chatter. Are you still taking your pictures?"

"That's become a bit difficult." He lifts the same hand he'd used to restrain Zanhua. It's only then that Yuliang registers the fact that it is withered and limp, a broken claw dangling at an odd angle off his wrist. "Oh, Qihua! What . . . ?"

"I ran into a few problems during the Generalissimo's little surprise party here. The one they're now calling the White Terror. Some thug wanted some information from me. He thought he'd get it more readily by tap-dancing on my fingers." He grins. "A small price to pay, really. Especially given what would have happened otherwise." He nods again, this time in Zanhua's direction. "But for your husband."

Zanhua shakes his head brusquely. "I did nothing." He is still visibly upset; a vein stands out over his left temple, pulsing. "And even so, I thought we'd agreed not to discuss it."

"It is hard to find heroes in times such as these," Qihua says quietly. "When we do, we should give them their due."

"I don't want dues." Zanhua hooks his cane over his arm. "I simply want to have my coffee in peace." To Yuliang he says, "I'll wait outside until you're done."

As he makes his way toward the door Yuliang watches him go, now completely confused. "I'm so sorry," she says at last. "He's . . . unpredictable these days."

"Nothing's predictable these days," Qihua says grimly. "Although I'll admit, I had hoped . . ." He sighs. "Perhaps it's for the best. I suppose we did have a sort of agreement in the end."

"Agreement?"

"He used his influence to secure my release from prison."

She sucks her breath in. "He never told me!"

"I'm not surprised. He has made it clear for years that he'd prefer we keep a safe distance apart. Oh, don't look so surprised. Not so long ago, even being seen with an old troublemaker like me could land you on the wrong side of the firing brigade. And you know our friend Chen Duxiu is still behind bars."

Yuliang nods slowly. "Still, I thought things were easier. They say the Generalissimo is making amends with the CCP now."

"Oh, we've patched things up for the duration of the war. Still, trusting the KMT is like trying to ride a tiger. Sooner or later, it's sure to bite us."

Yuliang bites her own lip, suddenly remembering Xing Xudun's comment to her more than a decade ago: *If anything, it's a marriage of convenience. And one I doubt will last.* With a twinge of guilt she looks after her husband.

"He has changed," she says softly.

"Everyone changes," Qihua answers. "Why, look at you! Who would have thought, in the days of Ocean Street, that you were on your way to being China's 'famous Western-style woman painter'?"

"Only thanks to you. If you hadn't convinced him to let me paint, I'd be little more than an official's concubine."

He grins wryly. "I wish I could take credit. But that, too, goes to your husband."

Yuliang frowns. "But you were the one who went after him that night."

"I did, yes. But by the time I found him he'd already decided to support you."

Yuliang blinks at him, dumbfounded.

"To be truthful, madame, I don't think he's ever really wanted much more. You are a very lucky woman."

For a moment, Yuliang is incapable of meeting his eyes. The morning's exchange with Curator Ma comes back to her, full-force: *Have you considered whether you support your husband?*

"I am," she says, touching the little boar in her pocket. "Far luckier than I deserve to be."

They stand together, sunk in separate thoughts. Then Qihua's face brightens. "Ah, Lao Zhou. How was your visit?" Zhou Enlai has returned.

"Reassuring," he says. "I hadn't seen those two since the march. I was half afraid they'd joined the ranks of the permanently missing." He smiles at Yuliang. "Has your esteemed husband left?"

Both the comment and its tone are nothing if not polite. And yet once more, Yuliang again finds herself speechless.

"He went outside to get some air," Qihua says for her, smoothly. "Actually, if you'll pardon me, I think I'll go join him for a moment. There is one last thing I'd like to communicate."

Nodding at them both, he makes his way to the door. Yuliang watches him leave, a knot forming in her throat.

Zhou Enlai lights a cigarette, then offers her the pack. "You—you were close," she says as he lights it for her. For some reason, she speaks in French.

"To Master Meng?"

"To Xudun."

"*Oui.*" He says it without a trace of emotion.

Lifting the cigarette, her hand trembles. "Were you there, then, that night?"

"*Helas, oui.* It's a miracle I escaped."

"And . . . he really did die."

"*Je l'ai enterré,*" he answers simply. *I buried him.*

A lone small hope that Yuliang hadn't even realized she'd harbored flickers briefly, then extinguishes. Yet the question flows from her, just as easily as Xudun's face did: "He told you about me?"

"Not in detail. But we all knew."

Outside, Meng Qihua is talking earnestly to Zanhua, who keeps his eyes fixed on the ground. It dawns on Yuliang suddenly: if Zhou Enlai knew, then did Qihua? Did Duxiu? Is it possible, even, that Zanhua . . . ? Her heart suddenly seems to turn over.

"You must think I'm a terrible woman," she manages at last. It takes effort to meet Zhou Enlai's bright gaze. When she does, she's surprised to see that it is filled with respect.

"Madame Pan," he says softly, "he couldn't have felt as he did if you were."

Stubbing out his cigarette in a nearby ashtray, he turns to go. Then he turns back again. "Keep fighting them," he adds quietly. "Whatever else you do. It would have made him even prouder."

Forty

THE DOORS TO THE EXHIBITION SPACE don't open until
eleven, which is about the earliest Shanghai's art elite can appear on
a Saturday, pressed, dressed, and driven out by their chauffeurs. Still,
Yuliang and Zanhua's carriage reaches Yan'an Road well before nine.
Only in part so she can look over the new hanging order.

It's a tradition Yuliang has developed these past years, taking one
last little walk among her paintings. She doesn't take notes, doesn't
repaint or change anything. She merely strolls, smokes, thinks. She
adjusts one frame here, rubs a smudge from another with a tongue-
moistened handkerchief. *You will be fine,* she tells her works, each
and every one of them. *You are beautiful. You make me proud.* Strangely
enough, it is this moment—not the awarding of prize or purse, nor
the flash of the reporters' cameras—to which she most looks forward. That bated-breath walk. That last quiet assessment. She and
her artwork, alone.

Today, however, as the rickshaw turns onto the tree-lined avenue,
Yuliang is surprised to see a small crowd already gathered. What's more,
the doors are already open. Not neatly hooked back as they usually are,
but swinging loosely on their hinges. Like two loose white teeth.

. "A good turnout," Zanhua says, either missing or discounting this detail. "Perhaps we'll see a sale or two."

When Yuliang doesn't answer, he touches her arm. "Don't worry," he says. "This will be your best one yet."

Yuliang forces a smile. It is both moving and inexplicable, his silent but unswerving support all of these years. "I'm not worried," she says.

Despite herself, though, she pats her pocket. All she feels is the ribbed texture of her stockings. She pats the other pocket: also empty.

Frowning, Yuliang slips her hand from her husband's arm. Turning in her seat, she probes the rickshaw cushions.

"What is it?" Zanhua asks.

"My boar." She checks her skirt again, then her jacket. She distinctly remembers slipping it into the day's planned outfit (a checked suit with puffed sleeves and a hemline a good inch or two above New Life standards). But again, it's not in any of her tiny, pointless pockets. Her embroidered handbag contains only its usual contents: cigarettes, her lipstick. Notes for an upcoming lecture at school. The rickshaw floor proves just as barren.

"Do you need to go back?" Zanhua asks.

And for a moment Yuliang actually considers it. After all, she carried the little sculpture with her to and from Europe, slept with it beneath her thin pillow in third class. She has taken it to almost every exhibit and major event ever since. It was even in her pocket when she first kowtowed to Guanyin. The thought of facing today, of all days, without it borders on terrifying. But she forces herself to sit up straight. "Don't be silly," she says, stiffly.

Still, as they draw even with the Exhibition Space, her anxiety hardens into a painful knot, slung low and tight in her stomach. The crowd isn't the usual sort that gathers before an art opening. It is more like one that gathers at the scene of a murder. French Concession policemen in their small flat hats and silver buckles are talking sternly and scribbling notes. Newsmen cluster with their cameramen. Pedestrians pause. Gallery personnel smoke and fan themselves in tense clusters. And as her rickshaw pulls up, the reporters swarm over, their faces alert, intent. Faintly gleeful. "Do you have any idea who did this?" one shouts. "Have you established what is missing?"

"And do you have any sense of where those pieces might have gone?"

Recognizing this last voice Yuliang whirls around quickly. Sure enough, it's Tang Leiyi, from the *Shenbao*. With a cool smile, he insinuates himself between Yuliang and her husband. "I've heard," he says in a low voice, "that the Blue Shirt Society was involved. Any comment?"

"That's outrageous!" Zanhua sputters, pushing him back. "And you have no right to bother us again." Taking Yuliang's arm, he tries to hustle her into the building.

Yuliang, however, remains rooted to the spot. She is suddenly aware of two somewhat hard-looking men across the street. When she stares at them, they stare right back. Expressionless. Smoking almost in unison.

"Did you say Blue Shirts?" she asks quietly. The society is well known in Nanjing, where it plays a key role in the eradication of Communists. Loosely modeled on Mussolini's Blackshirts, the Blue Shirts have a stated mandate of ensuring absolute allegiance to their Generalissimo, Chiang Kai-shek, in government, military, and society. Some claim they control everything from public schools to publishing houses. Up until now, though, Yuliang has never heard of them turning their steely gazes to painting.

"No one has confirmed it yet. But after what they've found here, there are whispers . . ."

Fear spreads blue-black wings in her chest. "What? *What* have they found here?"

"You mean to say they haven't called you?" He's scribbling furiously. "Do you suppose, then, that the Exhibition Space was in on it as well?"

"In on *what?*" Yuliang begins. But she's interrupted by a shrill exclamation: "Don't write that. Don't you write that!"

Curator Ma hurries over, glasses askew. For once his face is stripped of its smile. "We called Madame Pan right away," he tells the reporter. It's the angriest tone she's heard him use. "The concierge will confirm this, if you check at the Cathay. Surely you don't think that we had a hand—"

Yuliang can stand it no longer. "*Tell me!*" she shouts. "If someone doesn't tell me *now* what is going on, I—I will never speak to your paper again. And I—I'll take all my works somewhere else."

The curator blinks. The journalist's face creases into another smile. He writes something down, then underlines it. Twice. "I'll leave you to escort her inside, Master Ma." Turning to Yuliang, he adds ominously, "Madame. My condolences. We all know how hard you work." He saunters to the exhibition poster by the door.

Hands trembling, Curator Ma attempts to straighten his tie. "We rang your hotel three times, no less," he says helplessly. "Three times!"

"We had breakfast out," Yuliang tells him. "But I still—" She breaks off abruptly as her gaze lands again on Tang Leiyi, now positioned with his camera before the entrance. He's preparing to photograph a poster for the show, with the same wording Yuliang had asked to have changed. With a jolt, she suddenly sees that it *has* been changed—but not as she requested. Now not just *woman* but *painter* has been slashed out with red paint. Above are characters carrying a completely different meaning: 妓女.

Whore.

Yuliang shuts her eyes. *It's a dream,* she tells herself. *It's just another one of my dreams.*

But when she opens her eyes, the poster is still there. So are the two men, crushing out their cigarettes. One catches her eye. He grins—a hard, tight smile.

Stomache churning, Yuliang turns back to the curator. "Tell me what has happened."

Curator Ma attempts a smile that's so completely far from the mark that in other circumstances it might have made her laugh. "I—I think perhaps it's better if you see for yourself."

"I'll go with her," Zanhua says, stepping protectively in front of her.

But Yuliang shakes her head. "Let me go in first." She holds her hand out to the curator. "Please give me the key to the gallery."

For an instant the ghost of his old smile hovers at his lips. "Actually, madame," he says "you won't need it."

AS SHE ENTERS THE BUILDING she sees the posters inside, pulled from frames, ripped and hanging in shreds, and the doors slightly ajar. One doorknob is broken. Glass from several shattered panes lies in gleaming piles on the floor. Yuliang stares at the shards with a sense, as elusive as scent, that she has somehow lived through this moment before. But if she has, she can't recall it. And even if she could, she knows already, somehow, that it won't help to prepare her for what's to come. Wordlessly, she pushes her way through the battered door.

What strikes her first is the whiteness—the startling absence of color. It is almost what she imagines crossing over into the afterworld might be like. It takes a moment for her to realize that she is seeing only sunlight, bouncing blankly off the empty walls.

For the walls *are* empty, almost all of them: other than in the alcove, every single painting she'd ordered hung in the gallery has been yanked or knocked from its mounting. The ones the vandals left still litter the floor. Others are missing: They're simply not there.

Stunned, Yuliang scans the room, cataloguing the lost. She counts five: *Negress, Boy, Paris Nude, Dreaming Nude, Nursing Mother.* She sees it at once: All the nudes. It is only the nudes they've taken. For a split second she is baffled. Why take the very paintings they've decried the most?

The answer comes coldly: *They've stolen them to sell them.*

Behind her, a whisper. A pencil hitting a notebook. She feels

Zanhua behind her too, his hand firm on her shoulder. She shrugs him off sharply and walks around the room, continuing with her numb inventory: *Lotuses, Chrysanthemums, Still Life with Vase and Paper*. All of these have been left alone. But her cityscapes—from Rome and Venice, her Paris street scenes—have been scrawled on or slashed. And *The Bridge of Great Loyalty* has been almost completely destroyed: it's now little more than a row of gray-and-black-painted ribbons.

But worst of all is *Strong Man*. When Yuliang first leans over to inspect it, she gasps and quickly averts her face. It's as though she's identifying a body, but one that bears almost no resemblance to the strong, fluid form she's devoted herself to these past months.

They've embellished his lean form with cartoonish obscenities; breasts, a limp organ of impossible size. Little is left below the nose but poster paint. Even more chillingly, the eyes are gone—they've literally been cut out. They're blank and white, the eyes of a ghost. Across the top is scrawled, in the same meticulous hand she saw on the poster, "A Whore's Tribute to Her Client."

Her hands shaking, Yuliang lifts up the frame. "How did they do this?"

"We—we don't precisely know yet, madame," the curator says. "But it appears someone came through the western window."

He points. The window is open but, unlike the door, intact: no broken glass, no signs of damage or forced entry. "Are you saying it wasn't *locked*?"

"We've never thought," he begins. "That is, there has never been the need—"

"That's a lie!" she shouts. "You yourself warned me yesterday that there was danger!"

Behind them is a whispered chorus of pens. Zanhua takes her arm again as the first flare goes off. In the afterstink of the sulfur he attempts to comfort her: "Yuliang. We'll make them pay. We'll call my solicitor."

She laughs hoarsely. "Why? Can he paint?" Her eyes welling, she waves an arm at the decimated room. "It's gone. All gone. Half a lifetime of work."

As more flashes go off she holds her hands to her eyes, blocking it out—the explosions, the wreckage. That awful, blinding nullity. And yet even through her trembling fingers she still sees it—what *they'll* see when the papers come out tomorrow. Not a painter. Not even a victim. They'll see a weeping whore in the ruins of her career. For in the end, she suddenly realizes, the vandals' knives simply cut to the truth of what everyone already thinks of her.

"They wanted this," she murmurs. "All of them."

Her husband grips her arm. "Come. There's no reason to stay."

But Yuliang pushes him away. "No."

And with that one gesture, what remains of her self-control crumbles. Falling to her knees, she rips *Strong Man* from its frame. "Is *this* what you all wanted?" She hurls the frame to the ground. "And *this* . . . and *this* . . ." She stamps on the wood until it snaps. She tries to tear the painting as well, but the canvas, fortified with layers of hardened oils, resists her fingers. In the end, as cameras flash and click behind, she uses her feet, kicking the frame to pieces, grinding her heels into the varnish. She scrapes and stamps on the obscene scrawlings until they're indecipherable.

Then she turns back to the reporters.

"There," she says. "At least write that I finished the job. If you write anything, write that. I always finish the job."

Forty-one

IN THE END, the detectives assigned to the case confess to being at a complete loss. They have, they say, no idea who the vandals were, what their motives might have been. "These were very skilled," says one, who nevertheless can't quite meet Yuliang's eye. "I'd advise you to forget about them."

"About the vandals?"

"Forget about everything."

"Do you really think I can do that?" Yuliang snaps in disbelief.

The look he gives her is one of sheer scorn, only slightly leavened by pity. "Madame," he says, "they're just paintings. You can always paint new ones." His tone suggests that this is regrettable.

Even more insultingly, the amount the gallery offers by way of compensation is barely enough to cover painting expenses for three months, let alone replace twenty years' worth of work.

"We're aware that it's entirely inadequate," Curator Ma says, his smile retrieved and as infuriatingly cheerful as ever. "Unfortunately, we have our own troubles now. Our insurance barely covered the damages. And our artists for the next two shows have pulled out."

"Well," Zanhua says (for by this point Yuliang doesn't trust herself to speak), "I suppose that's a kind of payment in and of itself."

ZANHUA. HE IS, AS ALWAYS, attentive, thoughtful, sympathetic. He procures her sleep aids, French tobacco. Her favorite Pinot Noir. He urges her to return to Nanjing: "Please, Yuliang. There's nothing left for you here. Let's leave Shanghai tomorrow."

But Yuliang can't bring herself even to leave their hotel suite, much less to return to the stodgy city that is surely reveling in her misfortunes. She brushes off his attempts to woo her out: to Champion's Day at the races, to the French Club for dinner, to the new Dietrich film at the Lyceum. She refuses to see Liu Haisu, who arrives with flowers when the story hits the Shanghai papers the next morning (although she does read the little note he attaches to the gift: "The goal is not making art. It is living a life *through* art. Whatever else you do, do not give up"). She won't even see her stepson, who calls from the front desk the next day. "You two go out," Yuliang tells Zanhua dully. "Take him to lunch. Go see *The Devil Is a Woman.*" She laughs bitterly. "The papers will like that."

After he has gone she stares down at her quilt, smoking one Gitane lit from another. When the light starts to slant she finally picks up her sketchbook. She waits in the dimming evening for some event or sign, a moment she doesn't fully understand— inspiration, perhaps. Forgiveness. Rebirth. Cigarette after cigarette, though, the flawless white just stares back, as bleak and blank as the gallery walls were yesterday. Reverting to childhood comforts she recites Li Qingzhao's "Stream" over and over (*Its penetrating fragrance drives away my fond dreams of faraway places / How merciless!*). But even this does nothing at all. She is hollowed of hope, stripped clean of art spirit. Too beaten, even, to hurl her sketchbook across the room. And when, hours later, she finally drifts off to sleep, even her dreams are empty.

IT'S NEARLY A WEEK BEFORE Zanhua finally convinces her—mostly on the strength of their dwindling finances—to return home. He hires a closed car, discreetly pays the bill, smuggles Yuliang past reporters lurking outside. They board the Blue Steel Express well ahead of other travelers and retreat quickly to their private compartment. They dine quietly together, and sit in continued silence until the porter comes to turn down their berths. Zanhua promptly nods off, his distinguished-looking head falling forward onto his new edition of *The Heroic Life and Death of Sun Yat-sen.*

Yuliang cannot sleep at all. She nurses her wine, toasts her receding city. After the sleepless scream and neon of Shanghai, the Jiangsu countryside, with its moonlit fields and shadowed hills, seems almost ethereally quiet. There are no Tudor mansions here, no doormen. Only quiet little huts. The windows of most of them are shuttered, humble faces shielding their eyes from railborne intruders. "Windows are symbols," Yuliang has always told her students. "They are gateways—clues to mysterious unseen worlds. Don't think of them as simply lines and color values." For all her teachings, however, she herself has rarely wondered much about other people's lives.

Now, though, she does. Refilling her glass, Yuliang imagines families living behind these silent façades. She pictures fathers carving toys, smoking pipes by the *kang.* She sees mothers with lined faces, mending. For the first time she finds herself envious of such unmarked and ordinary existences, of lives made up of goals no more or less essential than ensuring that the rooms are clean, the tea hot, the children bountifully supplied. Running a hand over her own flat belly, she wishes anew for the motley badges of motherhood—the dimpled skin and aching back, bound endlessly to a howling infant. A body whose creative energies don't perpetually bypass the womb in their never-ending rush to a brush . . .

That's when it comes to her: perhaps she should just *stop.*

The thought, when it forms, feels wispy and unconvincing. Sipping her wine, Yuliang tests and tastes it. She fills in its outlines with detail, adds heft and substance. *Really,* she thinks. *Why not?* Surely by now she's acquired the skills to live like an ordinary woman; worrying about nothing more than her clothes, the house, her husband's needs and affections. Given Zanhua's moribund civil salary, she would have to keep teaching. But no one says that she has to keep painting. She could sell the few works she has left in her studio, cash in on her name . . . and then end it. After all, an end would be welcomed on all fronts. Even, at this point, on her own.

As Yuliang finishes off the wine, a kind of vertigo sweeps her, as though the train were flying straight off a cliff. But when she looks out again, it is still shuttling over the rails past all those reassuringly grounded little towns and cities. Before her lies the violet nightscape of her own vast, embattled nation, bound by ancient mountains, watched over by the Heavenly Cowherd and Celestial Weaver Girl. Behind her, her steadfast husband sleeps on.

Forty-two

Nanjing, 1936

A FULL HOUR AFTER Zanhua has risen, donned his clothes, and left for work, Yuliang sits at her dressing table. She is working furiously. Not on a sketch or self-portrait but on a proposal for a class she wants to teach in the fall, on the works of Lady Guan Daosheng. Yuliang anticipates some resistance to the idea of herself, a controversial "modern" painter, lecturing on a revered thirteenth-century artist. But she welcomes the debate. She welcomes, in fact, anything that takes her mind from her boredom; that fills the void her life seems to have become since her decision to stop painting.

When she first returned from Shanghai she spent a week in the house, dodging Guanyin inside as she avoided the newsmen, students, and sympathizers who continually rang the bell. Having locked up her studio, Yuliang was forced to find other, more mundane channels for her fury: lowering hems, sewing on buttons, mending the cloth-soled shoes that languished unworn in the far corner of her closet floor. She reorganized her clothes by color and style, pushing the Western-tailored items—her Parisian trousers and suits, her ties and hats and low-necked blouses—to one side. She wrapped her high-heeled shoes in flannel sacks, had new cheongsams made from silk and several pants sets made of heavy linen. All items of her new wardrobe adhere strictly to Madame Chiang's New Life standards. Wearing them, Yuliang feels strangely disguised—almost, in fact, the way she felt the first time Jinling painted her face for her at the Hall.

Her newly respectable role extends to the university as well. For the first time in her life, Yuliang is on committees. She votes on updating the art library, on examining teaching methods. She even sits in on Classroom Morality meetings, although more out of an interest in censoring budding gossip about herself than in any of the issues debated.

She has proctored six examinations, curated three student art exhibitions, and delivered two lectures ("Light in Painting: Impressionists vs. Pointillists," and "Fauves and Color: A Taste of the Wild"). The impressionist lecture pulled a mere five students. The fauves, just one—a lovesick boy who chases her around her lecture circuit with the fruitless ardor of a racecourse whippet.

Still, Yuliang delivered both lectures impeccably, with not a single pause, stumble, or complaint. She has stayed silent through the inevitable snickers at staff meetings and in hallways. She barely blinked, even, when someone slid a note beneath her office door, bearing just one suspiciously beautiful line of calligraphy:

自作自受

It serves you right.

In fact, overall she's been almost as serene as her own self-portraits—not to mention more conventionally attired.

Now she skims this class proposal quickly, searching for missing strokes or improper wording. She adds a list of proposed textbooks and picks out the day's clothes—a demure skirt and jacket—with care. She dons the round black spectacles she has until recently resisted wearing (as much from vanity as from the memories they bring back of her uncle) and brushes her hair back neatly from her face. She takes stock of herself.

For just an instant she feels it—the bleakness, seeping like damp mist through the tiny cracks in her resolution. Yuliang grits her teeth, forces a smile. "It's a beautiful day," she announces defiantly to herself, or perhaps to no one (but certainly not to Mirror Girl, whose taunting visage has been banished from Yuliang's presence). "I'll take a walk around the lake before the Library Committee meeting."

XUANWU LAKE PARK, THIS THURSDAY morning, is filled with the usual mix of schoolchildren, ambling visitors, strolling lovers. Yuliang walks among them, making her way unnoticed toward the lake's western side. As she follows the crumbling traces of walls erected by Ming Dynasty laborers, she keeps her eyes trained on the water. She loves the way its surface reflects the colors of each season —the lush spring greens, the aqua skies of summer. In the winter the lake is as black and opaque as onyx, the bare trees reflected as gray streaks breaking through. But now, in early fall, it is all golden earth tones, a shifting collage of wet leaf and reflected sky.

She pauses in her walk to give a visitor a clear view of the lake's most famous sight: five islets linked by old stone bridges. Watching the man shuffle and fiddle with his expensive, bulky camera, she very nearly pities him. The islands are famous for their chrysanthemums: autumnal bursts of saffron, fuchsia, and yellow. She has painted them scores of times, often with students. Even now, no longer a painter, she can't help but think they deserve more than photography's bleak palette of mourning.

The tourist takes his photograph, and Yuliang continues on, the sharp, short *snick* replaying in her inner ear. For an instant it comes back: the firestorm of camera flashes, the damning photos— particularly Tang Leiyi's shot of her and Zhou Enlai ("Nude Woman Painter Embraces CCP Cadre," read the caption). Zanhua, when he saw the piece (left conveniently for him by Guanyin), made no comment. But his stoic silence hurt Yuliang more than any spoken recrimination: it was as though her insides had been scraped out with a lathe.

Passing a lakeside tea vendor, she fishes out her change purse and hands the man a coin, watching aimlessly as steam floats toward the lake. When her gaze lands on a park bench and the man who is sitting there, she smiles, amused by the silver-tipped cane by his side. Zanhua seems to have started a trend. She takes her cup absently, her eyes drifting back to the cane's owner. Then she freezes and looks again.

For the man is none other than Zanhua himself.

She knows without a beat of question that it's he. His cane leans against the seat. Yuliang recognizes too the satchel he packed last night, when he told her he had nonstop meetings today. But clearly he isn't here to meet with anyone. He slumps, his news journal unread on his lap, his eyes bleakly on the summit of Purple Mountain.

"Your change," prompts the vendor.

Yuliang half turns and takes coins, her eyes still locked on her husband. Zanhua tosses his cigarette stub to the ground, where it joins a half-dozen others.

"Do you set up here every day?" she asks the vendor in a low voice.

"Every day there is no rain."

"Has he been here before?" She points.

The vendor squints. "Him? Oh, yes. He's always there. Sometimes he even sleeps there—takes a nap right on the bench. Can't be too comfortable." The man scratches behind his ear. "But mostly he just sits."

"How long has he been coming?"

The man frowns. "A month, maybe? A bit more perhaps."

It's been nearly eight weeks since they returned from Shanghai. Six since the picture of Yuliang and Zhou Enlai appeared. "You're sure it's the same man?" she asks shakily, though she knows the answer.

"Sure. At first I thought maybe he was a beggar. But he dresses too well—that cane and all. And he pays for his tea and seems to have some to spare." He narrows his gaze. "Why? Do you know him?"

How does one answer such a question? *Yes,* she imagines saying. *He's my husband, my savior. My conscience. Everything I have, I owe to him.*

Then again, how on earth, knowing what she now knows, can she even pretend that she knows him? She has been sleeping by this man's side these past eight weeks. Embracing him most nights in her continued hope that she'll conceive. Nestling into his softening arms and belly to sleep. In the morning she neatens up the tax forms and work papers he always seems to have left scattered around the room. Carelessly—or so she's believed. But clearly it's all a sham. The papers are a decoy: he has either lost his job, or is simply too ashamed to show his face there.

"Why not buy him a cup of tea?" the man is suggesting amiably. "I'm sure he'd welcome a little company."

"Why would you say that?"

The man shrugs. "He's always alone. Until you came, I didn't think he knew anyone at all."

Yuliang gazes at him fixedly, then turns back to her husband. "Please do me a favor," she says quietly. "Don't tell him I asked about him."

"I'd require something for my effort."

Numbly, she hands him back her change and the tea, which suddenly tastes like little more than steeped iron.

"My lips are sewn tight." The man drops her mug into a tin of yellow water, presumably to clean it. Yuliang turns away, preparing to hurry off the way she came. After a step or two, though, she stops.

What she really wants is to go to him, to put her arms around him. To sink her head onto his shoulder. She knows, though, that this would spell certain disaster. Catching Zanhua in his lie—the one true lie he has ever told her (and she shudders, for she certainly can't say the same)—would strip him of his last remnant of pride.

Instead she forces herself west again, back toward Zhongshan Road. It's eleven o'clock—she's going to miss her meeting. But suddenly this doesn't matter. Nothing matters but getting to the one place where she's all but certain she won't see Zanhua again before tonight—the home that now, all too clearly, is no refuge for him.

ARRIVING THERE A SHORT WHILE LATER, Yuliang picks up her mail and makes her way slowly upstairs, sifting through it. Two steps from the top she pauses, holding up a thin envelope stamped with a Paris return address. Curious, she breaks the seal and reads the note once, then twice. Then she turns her gaze to the wall.

Over Yuliang's objections, Guanyin has hung an insipid carp-and-stream scroll by some third-rate *guohua* artist her family knew. Yuliang has never given it a second glance. Now, however, she stares at it, the mundane sounds of the little house filling her ears: the *thunk-thunk* of the cook's cleaver, Guanyin's voice scolding the maid, the mournful croons of a passing corn vendor.

"*Xiao taitai!*" she hears a short moment later. "Are you there?"

Yuliang hesitates. But she doesn't answer. Wrenching her eyes from the painting, she refolds the note. Then she resumes her slow climb to the top.

Forty-three

A SHORT WHILE LATER, Yuliang unlocks the door to her studio for the first time in two months. She enters the little space with a strange sense of entering a home she once lived in but has since sold; stripped of clutter and free of its perpetual smell of solvent, the spare bedroom feels almost like that—a spare bedroom. Somehow, though, its very emptiness makes it seem ominous. Her easel looks like a spindly wooden skeleton. Her glass muller and inkstone look less like painting tools than potential weapons.

Yuliang makes her way over to her folding stool. She sits, staring out at the same horizon Zanhua had contemplated from his bench: Purple Mountain, its low slopes touched by jade green and light brown, the new observatory sparkling in the sunlight. It's a scene she's sketched aimlessly a thousand times in the past. Now, though, another image fills her thoughts: her husband by the lake. A pile of cigarette butts and an empty day before him.

After lighting her own first cigarette in nearly two months, Yuliang exhales deeply, relishing the feel of smoke freed from her lungs. Again she tries to understand it: what she has just seen. How she could have missed what was right before her own nose. After all, Zanhua certainly noticed her work stoppage—and, for once, talked to her about her career at some length. He'd seemed gratified by her goals, if troubled by her methods. "Are you sure you should stop painting *completely?*" he'd asked. "Can't you simply paint things that are considered . . . well, more acceptable?" Yuliang didn't have the heart to tell him that painting only "acceptable" work would be far worse for her than not painting at all. As Xu Beihong once said, dead dreams are poison . . .

For Zanhua's part, aside from that one trip to the Wuhu gardens, he himself never missed a day at work—at least, not in the days when Yuliang had first known him. "I may be ill," he'd say when she'd urge him to sleep off a wet cough or a hangover, "but the nation is even more ill than I am." It's true that he has stayed home in Nanjing more regularly. But Yuliang has neither asked nor particularly thought much about these absences. She has simply assumed that attendance in the bustling headquarters is more lax than it was in Wuhu. And if anything, she's welcomed his lighter workload for the opportunities it has given her to be with him; to complain about school, about the gossip. These days, Zanhua even walks her to classes, strolling across the campus with her. Discussing her lecture plans or her students.

And yet, staring at her empty easel, Yuliang realizes that for all the time they've spent together, for all their oaths of honesty and sacrifice, their life isn't what they've pretended it is. They have both been lying. And in the end, his life is as broken as hers.

For several moments she just sits there, ash dropping lightly from her smoke. At last the hot ember against her finger brings her back. Blinking, she stubs her cigarette out. She picks up the hand mirror she uses for her self-portraits, smooths her hair, picks a flake of tobacco from her front tooth. After a moment's hesitation, she reaches into her pocketbook and pulls out her Arden lipstick. Opening it, she suddenly has an odd impression that this is the first true color she has seen since the white walls of the gallery. As she applies it, Mirror Girl purses her mouth mockingly.

"Welcome back," Yuliang tells her. "I've missed you."

Forty-four

THAT NIGHT YULIANG SPENDS several more hours in her studio. Not painting, but sorting. She pores through notebooks, and the old or half-finished canvases she left leaning, faces turned to the wall. She leafs through the stack of reviews of her exhibits in China, of her entry into the Salon d'Automne, of her Shanghai-published book of prints. She rereads the handful of biographical pieces (all carefully edited by Yuliang herself) that ran when all of China seemed suddenly to want to know her story.

She also peruses a slim photograph album, and observes her own image evolving through the camera's drab lens: Here a teenage bride, posing somberly with Zanhua and Meng Qihua. There, taut and anxious outside the Shanghai Art Academy, on her very first day of class. Here she is, slightly seasick on the *Canadian Queen*; then, later, on the Boulevard de Clichy, the one face in a group of toasting Beaux Arts students not smiling at the prospect of term's end. There's a picture from Rome, Yuliang in her sculpture studio. There's another at the Silent Society exhibit.

The last photo was taken a little over four months ago, with sixteen of Yuliang's graduate-level students. In the image, Yuliang stands at the group's center, the atelier model beside her. The girl is naked, facing forward, as slim and pale as a slice of moonlight. Her small, high breasts are captured unabashedly on film. The only part of her body you can't see is her face, which she has turned away from the lens's gaze.

Studying the picture, Yuliang can't help noting of the odd duo they make: she in her fitted suit, Parisian scarf knotted stylishly at her neck, the model beside her a stripped and faceless shadow. If anyone had told her twenty years ago that she'd be the one in clothing—the learned one, the famous artist, the university professor!—she would quite simply have called them mad. Now, though, as she traces the photo's frame, a long-forgotten voice drifts dreamily into her head. *You see?* her uncle is saying. *You're very smart. You could be just about anything. A lady poet. A teacher.* The memory, she notes, is oddly devoid of the inner shudder that usually accompanies thoughts of her *jiujiu*. Is it possible that she has actually forgiven him?

She's just replacing her photos when she spies something else: a French biscuit tin, dust-coated, its red paint half-eaten by rust. With some effort Yuliang pries off the tarnished lid. The sheafs of paper inside are so tightly packed that several of them spring right out, and it's only then that she remembers what they are: Zanhua's letters, sent to her while she was in Europe. There must be well over two hundred.

Kneeling on the floor, Yuliang smooths one against her knee. *My dear Yuliang,* she reads. *It has been barely a week since you left our land. Not so much time, I suppose, in the space of one lifetime. And yet it feels like a small lifetime in itself . . .*

A lump takes shape in her throat. She remembers this—it's the first letter she received on arriving in Lyon. It was waiting for her at the Foreign Students Office. She reread it perhaps a dozen times during those first hazy days. The mere sight of his neat and yet sweeping handwriting had felt like a brief reprieve from an endless onslaught of foreign faces, sounds, food . . .

For a long while Yuliang sits, her old grief dampening her

thoughts. It's not until the travel clock on the painting table reads close to eleven that she returns the letters to their box. Making her way to her purse, Yuliang pulls out another envelope—the one from Paris she'd received earlier in the day. She reads it again, her mouth silently shaping French she feels she's already half forgotten.

Dear Madame Pan,

I hope this finds you well. I wanted to inform you that my colleague and I are finally opening the gallery we discussed. Located on Rue Ste.-Anne, it will present modern paintings by artists from China, Indochina, and Japan. We would still very much like to feature your work in the opening exhibition, and would of course reimburse shipping and traveling expenses. Should you agree, please telegraph at your earliest conveniencee.

Behind this envelope is another, stiff and scented with fresh ink. Yuliang leaves this one closed. Having bought it herself this afternoon, she already knows its contents: a one-way ticket to Marseille. The ship leaves in less than two months.

A LITTLE AFTER MIDNIGHT she hears the door downstairs. There's a rummaging in the kitchen, followed by Zanhua's measured tread up the creaking staircase. She visualizes her husband, passing first Weiyi's unused room, then Guanyin's, before finally reaching her own. The steps pause there, and Yuliang holds her breath. But Zanhua doesn't knock on his concubine's door tonight. He stands in silence for a moment, then continues on to the doorway closest to the studio—his own.

As Yuliang hears his door shut, her insides seem to contract. The sensation stays with her as she tiptoes down to her room, splashes her face in the basin, relieves herself in the tiny WC. It stays on, a cold coil in the center of her belly as she climbs into bed and begins reciting "The Double-Ninth Festival." Inevitably, though, she is sleepless again, beyond even the soothing reach of Li Qingzhao. Getting up at last, she crosses the room to her dresser and stares at herself in the mirror. She is greeted there not by Mirror Girl but by someone she barely recognizes: a middle-aged apparition, eyes lined by age. Her hair is tangled and lank. It seems pointless to pick up her hairbrush. Instead she turns and walks silently out the door.

Creeping down the hallway, Yuliang reaches Zanhua's door. She waits a moment, then enters. With each step across the polished floorboards she expects him to wake, to see her. But Zanhua remains sunk in sleep. He lies on his back, one hand flung toward the headboard, the other resting in its favorite spot, against his cheek. His face in the half-light appears far more serene than Yuliang can remember seeing it in past weeks. He also, she sees, needs a haircut—an unusually long lock of it sweeps from his hairline, an inky brushstroke against the pale span of his brow. Yuliang reaches down and pushes it back.

When she climbs onto the bed, Zanhua murmurs but doesn't move. Carefully, she frames her face against the pearl-toned square of the window: she wants to be the first thing he will see upon waking. She whispers his name: "Zanhua."

And again: "Zanhua."

His eyelids flutter. When he tries to sit up she presses him back again, gently pinning each of his limbs with her own. She travels down his length slowly, still holding his hands, keeping him in compliance until she knows for sure he is ready. When she moves back up, she kisses him again, brushing with her lips the features she's come to know almost better than her own: eyelids and curling lashes, nose, cheek, pulsing temple, the soft indent that marks the parting of his clavicle. As she starts her slow descent he lets loose a soft groan and wraps his arms around her. He pulls her back up, and his thin fingers fumble first to free himself, to find her. To find his way in.

But Yuliang refuses on this night to follow their usual pattern of efficient and unthinking consummation. She tightens her legs against him and around him. And when she finally opens to him, she draws it out, second by second. Forcing him, with a murmur or a silent, pointed squeeze, to slow or even stop altogether. Until in the end they are barely moving at all.

Gazing into his sleep-softened eyes, she tries to pour everything she feels into him—her discovery today, her fears. Her vast regrets. Her deceptions. Her unspeakable, unpayable debt. *I didn't choose to be this way,* she wants to say. *I've tried to change. I simply can't.* She searches his face for some sign of understanding as they slowly move together.

In the beginning it is barely a movement at all—simply the rise and fall of their twinned breathing. Gradually, though, she guides them both into an almost frantic rush. And in the end, the sensation that sweeps her is more profound than anything she has ever felt before, and almost painful. It seems to sweep not just her body but her whole being, carrying her high above him, crashing her back down like a kite.

And yet, lying on him after, his chest damp and smooth beneath hers and her own body bruised and empty and aching, she still feels strangely alone. Almost as though—despite his warm and familiar breath, the steadfast press of his limbs—she is already miles away.

Part NINE

The DEPARTURE

Another word for creativity is courage.

————

Henri Matisse

Your first-class stamp on this postcard allows us to use vital funds to save our national parks.

NO POSTAGE
NECESSARY
IF MAILED
IN THE
UNITED STATES

BUSINESS REPLY MAIL

FIRST-CLASS MAIL PERMIT NO. 1016 CINNAMINSON, NJ

POSTAGE WILL BE PAID BY ADDRESSEE

National Parks
PO BOX 413050
NAPLES, FL 34101-6887

National PARKS

Fall 2009 Reader Service

Planning a vacation? For information on ALL travel advertisers, circle:

100. Travel Destinations

For additional information on our advertisers, visit our web site at **www.npca.org/magazine** and click on "*search advertisers.*"

For free literature circle the appropriate number(s) and mail this card or for faster service, please fax this card to 1.888.847.6035.

1. Alpine Adventure Trail Tours
2. American Cruise Lines
3. Bose Corporation
4. Bradford Exchange
5. Forever Resorts
6. Hallo Bay
7. Harrison Middleton University
8. International Coin & Currency
9. Kennicott Glacier Lodge
10. Lajitas Resort
11. Littleton Coin Company
12. Microsoft
13. Mystic Stamp Company
14. NPCA ParkScapes
15. Outer Banks of North Carolina
16. PBS Distribution
17. Resole
18. Terra Incognita Ecotours
19. Texas Tourism

Name _____

Address _____

City / State _____ Zip _____

E-mail _____

The address on the reverse side of this card is for Reader Service inquiries only. We cannot process any other National Parks magazine mail at this address. Please allow 4-6 weeks for delivery. Offer expires December 31, 2009.

Forty-five

A WEEK INTO THE Western new year of 1937, Madame Pan Yuliang stands with her husband on the Canadian Maritime steamship pier. A sampan has been selected, vetted, and bargained down to two thirds the man's initial offering price. The weathered boatman, anxious to make the trip in time enough to come back for another late-arriving passenger, is busy loading Yuliang's two trunks, one carpetbag, and two well-wrapped portfolios—all of her work that is left—into the square stern of his craft. Yuliang herself carries her paintbox and her purse.

"You have your travel papers?" Zanhua asks.

"You've asked me four times."

"I suppose I keep hoping you've forgotten them." He smiles wanly.

Yuliang smiles back, although for a moment it feels as though her heart has already cracked, just a little.

Over the past week they've barely mentioned the looming specter of her departure. Instead, they've spent all the compensatory money from the disastrous exhibition. They've lived as though life starts and ends here in Shanghai; eating out virtually every meal, traversing the town's offerings from English pubs to French haute cuisine to the famous Yangzhou-style restaurant on Nanjing Road.

They've bought shoes and stockings at Wing On, hats at Grigorieff and Co., and undergarments at the China Tai Underwear Co. Yuliang has had four new dresses made at Madame Muriel's on Avenue Joffre. They've had tea at the Cathay, wine at the Palais, and gin at the Vienna Ballroom. On a whim, they've even joined the well-heeled throng at the annual New Year's Race Meeting at the posh Shanghai Race Club. Yuliang had never been to the races. But she found herself surprisingly swept up by them, as entranced by the sleek and thundering Mongolian ponies (on which a young Xu Beihong once honed his horse-sketching skills) as by the women sporting hats bedecked with moving still lifes: silk flowers and false fruits, birds and bows. They cheered and shouted themselves hoarse when the horse Zanhua called for second actually came in as predicted.

Even their lovemaking has had an air of frantic abandonment; as though it's just one more way they've deliberately put off this moment. On their last night they lay together, their bodies slick with sweat and one another, and there was no mention—not at all—of the dire event that was just hours away. Zanhua simply kissed her forehead, as he always does before sleep. Then he wrapped his arms around her and closed his eyes. Yuliang, for her part, stayed up nearly until dawn. But she didn't move; she was very, very careful not to wake him.

Standing here now, though, on the edge of their greatest divide yet, it suddenly strikes her as surreal that they could have existed in such a vacuum. *Then again,* she reminds herself, *this is Shanghai.* The entire city seems to live in a gay haze of denial, even as war grows more inevitable by the day. Nationalist planes screech through the skies, and Japanese soldiers swagger through Hongkou with impunity. They line China's northern borders, skirmishing for now but plotting "incidents" that will give them the excuse to invade in full force. Shanghainese, for their part, respond by shouting for another round. The drinks flow faster; the skirts grow shorter, the hours later, the dancehall dances longer and closer and more insinuating. Even now, recovering from what she senses will be the last hangover for at least a month, Yuliang sees among the scores of steamers, sampans, junks, and cargo ships the multirayed *Hi no Maru* flying from two destroyers against the horizon. The warships are well outside the League of Nations' "no sail" zone. But their presence is as sharply honed as two steel fangs.

"We should go now, madame," the boatman says gruffly, readying his oar in the boat's rear. The *Duchess of York* sits staunchly beyond him in the Huangpu. Its tiered decks are already lined with doll-sized figures waving and shouting, hefting cameras. Tossing food and dollars to the ever-present swarm of beggars below. The ship is scheduled to set sail in less than half an hour, and even now the huge horn on the upper deck lets loose its second-to-last warning blast. On the pier, other last-minute boarders hastily wrap up their own sampan negotiations and hug their loved ones one last time.

"You must hurry, madame," prompts Yuliang's ragged captain.

"I'm coming," she tells him. But she doesn't move.

"You *should* hurry," Zanhua says. "Or those papers won't even matter."

Shading his eyes he looks out at the ship, which will make port at Saigon, Singapore, and Colombo. It will round the great Horn of Africa, cover Djibouti's cobalt waters and coral reefs, and inch up the Suez Canal to Port Said before reaching its final destination: Marseille. It's Yuliang's third trip along this route—she has sketched these port towns from the deck. Suddenly, though, she hasn't the faintest recollection of what any of them look like. All she registers is the beloved, doomed city beyond the pier. That, and her husband's drawn face.

For an instant she's almost tempted to renounce her decision. *I have changed my mind*, she imagines saying. Instead, she takes his hand.

"I have a challenge," she says quietly.

He smiles weakly. "Very well. What are my clues?"

"Spring. Skiff. Heavy load."

His lips move in silence as he shuts his eyes. Then he opens them again.

> *They say that at the Twin Brooks, spring is still fair*
> *I, too, wish to row a boat there.*
> *But I am afraid that the little skiff on the Twin Brooks*
> *Could not bear the heavy load of my grief . . .*

His voice breaks on the last word. Jaw tightening, he looks away.

Lifting herself on tiptoe, Yuliang clasps her arms around his shoulders. "I *am* afraid," she whispers shakily. "I shouldn't leave you like this. Not now."

"You speak as though there might be a time that you *should* leave." He wraps his arms around her. His ridiculous cane pokes into her shoulder blade.

"It's just—I don't trust them to protect you."

"Who?"

"You know who." Her eyes are tearing—the wind, possibly. She dashes at them angrily. The last week has brought news of kidnappings and releases, of Japanese spies, contingency plans, backroom dealings. A new CCP-KMT alliance has been brokered—some say by Zhou Enlai himself, which might explain Zanhua's sudden welcome back to work (although certainly word of his scandalous concubine's departure didn't hurt). But Yuliang still doesn't trust them—not any of them. "I feel," she says, "like I'm leaving you to the tigers."

"Then stay. Protect me." Zanhua attempts another smile. "I don't know anyone more qualified to bargain with tigers."

"That's a lie." She wipes her eyes with her sleeves, laughing. "If I were brave I wouldn't be leaving in the first place."

"Why not? One needs to take holidays from fighting tigers."

This isn't just a holiday, she wants to say. But she doesn't. She follows their old rule, leaving the most painful things unsaid.

"Yuliang," Zanhua says. "Really. Perhaps you can still stay. Things here are on the verge of change. I feel it."

As she touches his cheek Yuliang knows this is the truth: that for all his bitterness, Pan Zanhua's faith in China is as ardent as it's ever been. Even if Guanyin and Weiyi weren't part of his picture, he would never do what she's doing: he wouldn't just leave.

"Then be part of the change," she tells him. "Find your friends. Hold fast to them. Don't worry about how you will be seen by others."

His lips tighten. "It's more difficult for some of us than for others."

The *Duchess* lets loose another blast—the final warning call. "Lady!" the boatman grumbles. "If you're not getting in, then take your bags back. I've got a business."

Yuliang takes another deep breath, then stands on tiptoes again. She gives her windblown husband one last kiss: French-style. On each cheek.

But as she's pulling away, he catches her back. Framing her face hard with his fingers, Zanhua presses his mouth forcefully against his wife's. His lips hurt her. But Yuliang doesn't pull away. And when he releases her, it's as though he has dropped her from some small height.

"I'll—I'll be on deck as we go," she whispers. She seats herself stiffly, gives a last, numb wave, then turns away, afraid that if she looks back even once, all her resolve will disappear. (*Don't think.*)

It's as the sampan driver plants his pole that she hears Zanhua call again. "Yuliang," he says. "Yuliang. Wait. I forgot to give you this . . ."

When she turns back, he's waving something at her, though it's too small for her to see. "I'll throw it," he calls over the widening distance.

"No, wait—"

But it's too late. He casts his arm, releases his fingers. The object arcs over gray water and bounces off the boat's rim. For a breathless moment Yuliang thinks the river will take it. But it tumbles in the other direction, rattling to the wet floor at her feet.

She leans over to pick it up. Wiping it on her trousers, she holds it up in disbelief: it's the little jade boar she lost on their last trip here.

"The hotel had it," he's shouting. "They found it under one of the beds." He shouts something else, but the sampan's clatter covers his words.

"What?" she shouts back, her voice cracking with the effort.

He shakes his head, takes a breath. He cups his mouth with his scholar's hands. And this time she makes out the words, just barely: *"It's for luck."*

Yuliang nods, clenching the tiny token so tightly her knuckles whiten.

She keeps her gaze on her husband as the sounds of the steamship overtake them—the shouted farewells, and one last, cryptic horn blast. She watches him as the sounds of Europe wash out onto the Huangpu. Until her bags are aboard and the sampan driver is finally casting off. Until the ship's loudspeaker announces the time, and the concierge standing by to help her leans over and inquires, in the oddly flattened French of North America, *"Venez-vous à bord, mademoiselle?"*

Yuliang turns and looks at him. *"C'est madame,"* she whispers.

"Pardon," he says. He switches to Chinese. "You're coming aboard?"

Yuliang looks down at the little boar. It gazes up with green eyes, as stony and as stubborn as ever. She gives it one last squeeze before slipping it into her pocket.

Epilogue

On July 13, 1937, the Japanese attacked Shanghai a second time, launching a bloody and grueling battle that, thanks to the determination and perseverance of both Chinese troops and Shanghai's own fearless citizens, lasted well over three months (and left tens of thousands of casualties) before the city was taken. By December 1937, Japan had taken Nanjing, launching a six-week orgy of rape, looting, and slaughter that took up to a half-million more lives. Chiang Kai-shek and his Republican government fled inland to Chongqing, where they again formed a shaky alliance with the Chinese Communist Party. That truce collapsed with Japan's surrender in 1945, plunging China into bloody civil war for four more years.

In December 1949, the last Republican stronghold of Chengdu fell, and Chiang's government fled again, this time to Taiwan. Following its establishment in October 1949, the Communist government of the People's Republic of China settled on social realism as the ideal art form for the new nation. Specifically formulated against more romantic Western movements, social realism focused on the ugly realities of modern life, particularly the plight of the poor. Traditional nudes were emphatically discouraged.

Some of Yuliang's former colleagues tried to adapt to the new aesthetic. Xu Beihong became president of the Central Academy of Fine Arts, and as

407

such pioneered the effort to integrate realism into traditional painting, but he died of a cerebral hemorrhage in 1953. Following liberation, Liu Haisu's Shanghai Art Academy was combined with two other art schools to form the East China College of Art, and ultimately was moved to Nanjing. Liu himself painted intensely throughout the 1950s and 1960s, slowing only temporarily after being declared an enemy to the Cultural Revolution and confined to house arrest. He died in 1994, painting indefatigably until the end.

Pan Zanhua died in 1959.

Pan Yuliang never returned to China. In the decade following her self-exile, she exhibited in the salon, the French National 53rd Art Exhibition, the Salon des Indépendants, and the 51st Salon Art Show. In 1945 she won a gold award for her entry in the Salon des Indépendants, and in 1958 she exhibited there again. In that same year her work was exhibited in Paris's Museum of Modern Art. Unwilling to change her painting style or overcome her aversion to dealers, she never became more than modestly successful in the commercial sense, and by most accounts lived out her last days in poverty and illness. She never relinquished her pride in her nationality, however, choosing to hold on to her Chinese citizenship until her death in 1977. She was buried in Paris's Cimetière du Montparnasse, in traditional Chinese robes.

Pan Yuliang's remarkable legacy includes more than four thousand works of art, including sculptures, sketches, oil paintings, and watercolors. Many of these can be found in her home province of Anhui, at the Anhui Museum.

Inevitably, it also includes controversy: in 1993, an exhibition of her work in Beijing caused enough concern that several of her nudes were removed.

Selected Bibliography

Ayscough, Florence. *Chinese Women: Yesterday and Today*. New York: Da Capo, 1975.

Baum, Vicki. *Shanghai, '37*. New York: Oxford University Press, 1987.

Birnbaum, Phyllis. *Glory in a Line: A Life of Foujita: The Artist Caught Between East and West*. New York: Faber and Faber, 2006.

Brassaï. *The Secret Paris of the 30's*. Translated by Richard Miller. New York: Pantheon, 1976.

Brettell, Richard. *Modern Art, 1851–1929*. London: Oxford University Press, 1999.

Chang, Iris. *The Rape of Nanking: The Forgotten Holocaust of World War II*. New York: Penguin, 1997.

Clark, David, et al. *Shanghai Modern: 1919–1945*. Ostfildern, Germany: Hadje Cantz, 2005.

Dong, Stella. *Shanghai: The Rise and Fall of a Decadent City*. New York: Harper Perennial, 2000.

Dunand, Frank, ed. *The Pavilion of Marital Harmony: Chinese Painting and Calligraphy Between Tradition and Modernity*. Chicago: Art Media Resources, 2002.

Evans, Richard. *Deng Xiaoping and the Making of Modern China.* Rev. ed. New York: Penguin, 1997.

Gronewald, Sue. *Beautiful Merchandise: Prostitution in China, 1850–1936.* New York: Harrington Park, 1985.

Hamilton, William Stenhouse. *Notes from Old Nanking, 1947–1949.* Canberra: Pandanus, 2004.

Hansen, Arlen J. *Expatriate Paris: A Cultural and Literary Guide to Paris of the 1920s.* New York: Arcade, 1991.

Henri, Robert. *The Art Spirit.* Boulder, Colo.: Westview, 1984.

Hershatter, Gail. *Dangerous Pleasures: Prostitution and Modernity in Twentieth-Century Shanghai.* Berkeley: University of California Press, 1997.

Ho, Lucy Chao. *"More Gracile Than Yellow Flowers": The Life and Works of Li Ching-chao.* Hong Kong: Mayfair, 1968.

Huddleston, Sisley. *In and About Paris.* London: Methuen, 1927.

Levine, Marilyn A. *The Found Generation: Chinese Communists in Europe During the Twenties.* Seattle: University of Washington Press, 1993.

Liao, Jingwen, and Ching-wen Liao. *Xu Beihong: Life of a Master Painter.* Translated by Zhang Peiji. San Francisco: China Books and Periodicals, 1987.

Lu, Hsun. *Selected Stories of Lu Hsun.* Translated by Yang Hsien-yi and Gladys Yang. New York: W. W. Norton, 2003.

Lucas, E. V. *A Wanderer in Paris.* London: Methuen, 1909.

Mason, Caroline Atwater. *The Spell of France.* Boston: L. C. Page, 1912.

Rose, June. *Suzanne Valadon: The Mistress of Montmartre.* New York: St. Martin's, 1999.

Shinan. *Huahun (Painter's Spirit: The Biography of Pan Yuliang).* Shanghai: Wenhui News/Wu Wenhuan, 1983.

Spence, Jonathan D. *The Search for Modern China.* New York: W. W. Norton, 1990.

Stein, Gertrude. *Paris, France.* New York: Liveright, 1996 (reissue).

Sullivan, Michael. *Art and Artists of Twentieth-Century China.* Berkeley: University of California Press, 1996.

Wakeman, Frederick. *The Fall of Imperial China.* New York: Free
 Press, 1975.

Wang, Ping. *Aching for Beauty: Footbinding in China.* New York: Anchor,
 2002.

Wheeler, K. W., and V. L. Lussier, eds. *Women, the Arts, and the 1920s
 in Paris and New York.* New York: Transaction, 1982.

Yang, Benjamin. *Deng: A Political Biography.* Armonk, N.Y.: M.E.
 Sharpe, 1998.

Ye, Zhaoyan. *Nanjing 1937: A Love Story.* Translated by Michael Berry.
 New York: Columbia University Press, 2002.

Acknowledgments

This has been a long-term, engrossing, and quite possibly far too ambitious project. That it succeeds to any extent is largely due to the people who have helped and supported it along the way, who include (but are certainly not limited to) Alan Ziegler and the Columbia School of the Arts Writing Division, for support and encouragement and for understanding the limits on a writing mother's time and finances; Helen Schulman, for helping me find my way early on; Binnie Kirshenbaum and Mary Gordon, for holding my feet to the fire and keeping me walking. Jeesoon Hong, Kailin Huang, Yeewan Koon, and Wei Zhong have all provided essential researching, translating, and proofreading help on the Chinese side of things, while Andrea LaFleur, Julia Lichtblau, Denis Bonnet, and Hillary Jordan have been equally helpful with the French. Tim Brewer and Erica Hope Charpentier suffered through my woeful attempts in the oil painting world. I'm indebted to Kuiyi Shen at the University of California, San Diego, who curated the exhibit that first brought Pan Yuliang's work to my attention. Borhua Wang at the Pratt Institute also provided early thought and insight into Pan's work, and Madeleine Zelin, of Columbia University's East Asian Languages and

Culture Department, pointed the way for reading, classwork, and further consultants. Suzette Cody traipsed tirelessly through Singapore, seeking out Pan Yuliang paintings; Tom Cody trolled the back streets of Shanghai for clues into Pan's life and formative influences. Liang Luo of the University of Michigan, Antonia Finnane of the University of Melbourne, and Anik Fournier of the Montréal Museum of Contemporary Art were all generous in sharing research, images and thoughts. I owe the Art Students League of New York—particularly Frank Mason and his talented class—great thanks for allowing me to intrude on their world for a day. Thanks, too, to the Art Retreat Museum in Singapore and to Sotheby's for access to and information on Pan Yuliang's amazing paintings

Between workshop colleagues and literature-loving friends, there are scores of people who have critiqued this novel for me as it's grown. I am especially grateful to Alison Bogert, Halle Eaton, Michael Epstein, Joanna Hershon, Hillary Jordan, Amy Sirot, Ellen Umansky, Josh Weil, and Michelle Wildgen for taking extra time to read, reread, and advise. My fabulous agent, Elizabeth Sheinkman, cheered me on at a courageously early point in this venture, and editors Jill Bialosky at Norton and Mary Mount at Viking U.K. made for an unstoppable duo; it has been a privilege to work with them. Copyeditor Liz Duvall made more life-saving catches than I can count. I'd also like to thank those who offered their homes, offices, and quiet spaces as my own little apartment filled with toys, joys, and tantrums; Marcy Lovitch, Susan Chaddick, and Andrea Reiff were especially generous.

Finally, and most importantly, my husband, Michael, deserves (even if he doesn't always receive) undying gratitude for spotting a good idea, daring me to try it, and offering truly heroic support, honest feedback, and continued marriage to me while I did. You are the Fire Horse of my soul. My daughters, Katie and Hannah—Dragon and Monkey, respectively—have been an endless (if sleepless) source of inspiration, mirth, and wonder. This, as everything, is for you all.

Permissions

THE PAINTER
FROM SHANGHAI

Jennifer Cody Epstein

THE PAINTER
FROM SHANGHAI

Jennifer Cody Epstein

JENNIFER CODY EPSTEIN ON HER
NOVEL *THE PAINTER FROM SHANGHAI*

If, twenty years ago, when I was plodding through what I thought was my first novel (a proverbial, semiautobiographical, coming-of-age saga with a plucky American reporter abroad as its main character), someone with a clear view of the future told me how my writing career would evolve—that I'd complete four stints overseas, three journalism jobs, two master's degrees, one marriage ceremony, and two childbirths before finally, tiredly, typing out those two magical words, The End—I'd have been surprised only that it took so long. If, however, that person then showed me the book I was to complete—a sprawling historical saga set in a land I'd never lived in, its heroine an obscure but fiercely talented Chinese painter—I'd have been shocked. *What on earth will I be thinking?* I'd have found myself wondering. *What would possibly possess me to take on this story?*

The answer lies in a progression of events, starting with a 1998 visit to the Guggenheim Museum. It was there that my husband and I attended an exhibit of modern Chinese art, and it was there that I saw my first Pan Yuliang painting—a lush and Cézannesque self-portrait, the artist seated serenely in a Parisian window. The work—hung among far more subdued watercolors and ink drawings as well as enormous revolution-era posters—drew me like a magnet. And while its unique East/West blend of brushstrokes struck me as fascinating, the accompanying bio of Pan's life literally stunned me. Breathlessly, I pulled my husband away from a Chairman Mao portrait and pointed. "Look," I said.

"This is an amazing story." Michael, a filmmaker with a good eye for plot and image, read Pan's bio, which briefly outlined her rise from prostitute to Parisian artist. He studied her portrait. Then he turned back to me. "This," he announced, with characteristic certainty, "is your first novel."

I blinked.

It was true that I had a master's in international relations. I'd lived in Japan, Thailand, and Hong Kong. I even—thanks to ten years of Japanese language studies—knew a little bit about written Chinese. But I knew nothing about Asian art or even about art in general. Indeed, at that point—freshly accepted to Columbia University's MFA program—I'd only started seriously writing fiction. When I finally managed a response, it was something along the lines of "You're nuts"—though also somewhat less polite.

Yet, like the idea of living in Asia in the first place, what seemed a startling proposal slowly took root. As I wrapped up my job at NBC, I scoured the Internet for glimpses of Pan Yuliang's work and life, and kept her Paris self-portrait as my screensaver. When I entered Columbia in the fall, I committed myself more fully, taking graduate-level courses in Chinese history, reading up on Chinese brothels, and hiring a Chinese translator to help with texts. I even signed up to take a few casual courses in oil painting—with decidedly mixed results.

I held off writing about Pan Yuliang, however, for several more months, long enough to complete my first year at Columbia. Long enough to take a maternity break for my first child. Long enough to spend three sleepless postpartum months wondering whether I'd ever write anything again.

And, finally, I did. After an early feeding one morning, I sat down in my still-sleeping household and clicked on my Pan Yuliang screensaver. I gazed at the extraordinary painted gaze and at the mother-child image Pan had titled *Motherlove*.

And I began.

DISCUSSION QUESTIONS

1. What happened to Yuliang's mother and father? How are Yuliang's experiences of family and intimacy shaped by her Uncle Wu and, later, her life in the brothel?

2. In rendering Yuliang's years working as a prostitute, Epstein depicts the intersection of the sexual economy, business elite, and political leadership. How do the intrigues of the brothel affect the economy and government in Wuhu?

3. How does poetry play a role in Yuliang and Zanhua's relationship? How does their shared appreciation for poetry stand in contrast to their feelings about visual art?

4. Yuliang's budding talent for sketching is not revealed until chapter 16. Do earlier chapters contain any hints of her artistic abilities?

5. How is Shanghai different than Wuhu? How does Yuliang's life change after she moves to Shanghai?

6. What results from Yuliang's confrontation with the women in the bathhouse in chapter 24? What does this scene reveal about Chinese female society—and what does it reveal about Yuliang?

7. Teacher Hong instructs Yuliang to "see the skin as more than simply skin." Jingling, as she mentors Yuliang in the brothel, advises her protégée to remember that "it's just skin." Whose advice does Yuliang follow, and why? Why is painting nude figures important for Yuliang?

8. How does politics play a role in the story? To what extent is Yuliang a political person?

9. Both Xudun and Zanhua have strong feelings about politics and government in China. What two ideologies do these men represent? Are they entirely opposed?

10. In the 1920s and '30s, Shanghai was often called "the Paris of the East." As depicted in the novel, how does Shanghai compare with the French capital? Both cities are cosmopolitan, but in different ways. How do you see those differences?

11. Why does Yuliang demand an abortion? Do you think she comes to regret that decision?

12. How does the course of Yuliang's personal and artistic career compare with that of her mentor, Xu Beihong?

13. In chapter 33, when Xudun takes Yuliang to the top of Notre Dame Cathedral—in what seems to be one of the most exciting and romantic moments of Yuliang's life—her thoughts return to her uncle, who sold her into prostitution. Yuliang, however, frequently professes a desire to stay "rooted in the present." To what extent is she able to do that? How do the wounds of her past manifest themselves later in Yuliang's life? How do they affect her art?

14. After she moves to Nanjing—after years in Paris and Rome and a stint as an outspoken teacher at the Shanghai Art Academy—why does Yuliang submit to acting as "the second woman" to Guanyin in Zanhua's household? Why does Yuliang feel sympathy for Zanhua's first wife? Do you think Guanyin deserves sympathy?

15. "It is hard to find heroes in times such as these," says Qihua, referring to Zanhua. After all that is revealed about him later in the book, does Zanhua emerge as a hero in this story? Does Xudun? Had Xudun lived, do you think Yuliang would have chosen him over her husband? Would you want her to?

16. In moving back to Paris, Yuliang chooses a life of free artistic expression over a more traditional life of marriage. The last chronological scene in the novel is the prologue. Based on that opening scene, how do you think Yuliang views her life's choices? How do you view them? Having finished the book, how has your feeling about her life and character changed? Why do you think Epstein chose to begin the novel with this scene?

17. At the end of her life, Pan Yuliang had become known in her Paris circle as the "Woman of Three 'No's'" for her steadfast refusal to work with dealers, take French citizenship, or enter into love affairs. Why do you think she was so firmly against each of these things? Are they in keeping with the image of her you've formed from reading *The Painter from Shanghai?*

*Available only on the Norton Web site: www.wwnorton.com/guides